GATEWAYS

BOOKS EDITED BY ELIZABETH ANNE HULL

Tales from the Planet Earth
(coedited with Frederik Pohl)

Gateways

GATEWAYS

EDITED BY

Elizabeth Anne Hull

TOR®

A TOM DOHERTY ASSOCIATES BOOK
NEW YORK

GATEWAYS

Copyright © 2010 by Elizabeth Anne Hull

A Tor Book
Published by Tom Doherty Associates, LLC
175 Fifth Avenue
New York, NY 10010

www.tor-forge.com

Tor® is a registered trademark of Tom Doherty Associates, LLC.

ISBN 978-0-7653-2662-1

First Edition: July 2010

Printed in the United States of America

0 9 8 7 6 5 4 3 2 1

I dedicate this *festschrift* to my beloved husband, Frederik, of course; and to those who are still alive but couldn't contribute—you know who you are—and to those I couldn't even ask, including Fred's boyhood friend Isaac (I would have loved to have had a story from you, and thanks to Janet, we do have your chapter on Fred from *I, Asimov*); Jack Williamson (no one jerked beef or made overnight oatmeal to equal yours); Judith Merril (my co-grandmother to the Canadian clan); Robert Sheckley (Fred always regretted not being your Best Man); Algis (A. J.) Budrys (a treasured friend before I ever met Fred); Charles N. Brown (how I wish I could share this book with you as we've shared so many others in our travels); Ian Ballantine (whom I used to translate for Fred when Ian spoke obliquely); Elsie (my "other mother") and Donald A. Wollheim; Judy-Lynn Benjamin (Fred's one-time assistant) and Lester Del Rey (our Best Man); Poul Anderson (who probably got as frustrated as Fred at the Poul/Pohl confusion among readers); Forrest J. Ackerman (no one else addresses me as Auntie Sci Fi now); Robert A. Heinlein (who thought I called him a prude even though I didn't); Fred W. Saberhagen (another pre-Fred friend); Frank Herbert (who graciously agreed with my critique of the movie *Dune*); Hal Clement (fellow teacher), Roger Zelazny (who shopped while we waited on the bus); Philip José Farmer (so nearby yet seldom visited except at cons—bless the cons!), and many, many more in the extended family that is the global SF community.

—Elizabeth Anne Hull

A DREAM OF FREDERIK POHL

to Fred, of course

I'm sorry, Fred. I didn't mean to frighten you.
It wasn't until I was on my way down,
free-falling, and saw the look on your face
that I realized this was the sort of thing
could make a person's heart stop.
It was just an impulse, Fred—there I was
on the balcony, thirty feet up,
looked down, saw you, thought *there's Fred*
and jumped. I was already feeling guilty
before impacting, ungainly meteorite,
four inches in front of your twisted features.
God, I'm sorry, man. You said something then
but gladly I don't remember what.
Your words were lost in the screams
as I turned to look up as you had before
and saw the little girl's leap
into space just beyond the clutch
of her mother's fingers. *My fault,*
my fault, my fault, I thought
in time with her giddy plunge. I'll never
forget the sound of her femurs shattering.
But it's okay, Fred, it was just a dream,
a stupid dream of unpremeditated acts,
falling bodies, and pointless guilt.
It has nothing to do with real life,
nothing to do with us at all.

—David Lunde

CONTENTS

GATEWAYS

ONE WAY INTO *GATEWAYS*
AN INTRODUCTION

"You two should know each other. You have a lot in common," Tom Clareson said. We were at a meet-the-authors party around the hotel pool on the first night of MidAmericon, the 1976 (and my first) Worldcon, in Kansas City. I had been teaching SF at my college for three years at that point and knew Tom, through the Midwest Modern Language Association and the Popular Culture Association annual meetings, and for his editing of the journal *Extrapolation*. I also knew of Fred already by his editing and by my reading his fiction, such as *The Space Merchants*. Over the years since then, I've always wondered what Tom saw in each of us that made him think we had anything significant in common. Fred was considerably older than I was, so I really don't imagine he thought we'd be *romantically* interested in one another. Years later, Tom told me that introducing us was one of his most proud accomplishments!

As we chatted, I reminded Fred that I had sent him a letter to attend the next year's PCA meeting, for which I was chairing the SF and fantasy track, to be interviewed by Tom. I boldly asked why he hadn't answered my request, one way or the other. At first he denied ever having seen that letter, but by the end of the weekend, Fred agreed that he would attend the PCA meeting the following April.

As it turned out, we soon realized that we saw the world from a similar political bias, although in the ensuing thirty-three years, we have not always agreed perfectly on every issue. We bonded as friends almost immediately when I offered to share my stash of instant coffee in my room. My roommate, Mary Kenny Badami, and I had planned a room party later that evening with some friends of ours from Madison and the Chicago area, and of course the BNF (Big Name Fan) Fred graciously agreed to join us even though Mary and I were relative neos to the world of fandom. My feet were killing me from traipsing around Kansas City in high heels, so I propped them up on the bed and demanded—where did I ever get the nerve?—that he massage them. I won't say I fell in love then and there, but I sure thought he was something special with his sensitive magic fingers.

At the time, Fred was still married and trying to make a go of it after having been separated from and reconciled with Carol. He told me, "At this point in my life it's easier to be married than not married." I responded that for me it was easier to be single, as I had been for over fifteen years at that time. Although we recently celebrated our silver anniversary, it's still true—he's a lot of work—but he certainly is worth it. We haven't had an easy or simple life, but it sure has been an interesting journey together.

We began to see one another romantically in the summer of 1977, shortly after Carol finally decided their marriage couldn't be saved. We met at first at SF cons we were both attending for our own interests. Then we began to look for cons that we both wanted to attend. We soon discovered another shared interest, travel. I had put myself through college as a travel agent and Fred had been lecturing on SF around the world, mostly behind the Iron Curtain, for the State Department. When Fred couldn't go with me to Italy because of previous commitments, he arranged for me to meet friends of his in Rome. When I went to Australia and New Zealand to see my godchild with her mother, we stopped in Tahiti and Moorea, which made Fred so envious that he arranged to go to the South Pacific himself for a few weeks the next winter. And when I traveled to China by myself, Fred influenced me to organize and lead another tour to China a year and a half later, so he could see what I had fallen in love with. With very few exceptions, we've traveled together ever since.

Since the late seventies, even before we married in 1984, one of our favorite domestic destinations has been Lawrence, Kansas, every July for the Campbell and Sturgeon Awards weekend. Fred has also helped to discover many new writers by serving as one of the judges of the finalists of the year for the Writers of the Future. Together and separately, we've taught classes and helped run workshops, judged novels and stories, and been honored guests at countless SF conventions in the United States and Canada as well as around the world.

Fred has even mentored me by encouraging me to become president of the Science Fiction Research Association and by supporting my campaign and giving me the courage to run for Congress in the eighth district of Illinois in 1996 as the Democratic nominee against our local representative, a long-time incumbent. We've also written both fiction and nonfiction together, though we both recognize that he is the writer who teaches occasionally while I am a professor of English (now emerita) who sometimes writes. The shared experiences have given us each the greatest respect for the other's professions.

We've visited seventy-some countries and been to see the ends of the earth, even living in London for a semester when I was teaching there. We've cruised into the polar ice cap within the Arctic Circle and in the Antarctic off Palmer Station, where I swam in the ship's (covered) pool. We've crossed the equator a number of times, and I've snorkeled around the islands and reefs in the Galápagos, and on the Great Barrier Reef off the coast of Australia, as well as on the smaller Great Barrier Reef off Belize and on the reefs around the Seychelles and around various islands in the Caribbean and Hawaii, "where the hukuhuku numunumu apa aa go swimming by."

In addition to all the usual tourist cities and well-known sights of China, we've been from Turfan and Urumqi in the Gobi to Chengdu to Tibet to Inner Mongolia. From the Mid-Atlantic ridge in Iceland, to Mauna Kea, to Patagonia, to Machu Picchu, to Mount Kirinyaga and the Maasai Mara in Kenya, and to Scandinavia and most of Eastern and Western Europe. We've visited east, west, and central Canada and all but three (Idaho, Wyoming, and Montana) of the United States together, and most of both Eastern and Western Europe, parts of Africa, five countries in Asia, many countries of South America, and many islands in the Caribbean and in the Pacific.

Wherever we've traveled, we've tried to meet SF fans and professionals, and we've made many good friends. We were part of the formation of World SF in the late 1970s (which Harry Harrison talks about in his afterword) and tried to help others network with their counterparts in various parts of the world. Although we're definitely Americans through and through, Fred and I feel like citizens of the world, and we try to work for peace and shared understanding, both locally and globally.

When we cruise, our favorite mode of travel in recent years (because we can use the ship as a hotel and avoid airport hassles and worries about missed connections), Fred usually lets me do the sightseeing for us both while he stays on board to write, having a nearly empty ship to himself while we're in port. People who've read a lot of Fred's stories will recognize that many of these places have become the settings for Fred's stories, as well as for a few of my own.

So it was natural that Fred and I were cruising in the South Pacific in January 2009, to revisit Tahiti together this time, when I conceived the project that would become this *festschrift* volume of tribute to my husband for his ninetieth year, marking his career in the world of science fiction—as a fan and as a professional writer, first and foremost, but also as an agent and editor of both magazines and books. He's also served as president of both the Science Fiction Writers of America and World SF. He's lectured at colleges and universities across the US and Canada and indeed around the world, and taught workshops and mentored many young writers, acted as a judge for various contests and competitions, and written insightful commentary on written SF and coauthored with his son, Frederik Pohl IV, a comprehensive book on the history of sci fi film. He's even published much nonfiction in areas outside the field.

He's won Hugos, Nebulas, and several Grand Masters trophies—so many awards, in fact, that we cannot contain them all in the rather large trophy case we finally bought especially for the purpose. He's done nearly everything a professional could do in our field, except be a publisher, a librarian, or an illustrator. And even though he never could draw—anyone who has his autograph realizes he never even mastered cursive—he's ordered artwork for countless magazine covers. Some of it graces the walls of our home today.

Above all, Fred has always remained a reader and an active fan, publishing fanzines and having been one of the founding members of the first science fiction convention in 1936 in Philadelphia. He was delighted several years ago to be the fan Guest of Honor at Westercon. He was at the heart of New York fandom in the 1940s and '50s. If you want to know what it was like in those early days, I recommend his early memoir, *The Way the Future Was.* I recently told him that I thought he should update this book, since it doesn't even mention me, having been finished before we knew one another. So he has started a blog, thewaythefutureblogs .com. He often writes about people he knew well in the SF field who are gone now, and couldn't be asked to contribute to this volume. I occasionally post on his site too.

Unfortunately, midway through our aforementioned tropical cruise we both picked up a virus that weakened us, such that Fred was hospitalized this year for six longish stays, not to mention several shorter trips to the ER, before finally stabilizing in the autumn with the installation of a pacemaker. I myself had laryngitis from January through April, and then, just as I was finally able to speak aloud and was breathing somewhat better, in mid-June I stumbled backward and fractured the L1 vertebra in my spine, which required a corrective "procedure" and the wearing of back braces for a few months, followed by more surgery to correct an abdominal hernia. It was touch-and-go whether we both would make it to celebrate our twenty-fifth anniversary in July.

But for nearly a year, I have worked on making this collection happen.

At first I planned to make it a surprise for Fred's ninetieth birthday. Then his doctor suggested that it might raise his morale and give him more will to live if he knew about it and had something else to look forward to, besides finishing his own current novel. Fred wanted it to be my project entirely, and the results are my sole responsibility, even though I was happy to have my husband's wisdom and vast experience to consult with. Previously Fred and I had coedited an anthology of stories from around the world, *Tales from the Planet Earth*, 1986, and from that experience I also learned much about encouraging original stories from a diverse group of writers.

Although most of the writers required very little persuasion to contribute a story to this tribute volume, the whole project ran less smoothly than we had anticipated because both of us were incapacitated for so long. But at last it has come together beautifully, rather like a poorly run SF con that is highly successful in spite of the inexperience of the neofan organizers, because of the experience of the fans in having a good time at conventions—the fans wouldn't let it be a failure. Trufans are prepared, perhaps by reading SF, to adapt to any situation. Likewise, the writers invited to write for this volume are all professionals who came though with stories of, in my estimation, extremely high quality, stories that exemplify their own characteristics in style and content. Fred was agent for some of the writers and editor for others, mentor or inspiration to still others. I have asked each contributor to write an afterword, in which they could discuss their own stories, and/or talk about the various ways they know Fred.

A few notes on particular stories: some of the stories are actually parts of a novel-in-progress, or they are being expanded into a novel. One writer, James Gunn, is allowing us to use four excerpts from his as-yet-unfinished novel, *Transcendental*; each is narrated by a representative of a different alien species—the four altogether create a rounded perspective on the way we humans look to others and help us to understand ourselves. Our friend and neighbor Gene Wolfe produced a story that he prophesied that I would hate, but I love it, and expect you will too. All the stories fit in with Fred's aim to always make the reader think twice—and then think again.

Several of those I invited to participate could not because of previous writing commitments, or because they were no longer writing short fiction, some were not writing fiction at all. A number of these writers contributed their own tributes, which are distributed between other stories. From the conception throughout the entire editing and compiling process, I have been encouraged and supported by my in-house editor, James Frenkel, an old friend and Fred's editor for many years, who wrote the final afterword for this anthology.

—Elizabeth Anne Hull, PhD
Professor Emerita, William Rainey Harper College
September 2009

DAVID BRIN

〉●〈

SHORESTEADING

A good traveler has no fixed plans and is not intent upon arriving. A good artist lets his intuition lead him wherever it wants. A good scientist has freed himself of concepts and keeps his mind open to what is. **—Lao-Tzu, *Tao Te Ching***

"Bu yao! Bu yao!"

Xin Pu Shi, the reclamation merchant, waved both hands in front of his face, glancing sourly at Wer's haul of salvage—corroded copper pipes, some salt-crusted window blinds, two small filing cabinets, and a mesh bag bulging with various metal odds and ends.

Wer tried to winch the sack lower, but the grizzled old gleaner used a gaffe to fend it away from his boat. "I don't want any of that garbage! Save it for the scrap barge, Peng Xiao Wer. Or dump it back into the sea."

"You know I can't do that," Wer complained, squeezing the calloused soles of both feet against one of the rusty poles that propped his home above the sloshing sea. His left hand gripped the rope, tugging at pulleys, causing the mesh bag to sway toward Xin. "There are camera-eyes on that buoy over there. They know I raised ninety kilos of salvage junk. If I dump this stuff back into the water, I'll be fined! I could lose my stake."

"Cry to the north wind," the merchant scolded, using his pole to push away from the ruined building. His flat-bottomed vessel shifted sluggishly, while eels grazed along its mossy hull. "Call me if you salvage something good. Or sell that trash to someone who can use it!"

"But—"

Wer watched helplessly as Xin spoke a sharp word and the dory's motor obediently started up, putting it in motion. Audible voice commands might be old-fashioned in the city. But out here, you couldn't afford subvocal mistakes. Anyway, old-fashioned was cheaper.

Muttering a curse upon the geezer's sleep, Wer tied off the rope and left his haul of salvage hanging there, for the cameras to see. Clambering up the strut, then vaulting across a gap, he managed to land, teetering, upon another, then stepped onto the main roof of the seaside villa—once a luxury retreat, worth two million Shanghai dollars. Now the half-drowned mansion was his. What was left of it. If he could work the claim.

Stretching under the hot sun, Wer adjusted a wide-brim straw hat and scanned the neighborhood. To his left extended the Huangpu Estuary, Huangzhou Bay, and the East China Sea, dotted with vessels of all kinds, from massive container ships—tugged by billowing kite-sails, as big as clouds—all the way down to gritty dust-spreaders and fishing sampans. Much closer, the tide was coming in, sending breakers crashing against a double line of ruined houses where he—and several hundred other "shoresteaders"—had erected hammock-homes, swaying like cocoons in the stiff breeze.

There may be a storm, he thought, sniffing the air. *I had better check.*

Turning, he headed across the sloping roof, in the direction of a glittering city that lay just a few hundred meters ahead, beyond the surfline and a heavy, gray seawall, that bore stains halfway up, from this year's highwater mark. A world of money and confident ambition lay on the other side. Much more lively than Old Shanghai, with its lingering afterglow from Awfulday.

Footing was tricky as he made his careful way between a dozen broad, lenslike evaporation pans that he filled each day, providing trickles of fresh water, voltage, and salt to sell in town. Elsewhere, one could easily fall through crumbling shingles and sodden plywood. So Wer kept to paths that had been braced, soon after he signed the papers and took over this mess. This dream of a better life.

And it could still be ours. If only luck would come back to stay awhile.

Out of habit, he made a quick visual check of every stiff pipe and tension rope that spanned above the roof, holding the hammock-home in place, like a sail above a ship going nowhwere. Like a hopeful cocoon. Or, maybe, a spider in its web.

And, like a spider, Ling must have sensed him coming. She pushed her head out through the funnel door. Jet-black hair was braided behind the ears and then tied under the chin, in a new, urban style that she had seen on-web.

"Xin Pu Shi didn't take the stuff," she surmised, from his expression.

Wer shrugged, while tightening one of the cables that kept the framework from collapsing. A few of the poles—all that he could afford so far—were made of noncorroding metlon, driven solidly into the old foundation. Given enough time, cash, and luck, something new would take shape here, a new and better home, as the old house died. That is, providing . . .

"Well?" Ling insisted. A muffled whimper, and then a cry, told him that the baby was awake. "What'll you do now?"

"The county scrap barge will be here Thursday," Wer said.

"And they pay *dung*. Barely enough to cover taking *our* dung away. What are we to live on, fish and salt?"

"People have done worse," he muttered, looking down through a gap in the roof, past what had been a stylish master bathroom, then through a shorn stretch of tiled floor, to the soggy, rotten panels of a once stately dining room. Of course, all the real valuables had been removed by the original owners when they evacuated long ago, and the best salvagable items got stripped during the first year of overflowing tides. A *slow* disaster. One that left little of value for late-coming scavengers, like Wer.

"Right," Ling laughed without humor. "And meanwhile, our claim expires in six months. It's either build up or clean out, remember? One or the other, or we're expelled!"

"I remember."

"Do you want to go back to work that's unfit for robots? Slaving in a geriatric ward, wiping drool and cleaning the diapers of little emperors?"

"There are farms, up in the highlands."

"And they only let in refugees if you can prove ancestral connection to the district. Or if you bring a useful skill. But our families were urban, going back two revolutions!"

Wer grimaced and shook his head, downcast. *We have been over this, so many times,* he thought. But Ling seemed in a mood to belabor the obvious.

"This time, we may not be *lucky* enough to get jobs in a geriatric ward. You'll have to work on a levee crew—and wind up buried in the cement. Then what will become of us?"

He lifted his gaze, squinting toward the long, concrete barrier, separating New Shanghai from the sea—part of a monumental construction that some called the New Great Wall, many times larger than the original—defending against an invader more implacable than any other—ocean tides that rose higher, every year. Here, along the abandoned shoreline, where wealthy export magnates once erected beachfront villas, you could gaze with envy at the glittering Xidong District, on the other side, whose inhabitants had turned their backs to the sea. It didn't interest them, anymore.

"I'll take the salvage to town," he said.

"What?"

"I ought to get a better price ashore. And I'll sell our extra catch, too. Anyway, we need some things."

"Yeah, like beer," Ling commented, sourly. But she didn't try to stop him, or even mention that the trip was hazardous. *Fading hopes do that to a relationship,* he thought. Especially one built on unlikely dreams.

They said nothing further to each other. She slipped back inside. At least the baby's crying soon stopped. Yet . . . Wer lingered for a moment, before going downstairs. He liked to picture his child—his son—at her breast. Despite being poor, ill-educated, and with a face that bore scars from a childhood mishap, Ling was still a healthy young woman, in a generation with too many single men. And fertile, too.

She is the one with options, he pondered, morosely. *The adoption merchants would set her up with a factory job that she could supplement with womb-work. Though they would take Xie Xie. He'd draw a good fee, and maybe grow up in a rich home, getting the new electronic implants and maybe . . .*

He chased the thought away with a harsh oath. *No! She came here with me. Because she believed we can make this work. And I will find a way.*

Using the mansion's crumbling grand staircase as an indoor dock, Wer built a makeshift float-raft consisting of a big square of polystyrene wrapped in fishing net, lashed to a pair of old surfboards with drapery cord. Then, before fetching the salvage, he took a quick tour to check his traps and fishing lines, bobbing at intervals around the house. It meant slipping on goggles and diving repeatedly, but by now he felt at home among the canted, soggy walls, festooned with seaweed and barnacles. At least there were a dozen or so nice catches this time, most of them even legal, including a big red lobster and a fat, angry wrasse. So, his luck wasn't uniformly bad.

Reluctantly, he released a tasty Jiaoxi crab to go about its way. You never knew when some random underwater monitor, disguised as a drifting piece of flotsam, might be looking. He sure hoped none had spotted a forbidden rockfish, dangling from a gill net in back, too dead to do anything about. He took a moment to dive deeper and conceal the carcass, under a paving stone of the sunken garden.

The legal items, including the wrasse, a grouper, and two sea bass, he pushed into another mesh sack.

Our poverty is a strange one. The last thing we worry about is food.

Other concerns? Sure. Typhoons and tsunamis. Robbers and police shakedowns. City sewage leaks and red tides. Low recycle prices and the high cost of living.

Perhaps a fair wind will blow from the south today, instead.

In part, Wer blamed the former owners of this house, for having designed it without any care for the laws of nature. Too many windows had faced too many directions, including north, allowed chi to leak, in and out, almost randomly. None of the sills had been raised, to retain good luck. How could supposedly smart people have ignored so many lessons of the revered past? Simply in order to maximize their scenic view? It had served them right, when melting glaciers in far-north Greenland drowned their fancy home.

Wer checked the most valuable tool in his possession—a tide-driven drill that was almost finished boring into the old foundation, ready for another metlon support. He inspected the watch-camera that protected the drill from being pilfered, carefully ensuring that it had unobstructed views. Just ten more holes and supports. Then he could anchor the hammock-home in place with a real, arched frame, as some of the other shoresteaders had done.

And after that? A tide-power generator. And a bigger rain catchment. And a smart gathernet with a commercial fishing license. And a storm shelter. And a real boat. And more metlon. He had even seen a shorestead where the settlers reached Phase Three: reinforcing and recoating all the wires and plumbing of the old house, in order to reconnect with the city grids. Then sealing all the walls to finish a true island of self-sufficiency— deserving a full transfer of deed. Every reclaimer's dream.

And about as likely as winning a lottery, it seemed.

I had better get going, he thought. *Or the tide will be against me.*

━●━●━

Propelling the raft was a complex art. Wer haunch-squatted on the poly-styrene square while sweeping a single oar in front of him, in a figure-eight pattern. It had taken months, after he and Ling first staked their claim, to learn how to do it just right, so there'd be almost no resistance on the forward stroke.

He tried to aim for one of the static pull-ropes used by other shoresteaders, which then led directly ashore, where the mammoth seawall swung backward for a hundred meters, far enough for a sandy beach to form. On occasion, he had been able to sell both fish and salvage right there, to middlemen who came out through a pair of massive gates. On weekends, a few families came down from nearby city towers, to visit salty surf and sand. Some would pay top rates to a shoresteader, for a fresh, wriggling catch.

But, while a rising tide helped push him closer, it also ensured the gates would be closed, when he arrived.

I'll tie up at the wall and wait. Or maybe climb over. Slip into town, till it ebbs. Wer had a few coins. Not enough to buy more metlon. But sufficient for a hardworking man to have a well-deserved beer.

As always, he peered downward as the raft moved with every stroke of the oar. Wer had modified the chunk of polystyrene to hold a hollow tube with a big, fish-eye lens at the bottom, and a matching lens up top. After much fiddling, he had finally contrived a good device for scanning the bottom while pushing along—a small advantage that he kept secret from the other steaders. You never knew when something might turn up below, revealed by the shifting sea. Mostly, house sites in this area had been bulldozed and cleared with drag lines, after the evacuation. Common practice in the early days, when people first retreated from the continental margins. Only later was steading seen as a cheaper alternative. Let some poor dope slave away at salvage and demolition, driven by a slender hope of ownership.

In large part, all that remained here were concrete foundations and fields of stubby utility pipes, along with tumbled lumps of stone and concrete too heavy to move. Still, out of habit, he kept scanning for any change, as a combination of curiosity and current drew him by what had been the biggest mansion along this stretch of coast. Some tech-baron oligarch had set up a seaside palace here, before he toppled spectacularly, in one of the big purges. Steader stories told that he was dragged off, one night, tried in secret, and shot. Quickly, so he would not spill secrets about mightier men. There had been a lot of that, all over the world, twenty years or so ago.

Of course government agents would have picked the place cleaner than a bone, before letting the bulldozers in. And other gleaners followed. Yet, Wer always felt a romantic allure, passing two or three meters overhead, imagining the place when walls and windows stood high, festooned with lights. When liveried servants patrolled with trays of luscious treats, satisfying guests in ways that—well—he probably couldn't imagine, though sometimes he liked to try.

Of course, the sand and broken crete still held detritus. Old pipes and conduits. Cans of paint and solvents still leaked from the ruin, rising as individual up-drips to pop at the surface and make it gleam. From their hammock-home, Wer and Ling used to watch sunsets reflect off the rainbow sheen. Back when all of this seemed exciting, romantic, and new.

Speaking of new . . .

Wer stopped kicking and twisted his body around to peer downward. A glitter had caught his eye. Something different.

There's been some kind of cave-in, he realized. *Under one edge of the main foundation slab.*

The sea was relatively calm, this far beyond the surfline. So he grabbed a length of tether from the raft, took several deep breaths, then flipped downward, diving for a better look.

It did look like a gap under the house, one that he never saw before. But, surely, someone else would have noticed this by now. Anyway, the government searchers would have been thorough. Wouldn't they? What were the odds that . . .

Tying the tether to a chunk of concrete, he moved close enough to peer inside the cavity, careful not to disturb much sediment with his flippers. Grabbing an ikelite from his belt, he sent its sharp beam lancing inside, where an underground wall had recently collapsed. During the brief interval before his lungs grew stale and needy, he could make out few details. Still, by the time he swiveled and kicked back toward the surface, one thing was clear.

The chamber contained things. Lots of things.

And, to Wer, almost anything down there would be worth going after, even if it meant squeezing through a narrow gap, into a crumbling basement underneath the sea.

TREASURE

Night had fallen some time ago and now his torch batteries were failing. That, plus sheer physical exhaustion, forced Wer, at last, to give up salvaging anything more from the hidden cache that he had found, underneath a sunken mansion. Anyway, with the compressed air bottle depleted, his chest now burned from repeated free-dives through that narrow opening, made on lung power alone, snatching whatever he could—whatever sparkle caught his eye down there.

You will die if you keep this up, he finally told himself. *And someone else will get the treasure.*

That thought made it firm. Still, even without any more trips inside, there was more work to do. Yanking some decayed boards off the upper story, Wer dropped them to cover the new entrance that he'd found, gaping underneath the house. And then one final dive through dark shallows, to kick sand over it all. Finally, he rested for a while with one arm draped over his makeshift raft, under the dim glow of a quarter moon.

Do not the sages counsel that a wise man must spread ambition, like honey across a bun? Only a greedy fool tries to swallow all of his good fortune in a single bite.

Oh, but wasn't it a tempting treasure trove? Carefully concealed by the one-time owner of this former beachfront mansion, who took the secret of a concealed basement with him—out of spite, perhaps—all the way to the execution-disassembly room.

If they had transplanted any of his brain, as well as the eyes and skin and organs, then someone might have remembered the hidden room, before this.

As it is, I am lucky that the rich man went to his death angry, never telling anybody what the rising sea was sure to bury.

Wer pondered the strangeness of fate, as he finally turned toward home, fighting the ebb tide that kept trying to haul him seaward, into the busy shipping lanes of the Huangpu. It was a grueling swim, dragging the raft behind him with a rope around one shoulder. Several times—obsessively—he stopped to check the sacks of salvage, counting them and securing their ties.

It is a good thing that basement also proved a good place to deposit my earlier load of garbage, those pipes and chipped tiles. A place to tuck them away, out of sight of any drifting environment monitors. Or I would have had to haul them, too.

The setting of the moon only made things harder, plunging the estuary into darkness. Except, that is, for the glitter of Shanghai East, a noisy galaxy of wealth, towering behind its massive seawall. And the soft glow of luminescence in the tide itself. A glow that proved especially valuable when his winding journey took him past some neighboring shoresteads, looming out of the night, like dark castles. Wer kept his splashing to a minimum, hurrying past the slumping walls and spidery tent poles with barely a sound. Until, at last, his own stead was next, its familiar tilt occulting a lopsided band of stars.

I can't wait to show Ling what I found. This time, she has to be impressed.

That hope propelled Wer the last few hundred meters, even though his lungs and legs felt as if they were on fire. Of course, he took a beating, as the raft crashed, half-sideways into the atrium of the ruined house. A couple of the salvage bags split open, spilling their glittery contents across the old parquet floor. But no matter, he told himself. The things were safe now, in easy reach.

In fact, it took all of Wer's remaining energy to drag just one bag upstairs, then to pick his way carefully across the slanted roof of broken tiles, and finally reach the tent-house where his woman and child waited.

◆—◆—

"Stones?" Ling asked, staring at the array of objects that Wer spread before her. A predawn glow was spreading across the east. Still, she had to lift a lantern to peer at his little trove, shading the light and speaking in a low voice, so as not to wake the baby.

"You are all excited about a bunch of stones?"

"They were on *shelves*, all neatly arranged and with labels," he explained, while spreading ointment across a sore on his left leg, one of several that had spread open again, after long immersion. "There used to be glass cabinets—"

"They don't look like gems. No diamonds or rubies," she interrupted. "Yes, some of them are pretty. But we find surf-polished pebbles everywhere."

"You should see the ones that were on a special pedestal, in the center of the room. Some of them were held in fancy boxes, made of wood and crystal. I tell you it was a *collection* of some sort. And it *must* have all been valuable, for the owner to hide them all so—"

"Boxes?" Her interest was piqued, at least a little "Did you bring any of those?"

"A few. I left them on the raft. I was so tired. And hungry." He sniffed pointedly toward the stewpot, where Ling was reheating last night's meal, the one that he had missed. Wer smelled some kind of fish that had been stir-fried with leeks, onions, and that reddish seaweed that she put into more than half of her dishes.

"Get some of those boxes, please," she insisted. "Your food will be warm by the time that you return."

Wer would have gladly wolfed it down cold. But he nodded with resignation and gathered himself together, somehow finding the will to move quivering muscles, once again. *I am still young, but I know how it will feel to be old.*

This time, at least, the spreading gray twilight helped him to cross the roof, then slide down the ladder and stairs without tripping. His hands trembled while untying two more of the bags of salvage, these bulging with sharply angular objects. Dragging them up and retraversing the roof was a pure exercise in mind-over-agony.

Most of our ancestors had it at least this bad, he reminded himself. *Till things got much better for a generation . . .*

. . . and then worse again. For the poor.

Hope was a dangerous thing, of course. One heard of shoresteaders striking it rich with a great haul, now and then. But, most of the time, reality shattered promise. *Perhaps it is only an amateur geologist's private rock collection,* he thought, struggling the last few meters. *One man's hobby—precious to him personally, but of little market value.*

Still, after collapsing on the floor of their tent-home for a second time, he found enough curiosity and strength to lift his head, as Ling's nimble fingers worked at the tie ropes. Upending one bag, she spilled out a pile of stony objects, along with three or four of the boxes he had mentioned, made of finely carved wood, featuring windows with beveled edges that glittered too beautifully to be made of simple glass.

For the first time, he saw a bit of fire in Ling's eyes. Or interest, at least. One by one, she lifted each piece, turning it in the lamplight . . . and then moved to push aside a curtain, letting in sharply horizontal rays of light, as the sun poked its leading edge above the East China Sea. The baby roused then, rocking from side to side and whimpering while Wer spooned some food from the reheating pot into a bowl.

"Open this," Ling insisted, forcing him to choose between the bowl and the largest box, that she thrust toward him. With a sigh, he put aside his meal and accepted the heavy thing, which was about the size and weight of his own head. Wer started to pry at the corroded clasp, while Ling picked up little Xie Xie in order to nurse the infant.

"It might be better to wait a bit and clean the box," he commented. "Rather than breaking it just to look inside. The container, itself, may be worth—"

Abruptly, the wood split along a grainy seam with a splintering crack. Murky water spilled across his lap, followed by a bulky object, so smooth and slippery that it almost squirted out of his grasp.

"What is it?" Ling asked. "Another stone?"

Wer turned it over in his hands. The thing was heavy and hard, with a greenish tint, like jade. Though that could just be slime that clung to its surface even after wiping with a rag. A piece of real jade this big could bring a handsome price, especially already shaped into a handsome contour—that of an elongated egg. So he kept rubbing and lifted it toward the horizontal shaft of sunbeams, in order to get a better look.

No, it isn't jade, after all.

But disappointment slowly turned into wonder, as sunlight striking the glossy surface seemed to sink *into* the glossy ovoid. Its surface darkened, as if it were drinking the beam, greedily.

Ling murmured in amazement . . . and then gasped as the stone changed color before their eyes . . .

. . . and then began to glow on its own.

MORE THAN ONE

The wooden box bore writing in French. Wer learned that much by carefully cleaning its small brass plate, then copying each letter, laboriously, onto the touch-sensitive face of a simple tutor-tablet.

"Unearthed in Harrapa, 1926," glimmered the translation in Updated Pinyin. "Demon-infested. Keep in the dark."

Of course that made no sense. The former owner of the opalescent relic had been a high-tech robotics tycoon, hardly the sort to believe in superstitions. Ling reacted to the warning with nervous fear, wrapping the scarred egg in dark cloth, but Wer figured it was just a case of bad translation.

The fault must lie in the touch-tablet—one of the few tech-items they had brought along to their shorestead, just outside the seawall of New Shanghai. Originally mass-produced for poor children, the dented unit later served senile patients for many years, at a Chungqing hospice—till Ling took it with her, when she quit working there. Cheap and obsolete, it was never even reported stolen, so the two of them could still use it to tap the World Mesh, at a rudimentary, free-access level. It sufficed for a couple with little education, and few interests beyond the struggle to survive.

"I'm sure the state will issue us something better next year, when little Xie Xie is big enough to register," she commented, whenever Wer complained about the slow conection and scratched screen. "They have to provide that much. A basic education. As part of the Big Deal."

Wer felt less sure. Grand promises seemed made for the poor to remember, while the mighty forgot. Things had always been that way. You could tell, even from the censored histories that flickered across the little display, as he and his wife sagged into fatigued sleep every night, rocked by the rising tides. The same tides that kept eroding the old beach house, faster than they could reinforce it.

Would they even let Xie Xie register? The baby's genetic samples had been filed when he was born. But would he get residency citizenship in New Shanghai? Or would the seawall keep out yet another kind of unwanted trash, along with a scum of plastic and resins that kept washing higher along the concrete barrier?

Clearly, in this world, you were a fool to count on beneficence from above.

Even good luck, when it arrived, could prove hard to exploit. Wer had hoped for time to figure out what kind of treasure lay in that secret room, underneath the biggest drowned mansion, a chamber filled with beautiful or bizarre rocks and crystals, or specimens of strangely twisted metal. Wer tried to inquire, using the little mesh tablet, only carefully. There were sniffer programs—billions of them—running loose across a million vir-levels, even the gritty layer called Reality. If he inquired too blatantly, or offered the items openly for sale, somebody might just come and take it all. The former owner had been declared a public enemy, his property forfeit to the state.

Plugging in crude goggles and using a cracked pair of interact-gloves, Wer wandered down low rent avenues of World Town and The Village and Big Bazaar, pretending to be idly interested in rock collecting, as a hobby. From those virtual markets, he learned enough to dare a physical trip into town, carrying just one bagful of nice—but unexceptional—specimens, unloading them for a quarter of their worth at a realshop in East Pudong. A place willing to deal in cash—no names or recordings.

After so long at sea, Wer found troubling the heavy rhythms of the street. The pavement seemed harsh and unyielding. Pulsating maglev trolleys somehow made him itch, all over, especially inside tight and sweaty shoes. The whole time, he pictured twenty million nearby residents as a pressing mass—felt no less intensely than the thousands who actually jostled past him on crowded sidewalks, many of them muttering and waggling their fingers, interacting with people and things that weren't even there.

Any profit from that first trip had been slim. Still, Wer thought he might venture to another shop soon, working his way up from mundane items to those that seemed more . . . unusual. Those kept in ornate boxes, on special shelves, in the old basement trove.

Though just one specimen glimmered, both in his dreams and daytime imaginings. Frustratingly, his careful online searches found nothing like the stone—a kind of mineral that glowed with its own light, after soaking in the sun. Its opal-like sheen featured starlike sparkles that seemed to recede into an inner distance, a depth that looked both brighter than day and deeper than night. That is, until Ling insisted it be wrapped up and put away.

Worse yet, time was running out. Fish had grown sparse, ever since the night of the jellyfish, when half the life seemed to vanish out of the Huangpu Estuary. Now, the stewpot was seldom full, and often empty.

Soon the small hoard of cash was gone again.

Luck is fickle. We try hard to control the flow of chi, by erecting our tent poles in symmetrical patterns and by facing our entrance toward the smiling south wind. But how can one strike a harmonious balance, down here at the shore, where the surf is so chaotic, where tides of air and water and stinging monsters rush however they choose?

No wonder the Chinese often turned their backs to the sea . . . and seem to be doing so again.

Already, several neighbors had given up, abandoning their shoresteads to the jellies and rising waters. Just a week ago, Wer and Ling joined a crowd of scavengers converging on one forsaken site, grabbing metlon poles and nanofiber webbing for use on their own stead, leaving little more than a stubble of rotting wood, concrete, and stucco. A brief boost to their prospects, benefiting from the misfortune of others—

—that is, until it's our own turn to face the inevitable. Forsaking all our hard work and dreams of ownership. Returning to beg our old jobs back in that stifling hospice, wiping spittle from the chins of little emperors. With each reproachful look from Ling, Wer grew more desperate. Then, during his third trip to town, carrying samples from the trove, he saw something that gave him both a thrill and a chill.

He was passing along Boulevard of the Sky Martyrs and about to cross the Street of October the Seventeenth, when the surrounding crowd seemed to halt, abruptly, all around him.

Well, not everybody, but enough people to bring the rhythmic bustle to a dead stall. Wer stumbled into the back of a well-padded pedestrian, who looked briefly as confused as he was. They turned to see that about a third of those around them were suddenly staring, as if into space, murmuring to themselves, some of them with jaws ajar, half open in some kind of surprise.

Swiftly he realized, these were people who had been linked-in with goggles, specs, tru-vus, or contacts, each person moving through some virtual overlay—perhaps following guide arrows to a destination, or doing business as they walked, while others simply liked their city overlain with flowers, or jungle foliage, or fairy-tale colors. It also made them receptive to a high-priority alert. Soon, half the people in sight were shuffling aside, half consciously moving toward the nearest wall or window in order to get away from traffic, while their minds soared far away.

Seeing so many others dive into a newstrance, the overweight gentleman muttered an oath and reached into his pocket to pull out some wraparound glasses. He, too, pressed close to the nearest building, emitting short grunts of interest while his aiware started filling him in.

Wer briefly wondered if he should be afraid. City life had many hazards, not all of them on the scale of Awfulday. But . . . the people clumping along the edges of the sidewalk didn't seem worried, as much as engrossed. Surely that meant there was no immediate danger.

Meanwhile, many of those who lacked gear were pestering their companions, demanding verbal updates. He overheard a few snippets.

"The artifact has spoken . . . ," and "The aliens have begun explaining their invitation, at last . . ."

Aliens. Artifact. Of course those words had been foaming around for a couple of weeks, part of life's background, just like the soapy tidal spume. It sounded like a silly thing, unworthy of the small amount of free time that he shared with Ling, each exhausted evening. A fad, surely, or hoax. Or, at best, none of his concern. Only now Wer blinked in surprise over how many people seemed to care. *Maybe we should scan for a free-access show about it tonight.* Instead of the usual medieval romance stories that Ling demanded.

Despite all the people who had stepped aside, into virtual newspace, that still left hundreds of pedestrians who didn't care, or who felt they could wait. They took advantage of the cleared sidewalks to hurry about their business. *As should I,* he thought, stepping quickly across the street while ai-piloted vehicles worked their way past, evading those with human drivers who had pulled aside.

Aliens. From outer space. Could it possibly be true? Wer had to admit, this was stirring his long-dormant imagination.

He turned onto the Avenue of Fragrant Hydroponics and suddenly came to a halt. People were beginning to stir from the mass newstrance, muttering to one another—in real life and across the mesh—while stepping back into the sidewalk and resuming their journeys. Only, now it was his turn to be distracted, to stop and stare, to push unapologetically past others and press close to the nearest building, bringing his face close to the window of a store selling visualization tools.

One of the new SEF ThreeVee displays sparkled within, offering that unique sense of ghostly semitransparency—and it showed three demons.

Or at least that's how Wer first thought of them. They looked like made-up characters in one of those cheap fantasy dramas that Ling loved—one like an imp, with flamelike fur, one horselike with nostrils that flared like caves, and another whose tentacles evoked some monster of the sea. A disturbing trio, in their own right.

Only, it wasn't the creatures that had Wer transfixed. It was their home. The context. The object framing, containing, perhaps imprisoning them. He recognized it, at once. Cleaner and more pristine—less pitted and scarred—nevertheless, it was clearly a cousin to the thing he had left behind this morning, in the surf-battered home that he shared with his wife and little son.

Wer swallowed hard.

I thought I was being careful, seeking information about that thing.

But *careful* was a relative word.

He left the bag of stones lying there, like an offering, in front of the image in the ThreeVee tank. It would only weigh him down now, as he ran for home.

PURSUIT

Despite his hurry to get home, Wer avoided the main gate through the massive seawall. For one thing, the giant doors were closed right now, for high tide. Even when they opened, that place would throng with fishermen, hawking their catch, and citydwellers visiting the last remaining beach of imported sand. So many eyes—and ais—and who knew how many were already sifting every passing face, searching for his unique biosignature?

I should never have posted queries about an egglike stone that glows mysteriously, after sitting in sunlight.

I should have left it in that hole under the sea.

His fear—ever since glimpsing the famous alien "artifact" on TV—was that somebody high and mighty wanted desperately to have whatever Wer discovered in a hidden basement cache, underneath a drowned mansion—and wanted it in secret. The former owner had been powerful and well connected, yet he wound up being hauled away and—according to legend—tortured, then brain-sifted, and finally silenced forever. Wer suspected now that it was because of an oval stone, very much like the one causing such fuss, around the world. Governments and megorps and reff-consortia would all seek one of their own.

If so, what would they do with the likes of me? When an object is merely valuable, a poor man who recovers it may ask for a finder's fee. But if it is a thing that might shake civilization?

In that case, all I could expect is death, just for knowing about it!

Yet, as some of the initial panic ebbed, Wer felt another part of his inner self rise up. The portion of his character that had dared to ask Ling to join him at the wild frontier, shoresteading a place of their own. *If there were a way to offer it up for bidding . . . a way to keep us safe . . . True, the former owner must have tried, and failed, to make a deal. But nobody knew about this kind of "artifact" then . . . at least not the public. Everything has changed, now that the Americans are showing theirs to the world. . . .*

None of which would matter, if he failed to make it home in time to hide the thing. Or to make some basic preparations. Above all, sending Ling and Xie Xie somewhere safe.

Hurrying through crowded streets, Wer carefully kept his pace short of a run. It wouldn't do to draw attention. Beyond the public-order cams on every ledge and lamppost, the state could tap into the lenses and private-ais worn by any pedestrian nearby. His long hair, now falling over his face, might stymie a routine or casual face-search, but not if the system really took an interest.

Veering away from the main gate, he sped through a shabbier section of town, where multistory residence blocks had gone through ramshackle evolution, ignoring every zoning ordinance. Laundry-laden clotheslines jostled solar collectors that shoved against semi-illegal rectennas, siphoning mesh-access and a little beamed power from the shiny towers of nearby Pudong.

Facing a dense crowd ahead, Wer tried pushing ahead for a while, then took a stab at a shortcut, worming past a delivery cart that wedged open a pair of giant doors. He found himself inside a vast cavity, where the lower floors had been gutted in order to host a great maze of glassy pipes and stainless steel reactor vessels, all linked in twisty patterns, frothing with multicolored concoctions. He chose a direction by dead reckoning, where there ought to be an exit on the other side. Wer meant to bluff his way clear, if anyone stopped him.

That didn't seem likely, amid the hubbub. At least a hundred laborers— many of them dressed little better than he was—patrolled creaky catwalks or clambered over lattice struts, meticulously cleaning and replacing tubes by hand. At ground level, inspectors wearing bulky, enhanced aiware, checked a continuous shower of some product—objects roughly the size and shape of a human thumb—waving laser pincers to grab a few of them before they fell into a waiting bin.

It's a nanofactory, Wer realized, after he passed halfway through. It was his first time seeing one up close, but he and Ling once saw a virtshow tour of a vast workshop like this one (though far cleaner) where basic ingredients were piped in and sophisticated parts shipped out—electroptic components, neuraugments, and organoplaques, whatever those were. And shape-to-order diamonds, as big as his fist. All produced by stacking atoms and molecules, one at a time, under programmed control.

People still played a part, of course. No robot could scramble or crawl about like humonkeys, or clean up after the machines with such dexterity. Or so cheaply.

Weren't they supposed to shrink these factories to the size of a toaster and sell them to everybody? Magic boxes that would let even poor folk make anything they wanted from raw materials. From seawater, even. No more work. No more want.

He felt like snorting, but instead Wer mostly held his breath the rest of the way, hurrying toward a loading dock, where sweltering workers filled maglev lorries at the other end. One heard rumors of nano-machines that got loose, that embedded in the lungs and then got busy trying to make copies of themselves. . . . Probably just tall tales. But Wer still had plans for his lungs. They mattered a lot, to a shoresteader.

He spilled out of gritty industry into a world of street-level commerce, where gaily decorated shops crowded this avenue. Sucking air, his nostrils filled with food aromas, wafting around innumerable grills, woks, and steam cookers, preparing everything from delicate skewered scorpions to vat-grown chickenmeat, stretched and streaked to look like the real thing. Wer's stomach growled, but he pushed ahead, then turned a corner and headed straight for the nearest section of massive wall separating Shanghai East from the rising ocean.

There were smugglers' routes. One used a building that formerly offered appealing panoramas overlooking the Hunangpu Estuary—till such views became unfashionable. Now, a lower class of urbanites occupied the tower.

The lobby's former coating of travertine and marble had been stripped and sold off years ago, replaced by spray-on corrugations that lay covered with long beards of damp algae. A good use of space—the three-story atrium probably grew enough to feed half the occupants a basic, gene-crafted diet. But the dank smell made Wer miss his little tent-home amid the waves.

We can't go back to living like this, he thought, glancing at the spindly bamboo scaffolding that crisscrossed the vast foyer, while bony, sweat-stained workers tended the crop, doing work unfit for robots. *I swore I would not raise our son on algae paste.*

The creaky elevator was staffed by a crone who flicked switches on a makeshift circuit board to set it in motion. The building must never have had its electronics repaired since the Crash. *It's been what, fifteen, sixteen years? Yes, people are cheap and people need work. But even I could fix this pile of junk.*

The car jerked and rattled while the operator glared at Wer. Clearly, she knew he did not work or live here. In turn, he gave the old lady a smile and ingratiating bow—no sense in antagonizing someone who might call up a face-query. But within, Wer muttered to himself about sour-minded "little emperors"—a generation raised as chubby only children, doted on by two parents, four grandparents and a nation that seemed filled with limitless potential. Boundless dreams and an ambition to rise infinitely high—until the Crash. Till the twenty-first century didn't turn out quite as promised.

Disappointment didn't sit well with little emperors—half a billion of them—so many that even the mysterious oligarchs in the Palace of Terrestrial Harmony had to cater to the vast population bulge. And they could be grouchy. Pinning the blame on Wer's outnumbered generation had become a national pastime.

The eleventh floor once boasted a ledge-top restaurant, overlooking a marina filled with opulent yachts, bordering a beach of brilliant, whitened sand. Now, stepping past rusty tables and chairs, Wer gazed beyond the nearby seawall, upon stubby remnants and broken masts, protruding from a brownish carpet of seaweed and sewage.

I remember it was right about here . . .

Leaning over, he groped over the balcony railing and along the building's fluted side, till he found a hidden pulley, attached to a slender rope leading downward. Near the bottom, it draped idly over the seawall and into the old marina, appearing to be nothing more than a pair of fallen wires.

Wer had never done anything like this before, trusting a slender line with his weight and his life. Though, on one occasion he had helped Quang Lu ferry mysterious cargo to the bottom end, holding Quang's boat steady while the smuggler attached dark bags, then hauled away. High overhead, shadowy figures claimed the load of contraband, and that was that. Wer never knew if it was drugs, or tech, or untaxed luxuries, nor did he care, so long as he was paid.

Quang Lu would not be happy if he ruined this route. But right now, Wer had other worries. He shaded his eyes to peer along the coast, toward a line of surfline ruins—the former beachfront mansions where his simple shorestead lay. Glare off the water stung his eye, but there seemed to be nothing unusual going on. He was pretty sure he could see the good luck banner from Ling's home county, fluttering in a vague breeze. She was supposed to take it down, in the event of trouble.

His heart pounded as he tore strips off an awning to wrap around his hands. Clambering over the guardrail, he tried not to look down as he slid down the other side, until he could support himself with one arm on the gravel deck, while the other hand groped and fumbled with the twin lines.

It was awkward, because holding on to just one strand wouldn't do. The pulley would let him plummet like a stone. So he wound up wrapping both slender ropes around his hand. Before swinging out, Wer closed his eyes for several seconds, breathing steadily and seeking serenity, or at least some calm. *All right, let's go.*

He let go of the ledge and swung down.

Not good! Full body weight tightened the rope like a noose around his hand, clamping a vice across his palm and fingers. Groaning till he was almost out of breath, Wer struggled to ease the pressue by grabbing both cables between his legs and tugging with his other hand, till he finally got out of the noose. Fortunately, his hands were so calloused that there appeared to be no damage. But it took a couple moments for the pain to stop blurring his vision . . .

. . . and when it cleared, he made the mistake of glancing straight down. He swallowed hard—or tried to. A terror that seemed to erupt from somewhere at the base of his spine, ran along his back like a monkey. An eel thrashed inside his belly.

Stop it! he told the animals within. *I am a man. A man with a duty to perform and luck to fulfill. And a man is all that I am.*

It seemed to work. Panic ebbed, like an unpleasant tide, and Wer felt buoyed by determination.

Next, he tried lowering himself, hand over hand, by strength alone. His wiry muscles were up to the task, and certainly he did not weigh enough to be much trouble. But it was hard to hold on to both strings equally. One or the other kept trying to snap free. Wer made it down three stories before one of them yanked out of his grip. It fled upward, toward the pulley while Wer, clinging to the remaining strand, plunged the other way, grabbing at the escapee desperately—

—and finally seized the wild cord. Friction quickly burned through the makeshift padding and into his flesh. By the time he came to a halt, smoke, anguish, and a foul stench wafed from his hand. Hanging there, swaying and bumping against a nearby window, he spent unknown minutes just holding on tight, waiting for his heart to settle and pain speckles to depart his eyes.

Did I cry out? he wondered. Fortunately, the window next to him was blocked by heavy drapes—the glare off the Huangpu was sharp this time of day. Many of the others were boarded up. People still used this building, but most would still be at work or school. Nor would there be much ai in a high-rise hovel.

I don't think I yelled. I think I'm all right. His descent should be masked by heat plumes and glaring sunlight reflections off metal and concrete, making daylight much preferable over making the passage at night, when his body temperature would flare on hundreds of infrared-sensitive cams, triggering anomaly-detection programs.

Learning by trial and error, Wer managed to hook one leg around each of the strands and experimented with letting them slide along his upper thighs, one heading upward and the other going down. It was awkward and painful, at first, but the tough pants could take it, if he took it slow and easy.

Gradually, he approached the dull gray concrete levee from above, and Wer found himself picturing how far it stretched—extending far beyond vision to the left, hugging the new coastline till it reached a great marsh that used to be Shandong Province . . . and to the right, continuing along the river all the way to happy regions far upstream, where the Chang became the Yangtze, and where people had no fear of rising waters. How many millions were employed building the *New Great Wall*? And how many millions more labored as prisoners, consigned on one excuse or another to the titanic task of staving off China's latest invader. The sea.

Drawing close, Wer kept a wary eye on the barrier. This section looked okay—a bit crumbly from cheap, hurried construction, two decades ago, after Typhoon Mariko nearly drowned the city. Still, he knew that some stretches were laced with nasty stuff—razor-sharp wires, barely visible to the eye, or heat-seeking tendrils tipped with toxins.

When the time came, he vaulted over, barely touching the obstacle with the sole of one sandal, landing in the old marina with a splash.

It was unpleasant, of course, a tangle of broken boats and dangerous cables that swirled in a murk of weeds and city waste. Wer lost no time clambering onto one wreck and then leaping to another, hurrying across the obstacle course with an agility learned in more drowned places than he could remember, spending as little time as possible in the muck.

Actually, it looks as if there might be a lot of salvage in here, he thought. Perhaps he might come back—if luck neither veered high nor low, but stayed on the same course as his life had been so far. Moderately, bearably miserable.

Maybe I will risk it, after all, he thought. *Try to find a broker who can offer the big white stone for sale, in some way that might keep us safe. . . .*

Before climbing over the final, rocky berm, separating the marina from the sea, he spotted a rescue buoy, bobbing behind the pilot house of one derelict. It would come in handy, during the long swim ahead.

●━●━

It was nearing nightfall when he approached the shorestead from the west, with the setting sun behind him.

Of course, by now the tide was low and the main gates were open—and Wer was feeling foolish. *I might have made it home by now, just by waiting in town.* In hindsight, his initial panic now seemed overwrought and exaggerated. *I might have sold those lesser stones, had a beer by the fishmonger stands, and already have made it home by now, having dinner while showing Ling a handful of cash.*

Soon, he faced the familiar outlines—the sagging northside wall . . . the metlon poles and supercord bracings . . . the solar distillery . . . the patches where he had begun preparing two of the upper-story rooms for occupation . . . he even caught a scent of that Vietnamese *nuk mam* sauce that Ling added to half her preparations. It all looked normal. Still, he circled the half-ruined mansion, checking for intruder signs. Oil in the water. Tracks in the muddy sand. Any kind of presence lurking below.

Nothing visible. So far so good.

A wasted day, then. A crazy, draining adventure that I could scarcely afford. Some lost stones . . .

. . . though there are more where those came from.

In fact, he had begun to fashion a plan in his head. The smuggler, Quang Lu, had many contacts. Perhaps, while keeping the matter vague at first, Wer might use Quang to set up a meeting, in such a time and place where treachery would be difficult. Perhaps arranging for several competitors to be present at once. How did one of the ancient sages put it?

In order not to be trampled by an elephant, get many of them to push against each other.

All right, maybe no sage actually said that. But one should have. Surely, Wer did not have to match the power of any of the great lords of government, wealth, and commerce. What he needed was a situation where they canceled out each other! Enough to get them openly bidding to obtain what he had. Open enough so that no one could benefit by keeping him quiet.

First thing, I must find a good hiding place for the stone. Then come up with the right story, for Quang.

It took real effort just to haul himself out of the water, Wer's body felt limp and soggy with fatigue. He was past hunger and exhaustion, making his way from the atrium dock to the stairs, then across the roof, and finally to the entrance of the tent-shelter. It flapped with a welcoming rhythm, emitting puffs of homecoming aromas that made his head swim.

Ducking to step inside, Wer blinked, adjusting to the dimmer light. "Oh, what a day I have had. You won't believe, when I tell you. Is that sautéed prawn? The ones I caught this morning? I'm glad you chose to cook those—"

Ling had been stirring the wok. At first, as she turned around, he thought she smiled. Only then Wer realized . . . it was a grimace. She did not speak, but fear glistened in her eyes, which darted to her left—alerting him to swivel and look—

A creature stood on their little dining table. A large *bird* of some kind, with a long, straight beak. It gazed back at Wer, regarding him with a tilt of its head, first one way and then the other. A moment later, it spread stubby wings, stretching them, and he numbly observed.

There are no feathers. A penguin? What would a penguin be doing here in sweltering Shanghai?

Then he noticed its talons. *Penguins don't have—*

The claws gripped something that still writhed on the tabletop, gashed and torn. It looked like a *snake* . . . Only, instead of oozing blood or guts, there were bright flashes and electric sizzles.

A machine. They are both machines.

Without moving its beak, the bird spoke.

"You must not fear. There is no time for fear."

Wer swallowed. His lips felt chapped and dry. "What . . . who are you?"

"I am an instrumentality, sent by those who might save your life." The bird-thing abruptly bent and pecked hard at the snake. Sparks flew. It went dark and limp. An effective demonstration, as if Wer needed one.

"Please go to the window," the winged mechanism resumed, gesturing with its beak. "And bring the stone here."

Well, at least it was courteous. He turned and saw that the white, egg-shaped relic lay on the ledge, soaking in sunlight—instead of wrapped in a dark cloth, as they had agreed. He glanced back sharply at his wife, but Ling was now holding little Xie Xie. She merely shrugged as the baby squirmed and whimpered, trying to nurse.

With a low sigh, Wer turned back toward the stone, whose opalescent surface seemed to glow with more than mere reflections, as he took two steps. Wer could sense the bird leaning forward, eagerly.

As he raised his hands, the whitish surface turned milky and began to swirl. Now it was plain to the eye, how this thing differed from the Havana Artifact that he had seen briefly through an ailectronics store window. It seemed a bit smaller, narrower, and considerably less smooth. One end was marred by pits, gouges, and blisters that tapered into thin streaks across the elongated center. And yet, the similarities were unmistakable. Especially when his hands approached within a few centimeters. A spinning sense of depth grew more intense. And, swiftly, a faint shape began to form, coalescing within, as if emerging from a fog.

Demons, Wer thought.

Or rather, *a* demon, as he realized—there was just a single figure, bipedal, shaped vaguely like a man.

With reluctance—wishing he had never laid eyes on it—Wer made himself plant hands on both tapered ends, gritting his teeth as a brief, faint tremor ran up the inner surface of his arms. He hefted the heavy stone, turned and carried it away from the sunlight. At which point, the glow seemed only to intensify, filling and chasing the dim shadows of the tent-shelter.

"Put it down here, on the table, but please do not release it from your grasp," the bird-thing commanded, still polite, but insistent. Wer obeyed, though he wanted to let go. The shape that gathered form within the stone was one that he had seen before. More humanlike than the demons he had glimpsed on TV, shown conversing with world delegates in Washington—but still a demon. Like the frightening penguin-creature, whose wing now brushed his arm as it bent next to him, eager for a closer look.

"The legends are true!" it murmured. Wer felt the bird's voice resonate, emitting from an area on its chest. "Worldstones are said to be picky. They may choose one human to work with, or sometimes none at all. Or so go the stories." The robot regarded Wer with a glassy eye. "You are fortunate in more ways than you might realize."

Nodding without much joy, Wer knew at least one way.

I am needed, then. It will work only for me.

That means they won't just take the thing and leave us be.

But it also means they must keep me alive. For now.

The demon within the stone—it had finished clarifying, though the image remained rippled and flawed. Approaching on two oddly-jointed legs, it reached forward with powerfully muscular arms, as if to touch or seize

Wer's enclosing hands. The mouth—appearing to have four lips arranged like a flattened diamond—moved underneath a slitlike nose and a single, ribbonlike organ where eyes would have been. With each opening and closing of the mouth, a faint buzzing quivered the surface under Wer's right palm.

"The stone is damaged," the penguinlike automaton observed. "It must have once possessed sound transducers. Perhaps, in a well-equipped laboratory—"

"Legends?" Wer suddenly asked, knowing he should not interrupt. But he couldn't help it. Fear and exhaustion and contact with demons—it all had him on the verge of hysteria. Anyway, the situation had changed. If he was special, needed, then the least that he could demand was an answer or two!

"What legends? You mean there have been more than one or two of these things? You mean they've appeared before?"

The bird-thing tore its gaze away from the the image of the humanoid creature, portrayed opening and closing its mouth in a pantomime of speech that timed roughly, but not perfectly, with the buzzing under Wer's right hand.

"You might as well know, Peng Xiao Wer, since yours is now a burden and a task assigned by Heaven." The penguinlike machine gathered itself to full height and then gave him a small bow of the head. "A truth that goes back farther than any other that is known."

Wer's mouth felt dry. "What truth?"

"That stones have fallen since time began. And men have spoken to them for at least nine thousand years.

"And in all that time, they have spoken of a day of culmination. And that day, long prophesied, may finally be at hand."

Wer felt warm contact at his back, as Ling pressed close—as near as she could, while nursing their child. He did not remove his hands from the object on the table. But he was glad that one of hers slid around his waist, clutching him tight and driving out some of the sudden chill he felt inside.

Meanwhile, the entity within the stone appeared frustrated, perhaps realizing that no one heard its words. The buzzing intensified, then stopped. Then, instead, the demon reached forward, as if toward Wer, and started to *draw a figure* in space, close to the boundary between them. Wherever it moved its scaly hand, a trail of inky darkness remained, until Wer realized.

Calligraphy. The creature was brushing a figure—an ideogram—in a flowing, archaic-looking style. It was a complicated symbol, containing at least twenty strokes. *I wish I had more education,* Wer thought, gazing in awe at the final shape, when it stood finished, throbbing across the face of the glowing worldstone. Both symmetrically beautiful and yet jagged, threatening, it somehow transfixed the eye and made his heart pound.

Wer did not know the character. But anyone with the slightest knowledge of Chinese would recognize the radical—the core symbol—that it was built from.

Danger.

DEPARTURE

The journey began with a bribe and a little air.

And a penguinlike robot, standing on the low dining table that Wer had salvaged from a flooded mansion. A mechanical creature that stayed punctiliously polite, while issuing commands that would forever disrupt the lives of Wer and Ling and their infant son.

"There is very little time," it said, gravely, in a Beijing-accented voice that emanated from somewhere on its glossy chest, well below the sharply pointed beak. "Others have sniffed the same suspicions that brought me here, drawn by your indiscreet queries about selling a *gleaming, egglike stone, with moving shapes within.*"

To illustrate what it meant by "others," the bird-thing scraped one metallic talon along the scaly flank of a large, robotic snake—an interloper that had climbed the crumbling walls and slithered across the roof of this once-opulent beachfront house, slipping into the shorestead shelter and terrifying Ling, while Wer was away on his ill-fated expedition to Shanghai East. Fortunately, the penguin-machine arrived soon after that. A brief, terrible battle ensued, leaving the false serpent torn and ruined, just before Wer returned home.

The reason for that fracas lay on the same table, shimmering with light energy that it had absorbed earlier, from sunshine. An ovoid shape, almost half a meter from tip to tip, opalescent and mesmerizing.

Only a week or two ago, Wer had been thrilled to discover a hidden cache, filled with beautiful things, mostly geological specimens. Which was all Wer thought the stone to be, at first. Or else he would have been more cautious—*far* more cautious—making queries on the Mesh.

The penguin-shaped robot took a step toward Wer.

"Those who sent the snake creature are just as eager as my owners are, to acquire the worldstone. I assure you they'll be less considerate than I have been if we are here when they send reinforcements. And my consideration has limits."

Though a poor man, with meager education, Wer had enough sense to recognize a veiled threat. Still, he felt reluctant to go charging off with his family, into a fading afternoon, with this entity . . . leaving behind, possibly forever, the little shorestead home that he and Ling had built by hand, on the ruins of a seaside mansion.

"You said that the . . . worldstone . . . picks only one person to speak to." He gestured at the elongated egg. Now that his hands weren't in contact with it, it no longer depicted the clear image of a demon . . . or space alien. (There was a difference?) Still, the lopsided orb remained transfixing. Swirling shapes, like storm-driven clouds, seemed to roil beneath its scarred and pitted surface, shining by their own light—as if the object were a lens into another world.

"Wouldn't your rivals have to talk to it *through me*," he finished. "Just as you must?"

One rule of commerce, that even a poor man understood—you can get a better deal when more than one customer is bidding.

"Perhaps, Peng Xiao Wer," the bird-thing replied, shifting its weight in what seemed a gesture of impatience. "On the other hand, you should not overestimate your value, or underestimate the ferocity of my adversaries. This is not a market situation, but akin to ruthless war.

"Furthermore, while very little is known about these worldstones, it is unlikely that you are indispensable. Legends suggest that it will simply pick *another* human counterpart—if the current one dies."

Ling gasped, seizing Wer's left arm in a tight grip, fingernails and all. But still, his mind raced. *It will say whatever it must, in order to get my cooperation. But appearances may be deceiving. The snake could have been sent by the same people, and the fight staged, in order to frighten us. That might explain why both machines showed up at about the same time.*

Wer knew he had few advantages. Possibly, the robot had sensors to read his pulse, blood pressure, iris dilation, skin flush response . . . and lots of other things that a more educated person might know about. Every suspicion or lie probably played out across his face—and Wer had never been a good gambler, even bluffing against humans.

"I . . . will need—"

"Payment is in order. We'll start with a bonus of ten times your current yearly income, just for coming along, followed by a salary of one thousand new yuan per month. As you might guess, this amount is trivial to my owners, so more is possible with good results. Perhaps much more."

It was a princely boon, but Wer frowned, and the machine seemed to read his thoughts.

"I can tell, you are more concerned about other things, like whether you can trust us."

Wer nodded—a tense jerk. The penguin gave a semblance of a shrug.

"That you must decide. Right now." Again, with that faint tone of threat. Still, Wer hesitated.

"I will pack some things for the baby," Ling announced, with resolution in her voice. "We can leave all the rest. Everything."

But the penguinoid stopped her, lifting one stubby wing.

"I regret, wife and child cannot come. It is too dangerous. There are no accommodations and they will slow us down." As Wer started to protest, it raised one stubby wing. "But you will not leave them to starve. I will provide part of your bonus now, in a form they can use."

Wer blinked, staring as the machine settled down into a squat, closing its eyes and straining, almost as if it were . . .

With an audible grunt, it stepped back, revealing a small pellet on the tabletop. "You'll find the funds readily accessible, at any city kiosk. As I said, the amount, though large for you, is too small for my owners to care about cheating from you."

"That is *not* what worries me," Ling said, though she stepped closer, leaned in, and snatched up the pellet. Wer saw that, while her voice was husky with fear, holding Xie Xie squirming against her chest, she wore a cold, pragmatic expression. "Your masters may find it inconvenient to leave witnesses. If you get the stone—how much better if nobody else knows? After . . . my husband departs with you . . . I may not live out the hour."

I hadn't thought of that, Wer realized, grimly. His jaw clenched. He took a step toward the table.

"Open your tutor tablet," the bird-thing snapped, no longer courteous. "Quickly! And speak your names aloud."

Wer hurried to activate the little Mesh device, made for preschoolers, but the only access unit they could afford. Their link was at the minimal, FreePublic level—still, when he spoke the words, a new posting erupted from the little screen. It showed his face . . . and Ling's . . . and the world-stone . . . plus a few dozen characters outlining an agreement.

"Now, your wife knows no more than is already published—which is little enough. Our rivals can extract nothing else, so *we* have no reason to silence her. Nor will anyone else. Does that reassure?

"Good. Only, by providing this reassurance, I have made our time predicament worse. Over the course of the next few minutes and hours, many new forces will notice and start to converge. So choose, Peng Xiao Wer. This instant! If you will not bring the stone, I will explode in twenty seconds, to prevent others from getting it. Agree, or flee! Sixteen . . . fifteen . . . fourteen . . ."

"I'll go!"

Wer grabbed up a heavy sack and rolled the gleaming ovoid inside. The worldstone brightened, briefly, at his touch, then seemed to give up and go dark, as he stuffed in some padding and slung the bag over a shoulder. The penguinoid was already at the flap of the little tent-shelter. Wer turned . . .

. . . as Ling held up their son—the one thing they both cared about, more than each other. "Thrive," he said, with his hand upon the boy's head.

"Survive," she commanded in turn. A moist glisten in her eye both surprised and warmed him, more than any words. He accepted the obligation with a hurried bow, then ducked under the flap, following the robot into the setting sun.

Halfway down the grand staircase, on the landing that Wer had turned into an indoor dock, the penguin split its belly open, revealing a small cavity and a slim, metal object within.

"Take it."

He recognized a miniature breathing device—a mouthpiece with a tiny, insulated capsule of highly compressed air. Quang Lu, the smuggler, had one—a bulkier model. Wer snatched it out of the fissure, which closed quickly, as the robot waddled to the edge, overlooking the greasy water of the Huangpu Estuary.

"Now, make speed!"

It dived in, then paused to swivel and regard Wer with beady, now luminescent eyes, watching the human's every move.

Wer took a brief, backward glance, wondering if he would ever return—then he slipped in the mouthpiece and took the biggest plunge of his life, following a sleek little robot into the murk.

SEASTEADING

The journey of a thousand li can begin with a first step into a pile of dogshit.

—popular Chinese expression, in cynical reply to Lao-Tzu

Ocean stretched in every direction.

Peng Xiao Wer had come to think of himself as a man of the sea. After all, for years he had spent most of his time in water—amid the scummy, sandy, tidal surges that swept up and down the Huangpu Estuary. He thought nothing of holding his breath while diving a dozen meters for crab, or prying salvage from the junk-strewn bottom, feeling more akin to the fish, or even drifting jellies, than to the landlubber he once had been. In a world of rising seas and drowning shorelines, it seemed a good way to adapt.

Only now, he realized, *I always counted on the nearness of dry land.*

The huge, ugly concrete seawall that China had erected, to defend its new coastline. And, beyond that New Great Wall, the shining towers of East Shanghai. Even the teetering, preflood mansions that poor men like me were tricked into shoresteading—a cheap way to clean up the mess left by other generations. Even those crumbling ruins were somehow re-assuring.

Compared to the real thing. Compared to this.

Ahead of him lay nothing but gray sea, daunting and seemingly endless, flecked with wind-driven froth and merging imperceptibly with a faraway, turbid horizon. Except where he now stood, on a balcony, projecting outward from a man-made island—a high-tech village on stilts—clinging to a reef that used to be a nation.

And that was now a nation, once again.

Looking carefully, he could follow the curve of breakers, where mutant corals had been planted in faint hope of enhancing the shoals. Below the surface, he knew, there lay stumps of what had once been buildings—homes and schools, shops and wharves. Only, here there had been no effort to preserve doomed properties against the rising sea. Explosives took care of that, years ago, making swift work of Old Pulupau, soon after most of the natives moved away. Anyway, the new inhabitants didn't want unpleasant reminders to spoil their view.

Of course there was a lot more hidden from the eye, just under the surface and beyond the reef. A vista of pulsating industry had been visible from the small submarine that brought him here, three days ago. Wave machines for generating electricity and siphons that sucked up bottom mud to spread into the currents, fertilizing plankton to enhance nearby fishing grounds and earn carbon credits at the same time. Through a tiny, circular window, Wer had also seen huge spheres, shaped like gigantic soccer balls, bobbing against anchor-tethers—pens where whole schools of tuna spent their lives, fed and fattened for market. A real industrial and economic infrastructure . . . all of it kept below the surface, out of sight of the residents.

A glint of white cloth and silvery metal . . . Wer winced as his right eye, fresh from surgery, overreacted to the sudden glare, reflecting off a twenty-meter sailing vessel that passed into view, around the far corner of Newer Newport. Sails billowed and figures hurried about the deck, tugging at lines. A call—distant but clear—bellowed across the still surface of the lagoon.

"Two-six, heave!"

Voices answered in unison as well-drilled teamwork rapidly set the main sail. Though the crew seemed to be working hard, nobody would call it "labor." Not when the poorest citizen of this independent nation could buy or sell a man like Wer, ten thousand times or more. Wer found the sight intriguing, in more ways than he could count.

I always thought that rich people would lay about, letting servants and robots do everything for them. Sure, you heard of wealthy athletes and hobbyists. But I had no idea so many others would also choose to sweat and strain . . . for fun. Or that it could be so—

He shook his head, lacking the vocabulary. Then something happened that he still found disturbing. A dark splotch appeared, as if by magic, in a lower corner of his right eye. The shadow resolved into a single Chinese character, with a small row of lesser figures underneath, offering both a definition and pronunciation guide.

Obsessive.

Yes. That word seemed close to what he had in mind. Or, rather, what the ai in his eye estimated, after following his gaze and reading subconscious signals in his throat, the subvocalized words that he had muttered within, without ever speaking them aloud.

This was going to take some getting used to.

"Peng Xiao Wer," a voice spoke behind him. "You have rested and the worldstone has recharged. It is time to return."

It was the same voice that he had come to associate with the penguin-machine, his constant companion during the hurried journey that began less than a hundred hours ago—first swimming away from his wife and child and the little shorestead they all shared, then aboard a midget submarine, followed by a fast coastal packet-freighter, then a hurried midnight transfer to a seaplane that made a rendezvous, in midocean, with yet another submarine . . . and all that way accompanied by a black birdlike robot. His guide, or keeper, or guard, it had spoken to him soothingly about his coming duties as keeper of the worldstone.

Only at journey's end, after surfacing and stepping onto Newer Newport, here in Pulupau, did Wer meet the original owner of the voice.

"Yes, Nguyen Ky," he answered, turning and nodding to a slight man, with Annamese features and long black hair braided in elegant rows.

"I come, sir."

He turned to gather up the off-white ovoid—the *worldstone*—from a nearby patio table, where it had lain in sunshine for an hour, soaking energy. A welcome break for him, as well.

As carefully as he would handle a baby, Wer hefted the artifact and followed Nguyen Ky between sliding doors of frosted glass, moving slowly, out of habit, in order to let his eyes adapt to interior dimness. Only, he might as well not have bothered. His right eye . . . or ai . . . now adjusted brightness and contrast for him, more quickly than any spreading of his natural iris.

The room was broad and well-appointed, with plush furnishings that adapted to each user's comfort preference. Programmable draperies were set to a soothing pattern that rippled gently, like a freshwater brook, though the farthest window was left open. Through it, Wer glimpsed the rest of Newer Newport—more than a hectare of sleek, multistoried luxury, perched on massive footings, firmly anchored over the spot where the ancestral kings of Pulupau once had their palace.

Some distance beyond, a series of other mammoth stilt-villages, each wildly different in style, followed one curve of the drowned atoll. They had odd names. like *Thielville, Minerva, Dzugasvilligrad, Bhodisathere,* and *Friedman's Freehold*. One of them—with architecture reminiscent of palm logs and thatch roofing—was set aside for the old royal family and a number of genuine Pulupauese. As legalistic insurance, in case any nation or consortium ever questioned the sovereign independence of this archipelago of wealth.

Seasteading. Of course, Wer had heard of such places. Along the spectrum of human wealth, these projects lay at the very opposite end from the *shore*stead that he had settled with Ling, in the garbage-strewn Huangpu. Here, and in a few dozen other locales, some of the world's richest families had pooled funds to buy up small nations to call their own, escaping responsibility to the continental states, with their teeming, populist masses. And taxes. Yet, there were essential traits shared in common by seastead and shorestead. Adaptation. Making the best of rising seas. Turning calamity into advantage.

Three technical experts—a graceful Filipina who never removed her wraparound immersion goggles; an islander, possibly an heir of the native

Pulupauans, who kept fingering his interactive crucifix; and an elderly
Chinese gentleman, who spoke in the soft tones of a scholar—watched
Wer gingerly replace the worldstone in its handcrafted cradle, surrounded
by instruments and sleek, ailectronic displays.

The ovoid had already started coming alive, in response to his touch.
Nobody knew why, as keeper of the worldstone, Wer alone could rouse
the object's power to create vivid images that shone within—like a whole
world or universe shining within an egglike capsule, half a meter long.
Whatever the reason, Wer was grateful for the honor, for the employment,
for a chance to participate in matters far above his normal station of life.

The now familiar entity *Courier of Warnings* lurked—or seemed to
lurk—just within the pitted, egglike curves, amid those ever-present swirling
clouds. *Courier*'s ribbon eye stared outward, resembling Anna Arroyo's un-
blinking goggles, while the creature's diamond-shaped, four-lipped mouth
pursed in a perpetual expression of worry or disapproval.

Wer carefully reattached a makeshift device at one end, which compen-
sated for some of the object's surface damage, partly restoring a sonic
connection. Of course, he had no idea how the mechanism—or anything
else in the room—worked. But he kept trying to learn every procedure. If
only so the others would consider him a colleague and not an experimen-
tal subject.

From their wary expressions, he could tell it would take time.

"Let us resume," Dr. Nguyen said. "We were attempting to learn about
the stone's arrival on Earth. Here are the ideograms we want you to try
next, please." The small man laid a sheet of e-paper in front of Wer, bearing a series of characters. They looked complex and very old—even archaic.

Fortunately, Wer did not have to hold the ovoid in his hands anymore.
Just standing nearby seemed to suffice. Bringing his right index finger
close—and sticking out his tongue a little in concentration—he copied the
first symbol by tracing it across the surface of the worldstone. Inky brush-
strokes seemed to follow his touch-path. Actually, it came out rather
pretty. *Calligraphy . . . one of the great Chinese art forms. Who figured I
would have a knack for it?*

He managed the next figure more quickly. And a third one. Evidently,
the ideograms were not in modern Chinese, but some older dialect and
writing system that preceded the unification standards of great Chin, the
first emperor. Fortunately, the implant in his eye went ahead and offered a
translation, which he spoke aloud.

"Date of arrival on Earth?"

There were two projects going on, at once. First, using the ancient symbols to ask questions. But Dr. Nguyen also wanted to expose the entity to modern words. Ideally—if it truly was much smarter than an earthly ai—it should learn the more recent version of Chinese, and other languages as well. Anyway, this would test the ovoid's adaptability.

After a brief pause, *Courier* appeared to lift one arm, with a weirdly flexible double-elbow, and knocked Wer's ideograms away, causing them to shatter and dissolve with a flick of one three-fingered hand. The simulated alien then proceeded to draw a series of new figures that jostled and arrayed themselves against the worldstone's inner face. Wer also sensed the bulbous right end of the stone emit faint vibrations. Sophisticated detectors fed these to a computer, whose vaice then uttered enhanced sounds that Wer didn't understand.

Fortunately, Yang Shenxiu, the white-haired Chinese scholar, could. He tapped a uniscroll in front of him.

"Yes, yes! So *that* is how those words used to be pronounced. Wonderful."

"And what do they mean, please?" demanded the Vietnamese mogul standing nearby.

"Oh, he . . . the being who resides within . . . says that he cannot track the passage of time, since he slept for so long. But he will offer something that should be just as good."

Dr. Nguyen stepped closer. "And pray, what is that?"

The alien brought its forearms together and then apart again. The ever-present clouds seemed to converge, bringing darkness upon a patch of the worldstone, till deep black reigned across the center. Wer caught a pointlike glitter . . . and another . . . and then two more . . . and another pair . . .

"Stars," announced Anna Arroyo. "Six of them, arrayed in a rough hexagon . . . with a final one in the middle, off-center . . . I'm searching the online constellation catalogs. . . . Damn. All present-day matches include some stars that are below seventh magnitude, so it's unlikely . . ."

"Please do not curse," said the islander, Patri Menelaua. "Let's recall that the topic at hand is time. Dates. *When*. Stars shift." Still fondling the animatronic cross that hung from a chain around his neck, he added. "Try going retrograde . . ."

The figure of Jesus seemed to squirm, a little, away from his touch. Anna frowned, but nodded. "I'm on it. Backsifting and doing a whole sky match-search in one hundred year intervals. This could take a while."

Wer grunted. Held back a moment. Then hurriedly blurted: "Seven!"

The scholar and the rich man turned to him. Wer had to swallow to gather courage, managing a low croak.

"Try the seven maidens. You know. The . . ." He groped for a name.

"Pleiades," the scholar finished for him. "Yes, that would be a good guess—"

The Filipina woman interrupted. "Got you. Scanning time-drift of just that one cluster, back . . . back . . . yes! It's a good match. The Pleiades, just under five thousand years ago. Wow."

Dr. Nguyen nodded. "I expected something like this. Peng Xiao Wer, the box that formerly held the worldstone—please tell us, what did the inscription say?"

Wer recited from memory.

"Unearthed in Harappa, 1926 . . ." He then spoke the second half with an involuntary shiver. "Demon-infested. Keep in the dark."

"Harappa, yes," Nguyen nodded, ignoring the other part. "A center of the Indus Valley culture . . . the poor third sister of the early days of urban civilization, after Mesopotamia and Egypt. Some think it was a stunted state—cramped, paranoid, and never fully literate. We don't really know what happened to the Indus civilization. Abandoned about 1700 BCE, they say. Possibly a great flood weakened both main cities, Harappa and Mohenjo-daro."

He shook his head, and the elegant braids swished. "But this makes no sense! Why would it be speaking to us in archaic Chinese, a dialect from a millennium later? Harappa was buried under sand, by then!"

Wer shrugged. "Shall I try to ask, sir?"

The small man waved a hand in front of his face. "No. I am following a script of questions, prioritized by colleagues and associates around the world. We'll keep to these points, then fill in gaps later. Go to the next set of characters, Peng Xiao Wer, if you would please."

Wer felt gratified, again, by Dr. Nguyen's unfailing politeness. The gentleman had been well brought up, for sure, skilled at how best to treat underlings. *Perhaps I will get to work for him, forever.* Not a harsh fate to contemplate, so long as Ling and the baby could join Wer, at some point soon.

He meant to prove his value to the man.

Bending over the stone, Wer carefully sketched four more of the complicated figures. Professor Yang Shenxiu had provided these versions of the questions, in a style from long ago, in order to communicate with the entity within. Dr. Nguyen's consortium could not wait for their own worldstone to learn modern Chinese. There wasn't time.

Not with the world in an uproar over dire things that were being said by the so-called Havana Artifact—another alien emissary-stone that an American astronaut recently retrieved from high orbit. *This* stone in front of Wer offered a way to check—in secret—on the stories being told by that other one in Washington. So far, they knew one thing.

Courier proclaimed that the Havana Artifact had been sent by "liars."

Wer concentrated on drawing the ancient characters right. When the last figure was finished, seeming to float, just below the surface of the egg-shaped thing, Wer spoke the question aloud, as well.

"*How* did you arrive on Earth?"

The reply came in two parts. While *Courier of Warnings* painted ideograms and uttered antiquated words, an *image* took shape nearby, starting as night's own darkness. Anna Arroyo quickly arranged for an expanded version of the picture to billow outward from their biggest 3D display, revealing a black space vista, dusted with stars.

Meanwhile, in arch tones that seemed beautifully and appropriately old-fashioned, Professor Yang Shenxiu translated the ancient ideograms, aloud.

Pellets, hurled from point of origin,
Thrown by godlike arms of light,
Cast to drift for time immeasurable,
Through emptiness unimaginable . . .

One star, amid a powdery myriad, seemed to pulsate, as if aiming narrow, sharp twinkles outward. . . .

"Capture those constellation images!" Dr. Nguyen commanded, with no time for courtesy.

"I'm on it!" Menelaua snapped. His fingers left the crucifix and waggled in the air with desperate speed, while the islander grunted and hopped a little in the seat of his chair.

Wer stared as several of the narrow, winking rays seemed to propel tiny dots in front of them. One of these zoomed straight toward his point of view, growing into a wide, reflective surface that loomed toward those watching.

"Photon sail!" Anna diagnosed. "A variant on the Nakamura design. Propelled by a laser at point of origin."

Wer grunted, amazed by her quickness—and that he actually grasped some of her meaning! The space windjammer hurtled past his viewpoint, which swiveled around to give chase—and he briefly glimpsed a tiny, smooth shape, dragged behind the giant sail, brilliantly radiant in the home star's propelling beam . . .

. . . which then dimmed. The diaphanous sail contracted, folding and collapsing into a small container at one end of a little egg, whose former brightness now faded, until it could only be made out as a seed-shaped ripple, hurtling at speeds Wer couldn't begin to contemplate.

"Neat trick with the sail," Patri commented. "Tuck it away, when it's not needed for propulsion or energy collection, so it won't snag interstellar particles. With bi-memory materials, it could expand or contract with very little effort. I bet they use it later to slow down."

Wer now grasped how the worldstone must have come across the incredible gulf between stars—a method sure to provoke feelings of kinship from this colony of wealthy yachting enthusiasts. At the same time, he wondered. What would ancient peoples, in China or India, have made of these images?

In fact, could anyone guarantee that modern humanity was much more advanced now? In ways that mattered most?

Meanwhile, Scholar Yang's narration continued.

Slow time passed while the galaxy turned,
A new star loomed—its light, a cushion.

The pellet turned around and redeployed its sail, which now took a gentler, braking push from a brightening light source ahead. *The sun,* Wer realized. It had to be.

"Knew it!" the islander exulted. "Of course there's no laser at this end. Just sunlight alone won't be enough."

As the star ahead grew from a pinpoint into a tiny, visible disk, a *new object* abruptly loomed in front of the worldstone—a great, banded sphere, replete with tier after tier of whirling, multicolored storms.

Chosen beforehand—a giant ball waited,
Ready to catch . . . pull . . . assist . . .

Yang Shenxiu's translation stumbled as, even with computer aissistance, he could only offer guesses. Well, after all, the Indus and archaic Chinese peoples knew very little about astronomy, planetary navigation, and all that.

"A gravity swing past Jupiter," Anna murmured in apparent admiration. "Like threading a microscopic needle across centuries and light-years. They had to time it perfectly."

The mighty gas planet swerved by unnervingly fast, and the pellet, with its sail still billowed open, now plunged slightly *away* from the sun, then plunged toward it again, from a different angle.

Patri interjected. "But it would still have loads of excess velocity. This needle would have been chosen to offer *multiple* swings past other planets, as well as Jupiter and the sun, again and again."

His appraisal was borne out, as the broiling solar sphere darted by, making Wer's eyes water. Just after nearest passage, the sail furled back into its container . . . and soon a smaller ball swung past, so close that Wer felt he was passing *through* the topmost of its churning, yellow clouds, while a brief, glowing aura surrounded the image.

"Atmospheric braking through the atmosphere of Venus. Dang! They'd need orbital figures down to ten decimals, in order to plan this from so far away, so long in advance."

Then, another sudden veer and gyre past Jupiter . . .

"Yes, though it could make small, real time adjustments, in between encounters, by tacking with the sail," Anna replied. "Still they wouldn't arrange it in such detail without a destination in mind." She made her own rapid finger movements. "They had to know about Earth already. From instruments, like our LifeSeeker Telescope . . . only far more advanced. They'd know it had an oxygen atmosphere, life, nonequilibrium methane, possibly chlorophyll. Even so—"

Without shifting his transfixed gaze, Wer had to shake his head. There was no way that ancient peoples could have made anything of this, even if *Courier* showed them all the same images and told them all about these worlds, named after their gods—or the other way around. Wer's head seemed to spin, nauseated, as the whirling, planetary dance went through several further encounters—more dizzying, gut-wrenching pirouettes—until the sense of pell-mell speed finally diminished. The pace grew sedate—if no less urgent.

Then a different-colored dot appeared, just ahead.

Once again, the storytelling image zoomed in upon the box at the front of the pellet. A little hatch opening, the sail reemerging.

At long last, the goal lay in sight,
Now to approach gently, and find a perch,
To focus, study, and appraise,
Then to sleep again and wait.
Wait until a time of claiming,
When allures are certain. Ready . . .

Only, this time, something went wrong, as the sail came out of its box—and one corner dimpled inward, crossing its own lines and causing a tangle.

"Uh-oh, that can't be good," Patri Menelaua commented. "How'd that happen?

Wer blinked in surprise and felt his guts clench as the sail rapidly collapsed, its slender cables knotted and spoiled. While this happened, Patri's commentary continued.

"It must have intended to fine-tune its approach to Earth, by gradually tacking on sunlight till entering a high, safe orbit, Perhaps at a Lagrange point. Then spend some time—centuries—evaluating the situation. Maybe use the sail as a telescope mirror, to make detailed observations from a secure distance. Then wait."

"Wait . . . for what?" Anna was doubtful. "For the planet to produce space travelers? But, the temporal coincidence is incredible! To launch this thing timed so it arrived only a few thousand years before we made it into space? How could they have known?"

Wer marveled that these skilled people could grasp so much, so quickly. Even allowing for all of their fancy tools and aids, it was a privilege to be in such company.

"Incredible, but implicit! Anyway, how do we know the solar system isn't filled with these stone-things, arriving all across the last billion years? We never surveyed the asteroid belt for objects this small. And that astronaut snagged one that drifted in—"

"It's still an appalling coincidence," Anna snapped. "There has to be—"

"Comrades, please," Professor Yang Shenxiu urged, raising his eyes briefly from his own workstation. "Evidently, something went wrong at the last minute. Let us observe."

Wer found that he could barely breathe from tension, watching a drama that had unfolded millennia ago. He felt sympathy for the world-stone. To have traveled so far, and come so close to success, only for it all to unravel . . .

Failure! Luck evades us,
While the ball-Earth reaches out,
To clutch me to her bosom.

Wer glanced at Yang Shenxiu, who was once again far away in time and space, his eyes glittering with soft laser reflections cast by his helper apparatus. Of course, the alien entity's vocabulary must have come from its encounters with early humans, in long-ago, more colorful days.

Will Earth embrace me?
Will I end in a fiery pyre?
Or will she fling me outward,
To tumble, forever—
—in cold and empty space?

Unable to maneuver, even a little, the pellet let go of its uselessly clotted sail as the planet loomed close, swinging by, once . . . twice . . . three times . . . and several more . . . From Patri's commentary, it seemed that some kind of safety margin was eroding with each orbital passage. Doom drew closer.

Then it came—the final plunge.

So, it will be fire.
Plummeting amid heat and pain,
Destined for extinction . . .

Starting with deceptive softness, the flames of atmospheric entry soon crackled around the image, accompanied by a roar that seemed almost wrathful. Wer realized, with a sharp intake of breath, that it would be just like the *Cheng He* expedition. He felt an agonized pang, as any Chinese person would . . .

. . . until new characters floated upward, to jitter and bump alongside the image-story, painted in brush strokes of tentative hope.

Then, once again,
Fate changed its mind.

The grand voyage might have ended then, in waters covering three-quarters of the globe, an epic journey climaxing in burial, under some muddy bottom. Or, impacting almost anywhere on land, to crush, shatter, and explode.

Instead, as they watched the egg-artifact ride a shallow trail of flame—shedding speed and scattering clouds—there loomed ahead a snow-covered mountainside! It struck the pinnacle along one flank, sending white spumes jetting skyward. Then another angled blow, and another . . . till the ovoid finally tumbled to rest, smoldering, on the fringes of a highland glacier.

Heat, quenched by cold, melted a shallow impression, much like a nest. Whereupon, soon after arriving in a gaudy blaze, the pellet from space seemed to fade—barely visible—into the icy surface. Wer had to blink away tears.

Wow, he thought, releasing tension. That was much better than any of the telenet dramas that Ling used to make him watch.

Meanwhile, archaic-looking ideograms continued to flow across the worldstone, next to the story-image. Yang Shenxiu was silent, as distracted and transfixed as any of them. So Wer glanced at some modern Chinese characters that formed in the corner of his right eye. A rougher, less poetical translation, offered by his own aissistant.

This was not the normal mission.
Nor any planned-for program.

For once, none of the smart people said a thing, joining Wer in silence as the picture narrative flowed on. Spot-sampled snapshots seemed to leap across countless seasons, innumerable years. The glacier underwent a time-sped series of transition flickers, at first growing and flowing down a starkly lifeless valley, carrying the stone along, sometimes burying it in white layers. Then (Wer guessed) more centuries passed as the ice river gradually thinned and receded, until the retreating whiteness departed completely, leaving the alien envoy-probe stranded, passive and helpless, upon a stony moraine.

But the makers left allowance,
For eventualities unexpected.

Appearing to give chase, grasses climbed the mountain, just behind the retiring ice wall. Soon, tendrils of forest followed, amid rippling, seasonal waves of wildflowers. Then, time seemed to put on the brakes, slowing down even more. Single trees stayed in place, the sun's transit decelerated, unnervingly, from a stop-action blur to the torpid movement of a shadow, on a single day.

Wer swayed in reaction, as if some vehicle he was riding had screeched to a halt. A bubble of bile rose in his throat. Still, he was unable to stop watching, or even blink . . .

. . . as two of the shadows moved closer, converging upon a pair of *legs*—clad in leather breeches and cross-laced moccasins—that entered the field of view in short, careful steps.

Then, a human hand, stained with soot. Soon joined by its partner—fingernails grimy with caked mud and ocher. Reaching down to touch.

Dour Storytellers

Wer tried hard to follow the conversation—partly out of fascination, but also because he felt desperate to please.

If I prove useful to them—more than a mere on-off switch for the worldstone—it could mean my life. It might even mean getting to see Ling and Xie Xie again.

That goal wasn't going to come easy, though. The others kept talking way over his head. Nor could he blame them. After all, who was he? *What* was he, but another piece of driftwood-trash, washed up on a beach, who happened to pick up a pretty rock? Should he demand they explain everything? *Dui niu tanqin* . . . it would be like playing a lute to a cow.

Except, of course, they needed his ongoing service as communicator/ambassador to the entity *within* that rock—and he seemed to be performing that task well enough. At least according to Dr. Nguyen, who always seemed friendly to Wer.

Still, the tech-search experts—Anna Arroyo and Patri Menelaua—clearly felt dubious about this ill-educated Huangpu shoresteader with weathered skin and rough diction, who kept taking up valuable time with foolish questions. Those two would be happier, he knew, if the honor of direct contact with the *Courier* entity were taken over by somebody else.

Only, can *the role be passed along at all? If I died, would it transfer to another?* Surely, they had mulled that tempting thought.

Or do I have some special trait—something that goes beyond being the first man in a decade or two, to lay eyes on the worldstone? Without me, might there be a long search, before they found another? That possibility, he knew, was the one he must foster. At some point, it might keep him breathing.

"Clearly, this mechanism in our possession was dispatched across interstellar space by different people, with different motives, than those who sent the Havana Artifact," commented Yang Shenxiu, the scholar from New Beijing, who rested one hand on the worldstone, without causing more than a ripple under its cloudy surface—giving Wer a touch of satisfaction. *It reacts a lot more actively to my touch!*

With his other hand, Yang motioned toward a large placard-image screen for comparison. In vivid three-vee, it showed the alien object under study in Virginia, America, surrounded by researchers from around the world—a bustle of activity watched by billions of people and supervised by Gerald Livingstone, the astronaut who had discovered and collected that "herald egg" from orbit.

To most of the world, that is the sole one in existence. Only a few suspect that such things have been encountered before, across the centuries. And even fewer have certain knowledge of another active stone, held in secret, here in the middle of the vast Pacific Ocean.

Wer contemplated the three-dimensional image of his counterpart, a clever and educated man, a scientist and spaceman and probably the world's most famous person, right now. In other words, different from poor little Peng Xiao Wer in every conceivable way. *Except that he looks as tired and worried as I feel.*

Watching the man portrayed in the placard-view, Wer felt a sense of connection, as if with another *chosen one.* Another keeper-guardian of a frightening oracle from space. Even if they found themselves on opposite sides of an ancient struggle.

Patri Menelaua answered Yang Shenxiu by describing a long list of physical differences in excruciating detail—the Havana Artifact was larger, longer, and more knobby at one end, for example. And, clearly, far less damaged. Well, it never had to suffer the indignities of fiery passage through Earth's atmosphere, or pummeling impact with a mountain glacier, or centuries of being poked at by curious or reverential or terrified tribal humans . . . not to mention a couple of thousand years buried in a debris pit, then a couple of decades soaking in polluted waters underneath a drowned mansion. Wer found himself reacting defensively on behalf of "his" worldstone.

I'd like to see Livingstone's object come through all that, and still be capable of telling scary stories.

Of course, that was the chief trait that both ovoids had in common. Differing somewhat in the details, each one seemed intent on frightening Earthlings with dire warnings they could do nothing about.

". . . so, yes, there are evident physical differences. Still, anyone can tell that at a glance that they use the same underlying technologies. Capacious and possibly unlimited holographic memory storage. Surface sonic transduction at the wider end . . . but with most communications handled visually, both in pictorial representation and through symbol manipulation. Some surface tactile sensitivity. And, of course, an utter absence of moving parts."

"Yes, there are those commonalities," Anna Arroyo put in. "Still, the

Havana Artifact projects across a wider spectrum than this one—and it portrays a whole community of simulated alien species, while ours depicts only one."

Dr. Nguyen nodded, his elegantly decorated braids rattling. "It would be a good guess to imagine that one species or civilization sent out waves of these things, and the technology was copied by others—"

"Who proceeded to cast forth modified stones of their own," concluded Anna. "Until one of those races decided to break the chain letter, somewhat. By offering a *dissenting* point of view."

Wer took advantage of this turn in the conversation—away from technical matters and back to the general story their own Worldstone had been telling.

"Isn't . . . is it not . . . clear who came second? *Courier* warns us not to pay attention to *liars*. It seems . . . I mean is it not clear that he refers to the tales that are . . . that have been told by the Havana Artifact?"

Of course they were amused by his stumbling attempts to speak a higher grade of Beijing dialect, with classier grammar and tones. But he also knew there were many *types* of amusement. And, while Anna and Patri might feel the contemptuous variety, it was the indulgent smile of Dr. Nguyen that mattered far more. He seemed approving of Wer's earnest efforts.

"Yes, Peng Xiao Wer. We can assume—for now—that our Worldstone is speaking of the Havana Artifact—or things like it—when it warns against *enemies and liars*. The question is—what should we do about this?"

"Warn everybody!" suggested Yang Shenxiu. "You've seen how the other worldstone has thrown the entire planet into a funk, with that story told by the *emissary* creatures who reside within. A tale of profound and disarmingly blithe *pessimism*, confidently assuring us that *nobody survives*. Already, there are rising waves of nihilism and despair, across every continent."

"Not everybody is reacting that way," Patri answered. "Perhaps the warning will have net positive effects. It may be enough to rouse humanity, to gird us with determination and make us decide at last to grow up. To bear down and concentrate on solving—"

Anna snorted with disdain. "You've seen the telecasts. Those artifact creatures insist, over and over again, that there is no way to accomplish it. Surviving as a technological civilization appears to be like crossing a vast minefield. Too many mistakes lie in wait for any sapient race. Too many bad trade-offs or ineludible paths of destruction. They say it's rare for any advanced culture to last for more than a few thousand years. At best. Barely long enough to learn how to make more of *these*"—she gestured at the worldstone—"and cast out more copies of the chain letter!"

Well, Wer thought, *even a few thousand years would be nice. We humans have only had high tech for a century or so, and we seem to have already blown it.*

Anna held up a finger.

"*Either* they are telling the truth about that inevitability, in which case it's all hopeless, and we should take up their offer . . . *or* . . ."—she held up another—"or they are telling this story *in order* to push us toward despair and self-destruction—the scenario that our *Courier* entity warns against."

Yang Shenxiu agreed. "This is bigger than any of us. Let us bring these terrifying stones together! Let them debate each other, before the world!"

All eyes turned to Dr. Nguyen, who rested both elbows on the teak tabletop and bridged his fingers, blowing a silent whistle through pursed lips. Finally, he shook his head.

"I am answerable to a consortium," he said at last, in impeccable Mandarin, with only a hint of his childhood Mekong accent. "My instructions were to start by getting this stone's story and determining if there were any differences from the Havana Artifact. That we have accomplished.

"Alas, the second imperative priority was made crystal clear—to seek advantageous technologies, at almost any cost. Either through interrogation or through dissection. Also, using such methods to determine if there are troves of information the thing is holding back."

With grim, tight lips, Patri Menelaua nodded. Meanwhile, Wer and the others stared, in various degrees of shock.

"The word *advantageous* . . . ," Anna protested. ". . . it assumes we can discover something that the researchers in Virginia aren't discovering—technologies that would give our consortium an edge. But we've already seen that these objects are similar. Moreover, the entire *premise* of the story being told by the creature-simulations inside the Havana Artifact . . . their whole narrative . . . revolves around a promise that they will give humanity every capability *to make more of these stones*!

"It's the reason they crossed so many light-years. Surely that means we'd gain nothing from tearing apart—"

"Not necessarily," Patri dissented. "If *Courier* is right, they have a hidden agenda. They'll hold back plenty. Sure, they're teaching humanity how to make copies. But really, what are they offering? These stone emissaries don't seem to be all that far in advance of our present capabilities, anyway. Now that we've seen them, we could probably duplicate everything—except maybe those super-propulsion lasers—in thirty years. Or less.

"No, what has to worry us is the possibility that there may be *a lot more to all of this*, underneath what they are telling us. Only, because the Havana Artifact is openly shared and in public hands, it will never be subjected to harsh scrutiny."

"But *we* can cut into *our* stone, because we're not answerable to public opinion, is that it?" Anna's voice cracked with disbelief. "Are you listening to yourself? If *Courier* is telling the truth, then *only he* can expose the other stone's lie! Yet, *because* we believe him, and have an opportunity to proceed in secret, *we'll* start sawing away at him, with drills and lasers?"

"Hey, look. I was only saying—"

"What about the others?"

Menelaua glared at Wer for interrupting, so fiercely that Wer shrank back and had to be coaxed into resuming.

"Please continue, son," Dr. Nguyen urged. "What others are you talking about?"

Wer swallowed.

"Other . . . stones."

Nguyen regarded him with a blank, cautious stare,

"Pray explain, Peng Xiao Wer. What other stones do you mean?"

"Well . . . ," he gathered his courage, speaking slowly, carefully. "When I first arrived here, you . . . graciously let me view that report . . . the *private report* describing legends about sacred crystals or globes or rocks that . . . were said to give some humans a chance to . . . to see strange or distant or fantastic things. Some of the stories are well known—crystal balls and dragon stones. Other tales were passed down for generations within families or secret societies. There is one that's supposed to go back nine thousand years, right? It's . . . it is interesting to compare those sagas to the truth we see before us . . . and yet . . ."

He paused, uncertain he should continue.

"Go on, Wer," urged the rich man—representing an association of many other rich men and women.

"Yet . . . what I don't understand is why that report, all by itself, would have made people so eager . . . spending so much money and effort . . . to actually *look* for such a thing! I mean, why would any modern people— sophisticated men like you, Dr. Nguyen—believe such stories, any more than fables about spirits and demons?" Wer shook his head, repressing the fact that he *had* always believed in spirits, at least a little. So did lots of people.

"I figure the former owner of our worldstone—"

"Lee Fang Lu." Yang Shenxiu interjected a name that Wer had never known, till now. The fellow who used to own that predeluge mansion, with the clandestine basement chamber where Wer had found a treasure trove of odd specimens. He nodded gratefully.

"Lee Fang Lu might have been arrested, tortured, and killed over rumors—"

"That he possessed something like this." Dr. Nguyen nodded and his beaded hair clattered softly. "Pray continue."

"Then there's the way you and your . . . competitors . . . pounced on me, after I put out just a *hint* about a glowing white egg. Clearly, when the Havana Artifact was announced, there were already powerful groups out there, who knew the . . . the . . ."

He groped for the right words. And abruptly a new, unfamiliar Chinese language character appeared in that ai-patch, overlain upon his lower right field of vision. Plus a row of tone-accented roman letters, for pronunciation. The ai-patch had been doing that more often as it grew more familiar with Wer—anticipating and assisting what he was trying to say.

". . . *the range-of-plausible-potentialities* . . . ," he carefully enunciated, while moving his finger over his palm, mimic-drawing the character in question—a common thing to do, when a word was obscure. He saw the others variously frown or smile a little. They were probably used to this sort of thing.

"I just find it hard to believe that powerful people would go to so much trouble . . . to search frantically for such a thing, even after learning about the Havana Artifact . . . unless they thought there was a real possibility of success. Unless they had strong reason to believe those legends were *more* than just legends."

He looked at Dr. Nguyen, surprised by his own boldness.

"I bet there was a lot left out of that report, sir. Is it possible that some groups have had worldstones before this? And maybe still do?"

Menelaua shook his head and snarled. "That's ridiculous."

"And why is that, Patri?" Anna Arroyo answered. "It'd take care of that *temporal coincidence*, at least a bit. Maybe these things have been crisscrossing our region of space for a long time, like messages in bottles, sent by neighbors squabbling and slandering each other. While most settled into far orbits, waiting for Earth to produce space-faring folk, others might have landed—accidentally, like this one. Or on purpose in some way. Most would shatter or get buried at sea. But just like a plant that sends out thousands of seeds, you need only one to take root . . ."

Yang Shenxiu protested. "If there were so many, would not geologists or gem seekers or collectors or plowing farmers have seen, by now, some of the fallen ones? Even if they were split or burned, they would stand out!"

Anna shrugged. "We have no idea how these things decay, if broken. Maybe they decompose quickly into a form that resembles typical rock crystal—like some of those that were worked into sacred skulls. Or they might dissolve into sand or dust, or even vapor. One more reason to leave this one intact, I say!" She turned to Wer. "But your point is that some clandestine group or groups may already have one or more of these things. Either complete or a partially working fragment. They might already have heard some variant on the tale told by the Havana Artifact . . ."

"In which case, *not* telling the world may have been merciful and wise," Yang Shenxiu muttered. "Better to let people continue in blissful ignorance, if all our efforts will be futile anyway. If humanity is simply doomed to ultimate failure."

Patri Menelaua pounded his fist on the table. His action-crucifix wriggled in rhythm to the vibrations. "I can't accept that. The Havana aliens *must* be lying! *That* stone should be dissected, instead of this one."

Silence stetched, while Yang Shenxiu seemed uncertain whether to interpret Patri's shouting as disrespect, or simply a matter of cultural or personality difference. Finally, the scholar shrugged.

"If we might get back on topic," he said.

"Indeed," Anna said. "I doubt any group would keep such an active stone secret out of pure altruism. Human beings tend to seek *advantage* while rationalizing that they mean well, for the greater good." She spoke in ironic tones, without looking directly at Dr. Nguyen. "But that's the problem with this hypothesis of Wer's. If any other group already had such a stone, would we not see new technologies similar to . . . similar to—"

Her voice stuttered to a stop, as if suddenly realizing what should come next.

Patri filled in for her. "Similar to the advances we've all seen, across the last century or so? As I just said, we're *already converging* on these abilities. More rapidly than any other kind of technology! Methods for advanced visual simulation, realistic avatar aindroids that pass Turing tests—"

"All of which may simply be incremental progress, propelled by the market, by popular culture, and by public demand," Dr. Nguyen pointed out. "Honestly, can you name a single breakthrough that did not seem to follow right on the heels of others, in a rapid but natural sequence of human ingenuity and desire? Isn't it a tiresome cliché to credit our own inventions to intervention from above? Must we devolve back to those lurid scenarios about secret laboratories where hordes of faceless technicians analyze alien corpses and flying saucers, without ever telling the citizenry? I thought we had outgrown such nonsense."

The others looked at their leader, and Wer could tell they were all thinking the same thing.

If anybody in this room does know about another, secret, stone, it would be him.

"But of course," Nguyen added, spreading his hands with a soft smile, "according to this hypothesis of Wer's, we should look carefully at those who have profited most from such technologies. Bollywood moguls. The owners of Believworld and Our-iverse. The AIs Haveit and Fabrique Zaire."

Wer felt a wave of satisfaction—briefly—upon hearing one of his ideas called a "hypothesis." Even so, he had an uneasy feeling about where this was heading.

"But that only makes our purpose here more pressing," Dr. Nguyen continued. "If there are human groups who already have this advantage— access to alien technologies—then they may turn desperate to prevent the International Commission from completing its study of the Havana Artifact. Even worse, there is no telling how long we can keep our own secret. Almost anything we do, any coding or shrouding that we use, could be penetrated by those who have had these methods for some time.

"Our only safe recourse would be to get as much out of this worldstone as possible, quickly, in order to catch up."

Wer realized something, watching Nguyen weave this chain of logic, even as the others nodded in agreement. *He is using this argument to support a decision that was already made, far above our heads.*

"Wer, I want to start asking the *Courier* entity for useful things. No more stories. We need technologies and methodologies, as quickly and practically as possible. Make clear how much depends upon—"

He paused as—ten meters across the lavish chamber—the far door opened. At the same instant, a curtain of obscuration fell across the table—a dazzle-drapery consisting of a myriad tiny, bright sparkles that prevented any newcomer from viewing the worldstone.

Too bad it *also* filled the air with a charged, ozone smell. Wer wrinkled his nose. He didn't understand how a Discretion Screen was generated by "laser ionization of air molecules," but he knew that a simple bolt of black velvet could have accomplished the same thing. Or else locking the door.

A moment later, a liveried servant hurried in—a young woman with strawberry hair. Wer had spoken to her a few times, a refugee from New Zealand, whose spoken Chinese was broken and coarse, but she lent the place a chaste, decorative charm.

"I asked that we not be disturbed for any—" Nguyen began.

"Sir, I am so sorry sir." She bowed low, as if this were Japan, where they still cared about such things. "Supervisor Chen sent me to come to you here with discreet message for you. He needs you at command center. Right away."

Nguyen started to get up, unfailingly polite. "Can you please say what it's about?"

"Sir, I think they have detected something approaching the security boundary at high speed, plus several other possible contacts—"

That was when the window behind Wer's back exploded into a million shards.

DISMEMBERMENT

> Those who cannot forgive others break the bridge over which they
> themselves must pass.   —Confucius

Wer felt shoved forward by the concussion—a fist of air striking his body from behind, as hard as any ocean wave. At almost the same instant, a spray of glass slivers impacted his back. Somebody screamed—it might have been him—as the cloud of brittle shards jetted past him to collide with the scintillating fog of the Discretion Screen. Dazzling sparkles flared as glass splinters met ionized nitrogen, appearing to frame his shadow in a vivid aura. It might have even been beautiful, if his mind had room for anything but shock . . . plus a single, stunned word.

What?

Stumbling to a halt right at the edge of the table, he glanced to the right and saw Dr. Nguyen—his left cheek bloody from a dozen cuts—turn toward him and shout. But Wer's ears didn't seem to be functioning. Only a low, growling hum penetrated.

Nguyen blinked. He pointed at Wer, then *into* the blinding haze above the tabletop—and finally jutted his finger southward, toward the exit farthest from the explosion. The ai-patch in Wer's lower right cone of vision started offering helpful interpretations, but he already understood.

Take the stone and get out of here!

This all took the barest moment. Another passed while Wer hesitated. Loyalty to his employer called for him to stay and fight. What would the others . . . Patri and Anna and Yang Shenxiu . . . think if they saw him run away?

But Nguyen jutted his finger again—emphatically—before turning to face something new, entering the room behind Wer. And Wer knew something with uncanny certainty. That just turning around to see might be the worst mistake of his life—

—so, instead, he dived into the drapery of fizzing sparks.

Naturally, it hurt like blazes. It was designed to. Keeping his eyes closed, he scooped up the worldstone by recall alone, along with its nearby container satchel. A shoresteader and reclamation diver needed good visual memory.

Tumbling out the other side of the dazzle curtain, he rolled across the carpeted floor and onto his left knee. By touch alone, Wer slid the ovoid into its carrier case, while he blinked rapidly, praying that clear vision would return—

—then instantly regretted the wish, when he saw what had become of the beautiful face of Anna Arroyo. She lay nearby, torn from forehead to ribs, the ever-present goggles now shattered into bits that only helped to ravage her face. Patri Menelaua, his own visage a mass of dribbling cuts with tiny glass daggers sticking out of some, held his dying comrade, offering Anna his crucifix. The animatronic Jesus moved its mouth, perhaps reciting some final prayer or death rite, while its hands, still pinned to the silver cross, opened in a gesture of welcome.

Hearing flooded back. Murky shouts erupted beyond the shrouded table, where he had just fled seconds ago. Dr. Nguyen's protesting voice argued with several others that were harsh, demanding. The floor vibrated with heavy footsteps. Grating rumbles carried through the shattered window—from war engines that had somehow crossed the broad Pacific undetected, all the way to this rich, isolated atoll. So much for the mercenary protection that wealth supposedly provided.

Wer gathered his strength to go . . . then spotted the New Beijing professor, Yang Shenxiu, cowering nearby, clutching a table leg. The scholar babbled and offered Wer something—a memory sheet, no thicker than a piece of paper and about the same size. Yang Shenxiu's fingernails clawed, involuntarily, at the fragile-looking polymer, leaving no tracks as Wer yanked it from the scholar's hand. Then, with a parting nod to Yang, he sprang away at a crouching run, dashing for a sliding door that gave way to a balcony, and then the sheltering sea.

Bless the frugal habits of a shoresteader. Waste nothing. Reuse everything. Upon arriving at Newer Newport, Wer had kept sly possession of the little disposable underwater breathing apparatus that the penguin-robot gave him, back in the murky waters of the Huangpu. Was it his fault they never asked for it back? In the well-equipped arcology kitchen, using a smuggler's trick, he had managed to refill the tiny reserve tank, while rehearsing speeches of forgetful innocence, should anyone find it in his pocket.

Now, splashing into a storm of saltwater bubbles and engine noise, Wer fumbled at the compact breather with one hand, struggling to unfold the mouthpiece and eye-shields, while the weight of the worldstone dragged him downward by his other arm. There was a scary moment when the survival gadget almost slipped out of his grasp. Only after slipping it snugly into place did Wer finally kick off his sandals and suck in a hopeful, tentative burst of needed air.

Okay. It's good, he noted with some relief. *But ease up. Breathe slow and steady. Move slow and steady.*

The normally clear waters roiled with turbid murk, a fog of churned gases, chopped seaweed, and fragments of shattered coral, along with a cloudy phosphorescence of stirred diatoms. Something foreign—perhaps leakage from those engines—filled his mouth with an oily tang. Still, Wer felt grateful for the obscuration as he kicked hard to grab a ladder stanchion along one of the massive concrete pillars, anchoring the arcology to the bottom.

Noises reverberated all around—more explosions and the *rattattat* of weapons being discharged somewhere nearby, while bits and pieces of debris fell from Newer Newport, splashing and tumbling to disturb the muddy bottom. Or else landing atop the drowned Royal Palace of Pulupau, just below. Part of him noted, with a shoresteader's eye for such things, that if the palace walls had not collapsed, the roofline would extend well above where he was, right now.

Wer clung to his perch, trying both to control his racing heartbeat and to seem very small. Especially when—after searching and peering about—he was able to make out several vessels, bobbing just beyond the reef, blocked from entering the lagoon by the shoreline ruins. Evidently they were submarines of some kind. *Sneakers*, designed for bringing commandos close to shore. Though Wer squinted, they were difficult to make out. The nearest submersible looked like a compact, tubular bulge of ghostly ripples, almost liquid amid the churning shoal currents. . . .

. . . until the aiware in his righthand field of view intervened, applying some kind of image processing magic to overcome the effects of blur-camouflage. Then, all at once, an augmented version of the scene—truer than reality—traced the warship for him, distinct enough to make out a sleek, sharklike shape, whose mouth still gaped after spewing raider troops, minutes ago.

Dr. Nguyen said this implant was only a simple one, to help me with translations. But it seems to be a whole lot more. Perhaps smart, too?

That thought must have conveyed to some nerves controlling speech, because Wer's unspoken question provoked an answer—one that floated briefly in the right eye's field of view. A single, simple character.

YES.

Wer shivered, realizing. He now had a companion—an ai—*inside* him. By one way of viewing things, it felt as much a violation as the painful cuts across his back. Which were oozing blood into the water, causing several sand sharks to start nosing up-current, heading this way, despite the turbulence. Not deadly in their own right. But more dangerous predators might soon converge, if the bleeding didn't stop.

He tried to bear down and think. *Shall I try to reach one of the other arcologies?* Even if Newer Newport was taken, the rest of the resort colony might be holding out. And, from the booming shockwaves still reverberating through the shallows, it seemed that they must be. Of course, his loyalty had been personal, to Dr. Nguyen, not to any consortium of rich folks. Still, the stipend they were paying into an account, for Ling and the baby, that was reason enough to try.

If it seemed at all possible, that is. The worldstone was too heavy a burden to haul through a long underwater slog, with limited air, while dodging both sharks and raiders. Anyway—

The enemy . . . they'll soon realize the stone isn't up top anymore. There'll be searchers in the water, any second now.

He decided, then.

It must be down.

He had already spotted several parts of the collapsed palace where the roof looked relatively intact, likely to host cavities and hiding places. Spots that only a shoresteader might notice. If he hid well, resting to minimize oxygen consumption, the invaders might give up after a quick scan, assuming that the worldstone was elsewhere—taken to another arcology, perhaps—and go chasing after it there.

Letting go of the stanchion, he allowed the stone's weight to drag him down till bottom mud met his feet . . . and he felt antediluvian pavement underneath a few centimeters of muck. The Pulupauan king's ceremonial driveway, perhaps. He shuffled along, grateful that none of the spiky, genetically engineered New Coral had yet taken root here. Hurrying, while trying not to exert himself, he slogged past several rusting hulks of automobiles—perhaps beloved, once upon a time, but not enough to take along, when the princely family fled rising seas.

There. That old window. The gable looks in good shape. Perfect.

Perhaps too perfect . . . it might occur to the enemy to search here. But he had no time to be choosy. Wer kicked through a series of hops that took him over the worst of the debris jumbles and clumps of rusty nails, arriving finally at the opening. He took a moment to grab the sill and frame, giving them a good shake to check for stability. But wealthy scuba divers would already have come exploring through here by now. It must be safe.

He slipped inside, and found the expected cavelike hollow. There was even a small air pocket at the ceiling vertex, probably stale, left here by those earlier diver-sightseers. Lacking a torch, Wer chose to settle in next to the opening, clutching the satchel and waiting. Either until the bad guys went away, or his breather ran empty, whichever came first. The goggle part included a crude timer display. With luck and a very slow use rate, there might be a bit more than half an hour of air left.

Before it runs out, and I have to surface, I'll hide the worldstone. And I'll never tell.

Something occurred to him: was that the very same vow made by the *last* owner of the alien relic, Lee Fang Lu? The man who kept a collection of strange minerals underneath his seaside mansion? Did that man resist every pressure to hand over the ancient interstellar messenger-stone, even unto death?

Wer wished he could be so certain of his own courage. But, above all, he yearned to know more about what was going on! Who were the parties fighting over these things? Dr. Nguyen seemed reluctant to talk about history, but there were hints . . . had factions really been wrangling secretly, in search of "magical stones" for thousands of years? Perhaps going farther back in time than reading and writing?

Only now, centuries of cryptic struggle seemed headed for some desperate climax, all because that American astronaut chose to let the whole world in on it. Or was all this frenzy for another reason? Because Earthling technology was at last ready—or nearly ready—to take up the tempting deal offered by those entities living inside the Havana Artifact?

A proposition, from a message in a bottle . . .

. . . to teach humanity *how to make more bottles.*

Wer blinked. He wanted to rub his eyes, in part because of irritation from the dazzle-curtain, along with all the debris and salt deposited on his lids and lashes. And waves of fatigue. His head hurt, in part from trying to think so hard, while the water shivered and boomed around, pummeling him with the din of fighting.

Of course he knew that explosions were far more dangerous underwater. If one occurred nearby, concussion alone could be lethal, even if the roof didn't collapse. Then there was the nagging worry over how long his air would last.

At least no big sharks could follow him inside this place. Perhaps his cuts would stop oozing before he had to leave.

To Wer's relief, the clamor of combat eased at last, diminishing toward relative silence. Only soon, he felt the drone of an engine drawing closer. His tension level spiked when a cone of sharp illumination speared through the murky water, just outside the dormer, panning and probing across the royal compound. His gut remained knotted until the rumble and the searchlight moved onward, following the line of ruins toward the old Parliament House and the soggy remnants of the town beyond.

Wer closed his eyes and concentrated on relaxing, slowing his pulse and metabolism. As the seconds passed, he felt gradually more able to remove himself from worry and fear. At least partly.

Serenity is good.

That pair of characters floated into the corner of his ai. Then three more, composed of elegant, brushlike strokes—

Contemplate the beauty of being.

For an instant, he felt irritated by the presumption of a machine program, telling hm to relax and meditate, under these conditions! But the ideograms *were* quite lovely, capturing wise advice in graceful calligraphy. And the ai had been a gift of Dr. Nguyen, after all. So . . . Wer decided to give in, allowing a sense of detachment to settle over him.

Of course sleep was out of the question. But to think of distant things . . . of little Xie Xie smiling . . . or of Ling in better days, when they had shared a dream . . . or the beauty he had glimpsed so briefly in the worldstone—those glowing planets and brittle-clear stars . . . the hypnotic veer and swing and swerve of that cosmic, gravity ballet, with eons compressed into moments and moments into ages . . .

Peng Xiao Wer, wake up!

Pay attention.

He startled out of a fetal curl and clutched reflexively at the heavy satchel—as the universe around him seemed to boom like the inside of a drum. The little attic cave rocked and shuddered from explosions that now pounded closer than ever. Wer fought to hold on to the windowsill, preparing to dive outside, if the shelter-hole started to collapse. Desperately, he tried to focus on the telltale indicator of the breather unit—*how long did I drift off?* But the tiny analog clock was a dancing blur before his eye.

Just when he felt he could take no more, as he was about to throw himself through the dormer to risk survival outside, no matter what—a *shape* suddenly loomed in the opening. A hulking form with huge shoulders and a bulletlike head, silhouetted against the brighter water outside.

Wer let out a low moan and a stream of bubbles, backing into a corner as the figure bent and twisted to squeeze inside, fleeing the watery maelstrom. The interloper squirmed about awkwardly, giving Wer a few moments to take measure.

It's a man . . . wearing some kind of military uniform . . . and one of those helmets that are equipped with emergency pop-out gills . . .

Oxygen-absorbing fronds had deployed out of recesses in the other fellow's headgear. Wer saw that he had a small tube in his mouth and was sucking at it desperately. Evidently a refugee from the renewed combat raging overhead, he wore goggles that were flooded and clearly *not* meant for underwater use. Wer watched as the soldier floundered, trying to stay upright while struggling for enough air.

He had better calm down, or he'll overwhelm those little gills. Also, Wer realized—*I'm darkness-adapted and my eye covers work. I can see him, but maybe he hasn't seen me.*

Evidently, the fellow wasn't as big as he had thought. Those hulking shoulders . . . had been inflated by air pockets inside the uniform, collapsing now as bubbles gradually escaped. The soldier—quite slim, he now realized—must have jumped into the sea in a hurry, much as Wer did earlier. Such haste suggested that—maybe—the tide of battle might have turned, outside.

Wer started edging toward the opening, lugging the worldstone satchel in short, careful shuffling steps, careful to avoid both broken timbers and the newcomer's feet.

Whoever he was, the soldier must have had good training. Wer could tell he was adapting, gathering himself, concentrating on solving problems. As the rollicking explosions diminished a little, the man stopped thrashing and his rapid gasps ebbed into more regular breathing. When he started to experiment with exhaling a vertical stream of bubbles, aimed at clearing and filling his goggles, Wer knew there was little time left to make a clean getaway. He picked up the pace, fumbling around behind himself to find the opening. Only it took a bit of effort while hauling the heavy . . .

He stopped, as sharp illumination erupted from an object in the soldier's hand, engulfing Wer and the dormer window.

Aided by the implant, Wer's right eye adapted, even as the left one was dazzled into uselessness. For several seconds, Wer stood and exchanged a long look with the soldier, who drifted almost within arm's reach. Because the implant laid a disk of blackness over the bright torchlight, he was able to tell that it was part of a weapon—a small sidearm—that the fellow aimed at Wer's chest.

Slowly, without jerky motions, Wer pointed at the torch . . . then at the dormer entrance . . . then jabbed his thumb upward several times.

Whoever is chasing you may see that light, streaming out of the ruins . . . and drop something unpleasant on us.

The soldier apparently grasped his meaning and slid a control or sent a subvocal command. The light source dimmed considerably and become all-directional, dimly illuminating the whole chamber so they could see each other . . .

. . . and Wer realized, he had been mistaken. The interloper was a woman.

Several more seconds passed, while the soldier looked Wer over. Then she laid the weapon down nearby—and used her right forefinger to draw several quick characters on the palm of her left hand.

You are Peng Wer.

Palm-writing was never a very good form of communication, all by itself. Normally, folks used it only to settle ambiguity between two spoken Chinese words that sounded the same. But down here, it was the best they could manage. Anyway, the flurry of movements sufficed for Wer to recognize his own name. And for him to realize—the invaders had come, all this way across the ocean, both knowledgeable and well prepared.

Only now, things seemed to be going rather badly for them.

But it would be rude to point out the obvious. So he finally responded with a brief nod. Anyway, she had expressed it as a statement, not a question.

The soldier finger-wrote three more ideograms.

Is that the thing?

She finished by pointing to the satchel holding the worldstone, that Wer clutched tightly. And he knew there was little use denying it. A simple shrug of the shoulders, then, to save air.

She spent the next few seconds concentrating on sucking air from the barely adequate emergency gill, then exhaled another stream of bubbles to fill her goggles. Her eyes were red from salt water and rimmed with creases that must have come from a life engaged in scrutiny. Perhaps a technical expert, then, rather than a frontline warrior—but still a member of an elite team. The kind who would never give up.

As combat sounds drifted farther away, she wrote another series of ideograms on her left palm. This time, however, he could not follow the finger movements well enough to understand. Not her fault, of course— probably his own, deficient education—and this time the aimplant in his eye offered no help.

He indicated confusion with a shake of his head.

Frustrated, she looked around, then shuffled half a meter closer to the nearest slanted attic wall. There, she used the same finger to disturb a layer of algae scum, leaving distinct trails wherever she wrote.

Are you a loyal citizen?

She then turned and patted a badge on her left shoulder. And Wer noticed, for the first time, the emblem of the armed forces of the People's Republic of China.

Taken aback, he had to blink.

Of course he was a loyal Chinese! But *citizen*? As a shoresteader, he had some rights . . . but no legal residency in either Shanghai or any of the great national cooperatives. Nor would he, till his reclamation contract was fulfilled. *All citizenship is local,* went the saying . . . and thus, two hundred million transients were cast adrift. Still, what did citizenship mean, anyway? Who ever got to vote above the province level? Nationwide, all "democracy" tended to blur into something else. Not tyranny— clearly the national government *listened* to the People—in much the same way that Heaven could be counted on to hear the prayers of mortals. There were constituent assemblies, trade congresses, party conclaves, dominated by half a billion little emperors . . . and it all had a loose, deliberately traditionally and proudly nonwestern flavor.

Still, am I proud to be Chinese? Sure. Why wouldn't I be? We lead the world.

Yet, that wasn't really what loomed foremost in his mind.

What mattered was that he had been noticed by great ones, somewhere high up the pyramid of power, obligation, and privilege. By people who were

high enough to order government special forces on a dangerous and politi-
cally risky mission, far from home.

*They know my name. They sent elite raiders across the sea, to fetch
me. Or, at least the worldstone.*

Not that it was certain they'd prevail. Even great powers like China had
been outmaneuvered, time and again, by the planetary New Elites. After
all, the woman soldier was hiding down here with him.

No. One consideration mattered, more than citizenship or national loyalty.

Even as the rich escaped to handmade sovereignties like New Pulupau,
old-fashioned governments still controlled the territories where *billions of
ordinary people* lived—the festering poor and middle classes. Which meant
one thing to Wer.

The high masters of China have Ling and Xie Xie in their hands.

I truly have no choice.

In fact, why did I ever believe I had one?

Wer shifted his weight in order to lean over and bring his own finger toward the slanted, algae-covered boards. Even as he drew a first character,
the ai in his eye remonstrated.

Don't do this, Wer.

There are other options.

But he shook his head and grunted the code word they had taught him
for clearing the irritation away. The artificial presence vanished from his
right field of vision, allowing him to see clearly the figures that he drew
through filmy scum. Fortunately, by now the explosions had faded away
almost completely, allowing him to trace his strokes carefully.

I will cooperate.

What must I do?

A look of satisfaction spread across the soldier's face. Clearly, this was
better fortune than she had figured on, only moments ago, when she jumped
from the balcony of Newer Newport into the uncertain refuge of ocean-
covered ruins. Perhaps, this little royal attic had unusually powerful chi.

She started to write again, across the scummy, steeply pitched ceiling.

Very good. We have little time . . .

Wer agreed. Less than five minutes of highly compressed gas remained
in the tiny air tank. That is, if he could even trust the tiny clock in his goggle lens.

She continued to write.

Nearby, we have a submerged emergency shelter where we can . . .

The soldier stopped suddenly, as if her body had gone frozen, her eyes masked in shadow. Then, he saw them glint with fear as she turned, like a marionette tugged by swirling currents.

He swiveled quickly . . . to see something very large, looming in the dormer opening. A slithering, snakelike shape—wider than a man—that wriggled upward, almost filling the slanted entrance. Robotic eyes began to glow, illuminating every crevice of the cavity within. Evidently a powerful fighting machine, it seemed to examine both of them—not only with light, but also pulses of sonar that frisked their bodies like ungentle fingers of sound.

A sharp spotlight swerved suddenly downward, at the soldier's pistol sidearm, laying on a broken chunk of wood. Abruptly, a whiplike tendril emerged from its mouth and snatched up the weapon, swallowing it before either human could move. Then, a booming voice filled the little hiding place, made only slightly murky by the watery echo chamber.

"*Come, Peng Xiao Wer,*" the mechanical creature commanded, as it began to open its jaw wide. "*Now. And bring the artifact.*"

Wer realized, with some horror, that the serpent-android wanted him to crawl inside, through that gaping mouth. He cringed back.

Perhaps sensing his terrified reluctance, the robot spoke again.

"*It is safe to do this . . . and unsafe to refuse.*"

A threat, then. Wer had plenty of experience with those. Familiarity actually calmed his nerves a little, allowing him to examine the odds.

Cornered, in a rickety sunken attic, facing some sort of ai superrobot, with my air supply about to give out . . . um do I have any choice?

Yet, he could not move. So the serpaint made things clear. From one eye, it fired a narrow, brilliant beam of light that made the water bubble and steam along its path. By the time Wer turned around, it had finished burning a single character in one of the old roof beams of the Pulupauan royal palace.

CHOOSE.

Still, he thought furiously. No doubt the machine could simply take the worldstone away from him, with one of those tendril things. So . . . it must realize . . . or its owners must . . . that the worldstone required him. Still, in order to make sure, he extended a finger and palm-wrote for the creature to see.

I am needed. It speaks to me. Only me.

The serpent-machine had no trouble parsing Wer's hand-writing. It nodded.

"*Agreed. Cooperation will be rewarded. But if I must take only the artifact, we will find a way.*"

That way would be to offer the stone new candidates. As many as it took. With Wer no longer alive.

"Choose now. There is little time."

Wer almost dug in his heels, right then. He was getting sick of people—and things—telling him that. Still, after a moment's stubborn fury, he managed to shrug it off, quashing both irritation and fear. Lugging the heavy satchel, he shuffled a step closer, and another.

Then he glanced back at the Chinese special forces soldier, who was still staring, wide-eyed. There was something in her expression, a pleading look.

Wer stood in front of the sea monster. He put the satchel down in the muck and raised both hands, to write on his palm again.

What about her?

The robot considered for just a moment, then answered.

"She knows nothing of my mission, owners, or destination. She may live."

Quiet thanks filled the woman's eyes, fortifying Wer and putting a sense of firmness in his step, as he drew close. Though he could not keep from trembling, as he lifted the satchel containing the worldstone and laid it inside that gaping maw. Then, without its weight holding him down, he rotated horizontal and turned his body to start worming inside.

It was the second strangest act he ever performed.

The very strangest—and it puzzled him for the next hour—was what he did *while* crawling inside . . . when he slipped one hand into his pocket, drawing out something filmy and almost translucent, tossing it backward to flutter out of the sea serpent's jaw, drifting below where its eyes could see . . . but where the soldier could not help but notice.

Yang Shenxiu gave it to me to protect from the attackers, and now I'm giving it to one of them? Does that even make sense? And yet, somehow, it felt right.

The gullet of the serpaint wasn't as gross as he expected. The walls were soft and he only had to crawl back a short distance to find a space that seemed shaped to fit a person, reclining on his back. While he twisted into the seat, Wer felt the jaw close with a solid thump and there was a sense of backward movement. Soon, by some mechanical wizardry, the small space around him began emptying of water, replaced by—

—Wer spat out the mouthpiece and took a tentative breath that turned into a shuddering gasp of pure relief. What little air had been left in the breather was stale beyond belief. The noseplug and gogglets went next, and he rubbed his itchy eyes, gratefully.

Then he realized, a patch of the machine's wall near his head . . . it was transparent! A window, then. How considerate. Really. It made him feel ever-so slightly less like a prisoner—or a meal—and more like a passenger. He pressed his face against the little viewing patch, peering at the dimness outside.

Now illuminated only by slanting moonlight, the palace ruins were a slanted jumble. It took him several moments, while the huge robot continued backing up, to spot the little attic opening where he had taken shelter.

Then, briefly, just before the machine began accelerating forward, Wer thought he glimpsed a shadow—a human silhouette—framed by a canted, twisted dormer window.

At least, he thought he did. Enough to hope.

It's a Buoy

The sea serpent took a circuitous route along the ocean floor, carrying Wer on a lengthy tour of murky canyons and muddy flats that seemed to stretch on endlessly.

Although the little cavity where he lay had clearly been intended for a passenger's comfort, there was almost no room in the padded space, between curved walls that kept twisting and throbbing as the machine beast propelled itself along. Nor was the robot vehicle as garrulous or friendly as Dr. Nguyen's penguin surrogate had been, giving only terse answers when he tried to start conversation and refusing his request for a webscreen or immersion specs or any other form of ailectronic diversion. For the most part, the apparatus kept silent.

As silent as a motorized python could be, while undulating secretively across a vast and mostly empty sea. Clearly, it was avoiding contact with humanity—not easily done in this day and age, even far away from shipping lanes and shorelines. Several times, Wer felt thrown to one side as the snake-submarine veered abruptly and dived to take shelter behind some mound, within a crevice, or even burying itself under a meter or so of mucky sediment, then falling eerily quiet, as if hiding from predators. On two of those occasions, Wer thought he heard the faint drone of some engine gradually rise and fall, in both pitch and volume, before fading away at last. Then, as the serpent shook itself free of mud, their journey resumed.

Of course there were still signs of mankind, everywhere. The ocean floor was an immense junkyard, even in the desert zones where no fish or plants or any kind of organism could be seen. Shipwrecks offered occasional sightseeing milestones, but far more often Wer saw mundane types of trash, like torn commercial fishing nets, resembling vast, diffuse, deadly clouds that drifted with the current, clogged with fish skeletons and empty turtle shells. Or swarms of plastic bags that drifted alongside jellyfish hordes—a creepy mimicry. Once, he spotted a dozen huge cargo containers that must have toppled from a mighty freighter, long ago, spilling what appeared to be bulky, old-fashioned computers and television screens across at least forty hectares.

I'm used to living amid garbage. But I always figured that the open sea was better off . . . more pure . . . than the Huangpu.

Losing track of time, he dozed at last, while the slithering robot hurried across a vast and empty plain, seeming almost as lifeless as the surface of the moon . . .

. . . then jerked awake, to look out through the tiny window and find himself being carried along a jagged underwater mountain range, an apparently endless series of stark ridges that speared upward from unfathomable depths, reaching almost to the glistening border between liquid and sky. It was as alien a landscape as he had ever seen, and even more transfixing because the rippling promontories vanished into bottomless gloom below.

If the mechanical creature that had swallowed him meant to shake off any pursuers, or avoid detection, weaving its way through this labyrinth would seem a pretty good approach.

Feeling somewhat recovered from exhaustion, Wer peeled open some ration bars that he found in a small compartment by his left arm. A little tap offered trickles of fresh water. There also was a washcloth, which he used to dab and clean his cuts, as well as possible in the cramped space. A simple suction tube—for waste—was self-explanatory, if a bit awkward to use. After which, the voyage became a battle against both tedium and claustrophobia—the frustration of limited movement and worry over what his future held.

No clues came from the sea serpent, which only spoke sparingly and answered no questions, not even when Wer asked about some roiling funnels of black water that he spotted, rising from fissures in a nearby ridgeline, like columns of smoke from a fierce fire.

It occurred to Wer that—perhaps—he shouldn't be so glad that the owners of this sophisticated device had included a window, after all. *In stories and teledramas, kidnappers always insist on a blindfold, if they plan to let you go.*

The time to worry is when they don't seem to care. If they let you watch the route to their lair, it often means they know you'll never talk.

On the other hand, who could possibly tell, from memory, one hazy sea ridge from another?

That reassured him for a while . . . till he remembered the visual helper unit that Dr. Nguyen installed in his right eye. Wer had come to take for granted the way the tiny aissistant augmented whatever he looked at, enhancing the dim scene beyond the window. Now he realized; without it, he wouldn't be seeing much at all.

Are they assuming that a poor man, like me, is unaugmented?

He wondered about the implant. Might it even be recording whatever he saw? In which case, was he like the kidnap victim who kept daring fate, by peeking under his blindfold?

Or am I headed for someplace that is so perfectly escape-proof that they don't care how much I know?

Or someplace that I'd never want to escape from?

Or am I to be altered, in ways that will make me placid?

Or do they figure that I'll only be needed for a little while—till a replacement can be arranged to speak with the worldstone? Must I try as hard to win over my next masters, as I did Anna and Patri and Dr. Nguyen?

Each scenario came accompanied by vivid fantasies. And Wer tried not to subvocalize any of them—there were modern devices that could track the impulses in a human throat and parse words that one never even spoke aloud. On the other hand, why would anyone bother doing that, with a mere shoresteader trashman, like him?

Ultimately, each fantasy ended in one thought. That he might never see his family again.

But the soldier . . . the woman in that drowned attic room . . . she will get the sheet recording that Yang Shenxiu made. She will know that I cooperated. The government will protect and reward Ling and Xie Xie. Surely?

It was all too worrisome and perplexing. In order to help divert his thoughts, Wer put the worldstone on his lap and tried talking to *Courier of Warnings.* True, without immersion in sunlight, the entity had to preserve energy, subduing its vivid animations—the images were dim and limited to a small surface area. Still, if he could learn some new things, that might prove his worth, a little, when they arrived.

It wasn't easy, at first. Without any sound-induction devices, he was limited to tracing characters on the ovoid's surface. *Courier* at first tried responding with ancient ideograms. But Wer knew few of those, so they resumed the process of updating its knowledge of written Chinese. The entity within offered pictures or pantomimed actions. Wer sketched the associated modern words—often helped by the ai-patch. Never having to repeat, it went remarkably quickly. Within half a day, they were communicating.

At last, Wer felt ready to ask a question that had been foremost in his mind. Why did *Courier* hate the aliens inside the Havana Artifact?

Why did he call them "liars"?

In a stream of characters, accompanied by low-resolution images, the entity explained.

Our world is farther from its sun than yours. Larger but less dense. Our gravity slighter. Our atmosphere thicker and rich with snow. It is a planet much easier to land upon than your Earth. Hence, if a solar sail is built especially sturdy in the middle, it can be used as a parachute, to cushion the fall.

And so, when they came to our world, many of the stones did not shy away, lurking at a safe distance. No, instead they sometimes chose a direct approach, raining down upon—

There appeared a new symbol, not at all like anything in Chinese, but made up of elegant, curling and looping lines that suggested waves churning a beach. The emblem reminded Wer of *turbulence* and so that became his word for the planet.

—from many sources.

My species rose up to sapience already knowing these things, finding them occasionally in mud or stone or ice. Foraging packs of our presapient ancestors cherished them. Early tribes fought over them, worshipped them, looked to them as oracles, seeking advice about the next hunt, about agriculture, about diplomacy . . . and marriage.

The alien made a gesture that Wer could not interpret—a writhing of both hands. And yet, he felt somehow sure that it expressed irony.

Thus, our evolution was guided. Accelerated. Certainly our cultures.

Painting characters with a finger, Wer wrote enviously that humanity never had such help. That is, unless you counted a few, vague strictures from Heaven. And, perhaps, some nudges from the rare messenger fragments that made it to Earth.

Do not envy too readily, Courier chided. *It might have gone smoothly, if there were only one kind of stone, with one inhabitant each! But there were scores, perhaps even hundreds of crystal seers, scattered across several continents! Only much later did we learn—they had come across space from several directions. At least six different alien points of origin. Turbulence planet sits at a meeting of galactic currents.*

Then add this irksome fact. That each stone held multitudes! Communities, accumulations, whole zoos of "gods," in many shapes, who bickered, even when they agreed.

We had the blessing—and the curse—of highly varied counsel. Except, of course, when they all wanted the same thing.

But still, Wer wrote, *they helped you rise up quickly.*

Courier nodded. Though whether the gesture was native to it, or learned from other humans, Wer could not tell.

One tribe—following advice—practiced fierce eugenics upon itself, in mountain isolation for fifty generations. When they burst forth, all other tribes were awed into submission. The females of our species wanted only to mate with their males.

The worldstone depicted a mob of naked primitives, bowing before another group that stood taller, more erect, wearing furs, with wide noses and thick manes—much like *Courier* himself.

Just a century later, we had cities. Within five, we were in space.

And then . . . only then . . . we learned what the emissaries wanted from us.

Wer felt tension, even though he knew the answer already. Everyone on Earth knew, thanks to the Havana Artifact. He had watched some news-informat shows about it, back in his small quarters at Newer Newport. Wer painted a summary with his finger.

They asked you to build more emissary stones—millions of duplicate bottles . . . And messengers to put inside them—and then to cast them forth toward new planets beyond.

An interstellar chain letter, people were calling it. Or a galactic pyramid scheme. The ultimate in "viral content"—getting neighbors to pass on more copies to more neighbors. In fact, that was exactly how one savant described it—a panelist on a show that Wer had seen, a renowned pandit from a top university in São Paulo.

"For a century and more," the Brazilian had said, "we kept sifting the skies for radio signals from other civilizations, because optimistic astronomers calculated that other spawning grounds for intelligent life just *had* to be there! Moreover, those astronomers assumed—naturally—that alien races would use radio, which travels far easier across space than physical objects do.

"But what if nobody happens to be listening right then? What do you do? Keep broadcasting? On and on, forever? Over the millennia—or eons—that it might take until that other star system develops technological people? *That* kind of commitment can get really expensive.

"Ah, but what if you send a probe, a tiny thing. True, the up-front cost is greater. But, with any luck, it can enter orbit above a likely planet and then wait, at no further cost to the civilization that sent it. Wait for people worth talking to.

"Some people dismissed the probe idea because they assumed that you must dispatch something fully capable. Of investigating and reporting back to the home world. Or mining local resources to make copies of itself. Any of these duties would demand heavy mass and fragile moving parts, rapidly increasing cost, reducing travel speed and cutting the numbers you can send. How much simpler to hurl just little, solid-state packets of information?

"Packets that can reproduce, simply by asking for that favor, at the other end!"

It had made sense to Wer . . . in a weird kind of way.

Only then the professor explained about the *viral* part. He talked further about how the Havana Artifact was indeed like a virus, moving from host to host, in order to get copies of its compact genes *sneezed onward*! Only, in this case, since the host would be an entire civilization, each packet had to be persuasive. It must sway an intelligent life form—a whole culture—to devote precious resources of their planet and solar system, in order to make huge telescopes and seek new planetary targets . . . then to manufacture vast numbers of new envoy-eggs and light sails . . . and giant lasers to propel them.

And what inducement could the little envoys use, to persuade such effort? Oh, the little eggs could offer knowledge. That might work with a few races with a strong sense of honor and quid pro quo. But something more was needed, an inducement more compelling.

"They offer to include some members of the host species, as new members of the community within," the scholar said. "Like adding a new signature to the bottom of a chain letter. It's what the Havana creatures propose. To show us how to download some of ourselves into crystal probes. A way for many humans to get to travel to the stars—as downloaded surrogates—and possibly live forever."

At the time, Wer felt that it was clear, the scholar thought this a pretty good deal. Of course, a man like him would certainly be among those who would get the honor, to file a fully aware duplicate in hundreds, thousands of little message bottles, cast heavenward on beams of light.

Recalling that explanation, Wer now wrote on the surface of the world-stone, summarizing it all, in part to check on his own understanding.

Again, *Courier* nodded.

It is the same deal they presented to us, back on Turbulence.

And we agreed! After all, these were the gods who had vexed and confused and guided and tormented and loved and taught us, as far back as our collective trace memory could penetrate the misty past. Even when we knew what they truly were—mere puppets sent by beings who once lived near faraway suns—we felt obligated to move forward.

Slowly, of course, while building a society of knowledge and serenity . . .

But no! They hectored that it should now be our top priority! They badgered us . . . until, at last, they confided a reason for haste.

And so came the great lie . . .

Black characters continued appearing under the surface of the stone, but the contrast was fading. Wer realized that it must be drawing low on its supply of stored energy. Moreover, his eyes hurt.

He painted a symbol on the ovoid—*WAIT*—and rubbed them. Time also for some water. The last protein bar . . .

A musical tone suddenly filled the little chamber. It might have been deafening, except for the padding on the walls. He looked about, voiced a question for the mechanical sea serpent, but got no answer.

Then a single word appeared in the lower right, offered by his ai-patch.

Ascent.

Sure enough, it felt as if the robot were now aiming upward, throbbing hard with swishing strokes of its long tail. Peering through the tiny window, Wer watched as an extinct volcano passed by—its eroded peak now crowned by a coral reef that shimmered with sunlit surf. Was this the secret base of whatever group had sent the serpent after him?

After the worldstone, that is?

But no, instead of entering the lagoon via a clear channel that Wer spied passing through the shoals, the machine undulated away, following a shoulder of the mountain toward a ridge of shallows, some distance from the atoll. And it began slowing down.

During one of the snake's looping movements, Wer caught sight of something . . . a metal *chain* leading from an anchoring point on the bottom, tethering something that bobbed at the surface. A wave-energy generator? Was the robot only stopping here to replenish its energy stores?

The thought that this might only be a brief stop, along a much longer journey, seemed to fill Wer's body with aches and his mind with a new-formed terror of confinement. The tiny space was suddenly even smaller and more stagnant than before. He flexed, involuntarily pushing with hands and feet against the close, padded space, breathing hard.

Wer

Focus

It is a weather and communications buoy.

The words, floating boldly, briefly, in his lower right field of view, both chided and calmed him. Wer even had the presence of mind not to subvocalize his relief. No doubt this was a rendezvous point. The serpent would use the buoy to summon another vehicle. A seaplane, perhaps. Wer had been on a similar journey before. Well, somewhat similar.

And yet, after all that covering of tracks, the Chinese Special Forces found us. Found the worldstone. Did they have a spy on Newer Newport? Or did one of their satellites pick up some special color of light, reflected by the stone when I left it outside, soaking in the sun?

Perhaps he would never know. Just as he might never learn the fate of Dr. Nguyen. Or Ling and their child.

Outside, through the little window, he could see a growing brightness as they rose toward daylight. The front end of the snake-bot broached and he abruptly had to shade his eyes against a sunshine dazzle off the ocean's rippling surface. Even with help from the ai-patch, it took a minute of blinking adjustment before he could make out something that bobbed nearby— a floating cluster of gray and green cylinders, with arrays of instruments and antennae on top.

Wriggling gingerly, carefully, the serpaint moved closer to curl its body around the buoy and grasp it firmly. Then Wer saw its mouth open and a tendril emerge.

It will tap in

to communicate

with its faction

The floating characters took on an edgy quality, drawn with strokes of urgency.

You must please act urgently

This won't be easy

Blink twice if willing

He was tempted to balk, to at least demand answers to a few basic questions . . . like *Willing to do what? For whom? To what end?*

But when it came right down to the truth, Wer didn't care about any of that. He had only one basis to pick and choose among the factions that were battling over the worldstone—and over his own miserable carcass.

Dr. Nguyen had been courteous and the snake-thing had been rude. That mattered. He closed his eyes, two times.

Good

Now you must press close to the window

Look at the buoy

Do not blink your right eye at all

He only hesitated a moment before complying. It was where curiosity compelled him to go, anyway.

At first he saw only an assembly of cylinders with writing on them— much of it in English, beyond his poor grasp of that language. Wer could make out various apertures, lenses, and devices. Some of them must sample air, or taste the water, part of a planetwide network of tools for measuring changes in a world under environmental stress. On the other side of the floating platform, he could make out the snake-robot's tendril, probing to plug itself into some kind of data port.

All right . . . so what are we trying to . . .

He stopped, and almost jerked back in surprise as the scene loomed *toward* him, zooming in on one part of the nearest cylinder. Of course there was nothing new about vision-zooming. But it had never happened *within* his own eye, before!

Wer kept as still as possible. Evidently, the patch had means of manipulating his organic lens . . . and using the surrounding muscles in order to aim the eye, as well. He quashed a feeling of hijacked helplessness.

When has my life ever really been my own?

Zooming and tracking . . . he found himself quickly zeroing-in upon one of those gleaming, glassy spots, where the buoy must stare day and night upon the seascape, stormy and clear, patiently watching, accumulating data for the great and growing Grand Model of the World. Suddenly, that gleaming lens filled Wer's right-hand field of view . . . and he closed the left eye, in order to let it become everything. A single disk of coated optical crystal . . .

. . . that *flared* with a sudden burst of bluish-green! More shocking, still, Wer realized that the color had come from *within his own eye*—spearing outward, spanning the gap and connecting . . .

I didn't know the implant could do that.

I wonder if even Dr. Nguyen knew.

It took every gram of grit and steadfastness to keep from drawing back, or at least blinking.

Almost in
But—
The floating characters stayed outside the cone of action, yet somehow remained readable. They throbbed with urgency.
—you must press your eye
against the window
Wer you must
or all is lost
A low moan fought to escape his throat and he barely managed to quell the sound, along with a sudden heaving in his gut. Gritting his teeth hard, all Wer could think about was the need to overcome raw, organic reflex—passed down all the way from when distant forebears climbed out of the sea. An overwhelming impulse to withdraw from pain, from damage, from fear—

—versus a command from far more recent parts of the brain. To go forward.

Using two fingers of his right hand to hold back the lids, Wer let out a soft grunt and pushed his head against the glass so hard that the eye had to come along.

It was bad.
Good
Not quite so hard
Hold it
Hold it
Hold it
He held, while greenish flares shot back and forth, between his lens and the glassy one on the buoy . . . and flashing internal reflections bounded around the inside of his right eye, like a maelstrom of cascading needle ricochets. At one point, his confused retina seemed to be looking at an image of *itself*, a cluster of blood vessels and sensor cells, and Wer felt boggled by an endless—bottomless—reflection of himself that seemed far more naked and soul-revealing than any mere contemplation of a face in a mirror.

And meanwhile, another part of him wondered in detachment: *How did I know what a "retina" is? Is even memory still mine, anymore?*

Worse. It got much worse, as the sea serpent seemed to catch on that something was going on. The thrashing intensified and a low growl resonated up and down the snakelike cloaca. Wer responded by clenching hard and holding even tighter.

All sense of time vanished, dissolved in pain. The little window felt like it was on fire. Using his feet and legs and back, he had to fight a war with himself, and the instinctive part seemed much more sane! As if he were trying to feed his own eye to a monster.

And then—

Black, floating letters returned. But he could not read the blurs. They clustered around his fovea, jostling for attention, interfering with his ability to concentrate. Wer sobbed aloud, even as the green reflections faded.

"I know! I'm . . . *trying* to hold on!"

Finally, the characters coalesced into a single one that filled every space within his agonized eye.

STOP

Meaning took a few more seconds to sink in. Then, with a moan that filled the little compartment, Wer let own body weight drag him back. He collapsed upon the passenger seat, quivering.

A minute or so passed. He rubbed his left eye free of tears. The right seemed too livid, too raw and damaged, to touch or even try to open. Instead of blindness, though, it seemed filled with specks and sparkles and random half-shapes. The kind that never came into focus, but seemed to hint at wonders and terrors, beyond reality.

Slowly, a few of the dazzles traded formlessness for pattern.

"Leave me alone!" he begged. But there was no way to escape messages that took shape inside your very own eye. Not without tearing it away. Oh, what a tempting thought.

While he cursed technology, clear characters formed. These featured a *brightness* around the edges that they never had before.

Wer, I represent a community

—a smart mob—with members

around the entire world . . .

and we want to help you.

Some small presence of mind was returning. At least, enough to notice a change. More than just the characters' shape and color were different. Indeed, they felt less like the simple responses of a partial ai. More like words sent by a living person.

He must have subvocalized it as a question, because when they next reconfigured, the figures offered an answer

Yes, Wer, my name is Tor Sagittarius.

I'm pleased to meet you.

Now I'm afraid we must insist.

Please get up and take action.

There is very little—

"I know! Very little time!" He felt on the verge of hysterical laughter.

So many factions. So many petty human groups wanted him to hurry, always hurry.

A groaning mechanical sound. The sea serpaint started to vibrate around him.

We've suborned the machine's software.

Ordered the jaws to stay open.

It may only be temporary.

He didn't need futher urging. While keeping his right eye closed, Wer bent to slip the worldstone into its carrier, then started crawling forward as the giant robot rocked and convulsed. Keeping the worldstone in front of him, he had to push and squeeze through constrictions, like a throat that kept trying to swallow him back down . . . only to then spasm the other way, as if vomiting something noxious.

Finally, spilling into the snake's mouth, he found that its head was rising and falling, slapping the water, splashing torrents of spume inside. The jaws kept juttering, as if trying desperately to close. And he knew, at any moment, they might succeed.

Scrambling desperately, Wer grabbed a garish tooth, hauling himself and the satchel toward the welcoming brightness outside—

—only to pause before making the final leap.

Don't be afraid, Wer . . .

He shouted: "Be quiet!"

And swung the valise with all his might, smashing it against the inner face of the serpent's left eye casing, which caved in with a satisfying, tinkling sound. He then cried out and did it again to the other one. Those things weren't going to aim burning lasers at him, once he was outside. Nor was he worried about the worldstone, which had survived deep space and collision with a mountain glacier.

Good thinking!

Now . . .

He didn't need urging. Not from any band of "smart mob" amateurs, sitting in comfortable homes and offices around the world, equipped with every kind of immersion hardware, software, and wetware that money could buy. Their help was welcome, so long as they shut up.

While the serpent-machine thrashed and its jaws kept threatening to snap shut, Wer heaved with all his might, scrambling like a monkey till he stood, teetering on the lower row of metal teeth—

—then leaped toward the buoy, as if for life itself, hurtling across intervening space—

—only to splash into the sea, just short, with the heavy satchel dragging him down by one hand. His other one clawed at the buoy, fingers seeking any sort of handhold . . .

. . . and failed, as he sank beneath the floating cylinders, hauled by the weight of his treasure bag, plummeting toward the depths, below.

Yet, Wer never fretted. Nor was he even tempted to let go of the world-stone, to save his life.

In fact, he suddenly felt just fine. Back in his element, at last. Doing his job and practicing his craft. Retrieving and recycling the dross of other days. Hauling some worth out of the salty, trash-strewn mess that "intelligent life" had made of the innocent sea.

His free hand grabbed at—and finally caught—the chain anchoring the buoy to the shoulder of a drowned mountain. Then, as the mechanical serpent thrashed nearby, crippled in its mind and body, but still dangerous as hell, Wer also seized the metal-linked tether with his toes.

Maybe there was enough air in his lungs to make it, he thought, while starting to climb.

If so? Then, once aboard the buoy, he might evade and outlast an angry robot. Possibly.

After that? Perhaps the help sent by his new friends in the "smart mob" would arrive before the snake's clandestine cabal did. Before the sun baked him. Or thirst or sharks claimed him.

And then?

Clambering awkwardly but steadily up the chain, Wer recalled something that Patri Menelaua said, back at Newer Newport, when the world-stone entity denounced the famous Havana Artifact, calling it a tool of interstellar liars.

"We have got to get these two together!"

Indeed. With the whole world watching. No more cabals and secret societies. Time to have it out, in front of everybody. And this time, Peng Xiao Wer would be in the conversation!

A bit amused by his temerity—the very nerve of such a vow, coming from the likes of him—Wer pondered as he kept climbing, dragging an ancient chain letter toward the light of day.

Yeah, right.

Just keep holding your breath.

Frederik Pohl—Architect of Worlds

I mused and fretted over what story to offer, for an anthology collected to honor Frederik Pohl. I finally chose "Shoresteading," in part, because it is about an ordinary man, swept up by extraordinary events—a theme that Fred evoked many times, over the course of an illustrious career.

A career that he spent both creating new worlds and helping others to do the same. Both as a prolifically creative author and as an agent-editor who coaxed other authorial visions into life, Fred Pohl may be responsible for more new "universes" coming into being than any other mortal . . . a point we'll return to, later.

Sure, they were all universes of the imagination—many of them so ephemeral that they only endured in human thought for the duration of a single monthly issue of *Galaxy* or *If*. Others, like *The Space Merchants* and *Jem* and *Man Plus* may actually divert the path of human destiny, forever, as we modify our policies and creative ambitions, diverting them a little, because of warnings and thought experiments erected by Frederik Pohl.

Even if Fred's visions had no lasting impact in the real world, there would be another reason for awed respect. I'll get to it in a moment. But first a personal note, as a longtime fan of Fred's work.

Wolfbane was one of the earliest SF novels I read, and at the time it certainly seemed the creepiest! In contrast, some of his other works with Cyril Kornbluth, such as *Gladiator at Law*, though fun adventures, also helped spur my lifelong habit of doubting all ends of the silly, nonsensical, so-called left-right political axis. Provoking people to rethink their own assumptions—now that's writing.

One nearly forgotten Pohl book ought to tower high on any shrine of modern techno-visionary prophecy. *The Age of the Pussyfoot* was one of the only science fiction stories of the fifties through seventies that envisioned computers becoming common household tools, owned and used, avidly, by nearly everybody. In fact, to my knowledge it is just about the *only* work of prophetic fiction to foresee citizens carrying about portable, computerized assistants that would fulfill all the functions we now see gathering together in our futuristic cell phones. And you can bet I salivate for the even better versions he foresaw. Pohl's "joy-maker" device is as marvelous an on-target prediction as Jules Verne predicting submarines or trips to the moon.

In *The Cool War*, Frederik Pohl showed a chillingly plausible failure mode for human civilization, one in which our nations and factions do not dare to wage open conflict, and so they settle upon tit-for-tat patterns of reciprocal sabotage, ruining one another's infrastructures and economies, propelling our shared planet on a gradual death spiral of lowered expectations degraded hopes. It is a cautionary tale that I cite often today, a recommended reading for those at the top of our social order.

I could go on and on, but have no more time or space for details. So let me just make a central point about a man who I am proud to call a colleague, in what may be the highest of all human professions. . . .

Wait a minute. Brin said what? Oh, sure, readers of this book probably like science fiction. But isn't that taking things a bit too far, calling sci fi writing the highest profession?

Well, in a profound irony that ought to amuse—or perhaps grate on—the many atheists and agnostics who write SF, let me suggest that no other calling, not even that of monk or priest, has a greater claim to sacred status.

After all, what was purportedly God's greatest act, other than creating the universe?

And what do science fiction authors do, almost every day, but erect new worlds, and characters to inhabit them?

If a father is proud of children who precociously try to pick up the parent's tools and apprentice in his craft, then whose play is more likely to rouse a smile from the Big Creator?

Oh, sure, Fred Pohl cannot parse Maxwell's equations very well and when he says "let there be light!" the incantation only flashes briefly, inside the heads of a few hundred thousand readers—a blaring supernova here, a slicing laser flash there, or else a brilliant insight into some small part of the human soul. Sure, that's small potatoes, on the cosmic scale of things. On the other hand, it is a step. And no human ever did it better.

I suppose that is why I urged the great asteroid-hunter, Dr. Eleanor Helin, to pick a couple of her discoveries and name them after two of the greatest . . . the two "poles" of sci fi . . . Frederik Pohl and Poul Anderson. They are out there now . . . glittering hunks of rock and metal and precious frozen vapors. Just waiting for our heirs to go out and—perhaps—mine those riches and turn them into wondrous things. And when they do, I am sure they'll hold another festschrift in honor of the dreamers who helped to make it all so.

—DAVID BRIN

PHYLLIS AND ALEX EISENSTEIN

VON NEUMANN'S BUG

Let's call our explorer Bert. His true designation was long and complicated and included elements vaguely similar to letters and numbers, but insofar as a human mouth could pronounce the first few sounds, they would be something like Bert.

Bert was endlessly curious, as befitted an explorer, and also endlessly patient, which was a good thing, since Bert had been traveling, at a substantial fraction of c, for a very long time, with little to show for the journey but stray hydrogen atoms. Thus, who could blame him for perking up at the first tenuous signals, at a variety of radio frequencies, from *that* direction?

With something potentially interesting waiting for him, there was braking to be done, and a slight course correction, not easy when all you had to work with was the lightly ionized interstellar medium. But at a high fraction of c, it could be done. The slower he went, though, the trickier it became. Fortunately, there was a convenient gas giant on the way, and Bert could use its gravity to swing into the inner system for a closer look at the source of the broadcasts.

Unfortunately, Bert was a trifle off in calculating his trajectory. This was forgivable, for he was, after all, the who-knows-how-many-hundredth generation removed from the first explorers sent out by their creators, and minor replication errors did occasionally occur. He had planned on going into orbit around the source of the broadcasts, data-mining as fully as possible from that vantage, sending information home on the tightbeam, and making a few copies of himself before moving on. Instead, this time, he found himself plunging into a nitrogen-oxygen atmosphere, sliding deep into the gravity well, and although he was far too sturdy to become a spark in that atmosphere, his vernier impellers were also too weak to escape that gravity field's grip. He made a crater many times his own size when he struck the surface.

—•—

Beneath Cheyenne Mountain, NORAD's massively integrated multiphase target acquisition computer, MIMTAC, barely noticed—via radar arrays and infrared eyes deployed from Nova Scotia to Saskatchewan—the bright streak that was Bert slamming through the atmosphere. Myriad bits of flotsam were sucked in daily by the planet's gravity well, but the complex algorithmic filters of MIMTAC's expert-system modules allowed the computer to ignore such cosmic debris, as it had no bearing on NORAD's imperatives for continental defense. Maintaining the nuclear peace of the world, not the launch of retaliatory strikes, was NORAD's fundamental mission; and thus the computer's role in that mission involved a highly refined ability not to respond with force to minimal threshold stimuli. Not even this one, with its faint gamma-ray emissions that no well-constructed warhead would ever leak past its jet-black polycarbon reentry cone.

—•—

Frank noticed the hole in the garage roof on Saturday, when he pulled out the mower for the first time that season. It wasn't a large hole, but the day was sunny and the bright spot on the lovingly polished hood of his car was hard to miss. He made a mental note to go up on the roof later and check it out. It might be easy to patch, or it might be a symptom of something worse; he hadn't been on the roof in a couple of years, and anything could be going on up there.

The front yard hardly needed cutting at all, but as always, the back had become a jungle after the first spring rains. He wasn't exactly sure why the grass grew so much faster in the back—more sun, better drainage, or just a superior variety of sod put down by the previous owners. Sometimes he thought it must be the bugs, aerating the soil or fertilizing it; there were a lot more bugs in the back. As the mower growled its way across the lawn, they swarmed upward, ricocheting off his legs, his arms, his face, and he slapped at them with one hand while he pushed the mower with the other. Some of them seemed larger than usual, little houseflies among the midges, which made him think that the neighbor's mutt had been in his yard again and left him a smelly gift, though he didn't find it. A few of these flies kept settling on the mower, though there didn't seem anything special to draw them there, except maybe the heat of the engine. As he finished the yard, he made sure he brushed them off, not wanting them to get into the house through the garage. Sliding the mower into its storage niche, he noticed a peppering of small pits in its plastic housing. He didn't remember them from the previous year. Had he kicked up pebbles while the bugs were distracting him? Well, it was nothing important. The mower wasn't exactly young.

Later that morning, when he had dealt with a couple of minor projects in the basement and decided to reward himself by driving down to the Mini-Mart for a six-pack, he realized there was also pitting on the hood of the car, the kind that might have been made by flying gravel. Except that he hadn't driven through any gravel since polishing the car that morning. He hadn't driven at all, and a shouted question to Liz resulted in the same answer from her. Had one of the kids been playing around with something like chips of crumbled alley pavement while he, Frank, was in the basement? They both denied it, though he wasn't sure they'd confess if they had. He wondered if a blast of something, some mini-tornado dumping stones or maybe hail, had caused the hole in the roof and sprayed the car and mower. Two blasts: the second while he was in the basement, since the hole in the roof preceded the pits on the car.

It all sounded pretty unlikely. Still, he circled the car, scanning the garage floor for any small hard particles that might have bounced off it. But the cement seemed clean, as always; not even a fresh oil stain. Then he spotted something gritty behind the right front tire, went down on his hands and knees for a closer look, and found a depression in the floor the size of a silver dollar, surrounded by radiating streaks of whitish dust. Where had *that* come from? It had to have happened during the week, while the car was out of the garage. Something really heavy. There was nothing in the garage that could have done it—and again Liz and the kids pleaded innocent, even after he shouted. When he had calmed down, he was more politic about grilling his neighbors on either side, but he didn't get any better answers.

He went up on the roof, then, to inspect the golf ball–size hole. There was no sign of the culprit, no stones, no ice, just sun-warmed shingles and a smooth-bored hole barely large enough to slide three fingers into. Of course hail would have melted and run off or evaporated by now. He plugged the hole with a good grade of patching compound, and when he came down, he decided he really needed that beer. He drove over to the Mini-Mart, and ended up with more than one six-pack and a few bags of chips, too; fortification for getting rid of those pits. He hadn't intended to work on the car so much this weekend, but he couldn't let corrosion get a foothold on the otherwise bright finish.

There were more flies in the garage when he came back. He found a swatter under the tool bench and swung at a few of them, several satisfying snaps proving his aim and reflexes were as good as ever. He wondered what could be attracting them. A quick search turned up nothing, not a partly eaten sandwich tossed by one of the kids, not a dead opossum—there'd been one of those once, behind the peonies a few summers back, but not this time. He picked up the swatter again and batted at a few more flies before noticing the hole in its plastic mesh. He didn't remember the hole, but then he hadn't looked at it very closely. He should have checked it out before he went to the store; he could have picked up a new one, or a couple. He covered the hole with a strip of duct tape. Good enough. He hit a few more flies.

Two beers later, he was dismayed to find that most of the pits on the car went all the way through: with the hood up, he could see pinpoints of daylight, like the bright stars of outer space scattered across the dark underside. He swore loudly, which brought Liz out to see what was going on . . . and tell him to watch his language while the kids were home.

Of one thing he was certain: this was going to take longer than he had thought.

▬▬

There was plenty of data to be gathered at the bottom of a gravity well, and Bert was a good little machine, with a complex array of picosystems that had no trouble gathering that data and sending it back to his creators. But getting out of that gravity well and continuing his exploration was another problem entirely. His propulsion capacities, intended for interstellar and even intergalactic travel, were wholly inadequate for that, and his picosystems offered his tiny artificial intelligence only limited options. Aside from the primary task of data gathering, he had been designed to replicate himself, as and where possible, extracting raw materials for the process from whatever resources were available in the vacuum of space, be they stony, metallic, or carbonaceous. In the gravity well, with its rich planetary surface, the only obstacle to this replication was the speed at which he could manufacture individuals that, if the local inhabitants had built them, might be considered the F1 generation of Berts. As always, the good little machine followed his Designers' instructions. And so did the F1 generation. This would be a very thoroughly examined gravity well.

▬▬

Frank was smoothing sealer over the eighth pit when something stung his bare leg. He yelped. The sudden sharp pain made him drop the can, and fast-drying sealer spattered an undamaged part of the fender and made him swear again, more softly this time, as he caught up a clean rag to wipe it away. He looked around for the bee or wasp that had gotten him, but all he saw were the flies that were treating his garage like a vacation spot. There was a dot of blood on his leg, but no stinger and no swelling, so he ignored it.

By the time Liz called him for dinner, he had finished the first six-pack. The car would be ready for paint touch-ups in the morning. He had acquired a jar of the right color paint shortly after buying the car, because you never knew when you might need to deal with a ding. Frank was a man who prided himself on his foresight.

In the morning, there were even more pits than before.

●—●—

Bert was now the patriarch of a family of explorers, in continuous contact with his offspring—not exactly coordinating their activities, for there was no need to do so, but acting as the backup for all of them, in case something unexpected happened while they went about their business, such as a localized nuclear explosion. That was one of the events they had been programmed to avoid, along with supernovas, nodules of antimatter, and black holes of any substantial mass. Bert himself had never encountered any such in close proximity, but his internal library contained relevant information on each. More trivial impediments, like the flexible planiform squasher that so easily destroyed those organic creatures that vaguely resembled him in their outward conformation, were of no concern.

●—●—

Frank decided there had to be some chemical in the garage that was causing the damage to his car, and on Sunday he duct-taped all around the door between the house and the garage, left the outside garage door open, and parked the car at the curb. He told Liz to stay out of the garage and to keep the kids out, too, because if that chemical was bad for the car, it had to be bad for people as well, and come Monday morning she should call someone to check it out. She did that, making quite a few calls not just on Monday morning but through the rest of the week, and a parade of inspectors from the gas and electric companies, the city, the state, and even the EPA began trooping through the garage. They tested the air, the floor, the walls, the surrounding soil, the tools, and every half-empty can that Frank had carefully resealed on the assumption that he might need the contents again someday. None of them found anything suspicious, and most suggested Frank must be using something corrosive on the car, though they couldn't find any trace of that, either. Liz pointed out that the mower, too, was pitted, but the inspectors thought that was just the result of age and use. Still, several of them took away samples of almost everything for laboratory analysis.

Weeks passed before the final verdict was in.

In the meantime, Frank continued to park at the curb and to leave the garage open, though he wasn't very happy about that. He was on reasonable terms with the neighbors, even the ones with the dog. and didn't really expect them to "borrow" anything while the garage was open. But after a couple of days, just to be sure, he went to the nearest home improvement center and bought a metal cabinet, a length of chain, and a heavy-duty bicycle lock to secure it all. And every evening when he came home, there were pits in the cabinet walls, the chain, and even the bicycle lock.

Eventually, he lost his patience waiting for the authorities and bought himself a gas mask so that he could scrub down every inch of the garage and its contents. He also packed all those half-empty containers in a large cardboard box and set it in the farthest corner of the backyard, to be thrown away if the testing showed any of that material was responsible for the damage. Then he sanded and filled (it had a stubborn little rim around it) the hole in the floor, resealed the entire surface, and painted the walls, ceiling, and workbench with deck enamel. Last, since in spite of all his cleaning the flies were thicker than ever, he hung spiral flypaper from the rafters.

The lab tests all came back negative.

The flypaper caught two houseflies and a ladybug. The rest of the flies (the ones that seemed to glitter greenly when sunlight struck them at just the right, low angle in late afternoon) seemed very good at avoiding it.

Frank lost ten pounds between working on the garage and refinishing his car. And in spite of the car being parked in the open air, the pitting continued to appear; and not just on the outside, but under the hood, on the manifold, the battery, and the plastic windshield wiper fluid reservoir, which was soon leaking drops of pale blue liquid onto the asphalt. He patched the reservoir with duct tape and began parking at the other end of the block each evening, but that didn't seem to make any difference. When the neighbors on either side pointed out that whatever was damaging his property was starting to work on theirs, too, and they were thinking of taking legal action against him, he didn't know what to say. Although he said it very loudly.

━━ ━━

Bert and the F1, F2, F3, and F4 generations were of course identical in all but their serial designations, except for one individual, whose tiny variation caused him to become trapped in a behavioral loop of tight right turns around a large metallic container. Observing both his internal and external activities, the other members of the group determined that he was unsalvageable, and as their collective senior, Bert took responsibility for sending the self-destruct signal. The defective machine collapsed into a fine greenish powder.

The irony of that fate did not escape the rest of them. Bert himself had been replicated imperfectly enough that his calculation errors had resulted in their current situation. But he—and by the nature of proper replication, they—had learned from that experience, as the Designers had intended. Now, with five generations of Bert in existence, it was time for a final test of the skills and ingenuity of those Designers. This planet had been explored sufficiently, and the tightbeam was crammed with information on its way to a distant data port of the receiver network. The good little machines that were identical to Bert did not care that they themselves would never go home. But they cared very much (ever so much!) about their mission.

●—●—●

After Frank's lawyer assured him that, based on the investigations of the various governmental bodies, the neighbors had no grounds for suing him successfully, he calmed down enough to think. As he saw it, he had three options. He could do nothing, and take a chance on all of this just stopping. He could have the garage torn down and rebuilt completely, which would probably mean breaking up and repouring the slab, too. Or he and his family could sell the house and move someplace else.

The third option attracted him the most, but Liz and the kids, who liked the house, the neighborhood, the school, and the shopping, vetoed it.

The second option would be expensive, and there was no guarantee that it would work.

The first option was what they were already doing, and he didn't see anything positive coming out of it.

After a long, sleepless night he found himself wondering if maybe the house had been built on some old graveyard, and the spirits of the dead were causing this; although when he suggested that to Liz, she looked at him as if he had lost his mind. It sounded crazy to him, too, but what other explanation was there? He wasn't Catholic, but he was strongly tempted to go to the local parish and beg a priest to come out and exorcise the property. It couldn't hurt anything. Still, it seemed a bit extreme. Then the car's catalytic converter blew due to a myriad of perforations, and Frank was at the end of his rope. The following Sunday, he went to St. Catherine's with his concerns. The priest listened to the whole story before gently suggesting that he seek psychiatric help.

On Monday morning, he told Liz to call a contractor about demolishing the garage.

●—●—●

The signal went out across the planet, an ultra-high frequency reveille summoning all the generations of Bert back to their progenitor, and they came at speeds that no natural denizen of the land, the water, or the atmosphere could match. They were powerful little machines. They could drill out or chip away particles of any substance this planet had to offer, whether stony, metallic, or carbonaceous. They could not be harmed by being swatted, stepped on, or eaten. But they had their limits. Like Bert himself, not one of them had the strength and speed to achieve escape velocity—not to mention that in this planet's thick atmosphere, they could barely attain the hypersonic. Like Bert himself, they were all trapped at the bottom of this planet's steep gravity well.

Of course, in spite of their individual artificial intelligences, they were only individuals in a technical sense. Now, knowing the new plan and agreeing to it unanimously—and why would they not?—they assembled themselves like a three-dimensional jigsaw puzzle, each fresh arrival fitting into his place, snug against his fellows. The final construct was sleek and slim and iridescent as the back of a housefly.

▬▬

The noise woke him: a clicking like a child's blocks tapping together, or a key turning a deadbolt over and over. At first he thought it was the contractor, arriving a few days early and at an ungodly hour. But it wasn't really a knock, so then he thought it must be a branch bumping against the side of the house, or even a loose siding board flapping in the wind. It was much too early to get up; dawn twilight was showing at the bedroom windows, Liz was still asleep beside him, and he didn't hear the usual morning racket from the kids. He almost turned over and went back to sleep, but the sound was just loud enough and puzzling enough to pull him all the way to wakefulness.

It seemed to be coming from the garage.

He threw on jeans and sneakers, and almost tried to open the door to the garage before he remembered the duct tape. He went out the front door instead, out to the sidewalk, expecting to see some animal nosing about in the garage—a stray dog, a raccoon, an opossum; even a deer. Antlers might be making that clicking noise, knocking against a wall, or little hooves on the garage floor. Or claws. A cornered animal, he thought, and wondered if he should have taken a broom from the kitchen. He stayed well back from the garage entrance, to give it plenty of room to escape.

From the sidewalk, he peered into the open garage. At first, in the uncertain light, he couldn't make sense of what stood inside. Was it a big roll of wrapping paper? A floor lamp? A scale model of the Washington Monument? Then he thought, No, it was one of those model rockets he had seen in a movie once. Had the kids found yet another hobby? He swore under his breath, because he had warned them, ordered them, to stay out of the garage.

He took a few steps toward it, not enough to actually go into the garage, but enough to get a better look at the thing. It was a little taller than he was, slim enough for him to circle with one arm, though he didn't feel any need to try that, and its surface seemed to flicker as if it were made of thousands of tiny parts that vibrated constantly, like the wings of insects. And as he watched, a dozen smallish flies landed on that surface with the tiny clicks he had already heard and seemed to merge with it. The vibration stilled abruptly, and then the thing rose a few inches from the garage floor, moved sideways until it was clear of the building, and shot upward into the pale morning sky. While Frank stood outside the garage with his mouth hanging open, it vanished into the distance.

After a long moment of staring, Frank rubbed at his eyes. Either he was still asleep or the kids were somewhere snickering at him. He was pretty sure he wasn't asleep. With a last, long look upward, he went back into the house. He checked on the kids. They were in bed, but that didn't prove anything. They could be faking, or there might have been a timer on the thing. He heated a cup of last night's coffee in the microwave. It was lousy, but it was something to occupy him until the sun rose above the houses across the street, at which point he woke the kids and yelled at them, assuming they would deny everything, which they did. A minute later, Liz was standing beside him, yelling at him not to yell at the kids. It was probably somebody else's kids, she said, using the open garage.

That sounded pretty reasonable to him. After all, neighbors who would threaten lawsuits would probably have rotten kids.

Really smart rotten kids.

At least the thing hadn't come back down on his property.

••┼••

As they had calculated, the united generations of Bert successfully achieved escape velocity from the gravity well they had so thoroughly explored. They then used the nearby natural satellite, the next planet closer to the primary, and finally the primary itself, to sling their construct out of the stellar system entirely. You and I would be impressed by the calculating power of so many good little machines working in concert, and we might think that, having experienced that success—because, of course, they learned from experience—they would remain together to continue their mission with even greater effectiveness. Yet some time later, though the exact time elapsed did not matter to them, the smooth, sleek, iridescent object they had created of themselves broke apart, and each of the Berts used his tiny power to leave his fellows and resume his exploration as the original Designers had always intended.

To maintain such a clear and constant purpose was an excellent thing for the good little machines. With such a singleness of purpose, it would never matter to any of the Berts whether the race that created them, or any race arising from it, still existed to receive the tightbeam crammed with all their meticulously gathered information.

The Mission was the thing; the Mission.

In the bowels of NORAD, the strategic operations computer named MIM-TAC noted the accelerating outward trajectory of a familiar-looking object, but raised no alarm. The reasons for this were several: the two-meter-long spindle was oddly porous; its infrared signature was not that of any known rocket or ramjet engine; its mean path appeared to speed it well beyond Earth's ionosphere; and it displayed an incessant random flickering along its entire surface, like a swarm of eddying dust motes. The computer's multivariable analysis determined that the object best fit the category of "rare atmospheric plasma phenomena," which offered no discernible threat to the security of North America. Someday an even smarter computer system might identify this anomaly's physical cause. But the current generation of machine intelligence known to properly cleared humans as MIMTAC just filed it under a code that translated roughly as "unusual but innocuous entity." And kept on watching the skies.

Frank decided to cancel the demolition of the garage.

Instead, he put the car back inside, stripped the duct tape off the door to the house, took down the dangling, bug-dotted flypaper, and lowered the garage door. There was work to be done on the car, some parts to be replaced, the finish to smooth out and repaint; he would get on that next weekend. The duct tape hadn't done the woodwork any good, so that was another project to start soon. But there was no need to buy a new mower; the old one worked well enough, in spite of the awful way it looked.

With the damage halted, the neighbors finally gave up on their preposterous lawsuit. Still, Frank never spoke to any of them again. Because, you know, in the great cosmic scheme of things, it simply didn't matter.

Little did he know.

Afterword

This story was inspired by the way Frederik Pohl wrote "Day Million"—though this may not be obvious in the result, partly because it is not about the same things "Day Million" is about. Yes, it is an entirely different story, written in an entirely different way. What's so surprising about that? That's as it should be, isn't it? *I* think so. But I still think it reads like a story written under the influence of Fred Pohl's short science fiction. Not any one story, but a mélange of a whole raft of his stories that are told by a friendly narrator who is not really an actor within the framework of the storyline itself.

When I was a teenager, my primary goals in life were to write science fiction and to meet all the science-fiction writers whose work I loved. It shouldn't surprise anyone that Fred's name was high on the list. After all, I had every one of his short story collections—*all* of them. And eventually, most of the novels, too.

I first actually met Fred a mere few decades ago. Sometime in our early acquaintance, when he was an editor at Bantam, I tried to sell him a novel; and while he thought the one I had written was not uninteresting, he insisted he would rather see its sequel. Since I never wrote that sequel, and someone else published the novel, Fred never became my editor. Instead, he married my friend Betty, which gave us an entirely different (and I believe more salutary) relationship. Had he become my editor, I would never have discovered, for example, that he made instant coffee with hot water straight from the tap. And many other things that I would never reveal, no matter how much you paid me.

But I will say that, even though Fred Pohl is one of science fiction's preeminent satirists, underneath that wry and sardonic exterior of Fred-the-writer, he's a kind and very approachable human being. And anyone who knows him well also knows this very well.

—PHYLLIS AND ALEX EISENSTEIN (MOSTLY PHYLLIS)

Isaac Asimov

><:o:><

FREDERIK POHL

Frederik Pohl was born in 1919 and is just a few weeks older than I am. When we met as fellow Futurians in September 1938, we were each of us edging toward his nineteenth birthday. Despite the equality of our chronological age, he has always been more worldly-wise and possessed of more common sense than I. I recognized this and I would turn to him for advice without any hesitation.

Fred is taller than I, very soft-spoken. He has a pronounced overbite and an often quizzical expression on his face that makes him look a bit rabbity but, in my eyes, cute, because I am very fond of him. He has light hair that was already thinning when I met him.

Fred is a very unusual fellow. He does not flash from time to time as I do, and as several of the other Futurians did. Instead, he burns with a clear, steady light. He is one of the most intelligent men I have ever met, and he frequently writes letters or columns for the fan magazines or professional magazines, expressing his views on scientific or social issues. I read them avidly, for he writes with clarity and charm, and I have never in fifty years had occasion to disagree with a word he has said. On a very few occasions when he expressed a point of view differing from one I had expressed, I would see at once that I had been wrong, he right. I think he is the only person with whose views I have never disagreed.

I always felt closer to him than to any other Futurian, even though our personalities and circumstances were so different. He had had an unsettled childhood, though he never spoke of it in detail, and the Great Depression had forced him out of high school. He makes the best of it by treating the matter humorously and referring to himself as a "high school dropout." Don't let him kid you, though. He continued his program of self-education to the point where he knows a great deal more about a great many more things than does many a person with my own intensive education.

His social life has been more hectic than mine. For one thing, he has been married five times, but his present marriage, his fifth, to Betty, seems stable and happy.

At the time we met, he and the other Futurians were writing science fiction at a mad pace, alone and in collaboration, under a variety of pseudonyms. I did not join them in this, insisting on writing my stories on my own and using my own name. As it happened, I was the first Futurian to begin to sell consistently, but they tumbled into the field on my heels.

He began to use his own name on his stories in 1952, when he, in collaboration with another Futurian, Cyril Kornbluth, published a three-part serial in *Galaxy* entitled "Gravy Planet." It appeared in novel form as *The Space Merchants* in 1953 and made the reputation of both Fred and Cyril. Each was a major science fiction writer thereafter.

His connection with me?

In 1939, he looked over my rejected short stories, called them "the best rejections I have ever seen" (which was very heartening), and gave me solid hints on how to improve my writing. Then, in 1940, when he was still only twenty years old, he became the editor (and a very good editor too) of two new science fiction magazines, *Astonishing Stories* and *Super Science Stories*. For those magazines he bought several of my early stories. This kept me going till I got the range of the best magazine in the field, *Astounding*. Fred and I even collaborated on two stories, though not very good ones, I'm afraid.

In 1942, when I was stuck and could not proceed with a novelette I was writing that *had* to be submitted in a week or so, he told me how to get out of the spot I had written myself into. I remember that we were standing on the Brooklyn Bridge at the time, but what my difficulty was and what his solution was, I don't remember. (We were standing on the Brooklyn Bridge, I found out many years later, because Fred's first wife, Doris, thought I was a "creep" and wouldn't have me in the apartment. I was struck in a heap when I found this in Fred's autobiography because I had liked her and had never dreamed of her distaste. Nor could I make it up with her, for she had died young.)

In 1950, Pohl was instrumental in the highest degree in getting my first novel published. In short, Fred, more than anyone else but John W. Campbell Jr., made my career possible.

Joe Haldeman

✠

SLEEPING DOGS

The cab took my eyeprint and the door swung open. I was glad to get out. No driver to care how rough the ride was, on a road that wouldn't even be called a road on Earth. The place had gone downhill in the thirty years I'd been away.

Low gravity and low oxygen. My heart was going too fast. I stood for a moment, concentrating, and brought it down to a hundred, then ninety. The air had more sulfur sting than I remembered. It seemed a lot warmer than I remembered that summer, too, but then if I could remember it all I wouldn't have to be here. My missing finger throbbed.

Six identical buildings on the block, half-cylinders of stained pale green plastic. I walked up the dirt path to number three: OFFWORLD AFFAIRS AND CONFEDERACIÓN LIAISON. I almost ran into the door when it didn't open. Pushed and pulled and it reluctantly let me inside.

It was a little cooler and less sulfurous. I went to the second door on the right, TRAVEL DOCUMENTS AND PERMISSIONS, and went in.

"You don't knock on Earth?" A cadaverous tall man, skin too white and hair too black.

"Actually, no," I said, "not public buildings. But I apologize for my ignorance."

He looked at a monitor built into his desk. "You would be Flann Spivey, from Japan on Earth. You don't look Japanese."

"I'm Irish," I said. "I work for a Japanese company, Ichiban Imaging."

He touched a word on the screen. "Means 'number one.' Best, or first?"

"Both, I think."

"Papers." I laid out two passports and a folder of travel documents. He spent several minutes inspecting them carefully. Then he slipped them into a primitive scanning machine, which flipped through them one by one, page by page.

He finally handed them back. "When you were here twenty-nine Earth years ago, there were only eight countries on Seca, representing two competing powers. Now there are seventy-nine countries, two of them off-planet, in a political situation that's . . . impossible to describe simply. Most of the other seventy-eight countries are more comfortable than Space-port. Nicer."

"So I was told. I'm not here for comfort, though." There weren't many planets where they put their spaceports in nice places.

He nodded slowly as he selected two forms from a drawer. "So what does a 'thanatopic counselor' do?"

"I prepare people for dying." For living completely, actually, before they leave.

"Curious." He smiled. "It pays well?"

"Adequately."

He handed me the forms. "I've never seen a poor person come through that door. Take these down the hall to Immunization."

"I've had all the shots."

"All that the Confederación requires. Seca has a couple of special tests for returning veterans. Of the Consolidation War."

"Of course. The nanobiota. But I was tested before they let me return to Earth."

He shrugged. "Rules. What do you tell them?"

"Tell?"

"The people who are going to die. We just sort of let it catch up with us. Avoid it as long as possible, but . . ."

"That's a way." I took the forms. "Not the only way."

I had the door partly open when he cleared his throat. "Dr. Spivey? If you don't have any plans, I would be pleased to have midmeal with you."

Interesting. "Sure. I don't know how long this will take . . ."

"Ten minims, fifteen. I'll call us a floater, so we don't have to endure the road."

◆━ ◆━

The blood and saliva samples took less time than filling out the forms. When I went back outside, the floater was humming down and Braz Nitian was watching it land from the walkway.

It was a fast two-minute hop to the center of town, the last thirty seconds disconcerting free fall. The place he'd chosen was Kaffee Rembrandt, a rough-hewn place with a low ceiling and guttering oil lamps in pursuit of a sixteenth-century ambience, somewhat diluted by the fact that the dozens of Rembrandt reproductions glowed with apparently sourceless illumination.

A busty waitress in period flounce showed us to a small table, dwarfed by a large self-portrait of the artist posed as "Prodigal Son with a Whore."

I'd never seen an actual flagon, a metal container with a hinged top. It appeared to hold enough wine to support a meal and some conversation.

I ordered a plate of braised vegetables, following conservative dietary advice—the odd proteins in Seca's animals and fish might lay me low with a xeno-allergy. Among the things I didn't remember about my previous time here was whether our rations had included any native flesh or fish. But even if I'd safely eaten them thirty years ago, the Hartford doctor said, I could have a protein allergy now, since an older digestive system might not completely break down those alien proteins into safe amino acids.

Braz had gone to college on Earth, UCLA, an expensive proposition that obligated him to work for the government for ten years (which would be fourteen Earth years). He had degrees in mathematics and macroeconomics, neither of which he used in his office job. He taught three nights a week and wrote papers that nine or ten people read and disagreed with.

"So how did you become a thanatopic counselor? Something you always wanted to be when you grew up?"

"Yeah, after cowboy and pirate."

He smiled. "I never saw a cowboy on Earth."

"Pirates tracked them down and made them walk the plank. Actually, I was an accountant when I joined the military, and then started out in pre-med after I was discharged, but switched over to psychology and moved into studying veterans."

"Natural enough. Know thyself."

"Literally." Find thyself, I thought. "You get a lot of us coming through?"

"Well, not so many, not from Earth or other foreign planets. Being a veteran doesn't correlate well with wealth."

"That's for sure." And a trip from Earth to Seca and back costs as much as a big house.

"I imagine that treating veterans doesn't generate a lot of money, either." Eyebrows lifting.

"A life of crime does." I smiled and he laughed politely. "But most of the veterans I do see are well off. Almost nobody with a normal life span needs my services. They're mostly for people who've lived some centuries, and you couldn't do that without wealth."

"They get tired of life?"

"Not the way you or I could become tired of a game, or a relationship. It's something deeper than running out of novelty. People with that little imagination don't need me. They can stop existing for the price of a bullet or a rope—or a painless prescription, where I come from."

"Not legal here," he said neutrally.

"I know. I'm not enthusiastic about it, myself."

"You'd have more customers?"

I shrugged. "You never know." The waitress brought us our first plates, grilled fungi on a stick for me. Braz had a bowl of small animals with tails, deep-fried. Finger food; you hold them by the tail and dip them into a pungent yellow sauce.

It was much better than I'd expected; the fungi were threaded onto a stick of some aromatic wood like laurel; she brought a small glass of a lavender-colored drink, tasting like dry sherry, to go with them.

"So it's not about getting bored?" he asked. "That's how you normally see it. In books, on the cube . . ."

"Maybe the reality isn't dramatic enough. Or too complicated to tell as a simple drama.

"You live a few hundred years, at least on Earth, you slowly leave your native culture behind. You're an immortal—culturally true if not literally—and your nonimmortal friends and family and business associates die off. The longer you live, the deeper you go into the immortal community."

"There must be some nonconformists."

" 'Mavericks,' the cowboys used to say."

"Before the pirates did them in."

"Right. There aren't many mavericks past their first century of life extension. The people you grew up with are either fellow immortals or dead. Together, the survivors form a society that's unusually cohesive. So when someone decides to leave, decides to stop living, the arrangements are complex and may involve hundreds of people.

"That's where I come in, the practical part of my job: I'm a kind of overall estate manager. They all have significant wealth; few have any living relatives closer than great-great-grandchildren."

"You help them split up their fortunes?"

"It's more interesting than that. The custom for centuries has been to put together a legacy, so called, that is a complex and personal aesthetic expression. To simply die, and let the lawyers sort it out, would trivialize your life as well as your death. It's my job to make sure that the legacy is a meaningful and permanent extension of the person's life.

"Sometimes a physical monument is involved; more often a financial one, through endowments and sponsorships. Which is what brings me here."

Our main courses came; Braz had a kind of eel, bright green with black antennae, apparently raw, but my braised vegetables were reassuringly familiar.

"So one of your clients is financing something here on Seca?"

"Financing me, actually. It's partly a gift; we get along well. But it's part of a pattern of similar bequests to nonimmortals, to give us back lost memories."

"How lost?"

"It was a military program, to counteract the stress of combat. They called the drug aqualethe. Have you heard of it?"

He shook his head. "Water of what?"

"It's a linguistic mangling, or mingling. Latin and Greek. Lethe was a river in Hell; a spirit drank from it to forget his old life, so he could be reincarnated.

"A pretty accurate name. It basically disconnects your long-term memory as a way of diverting combat stress, so-called post-traumatic stress disorder."

"It worked?"

"Too well. I spent eight months here as a soldier, when I was in my early twenties. I don't remember anything specific between the voyage here and the voyage back."

"It was a horrible war. Short but harsh. Maybe you don't want the memory back. 'Let sleeping dogs lie,' we say here."

"We say that, too. But for me . . . well, you could say it's a professional handicap. Though actually it goes deeper.

"Part of what I do with my clients is a mix of meditation and dialogue. I try to help them form a coherent tapestry of their lives, the good and the bad, as a basic grounding for their legacy. The fact that I could never do that for myself hinders me as a counselor. Especially when the client, like this one, had his own combat experiences to deal with."

"He's, um, dead now?"

"Oh, no. Like many of them, he's in no particular hurry. He just wants to be ready."

"How old is he?"

"Three hundred and ninety Earth years. Aiming for four centuries, he thinks."

Braz sawed away at his eel and looked thoughtful. "I can't imagine. I mean, I sort of understand when a normal man gets so old he gives up. Their hold on life becomes weak, and they let go. But your man is presumably fit and sane."

"More than I, I think."

"So why four hundred years rather than five? Or three? Why not try for a thousand? That's what I would do, if I were that rich."

"So would I. At least that's how I feel now. My patron says he felt that way when he was mortal. But he can't really articulate what happened to slowly change his attitude.

"He says it would be like trying to explain married love to a babe just learning to talk. The babe thinks it knows what love is, and can apply the word to its own circumstances. But it doesn't have the vocabulary or life experience to approach the larger meaning."

"An odd comparison, marriage," he said, delicately separating the black antennae from the head. "You can become unmarried. But not un-dead."

"The babe wouldn't know about divorce. Maybe there is a level of analogy there."

"We don't know what death is?"

"Perhaps not as well as they."

●—●—●

I liked Braz and needed to hire a guide; he had some leave coming and could use the side income. His Spanish was good, and that was rare on Seca; they spoke a kind of patchwork of Portuguese and English. If I'd studied it thirty years before, I'd retained none.

The therapy to counteract aqualethe was a mixture of brain chemistry and environment. Simply put, the long-term memories were not destroyed by aqualethe, but the connection to them had been weakened. There was a regimen of twenty pills I had to take twice daily, and I had to take them in surroundings that would jog my memory.

That meant going back to some ugly territory.

There were no direct flights to Serraro, the mountainous desert where my platoon had been sent to deal with a situation now buried in secrecy, perhaps shame. We could get within a hundred kilometers of it, an oasis town called Console Verde. I made arrangements to rent a general-purpose vehicle there, a jépe.

After Braz and I made those arrangements, I got a note from some Chief of Internal Security saying that my activities were of questionable legality, and I should report to his office at 0900 tomorrow to defend my actions. We were in the airport, fortunately, when I got the message, and we jumped on a flight that was leaving in twenty minutes, paying cash. Impossible on Earth.

I told Braz I would buy us a couple of changes of clothing and such at the Oasis, and we got on the jet with nothing but our papers, my medications, and the clothes on our backs—and my purse, providentially stuffed with the paper notes they use instead of plastic. (I'd learned that the exchange rate was much better on Earth, and was carrying half a year's salary in those notes.)

The flight wasn't even suborbital, and took four hours to go about a tenth of the planet's circumference. We slept most of the way; it didn't take me twenty minutes to tell him everything I had been able to find out about that two-thirds year that was taken from me.

Serraro is not exactly a bastion of freedom of information under the best of circumstances, and that was a period in their history that many would just as soon forget.

It was not a poor country. The desert was rich in the rare earths that interstellar jumps required. There had been lots of small mines around the countryside (no farms) and only one city of any size. That was Novo B, short for Novo Brasil, and it was still not the safest spot in the Confederación. Not on our itinerary.

My platoon had begun its work in Console Verde as part of a force of one thousand. When we returned to that oasis, there were barely six hundred of us left. But the country had been "unified." Where there had been seventy-eight mines there now was one, Preciosa, and no one wanted to talk about how that happened.

The official history says that the consolidation of those seventy-eight mines was a model of self-determinism, the independent miners banding together for strength and bargaining power. There was some resistance, even some outlaw guerilla action. But the authorities—I among them, evidently—got things under control in less than a year.

Travel and residence records had all been destroyed by a powerful explosion blamed on the guerillas, but in the next census, Serarro had lost 35 percent of its population. Perhaps they walked away.

We stood out as foreigners in our business suits; most men who were not in uniform wore a plain loose white robe. I went immediately into a shop next to the airport and bought two of them, and two sidearms. Braz hadn't fired a pistol in years, but he had to agree he would look conspicuous here without one.

We stood out anyway, pale and tall. The men here were all sunburned and most wore long braided black hair. Our presence couldn't be kept secret; I wondered how long it would be before that Chief of Internal Security caught up with me. I was hoping it was just routine harassment, and they wouldn't follow us here.

There was only one room at the small inn, but Braz didn't mind sharing. In fact, he suggested we pass the time with sex, which caught me off
guard. I told him men don't routinely do that on Earth, at least not the
place and time I came from. He accepted that with a nod.

I asked the innkeeper whether the town had a library, and he said no, but
I could try the schoolhouse on the other side of town. Braz was napping, so
I left a note and took off on my own, confident in my ability to turn right
and go to the end of the road.

Although I'd been many places on Earth, the only time I'd been in
space was that eight-month tour here. So I kept my eyes open for "alien"
details.

Seca had a Drake index of 0.95, which by rule of thumb meant that
only 5 percent of it was more harsh than the worst the Earth had to offer.
The equatorial desert, I supposed. We were in what would have been a
temperate latitude on Earth, and I was sweating freely in the dry heat.

The people here were only five generations away from Earth, but some
genetic drift was apparent. No more profound than you would find on
some islands and other isolated communities on Earth. But I didn't see a
single blonde or redhead in the short, solidly built population here.

The men wore scowls as well as guns. The women, brighter colors and
neutral distant expressions.

Some of the men, mostly younger, wore a dagger as well as a sidearm.
I wondered whether there was some kind of code duello that I would have
to watch out for. Probably *not* wearing a dagger would protect you from
that.

Aside from a pawnshop, with three balls, and a tavern with bright
signs announcing berbesa and bino, most of the shops were not identified.
I supposed that in a small isolated town, everybody knew where everything was.

Two men stopped together, blocking the sidewalk. One of them touched
his pistol and said something incomprehensible, loudly.

"From Earth," I said, in unexcited Confederación Spanish. "*Soy de la
Tierra.*" They looked at each other and went by me. I tried to ignore the
crawling feeling in the middle of my back.

I reflected on my lack of soldierly instincts. Should I have touched my
gun as well? Probably not. If they'd started shooting, what should I do?
Hurl my sixty-year-old body to the ground, roll over with the pistol in my
hand, and aim for the chest?

"Two in the chest, then one in the head," I remembered from crime
drama. But I didn't remember anything that basic from having been a

soldier. My training on Earth had mainly been calisthenics and harassment. Endless hours of parade-ground drill. Weapons training would come
later, they said. The only thing "later" meant to me was months later,
slowly regaining my identity on the trip back to Earth.

By the time I'd gotten off the ship, I seemed to have all my memories
back through basic training, and the lift ride up to the troop carrier. We
had 1.5-gee acceleration to the Oort portal, but somewhere along there I
lost my memory, and didn't get it back till the return trip. Then they
dropped me on Earth—me and the other survivors—with a big check and
a leather case full of medals. Plus a smaller check, every month, for my
lost finger.

I knew I was approaching the school by the small tide of children running in my direction, about fifty of them, ranging from seven or eight to
about twelve, in Earth years.

The schoolhouse was small, three or four rooms. A gray-bearded man,
unarmed, stepped out and I hailed him. We established that we had English
in common and I asked whether the school had a library. He said yes,
and it would be open for two hours yet. "Mostly children's books, of course.
What are you interested in?"

"History," I said. "Recent. The Consolidation War."

"Ah. Follow me." He led me through a dusty playground, to the rear of
the school. "You were a Confederación soldier?"

"I guess that's obvious."

He paused with his hand on the doorknob. "You know to be careful?"
I said I did. "Don't go out at night alone. Your size is like a beacon." He
opened the door and said, "Suela? A traveler is looking for a history
book."

The room was high-ceilinged and cool, with thick stone walls and plenty
of light from the uniform glow of the ceiling. An elderly woman with white
hair was taking paper books from a cart and reshelving them.

"Pardon my poor English," she said, with an accent better than mine.
"But what do you want in a paper book that you can't as easily download?"

"I was curious to see what children are taught about the Consolidation
War."

"The same truth as everyone," she said with a wry expression, and
stepped over to another shelf. "Here . . ." she read titles, "this is the only
one in English. I can't let you take it away, but you're welcome to read it
here."

I thanked her and took the book to an adult-size table and chair at the other end of the room. Most of the study area was scaled down. A girl of seven or eight stared at me.

I didn't know, really, what I expected to find in the book. It had four pages on the Consolidation and Preciosa, and in broad outline there was not much surprising. A coalition of mines decided that the Confederación wasn't paying enough for dysprosium, and they got most of the others to go along with the scheme of hiding the stuff and holding out for a fair price—what the book called profiteering and restraint of trade. Preciosa was the biggest mine, and they made a separate deal with the Confederación, guaranteeing a low price, freezing all their competitors out. Which led to war.

Seca—actually Preciosa—asked for support from the Confederación, and the war became interstellar.

The book said that most of the war took place far from population centers, in the bleak high desert where the mines were. Here.

It struck me that I hadn't noticed many old buildings, older than about thirty years. I remembered a quote from a twentieth-century American war: "We had to destroy the village in order to save it."

The elderly librarian sat down across from me. She had a soft voice. "You were here as a soldier. But you don't remember anything about it."

"That's true. That's exactly it."

"There are those of us who do remember."

I pushed the book a couple of inches toward her. "Is any of this true?"

She turned the book around and scanned the pages it was open to, and shook her head with a grim smile. "Even children know better. What do you think the Confederación is?"

I thought for a moment. "At one level, it's a loose federation of forty-eight or forty-nine planets with a charter protecting the rights of humans and nonhumans, and with trade rules that encourage fairness and transparency. At another level, it's the Hartford Corporation, the wealthiest enterprise in human history. Which can do anything it wants, presumably."

"And on a personal level? What is it to you?"

"It's an organization that gave me a job when jobs were scarce. Security specialist. Although I wasn't a 'specialist' in any sense of the word. A generalist, so called."

"A mercenary."

"Not so called. Nothing immoral or illegal."

"But they took your memory of it away. So it could have been either, or both."

"Could have been," I admitted. "I'm going to find out. Do you know about the therapy that counteracts aqualethe?"

"No . . . it gives you your memories back?"

"So they say. I'm going to drive down into Serarro tomorrow, and see what happens. You take the pills in the place you want to remember."

"Do me a favor," she said, sliding the book back, "and yourself, perhaps. Take the pills here, too."

"I will. We had a headquarters here. I must have at least passed through."

"Look for me in the crowd, welcoming you. You were all so exotic and handsome. I was a girl, just ten."

Ten here would be fourteen on Earth. This old lady was younger than me. No juve treatments. "I don't think the memories will be that detailed. I'll look for you, though."

She patted my hand and smiled. "You do that."

Braz was still sleeping when I got back to the inn. Six time zones to adjust to; might as well let him sleep. My body was still on meaningless starship time, but I've never had much trouble adjusting. My counseling job is a constant whirl of time zones.

I quietly slipped into the other bunk and put some Handel in my earbuds to drown out his snoring.

━ ━

The inn didn't have any vegetables for breakfast, so I had a couple of eggs that I hoped had come from a bird, and a large dry flavorless cracker. Our jepé arrived at 8:30 and I went out to pay the substantial deposit and inspect it. Guaranteed bulletproof except for the windows, nice to know.

I took the first leg of driving, since I'd be taking the memory drug later, and the label had the sensible advice DO NOT OPERATE MACHINERY WHILE HALLUCINATING. Words to live by.

The city, such as it was, didn't dwindle off into suburbs. It's an oasis, and where the green stopped, the houses stopped.

I drove very cautiously at first. My car in LA is restricted to autopilot, and it had been several years since I was last behind a steering wheel. A little exhilarating.

After about thirty kilometers, the road suddenly got very rough. Braz suggested that we'd left the state of Console Verde and had entered Pretorocha, whose tax base wouldn't pay for a shovel. I gave the wheel to him after a slow hour, when we got to the first pile of tailings. Time to take the first twenty pills.

I didn't really know what to expect. I knew the unsupervised use of the aqualethe remedy was discouraged, because some people had extreme reactions. I'd given Braz an emergency poke of sedative to administer to me if I really lost control.

Rubble and craters. Black grit over everything. Building ruins that hadn't weathered much; this place didn't have much weather. Hot and dry in the summer, slightly less hot and more dry in the winter. We drove around and around and absolutely nothing happened. After two hours, the minimum wait, I swallowed another twenty.

Pretorocha was where they said I'd lost my finger, and it was where the most Confederación casualties had been recorded. Was it possible that the drug just didn't work on me?

What was more likely, if I properly understood the literature, was one of two things: one, the place had changed so much that my recovering memory didn't pick up any specifics; two, that I'd never actually been here.

That second didn't seem possible. I'd left a finger here, and the Confederación verified that; it had been paying for the lost digit for thirty years.

The first explanation? Pictures of the battle looked about as bleak as this blasted landscape. Maybe I was missing something basic, like a smell or the summer heat. But the literature said the drug required visual stimuli.

"Maybe it doesn't work as well on some as on others," Braz said. "Or maybe you got a bad batch. How long do we keep driving around?"

I had six tubes of pills left. The drug was in my system for sure: cold sweat, shortness of breath, ocular pressure. "Hell, I guess we've seen enough. Take a pee break and head back."

Standing by the side of the road there, under the low hot sun, urinating into black ash, somehow I knew for certain that I'd never been there before. A hellish place like this would burn itself into your subconscious.

But aqualethe was strong. Maybe too strong for the remedy to counter.

I took the wheel for the trip back to Console Verde. The air-conditioning had only two settings, frigid and off. We agreed to turn it off and open the nonbulletproof windows to the waning heat.

There was a kind of lunar beauty to the place. That would have made an impression on me back then. When I was still a poet. An odd thing to remember. Something did happen that year to end that. Maybe I lost it with the music, with the finger.

When the road got better I let Braz take over. I was out of practice with traffic, and they drove on the wrong side of the road anyhow.

The feeling hit me when the first buildings rose up out of the rock. My throat. Not like choking; a gentler pressure, like tightening a necktie.

Everything shimmered and glowed. *This* was where I'd been. This side of the city.

"Braz . . . it's happening. Go slow." He pulled over to the left and I heard warning lights go *click-click-click*.

"You weren't . . . down there at all? You were here?"

"I don't know! Maybe. I don't know." It was coming on stronger and stronger. Like seeing double, but with all your body. "Get into the right lane." It was getting hard to see, a brilliant fog. "What is that big building?"

"Doesn't have a name," he said. "Confederación sigil over the parking lot."

"Go there . . . go there . . . I'm losing it, Braz."

"Maybe you're finding it."

The car was fading around me, and I seemed to drift forward and up. Through the wall of the building. Down a corridor. Through a closed door. Into an office.

I was sitting there, a young me. Coal-black beard, neatly trimmed. Dress uniform. All my fingers.

Most of the wall behind me was taken up by a glowing spreadsheet. I knew what it represented.

Two long tables flanked my workstation. They were covered with old ledgers and folders full of paper correspondence and records.

My job was to steal the planet from its rightful owners—but not the whole planet. Just the TREO rights, Total Rare Earth Oxides.

There was not much else on the planet of any commercial interest to the Confederación. When they found a tachyon nexus, they went off in search of dysprosium nearby, necessary for getting back to where you came from, or continuing farther out. Automated probes had found a convenient source in a mercurian planet close to the nexus star Poucoyellow. But after a few thousand pioneers had staked homestead claims on Seca, someone stumbled on a mother lode of dysprosium and other rare earths in the sterile hell of Serarro.

It was the most concentrated source of dysprosium ever found, on any planet, easily a thousand times the output of Earth's mines.

The natives knew what they had their hands on, and they were cagey. They quietly passed a law that required all mineral rights to be deeded on paper; no electronic record. For years, seventy-eight mines sold 2 percent of the dysprosium they dug up, and stockpiled the rest—as much as the Confederación could muster from two dozen other planets. Once they had hoarded enough, they could absolutely corner the market.

But they only had one customer.

Routine satellite mapping gave them away; the gamma ray signature of monazite-allenite stuck out like a flag. The Confederación deduced what was going on, and trained a few people like me to go in and remedy the situation, along with enough soldiers to supply the fog of war.

While the economy was going crazy, dealing with war, I was quietly buying up small shares in the rare earth mines, through hundreds of fictitious proxies.

When we had voting control of 51 percent of the planet's dysprosium, and thus its price, the soldiers did an about-face and went home, first stopping at the infirmary for a shot of aqualethe.

I was a problem, evidently. Aqualethe erased the memory of trauma, but I hadn't experienced any. All I had done was push numbers around, and occasionally forge signatures.

So one day three big men wearing black hoods kicked in my door and took me to a basement somewhere. They beat me monotonously for hours, wearing thick gloves, not breaking bones or rupturing organs. I was blindfolded and handcuffed, sealed up in a universe of constant pain.

Then they took off the blindfold and handcuffs and those three men held my arm and hand while a fourth used heavy bolt-cutters to snip off the ring finger of my left hand, making sure I watched. Then they dressed the stump and gave me a shot.

I woke up approaching Earth, with medals and money and no memory. And one less finger.

◆━◆

Woke again on my bunk at the inn. Braz sitting there with a carafe of *melán*, what they had at the inn instead of coffee. "Are you coming to?" he said quietly. "I helped you up the stairs." Dawn light at the window. "It was pretty bad?"

"It was . . . not what I expected." I levered myself upright and accepted a cup. "I wasn't really a soldier. In uniform, but just a clerk. Or a con man." I sketched out the story for him.

"So they actually chopped off your finger? I mean, beat you senseless and then snipped it off?"

I squeezed the short stump gingerly. "So the drug would work.

"I played guitar, before. So I spent a year or so working out alternative fingerings, formations, without the third finger. Didn't really work."

I took a sip. It was like kava, a bitter alkaloid. "So I changed careers."

"You were going to be a singer?"

"No. Classical guitar. So I went back to university instead, pre-med and then psychology and philosophy. Got an easy doctorate in Generalist Studies. And became this modern version of the boatman, ferryman . . . Charon—the one who takes people to the other side."

"So what are you going to do? With the truth."

"Spread it around, I guess. Make people mad."

He rocked back in his chair. "Who?"

"What do you mean? Everybody."

"Everybody?" He shook his head. "Your story's interesting, and your part in it is dramatic and sad, but there's not a bit of it that would surprise anyone over the age of twenty. Everyone knows what the war was really about.

"It's even more cynical and manipulative than I thought, but you know? That won't make people mad. When it's the government, especially the Confederación, people just nod and say, 'more of the same.'"

"Same old, we say. Same old shit."

"They settled death and damage claims generously; rebuilt the town. And it was half a lifetime ago, our lifetimes. Only the old remember, and most of them don't care anymore."

That shouldn't have surprised me; I've been too close to it. Too close to my own loss, small compared to the losses of others.

I sipped at the horrible stuff and put it back down. "I should do something. I can't just sit on this."

"But you can. Maybe you should."

I made a dismissive gesture and he leaned forward and continued with force. "Look, Spivey. I'm not just a backsystem hick—or I am, but I'm a hick with a rusty doctorate in macroeconomics—and you're not seeing or thinking clearly. About the war and the Confederación. Let the drugs dry out before you do something that you might regret."

"That's pretty dramatic."

"Well, the situation you're in is *melo*dramatic! You want to go back to Earth and say you have proof that the Confederación used you to subvert the will of a planet, to the tune of more than a thousand dead and a trillion hartfords of real estate, then tortured and mutilated you in order to blank out your memory of it?"

"Well? That's what happened."

He got up. "You think about it for a while. Think about the next thing that's going to happen." He left and closed the door quietly behind him.

I didn't have to think too long. He was right.

Before I came to Seca, of course I searched every resource for verifiable information about the war. That there was so little should have set off an alarm in my head.

It's a wonderful thing to be able to travel from star to star, collecting exotic memories. But you have no choice of carrier. To take your memories back to Earth, you have to rely on the Confederación.

And if those memories are unpleasant, or just inconvenient . . . they can fix that for you.

Over and over.

Afterword

I sent my first SF story, "Out of Phase," to *Galaxy Magazine* when Fred was editor, and he sent me back a tiny note (less than two inches square, typed), saying that if I could boil the first four pages down to one, he would look at it again.

In fact, I boiled the pages down to one word. I sent the revised story back to him with a one-line cover letter, as the writing magazines at the time advised: "Dear Mr. Pohl—Here is the story with the changes you requested."

But Mr. Pohl had meanwhile quit the job at *Galaxy*! His replacement, Ejler Jakobsen, hadn't edited a science fiction magazine in twenty-some years, and he probably didn't know Haldeman from Heinlein. I suspect he read the cover letter and, under deadline pressure, accepted the story without reading it.

Years later I met Fred at a cocktail party and told him he might have been responsible for my becoming a science fiction writer. He shrugged and said, "Everybody makes mistakes."

—JOE HALDEMAN

LARRY NIVEN

✠

GATES (VARIATIONS)

1

Outside the Coffee Bean they found an empty table, and sat. Traffic was noisy, and they had to raise their voices. Todd Varney didn't care who overheard.

"I haven't tried this notion on my agent," Varney said. "Roy, would you know what I mean by 'the singularity'?"

Roy was Varney's nephew. He taught grade school. He said, "I know some math teachers. A singularity is a place where the math doesn't work. It's not magical. In a polar coordinate system you define a point as an angle plus the radial distance from the center, but the center is zero plus any angle you like. That's a singularity."

"Not . . . *quite* what the science fiction writers mean. This is a predictive thing. One variation is, when someone learns how to increase his own intelligence, makes himself smarter, learns how to increase his intelligence again—"

"Or hers?"

"Or its. Could be a computer. The point is that the curve goes to infinity. Once you're smart enough, you can *see* how to get smarter yet. The singularity, the way writers like Greg Bear see it, is the point where *all* the curves start going to infinity. Intelligence. Available energy. Lifespan. Price of oil, or bread. Computer power per dollar. And after the singularity comes, you can't predict a future."

"I don't know this Greg Bear."

"He's another science fiction writer, like me. The point is, it's *hard work* writing about the singularity. Nothing's harder than writing about a character who's smarter than the author. Even so, the singularity could be coming right down our throats. Bear wonders if the next generation will be recognizably human."

"Write about something else," Roy suggested.

Varney smiled. "Well, but this is the cutting edge in the science fiction field. And I got to thinking. We should have the singularity *now*. Some man or woman or machine, someone out there is increasing his intelligence toward infinity."

"This is not a new thing, Uncle," Roy said patiently. "A child does that growing up. It's a big breakthrough when he learns to read."

"A child growing up reaches a limit. A computer might not. A computer programmer might not. I was thinking that we'd be there already if it weren't that nerds get distracted. What if we went looking for the fated ones? We might find someone like Diane Hire."

"Name-dropper."

"Roy, she's been in the news. Diane Hire suffered from depression. None of the usual treatments worked. Twenty years of despair in a mental institution, and then some doctors put electrodes in her brain and batteries under the skin in her upper chest. The current runs through what we used to call the pleasure center in her brain. She's smiling for the first time in decades. Roy, she's got a wonderful smile! She grins like she means it, with faith and energy and a plan for the future. You look at her, you want to elect her, or invest money."

Roy was laughing.

His uncle said, "But could she have gone further? Suppose her doctors had linked her directly to a computer instead, and kept on fiddling. She might have been the first of the . . . call 'em 'singular ones.' Bought stocks on the Internet. Bought more memory. Wound up owning the world. Or take Richard Feynman, a real seminal genius, worked on the atomic bomb, the founder—"

"Quantum electrodynamics. QED."

"Yeah. What if Feynman hadn't been distracted by bongo drums and wine and women and song? Or Bill Gates. *He* could have been the one, but he went for wealth instead, and social interactions, a wife and family, and happiness. Just as soon as he was able."

"I think he should have all that," Roy said positively.

"Okay," said Varney, and sucked up the last of his cappuccino.

Roy sipped at his iced mocha latte. "But that's doing nothing for you. Uncle, what if Bill Gates *did* it? Linked to one of his own computers. Boosted his intelligence. Didn't tell the rest of us."

"Mmm?"

"You know, Gates works all his minions half to death, but the implied payoff is that they all get rich. They *did* get rich, all of them. He's been shar-

ing the secret with all the bright guys who accept his offer, and work their decade or two with no thought for anything but Microsoft, and come out owning half the planet. How many are they? Could that many keep the secret?"

"If you can't keep the secret, you disappear," his uncle said. "Any decent writer of fiction would tell you that."

Roy's laugh somehow dried up. "Maybe you should write some other
story."

Varney smiled.

2

The Boss was an old man, feeling his mortality. He'd be wealthy if he
hadn't spent everything on constant upgrades to his market, his computers. He'd have friends and a family if he'd trusted enough, but he might
have lost control too. The computers had been everything to him.

And he finally had the computer power he needed.

Each of the four employees here present was crazy in his own way.
Nerds together. Elmer Haines and Guy Towers had built the Kaiser super-
computer; Gary Hoberman had been invaluable in shaping the Solipsist
program; but they didn't understand what they'd built. He still needed
them all, and Orren too, to make it all work.

Of course it was all for him. *His* daydream. The old man should have
known that they wouldn't share his enthusiasm.

He tried talking money. "It'll make us all indecently rich. What I've put
together here is the ultimate entertainment—"

Orren Garvey broke in, a thing the lawyer wouldn't usually do. "It's
too big. We couldn't sell it—no, lease it, more likely—for less than a hundred million dollars a year. Who'd pay that?"

"Half a dozen oil sheiks, maybe. Some of the other computer companies, if only to copy us. Orren, the price will drop. Once we've got the
kinks out, we'll have customers. I know a guy who paid twenty million
dollars to live in the Space Station for a week. Now it'd be thirty million."

"We've got maybe a hundred possible customers, worldwide. Willy,
when they see the interface, they'll flinch. Wires in the brain! You want to
test it yourself, don't you? But you'll *feel* the bad programming, the bugs,
they'll be in your *head* before you can write them out."

"Orren, I've already tried the prototype."

Orren was silent.

"It'll get cheaper again. Moore's Law: you get double the computer power per dollar every year and a half. When it gets cheap enough, we could have the whole human race living inside the hard drive."

Orren was frowning. Was he having ethical problems? Orren could be talked around, but later. The lawyer could always play catch-up.

Gary was fascinated.

Guy wasn't, but he was following all right. He wasn't a leader anyway.

But Elmer Haines had a sleepy look, and that wasn't so good. So the old man said, "You won't have to wait to get rich, Elmer. Hook up and you're already there. A whole world, and you own it. The Kaiser has the capacity to simulate billions of units. Virtual people, and anyone can play, but I'll be in there first. I'm going to create a utopia with the Solipsist program. The world as we always wanted it to be. When I've got the bugs out, you can just hook in."

Elmer asked, "What'll you call yourself?"

"What?"

Elmer said, "*Second Life* and the like, the users give their avatars names—"

The old man shook his head hard. "I'll use my own name. William Gates."

"What's your perfect world like, Willy?"

"Well—" He stopped. His sudden horrifying insight was that he hadn't done enough daydreaming. Computers, programming, tiny components growing tinier, competing machines: these had been his life, but they were not the kind of dream that can give a world its shape.

"I suppose I'll make myself the richest man on Earth. I'll make you all rich too, everone who's worked for me or with me. There've been too many computers in my life. In the next I'll have family and children. I'll have presidents and kings for friends. I'll be strong. Healthy. Better eyesight."

"That's just you. What about the world? What's in it for us?" Gary Hoberman asked.

"I hadn't thought . . . oh, all right." This wasn't coming easily. "I'll take down the Soviet Union. Make the United States the most powerful nation in the world."

"Won't the Soviets just nuke everything?"

"I won't write it that way."

"Cities on the moon? Base on Mars?"

The old man laughed, then coughed. When he had it under control he said, "The Kaiser doesn't have *that* much capacity. Maybe the 2.0 version. Or I can say we went to the moon and came back and stopped. Leave it at that."

Elmer said, "I wonder if those six billion people you're going to program in could be self-aware?"

"Hah! Maybe with the 2.0 version."

"We should think about it now. Orren, is it ethical to build people into an artificial world? Willy, you know perfectly well that it won't stay peaceful. Peace is dull. You can't sell dull. You'll end with a shoot-'em-up game."

The lawyer said, "Willy, what if you're right, what if they'll be self-aware? Is it ethical to deny all these people their existence? It's like the ethics of abortion. There are two sides."

Elmer shook his head violently, and the old man said, "I never would have thought of that one. You think I *owe* it to them?" He laughed out loud, but he was the only one.

He didn't wait for an answer. "Let's do it. We'll start tomorrow," he said, and that was that.

Afterword

Frederik Pohl bought my first four stories. From that point on he got first look at almost everything.

The third of those stories was a novelette. He retitled it *World of Ptavvs,* using a word I'd made up for the story background. And he ran the novelette down the street to Betty Ballantine and suggested it could become a novel. Ballantine Books published it, my first.

Fred saw the short story "Becalmed in Hell" first. I got back a letter telling me everything he thought was wrong with it. I rewrote the story, and sent it to *F&SF*, which bought and published it. The next time we met, he explained that a long letter from an editor means he'd like to see an altered version: a thing I should have realized myself.

I sent him "Neutron Star." He didn't just publish it; he suggested a series of stories about the weirdest objects in the universe, paired with articles about the same objects. That series never quite jelled, but Fred did start me looking for the weirdness about us, and I've continued to do that.

This is for Fred.

—LARRY NIVEN

GARDNER DOZOIS

※·※

APPRECIATION

While Fred Pohl's writing career will almost certainly be the thing most celebrated and talked about in this anthology, there's one other thing I wouldn't want to see overlooked: his career as a magazine editor. Although most people would name John W. Campbell for this role, for me Fred was quite probably the best SF magazine editor who ever lived, and when I became an SF magazine editor myself, back in the early eighties, the editor I consciously modeled myself upon was not John W. Campbell, but Fred Pohl.

I'm more jealous of Fred for having been the one who got to publish all those great Cordwainer Smith and Jack Vance stories than I am of any other editor; the publication of Smith's "On the Storm Planet," "The Ballad of Lost C'Mell," "A Planet Named Shayol," "Mother Hitton's Littul Kittons," and "The Game of Rat and Dragon," and Vance's *The Dragon Masters*, *The Last Castle*, and "The Moon Moth" would be enough all by themselves to cement Fred's position in the hierarchy of great SF editors, to say nothing of all the other first-rate fiction by first-rate authors that appeared in both *Galaxy* and *Worlds of If* during the years that he edited them.

Although Fred thought of *Worlds of If* as *Galaxy*'s remainder outlet, a magazine in which to dump stuff that was good but not good enough for Pohl's frontline magazine, *Galaxy*, I must admit that it was *Worlds of If* that owned my adolescent heart as it apparently did the hearts of many another fan, as, seemingly almost to Fred's annoyance, it kept winning the Hugo Award for best magazine year after year instead of the more "respectable" *Galaxy*. *Galaxy* may have been more substantial, but *Worlds of If* was more fun, a magazine that specialized in the sort of colorful ripsnorting adventure tales that had become rarer in more somber magazines such as *Analog* by then. Fred used *Worlds of If* as a platform to revitalize the space adventure tale by publishing Larry Niven's early "Known Space" stories and Fred Saberhagen's long sequence of "Berserker" stories, and a little later started something of a miniboom in the even-more-specialized form of the "interstellar espionage" story, with Keith Laumer's hugely popular "Retief" stories; they were later joined by similar stories by C. C. MacApp, James H. Schmitz, and others, and there was also always highly entertaining work to be found in the pages of *If* by Roger Zelazny, Robert Silverberg, Samuel R. Delany, James Tiptree Jr., Philip K. Dick, R. A. Lafferty, and others.

Remainder outlet or not, Fred made *If* a loose, lively, and entertaining magazine. Not the least of the lessons from Fred's work that I kept in mind when I began editing a monthly SF magazine was that in addition to whatever work of great profundity and social worth you could find to publish, such a magazine also always had to be fun, and that it was the reasonable expectation of finding fun there that would keep the readers coming back month after month.

Speaking of which, the one thing I quite consciously stole from Fred's *If* when I took over *Asimov's* was a device known as the Next Issue Box. Fred used these Coming Attractions very shrewdly not only to whip up anticipation for the wonders that could be found in the next issue, but to create a sense of community, of readers joined together in excitement and expectation, all of them looking forward eagerly to what was to come. I followed his example at *Asimov's*, where the Next Issue Boxes had previously often been nothing more than a list of author names. I made them lurid and hucksterish, trying my best to drum up excitement and anticipation for the stories that were going to be in the next issue. Now that kind of Coming Attractions announcement is pretty much the industry standard. It may be a small one, but that also is a part of Fred's legacy.

There have ever only been a handful of great SF magazine editors, and, in my opinion, Fred deserves to be ranked right at the very top.

James Gunn

)•I•(

TALES FROM THE SPACESHIP *GEOFFREY*

The following four stories are part of a novel-in-progress *Transcendental*. Taking place about a thousand years in the future, it's about a group of human and alien pilgrims on a long space journey seeking the site of a transcendental machine, who pass the time by telling stories about what brought them on this quest.

TORDOR'S STORY

Tordor said:

I was born on an ideal world of great sweeping plains and flowing rivers of sweet water and oases of trees where we could doze in the heat of the day. The sun was yellow, the pull of the world was solid, and the days were long, and I was happy to eat and sleep and play mock battles with my tribe-mates. I had two good friends: a male my age named Samdor, who was my constant companion, and a pleasingly muscled female named Alidor that I secretly admired and allowed to beat me in our games. And then I turned five and the recruiters came from the distant cities and my parents said I must go with them. I was bewildered and afraid. Why should my parents send me away? What had I done wrong?

The recruiters were thinner than we grass-eaters but tall, strong, and distant. They came in a big, gas-filled aeronef, and they spoke to the recruits only to give orders and said nothing to each other. Some fifty of us had been collected from the plains tribes, most of them my age, a few younger and a couple a year older and meaner. They bullied the younger ones, stole their food and made them fight each other until they rebelled, and then the older recruits beat them. The recruiters did not seem to care. Later I learned that letting the recruits fight among themselves and establish their hierarchy was the custom, that children had to learn how to survive under difficult circumstances, in strange lands, and without friends. We were being transformed into good Dorians.

Only two of us died on the long trip to the northern highlands. One of them was Alidor.

I had never seen a city before. My parents had told me stories about powerful Dorians who flew through the sky and traversed the great void between the stars, but I thought they were fairy tales, like the fanciful stories my tribe-mates spun during the long evenings. But the city of Grandor, the great city of Doria, grew out of the northern mountain range like a forest of fairy palaces, glittering with crystalline reflections in the evening sun and, as the sun dropped behind the mountains, glowing with light. The spires of the city seemed to rise above even the peaks that surrounded it.

It was as marvelous as my parents had described it, and I would have exclaimed at its beauty, and the people who had built it, if I had not been bruised and afraid. We were herded off the ship and prodded into crude quarters, little more than stalls for sleeping, without privacy. Drink was available at a central trough; to eat we had a poor quality of grass, without grains or fruit. Later I learned that this treatment was intended to toughen us against future hardship, and, anyway, quality food was expensive to bring from the plains and was reserved for the citizens who governed the city and the world and the worlds beyond.

We got used to it, as young people will, and to the morning run up and down the mountainsides, to the mock combat in the afternoon, with and without weapons, and to the classrooms where we were taught mathematics and engineering and spacecraft and the military history of Doria, and the minor skills of computers and accounting. The classrooms were the good times when it was possible to doze off if one had a classmate willing to nudge one awake when the instructor looked one's way. Otherwise, a club was likely to come crashing down upon one's skull, and more than one young Dorian met his end that way. I was lucky. I got only a lump or two, but I had a thicker skin and a thicker skull than most. My classmate died. Sometimes I envied him.

In the evenings Dorian heroes would tell us stirring tales of combat, and I wondered if I would ever be like them: strong, confident, swaggering, deadly, full of honors, mating at will. I could not imagine it. None of us dozed then. Sometimes they showed us patriotic films or films of space combat. The ones we could follow seem staged for the cameras. The real ones were almost impossible to observe anything at all except for moments when they were too confused to distinguish friend from enemy. We were always tired. If we napped then, nobody cared.

So it went, year after year, as I grew to be even taller than the recruiters and my plains fat was converted into muscle. I was the one who triumphed in the mock battles, even when I faced our instructors, and I gloried in my newfound strength and skill. One by one my fellow students recognized my preeminence, those that survived. Of my cohort of fifty, only twenty reached the age of decision. I personally killed the two older ones who had bullied us on the way to Grandor.

The age of decision was ten. I no longer wept for my parents and my siblings. I had given up ever seeing them again. I knew that if I returned they would be required to put me to death as a disgrace to the family and the tribe, and I would have to kill them instead. So I only dreamed about the flowing plains of grass and the sweet streams and the clear blue sky, and about running, running endlessly and untiringly under that yellow sun, knowing that it could never be anything but a dream.

We lined up at graduation to learn our fates, and heard our records read aloud and our destinations announced. Some fulfilled my worst nightmare: they were rejects, to be returned to their families and certain death or to wander the plains as rogue males, ostracized by everyone they met and subject to termination by anyone. Some became factory supervisors. Some became engineers or scientists. Some were assigned to bureaucratic posts within Grandor or one of the lesser cities scattered along the coasts to the far southernmost tip of land. Some received postings to other planets under Dorian rule. Some became recruiters, like those that came for us five years before.

And a few were appointed to the military academy.

I was one of those.

❧

The military academy was situated in a valley among tall mountains that divided the southern continent from the north, and near the spaceport at the equator, with its space elevator that we were told had been invented by a Dorian scientist but I later learned had been acquired from humans—perhaps the only thing we learned from them besides ferocity. We had our own taste of ferocity, among ourselves and among the savage Dorians who occupied the southern continent, separated for long ages by the mountain range. With the superior technologies of the north, they could have been subdued centuries before, I learned from a wise master, but our rulers had decided they were of greater utility as anvils on which to hammer out the blades of our soldiers.

We fought them with their own weapons, not with ours, and we prevailed, not because we were stronger or more bloodthirsty but because we were disciplined. That was our first lesson—discipline or death. Fight as a group or die as an individual.

Sometimes, as if by prearrangement, the savages attacked the academy, and we were roused from our stalls to grab our weapons and repel them from our walls. More often we ventured forth in hunting groups and fell upon them in their villages, killing them all, males, females, and children; we did not venture too far south lest we reduce their numbers beyond repletion. Sometimes they ambushed our groups, and we had to fight for our own lives. Often groups returned with their numbers depleted. Those who returned without their fellows were beaten and those who returned without their fellows' bodies were expelled—south of the mountains. Sometimes groups did not return at all.

In my first five years I had learned survival. The cadets among whom we were thrown would have treated us in the same way as the bullies in the aeronef, but I had prepared the dozen of appointees sent with me. We would present a united front. We would not fight among ourselves, but we would fight anyone else as a group. And we would fight before we would submit.

I fought the cadet leader on the first day of our arrival. He was older and more experienced than I, but he was overconfident, and I was determined not to surrender to his official sadism. His cohort carried him off the field, unable to intervene because my cohort stood solidly behind me. After that no one touched us, no one taunted us. Another leader was chosen, but unofficially I was the leader, and consulted about plans and procedures affecting my group. My group was not sent on missions without strategic goals and training. We operated as a unit with advance scouts and side scouts and rear scouts, and we knew the terrain and its ambush points as well as we knew our own plains. None of my group died.

Even the academy instructors began to notice. Ordinarily they let the cadets create their own culture, but now they understood that the culture had been taken over by a newcomer who was flouting tradition and its custodians. They feared novelty, since their familiar practices had worked for so long. They tried to break my will and my power over the group. They separated me from the others, but I had warned them of this possibility and deputized Samdor to serve in my absence. They imprisoned me for a time on imaginary charges and sent me out to do battle alone. I survived and returned with grisly proof of my success.

Finally they recognized my leadership and the success of my organization, and let me install my program for the entire academy, forming the cadets into cohesive units and letting each choose a commander—with my approval—and preparing for battle with the same kind of strategic planning. Casualties dropped. Successes mounted.

Life at the academy was not all skirmishes with the savages or combat training within the yard. We were being prepared as the new Dorian military leaders. We studied military strategies, combat maneuvers, enough space navigation to understand—and sometimes check upon—the navigators, weapons and weapon repair, chemistry and physics and mathematics, but no literature or art. That we had to acquire—if we had the taste for it—in our leisure hours, such as they were, and secretly, for they were considered suspicious if not, perhaps, subversive.

We had only limited exposure to current events and politics. We knew about alien civilizations—they were considered lesser creatures who had ventured, almost by accident, into space and could serve, at best, as suppliers to Doria, and, at worst, as servants and their lands potential Dorian dominions. Alien languages were not part of the curriculum. Let them learn Dorian was the official attitude. Although I did not understand why this was so, I sensed that this was a mistake. We could not depend upon translators, particularly alien translators, nor even upon mechanical translators. Within each language, I came to believe, was the heart and soul of the people who spoke it. So, like literature and art, I studied alien languages, beginning with the language of the savages to the south. It was then I learned what moved them and how to work with them in other ways than combat.

In our fourth year we learned of humans—these pretentious interlopers who emerged from their single system as if they were the equals of the long-established Dorians and the others, who, though unequal, had been part of the galactic scene for millennia. Our instructors let us know, not by word but by intonation, that humans were inconsequential, that they were nothing to be concerned about except as they disturbed the aliens whom we allowed to coexist.

This, perhaps, was a Dorian error that was almost fatal, not simply to us but to the entire galactic civilization that had existed for so many millennia in equilibrium—an uneasy equilibrium like supercooled water but equilibrium all the same.

And then it was time for graduation, deliverance from the petty tyranny of the academy and into the great tyranny of military service. But our instructors had one more graduation barrier for us to hurdle—one final hand-to-hand combat to the death for a pair of matched champions—and I learned that the academy may yield but it does not forget. It matched me against my old tribe-mate and second-in-command, my best friend Samdor.

I would have refused, but it would have meant death to us both. Samdor did refuse, but I persuaded him that it was better to kill or be killed in combat than to be executed as a coward. I knew he was no coward. He loved me, as he, like me, had loved Alidor. I wanted him to kill me, to end this misery we Dorians called living, but in the end, in front of the jeering instructors and the quiet cadets, something in me deflected his blows and parried his thrusts. I had practiced survival too long.

I killed Samdor and with that blow became a true Dorian.

●▬ ▬●

Our superiors assigned us to military posts by lot, they said. Only later did I learn that the system was manipulated to place the new officers where they thought we should go, just as the combat by lots was fixed to pit friend against friend. I went to my post as the gunnery officer on a Dorian light-cruiser off the farthest Dorian outpost, where our empire met the humans. They were always encroaching with their inexhaustible numbers and appetites for land and conquest. I went with an empty heart, always seeing the eyes of Samdor as he accepted my fatal blow, seeing the light behind those eyes fade and go out. I tried to accept that, but what I could not accept was the expression of gratitude that flashed over his face at the moment of his death.

Was death so welcome? Or was his love so much greater than mine that he wished to buy my life with his death?

The journey to the outpost was long. They did not waste wormhole technology on newly commissioned officers, and we were jammed into the hold of a cargo ship like bales of hay. But we had little hay. We were on short rations from the start of the journey, and many would have died along the way had we been left on our own. Like the military academy, the fittest were intended to survive. But I organized a small group of natural leaders to see that the rations were divided equally, and that we all lived in a state of semistarvation. Only one died.

When we reached the fleet, I reported to the commanding officer. His name was Bildor. He was the biggest Dorian I had met, and his body was crisscrossed with the scars of battle—Dorian battle, I learned later. He looked at me as if he saw me as a potential rival, but I was clearly his inferior in everything but promise. He would gain nothing by challenging me, but he challenged my ideas instead. "So, you are the newly commissioned officer who thinks he has a better way of doing things?"

"There is always a better way," I replied with proper deference.

"Tradition has brought us to this mighty empire," he said.

"New challenges arrive daily," I said, "for which tradition has no responses."

"You will perform your duties as a proper Dorian," Bildor said.

I bowed my head and was dismissed. But I knew that Bildor was watching through his senior officers.

We had skirmishes with the human ships when we came across them. But between skirmishes we socialized. I met them, and other aliens, in bars or theaters. I learned a bit of human speech and what passed for humor between us both. We told jokes. I learned something of human history and the history of other species in the galaxy and compared them to our own. That was my education in xenology. I learned what made them drunk and broke down their limited reserves, and tried to hide from them what made Dorians drunk. Not that it would have mattered. Dorians become sullen and withdrawn when drunk on—shall I reveal it?—fermented hay.

I even grew to like the humans, perhaps even more than I liked my superiors. My superiors were determined to make us hate the humans as much as we hated each other. They pitted us against each other for promotions, in what they called "fight days" that were carryovers from the military-school survival programs. I was clearly the best at personal combat, but after Samdor I refused to fight to the death. I defeated my opponent and spared his life. Only one of my superiors dared to challenge me, and in his case I made an exception and killed him. That gained me a promotion to his position as second navigator and freedom from challenges from below or above. Even Bildor seemed to relax his vigilance.

So I made my way up in the Dorian service, from lowly officer to second in command, and then, when Bildor got killed in a personal duel with the commander of another ship, I got my own ship. I changed the discipline. I did away with fight days. I encouraged my subordinates to come to me with their problems, to make suggestions, to work toward a harmonious crew.

Change didn't come easy. Dorians are herd creatures, as are most grazers, elevated to sentience millennia before by hard times. Some historians have traced the transformation to a tumultuous period of volcanic activity that contaminated the Dorian atmosphere with smoke and ash, causing the death of grass almost everywhere and the near extermination of the Dorian people. Other scientists point to deep pits in the Dorian soil caused, they say, by meteoric bombardment raising clouds of dust and smoke that caused similar death and near starvation. Whichever is correct—and perhaps both are—Dorians were forced to change. They had to learn. They had to invent. Most of all, they had to survive, and often at the expense of another group or another individual. The most successful of these founded Grandor, so remote from Dorian experience and nature, and then the other cities of the northern hemisphere, and, more recently, the southern.

When the crisis passed, those who had founded the cities under the pressure of necessity saw Dorians relapsing into their former indolence and herd mentality, and began a regime of recruitment and training such as I had experienced, with a system that set out to replicate the conditions that had produced the Grandorians. If nature could not be trusted to provide harsh necessity, the system would supply something similar.

Humans, I learned, were more fortunate, if that is how it might be termed: Earth was not as benign as Doria, and humans had competitors against which they had to struggle, along with more frequent moments of cosmic catastrophe and mutating radiation. Humans' view of their environment was not the gentle Doria but, as one human poet described it, "Nature, red in tooth and claw." Fortunate, I say, because humans evolved through struggle and their social systems evolved to ameliorate the pain of survival, not to replicate it. Their aggressive attitudes toward the universe are innate rather than nurtured. Dorians have to be brutalized.

I thought it was time to change. Perhaps the Grandor system was needed at one time, but Dorians had passed that point. Curiosity, learning, the need to achieve, could be instilled at an early age through programs of education. Skills in battle and obedience to command could be developed through programs that emulated real conditions rather than replicated them. Dorians, I thought, could be more like humans.

I had two long-time periods to retrain my crew. The lower-ranking crew members were as resistant as the officers. Like them, they had survived the Dorian survival-of-the-fittest system, and they would surrender their attitudes, and their positions of privilege, reluctantly if at all. The process was like retraining an abused animal: repeated kindnesses and frequent strokings are required to reverse a lifetime of avoiding predators and the blows of masters.

I was succeeding, I thought. Morale was higher. The crew seemed once more like my childhood herd, happy, responding better to requests than to orders, coming forward with suggestions, developing into a team rather than a group of individuals. There were throwbacks, to be sure, quarrels, batterings, surly responses, but they were growing fewer and infrequent.

And then the war broke out.

- - -

We never knew what started the war, or what was at stake. For millennia, after the legendary galactic war, which probably was a series of wars initiated by a new emerging species, the star empires had worked at keeping the peace. And the uneasy truce that followed the human emergence had seemed a recognition of earlier folly. But it was a truce easily destroyed by a careless action, a misunderstood intrusion, a failure of communication. And then every empire turned upon every other.

Wars are mass confusion; no one knows who is winning until one side turns and runs or loses its will to continue and sues for peace. Only the historians are able to decide who came out ahead and on what terms, and they are often wrong. Interstellar wars are far more difficult to evaluate. News of battles comes only after many cycles, and even then the information is unreliable. How many of the enemy ships were destroyed? How were they identified? What was their mission? How many ships did the Dorians lose? What were our casualties? How many colonies were destroyed on each side, how many planets laid waste? How many replacement ships have been built? How many crews have been trained? Are our resources capable of withstanding the terrible drain of conflict?

Many cycles will be required before any of this becomes clear. The historians are still computing.

At first our enemy was the humans. They were the newcomers; they were the troublemakers. We fell upon them near the Sirian frontier, and massacred their ships. I tried to stop it, but I had no time after the orders came. And then the humans retaliated, their ships appearing in our midst out of wormholes that we did not suspect, or detect, and wreaked havoc in our fleet. Only the superior organization of my crew allowed the *Ardor* to survive, damaged as it was. We were the only ship in the fleet to emerge without a casualty, despite being in the midst of the action.

At first we were accused of cowardice by the high command, but visual records proved the opposite. And then I was given command of a fleet and told to attack the humans in return. I disobeyed. I contacted the human fleet commander and spoke to her in my broken glish and arranged a meeting. Face to face we worked out our differences and I returned to my superiors with the offer of peace. Again I was placed on trial for treason. I almost resorted to a personal challenge of the court, once more, but refrained and argued my case with all the urgency and eloquence that I could command.

Reluctantly they accepted the terms, and we allied ourselves with the humans against the Sirians and then with the humans and the Sirians against the Aldebarans, and with the humans, the Sirians, and the Aldebarans against the Alpha Centaurans. Finally, exhausted with battle, the galaxy strewn with broken ships, broken worlds, and broken creatures, we made a peace. Ten years of war, a thousand broken planets, and a thousand million casualties, and nothing more. Never again, we vowed, would we go to war. Anyone who broke the peace would be turned upon by all the others. Boundaries were established, spheres of influence were agreed upon, mechanisms for settling disputes were created. We would study war no more.

I returned to Doria a hero, commander of a battle group that had won every engagement, the inventor of new strategies of command and tactics, but most of all, the crafter of peace. I thought I could challenge the high command. I thought my innovations in training and organization would provide a strategy for change. I thought I might even compete to be the successor to the Hierarch. But instead I was once more placed on trial for disobedience and treason, and escaped punishment only through the basic right of personal combat. The High Command had succeeded once more. Doria had won but not in the Dorian way, and the High Command, and Doria itself, was not ready to accept victory on any terms but those that emerged from its own traditions. It had used me and now was prepared to throw me away.

I did not blame the High Command or Doria. I wasn't good enough. I realized my failings as a Dorian, as a sentient creature. Perhaps no one was good enough. Not on Doria, nor on any world. At least we had peace, and I decided to retire to a world at peace, to a galaxy at peace.

But peace was not so simple. The Galactic Powers had to set up an interspecies board to evaluate new inventions and their potential for creating change and conferring superiority on one species or another. All such developments, like the human space elevator, had to be shared by all.

And then came Transcendentalism with all its mystery, with all its promise. Now, perhaps, I could be good enough, and here I am.

XI'S STORY

Xifor is a cruel world of rocky continents and cold seas whose misery is relieved by a few fertile valleys near the equator. According to Xifora scientists, Xifor life began and civilization emerged in those valleys. Xifor's sun is old and dim. Xifora scientists speculate that Xifor was a rocky wanderer from outer space that strayed into the Xifor system late in its evolution and was captured and dropped into orbit by the competing tyranny of its gas giants. Certainly Xifor is unique among the other planets of the system, which are all gas giants, although some have Xifor-size satellites. Some scientists insist that Xifor is one of those satellites torn free by the attraction of a massive passing body and condemned to an obscure orbit among the giants.

No matter. Xifora have always felt that Xifora must fight to stay alive in a universe that does not love these persons. The geology of Xifor means that most Xifora are born and raised in the unforgiving mountains. Many creatures love their planet of origin, but Xifora do not love Xifor. Xifor is respected, like the whip that transforms a weakling into a creature of strength and endurance, but not loved.

Today's Xifora are the descendants of ancestors driven from the fertile valleys by the privileged few, the hereditary nobility that were strong when the land was weak, and seized possession when the land was held by all. When population grew too great, the nobility cast out the persons who tilled the fields and harvested the grain. The exiled Xifora's only food became what these persons could steal from the valley-dwellers or hunt down upon the crags among creatures as hungry as these persons. But these persons scratched terraces out of mountain slopes, domesticated animals for food and clothing and their dung to fertilize their terraces, stared at the stars, dug deep in the land, and built machines.

Out of deprivation came strength. Out of suffering came a people for whom suffering was a familiar companion. Out of these persons' pain-filled past came these persons' glorious future. Being cast out of paradise made mountain Xifora strong and proud. These persons prospered and the valley-dwellers decayed until these persons prevailed and created a new world—still harsh and beautiful in its harshness, but fair. When the mountain Xifora were strong enough these persons took back the valleys from those persons who had grown soft and weak from lack of struggle.

The mountain Xifora cast out the valley-dwellers to live or die, as the mountain Xifora were forced to do in millennia past. From the history of mountain Xifora the Xifora learned the essential lesson the universe has to offer: suffering is good, the easy life is the way to racial ruin, Xifora cannot depend upon the kindness of others, that the only resource Xifora have is these persons' own strength and resolve, even when soaring hatchling rates caused these persons to resort to the same solution as that of the hereditary nobility.

To cope with the ugly reality of their circumstances, Xifora turned to technology. The machines Xifora had developed to make these persons' existence possible and to take back the valleys from the decadent valley Xifora, these persons now adapted to fly above the mountains rather than to crawl upon those cold and cruel excrescences of these persons' world. And then these persons looked at the gas giants that oppressed Xifor and Xifora, and saw those worlds, like the valley Xifora, hoarding resources that Xifora could use and the satellites that could provide a home for more Xifora, perhaps more hospitable than the Xifor mountains.

Xifora dug ore out of the Xifor mountains and smelted the ore into metal and worked the metal into ships that conquered empty space, mined the atmospheres of the gas giants for precious fuel and materials, and took the satellites as these persons' own. Within a few centuries the Xifora had turned this oppressive system into new and better Xifors. The pygmy interloper became the master of the entire system. The Xifor will conquered the giants' power.

Life went too well. Some of the satellites were more favored by geology and climate than rocky Xifor, and their Xifora became as soft and decadent as the valley-dwellers. The governors responded, acting with stern kindness to transport children to the remote areas of the home planet to harden or die. Many died, but many survived, prepared now to suffer as a way of life and to act as needed without direction.

But with machines to protect these persons from the cruelties of nature, even Xifor became too soft, and the Xifora turned these persons' eyes to the stars, knowing that the stars were cold and distant and uncaring, and that space itself, like the remote regions of Xifor, was the ultimate test of Xifor will and strength. Xifora ventured forth and discovered that the galaxy was not as empty as the giants' satellites; like the valleys, it was already owned. Once more the Xifora were thwarted, deprived of the Xifora birthright. Here, again, the Xifor past informed the Xifor present: Xifora would be better and tougher, more determined to succeed and more willing to persist over millennia, over failures, than other Galactics.

So events have gone, these millennia past. Gradually, through faith and perseverance, the Xifora have become one of the coequal members of the Galactic ruling council, recognized for Xifora determination to succeed over obstacles, Xifora willingness to sacrifice for Xifora beliefs, Xifora inventiveness in solving great problems, and Xifora—but Xifora must not be boastful. It suits Xifora temperament best to suffer in silence and revenge at length.

All this account is one reason for Xifora sympathy for humans, who emerged into the galaxy to find it already populated and settled and governed by others, just as Xifora discovered, in millennia past. But impatience and complaint Xifora find offensive, and for these barbarisms Xifora do not like humans.

◆▬ ▬◆

All this is prologue to this person's story. Xifora are hatchlings, but like all hatchlings, dangerous companions. Xifora know that in the mountains Xifora live or die alone. So life was for this person. This person was the smallest of a brood of a dozen hatchlings, of which five died and were eaten in the nest. This person would have been eaten as well had not this person's cleverness and will led to survival in this person's first days out of the shell. This is the way of the nest: hatchlings eat or are eaten. Those that the stronger hatchlings cannot fall upon and eat, delight in tormenting the weaker hatchlings, depriving them of food, tearing away limbs in sport, or so the stronger hatchlings say. Those persons called it part of the Xifor way, to make sure the fittest survive, but the game is actually survival itself. The fewer that survive mean more food and more status for those who live.

This person survived the loss of numerous limbs, usually one but never more than two at one time. Others, in this nest and neighboring nests, were less fortunate: if three limbs are lost, the game is lost. The fourth limb is doomed, and the hatchling will be consumed before the limbs can grow back. This person understood that consequence early, concealed food in a corner of the home nest where a rock could be rolled into place, and retreated there furtively and in haste as soon as a limb was lost. Many periods were spent growing new limbs.

The only safe time was during school hours when hatchlings were taught the history of oppression and the language and tools of justice. Science explained the unloved place of Xifora in the universe, and technology provided the means by which Xifora could liberate Xifora from the cruel Xifor environment. School was good, not least because it provided a period when survival was not at stake and wits could be turned to the larger issues that lay ahead. And the best part was that the worst hatchling tormentors were the poorest students; those persons who depend upon size and power discover that strength alone is not enough, that the mind has powers beside which the greatest physical endowments dwindle to insignificance.

Where were these persons' parents while these cruel games continued, the listener to this story may ask. Such a question would never have occurred before Xifora encountered the Galactic Federation, where mercy is considered a virtue. Xifora parents are like Xifor itself: hard, demanding, unsentimental. Like Xifor, parents breed offspring hardy and self-reliant. Those persons survive who should survive because those persons are strong of body or will; the weak fail and are eaten; and thus Xifora grow stronger and more capable with each generation. Xifora not only embrace evolution, they enhance it.

Before this person left the nest, this person found a piece of unusually hard wood that this person sharpened to a point by rubbing it hour after hour against a rock, and this stick became a defense against this person's nestlings. After a few accidents to other hatchlings, this person lost no limbs from personal teasing. Instead this person took vengeance against this person's chief tormentor, Vi, the largest and most promising of the nestlings. When attacked once more, rather than losing a limb this person raised his pointed stick and Vi ran upon it, in that person's vulnerable eating sack. After the accident, this person stood aside while the tormentor was consumed by the other nestlings. Vi was gone and would torment no more; this person did not need to consume any of the remains to be strong.

As soon as the feast was over, this person left the nest and began existence in the mountains of northern Xifor. The nights were cold and the days only slightly warmer, but this person soon trapped a furry creature and fashioned warm garments from its hide. This person stole fire, cooked meat, and fashioned weapons, first a sling for propelling rocks, then a mechanism for projecting small, pointed spears, and finally, when a dump of discarded materials was stumbled upon, weapons shaped from metal scraps, and then tools that this person used to build smelters for ore, and finally to construct machines.

When this person was nearly adult, this person encountered this person's parents once more. This person recognized them by their resemblance to Vi and by their family pheromones, and for a moment ancient fears and hatreds flared. The natural attempt to kill this person was anticipated and foiled, with only the loss of a single limb by the female parent. Then this person convinced the parents that this person was indeed a member of the parents' brood, and that the killing of the largest and most promising of the brood was justified and that this person's survival should be celebrated and not condemned. This person demonstrated the machines this person had built. Suitably impressed, the parents accepted this person as a member of their family and enrolled this person in a scientific academy situated near the equator.

There, not far from the valleys where the Xifora had developed from clumsy beasts crawling out of the sea onto the land, this person learned Xifor history, Xifor art, Xifor science, and Xifor technology. This person also learned that the machines in which this person had placed so much pride had been invented before, and better. The discovery was a lesson in humility that this person carries to this moment. With that insight, this person's career as an inventor and a scientist came to an abrupt end. Instead, this person became a philosopher and a politician. On Xifor the callings are almost identical.

Then, fatefully, this person was discovered. Not by the most able leader of Xifora history, Xidan, but by that person's chief assistant, Xibil, who had been the philosopher behind Xidan's resplendent political career. In this person Xibil saw a promise that no other person had observed: the ability to produce new solutions to old problems. This person's real life began.

•◄•►•

Xidan had not been responsible for the invention and production of spaceships that occupied the satellites of the gas giants, nor the interstellar flight that made contact with the Galactic Federation, nor, indeed, the negotiations that resulted in the acceptance of Xifor as a junior member of the Federation. All these events happened countless millennia earlier. Xidan's great accomplishment was to bring all the colonies of Xifor under the absolute control of the native world and with the loss of only a few million Xifora lives and only a single satellite. Under Xidan, Xifor finally gained full membership on the Galactic Council.

All was good; Xifor was beginning to reap the benefits of Galactic goodwill and the full range of Galactic science and invention. Xifora basked in the illusion that the universe had changed and the sneer of hatred had become the smile of love. And then humans emerged into the galaxy. Unlike the Xifora, humans were unwilling to accept a proper role as apprentice Galactics. Humans insisted on full membership immediately. Old allegiances were threatened. Ancient agreements were broken. War happened.

War, Xifora understand, is the natural condition of the Universe. Xifora are born with this knowledge. Xifora must kill or be killed, eat or be eaten. But, as Xibil has eloquently explained, sublimation of this instinct to survive by all and any means, and the sublimation of the instinct to defend these persons' territory and these persons' honor to the death, is the price of civilization. To honor that hard-won principle Xifor produced warships for the Federation and manned them and thrust them into battle. No longer were hatchlings killed, but instead sent forth in geometric numbers to Xifora the battleships. Xifora pride themselves that Xifora numbers and Xifora production were a major component of Galactic strategy.

Humans would have been defeated within hours and forced back into the nothingness from which they came if other Galactics, less committed than Xifor to the consensus principles of the Federation or sensing an opportunity for political advantage, had not protected the humans from the righteous rebuke of the Galactic Federation.

This person volunteered to be among the warriors, but Xibul insisted that this person's best place was in Xifor councils, to help plan the tactics of battle and the strategies of the peace that would, sooner or later, follow. The end of war, Xibul counseled, is the time when scales are rebalanced and adjustments are made, when the ready have the chance to seize power and to hold it, just as the Xifora nobility had seized the valleys millennia before. Xifor could become one of the major powers, perhaps the major power, in the Council rather than a junior member, seldom heard, often ignored. Xifora are small but Xifora will not be overlooked.

One of the tactics this person proposed, which became standard battle procedure, was the sacrifice of a part—a ship, a fleet, or a world—to gain an overall advantage. The peculiar advantage of this tactic is that it is rooted in Xifora physiology and evolution: in personal strife, clever Xifora emerge victorious by offering an arm while the other appendage wields a deadly weapon.

Envious rivals spread the rumor that the tactic originated with a subordinate and not with this person. Every administration is rife with such knife wielders; the secret to survival is not to offer a back to colleagues. Such an accusation was easy to dismiss: Xifor tradition and law prescribe that all products of labor or thought are the rightful property of the superior; the unfortunate subordinate died by accident before the subordinate could confirm this person's primacy, but after that no question was raised.

Before the subordinate's body was cold, the tactic was communicated to Xidan directly. Xibil was involved in discussions concerning the next envoy to the Galactic Council, the previous envoy having been killed when the envoy's ship was attacked by a human vessel.

Only after the war did this person discover that the tactic of sacrifice had been discovered independently by humans. Even though humans are too soft to accept sacrifice willingly, humans have a strange custom in which those persons model human behavior in something called "games," which those persons then apply to everyday behavior including war. Thus the tactic was not as successful as this person or Xidan had hoped, nor as Xibil had feared.

Xibil, to be sure, had accepted this person's strategy as proper Xifora behavior, recognizing the fate of ingenious subordinates. Then as quickly as the war had begun the war ended in a truce. Xifor opposed the end of hostilities, but the envoy's death left it with little influence, and even the passionate words of the assistant envoy, who had fortunately survived the attack that killed the envoy, went unheeded. Less hardened Galactics had tired of sacrifice and traded honor for peace.

Now was the time for Xifor to act. While other Galactics were fatigued by war and eager for peace at any price, Xifor determination and willingness to sacrifice would give Xifor the opportunity to seize the Galactic Council and shape the Federation future. Xidan turned to Xibil and asked

Xibil to accept the position of envoy to the Council. Xibil accepted on the condition that Xifor sacrifice its ambitions in behalf of Federation harmony and civilization.

Then Xibil met with an unfortunate accident.

●▪●▪

In the tradition of Xifor, Xidan turned to Xibil's assistant, and this person was named envoy but without the unnatural conditions for sublimating Xifora behavior that Xibil had urged. Many time periods elapsed before this person joined the Council and came to an understanding of the Council's operation and secret levers of power. The Council is a large and deliberative body that, like a glacier, moves slowly but inexorably down hill. The Council is hard to stop and impossible to steer; the Council can only be shattered into maneuverable segments.

The Council was a devastating disappointment. This person had expected opposition but found turgid indifference. Other Council members were older and, let this be admitted in all humility, wiser. This person tried to move the inertia of the Council into action, with Xifor at its head. This person was listened to and agreed with but nothing happened. No opposition could be identified; no other person stood in the way; an accident to any person or group of persons would change nothing.

This person learned patience.

Patience brings with it an acceptance of the way things are, and a hope that change will emerge through a slow accumulation of minor alterations. That is not the Xifor way. It was the Galactic Federation way. The galaxy turns slowly, and the spiral arms are distant. The Federation is old, and it had gotten old by minimizing change and its accompanying potential for conflict. The emergence of humans had disturbed the Galactic balance; change had occurred, and the Federation didn't like change. Now, with the Great Truce established, the Federation was ready to return to the ancient ways that had worked so well for so many eons, keeping aliens from the breathing tubes of other aliens.

And then word came of a new prophet emerging. Without a name, without an origin or place, without a species identification or description, a creature was rumored to have announced the possibility of transcendence—not the long Xifora way of deprivation and inner strength but an instantaneous mechanical ascension. This person cannot describe the state of chaos in the Federation Council that followed this unsubstantiated rumor. The old and wise Councilors became frantic and frightened. Evolution was understood by all, but evolution was slow and the massive Federation could adjust. Physical transcendence could happen instantly. A person or a species could gain superiority. The current balance—some have called the condition "stasis"—was threatened. All sentient life might be terminated.

Councilors dispersed across the galaxy, fleeing home for consultation or consolation. This person did not, knowing that the change this person had sought had become change of another sort, but change nevertheless, and in change is the possibility of something better. Xifora share that with humans.

Xifora also share with humans a passion for transcendence. Not in the human way, for humans already believe they are a favored species, chosen for greatness, deserving of good fortune; while Xifora know that all life is a cosmic accident, an improbable joke, and that Xifora have been badly treated from Xifora's earliest existence and must fight for everything. Somewhere, somehow, the universe owes Xifora transcendence.

Then came an intervention. This person was summoned to a meeting of soft-spoken aliens. What kind of aliens this person could not identify, for the aliens used distortion fields and translation devices to conceal their species. But the aliens made clear what this person had not yet suspected, that the Galactic Council was not the supreme legislators of the galaxy, or perhaps not the only supreme legislators, that other, unknown forces operated at a distance though perhaps even more effectively.

Whether economic, political, or religious, these forces acted with great decision and foresight. The aliens informed this person that the new religious fervor sweeping the galaxy could be a blessing or a threat. If true, transcendentalism could be the start of a new war that would destroy the galaxy, when one species achieved transcendence and tried to exert its superiority; or it could be the beginning of a new and greater Federation in which every species would achieve its own perfection and the galaxy would blossom with wealth, art, and goodwill. If untrue, transcendentalism could send the galaxy into a depression of disappointed expectations from which it might not emerge for millennia; or the concept of the new religion could be adopted by the proper authorities to set the galaxy on a path toward individual species betterment that would launch a new era of mutual aspiration and tolerance.

What transcendentalism is, the aliens said, must be discovered, and this person was ordered to find out, to join the pilgrimage, to determine if the Prophet was on board the ship, and to learn whether the Transcendental Machine was real and how it worked and to bring it back, or if this person could not do one of those things, to destroy the Prophet or the Machine before the Prophet or the Machine could be misused by the wrong persons or species.

This person reveals these truths now because the facts have become apparent: the Prophet is aboard the *Geoffrey*, although not revealed; and the Machine, therefore, may well be real; and other creatures aboard also have been commissioned by unknown powers—Jon and Jan, no doubt, and perhaps others. This person's revelation may be doubted. Why should this person reveal this person's mission? Reasons are many; the time for revelation is at hand. If this pilgrimage is to succeed, all must work for all.

And so, in full knowledge that this person was betraying Xidan's trust and this person's opportunity to seize greatness for this person and for Xifor, this person abandoned this person's post without informing Xidan, found resources unexpectedly in this person's accounts, and took passage for Terminal.

This person chose Terminal because of the direction of the Secret Power, but why did the many persons gathered here choose Terminal? This person will not recount the many difficulties this person had to overcome to reach the place from which this ship departed. All persons gathered here survived similar obstacles, and many others surely misread the signs and flocked elsewhere to wait for a ship that never came.

That would have been a proper fate for a Xifora.

KOM'S STORY

The life of Sirians is dominated by their suns. Sirius is a hot, bluish-white star with a white-dwarf companion, and its planets are all gas giants except for a few rocky quasiplanets beyond the farthest giant's orbit. The habitable worlds are all satellites, some of them larger than the planets of less dominant suns, and Komran is one of them. It revolves around the gas giant Sirians call Kilran.

Komran is the second-largest satellite of the fourth gas giant from the sun. As a satellite, it bakes in Sirius's glare half a day and freezes in Kilran's shadow for the other half, while Komran rotates a half-turn to bring each of its hemispheres alternately into the light and the shadow. Komran, then, is enslaved to Kilran but tyrannized by Sirius. Sirians must adjust to this complex climatic state.

Earth, I have learned, has a hot period of half a year over most of its surface followed by a cold period that lasts the other half. Komran has a summer and winter every day, a cycle moderated only by Kilran's gravitational attraction, which Komran translates into internal warmth, and by planet-shine.

Life struggled to come into existence on Komran. Not only was life inhibited by temperature extremes, but the incessant movement of the world's crust caused by Kilran's constant push and pull trapped life-forms under falls of rock and surging seas, and the creatures that finally emerged were hardy and temperature-sensitive. They thrived for half a day in the warmth and shut down for half a day in the cold until, finally, they evolved more efficient mechanisms for controlling internal temperature in the form of their present beautiful radiating fins. It is this triumph of matter over energy that makes Sirians fierce competitors and even fiercer friends, and it is their unique planetary situation that makes Sirians special in the galaxy.

Sirians are live-born but immature, like larvae. They develop inside their fathers' bodies for a period as long as they gestate inside their mothers. The maturing process, consuming special food stored for their nurturing during the mother's gestation, is idyllic, and remembered by adults as the happy time when food was always available, when temperature was constant, and when there was no competition. It is this time that Sirians long to regain, that controls their lives and shapes their dreams.

For reasons that are beyond rational analysis, Sirians associate that dream with Sirius's companion star. That white-dwarf sun is always assumed, never named. Although Sirius gave us birth, the companion gives us aspirations. To live in the feeble glow of its blessed rays is every Sirians' consuming passion. But the companion star has no planets. Creation myths tell Sirians that our companion sun is the source of our existence, that it once was even larger than Sirius but was diminished by the nurturing of a group of worlds that were stolen away by his mate and given as satellites to the gas giants. In sorrow and dismay at the inevitable end of love, the companion sun at first became angry and red with rage, but weakened by the nurturing process and by the betrayal of its mate it collapsed into its present shrunken state, all life gone but a feeble glow.

Some astronomers confirm these myths with speculation that the satellites of the gas giants such as Kilran were indeed the offspring of the white dwarf who shall not be named. Others, less mystical, believe that they were once independent worlds of Sirius captured by the gas giants, or worlds drawn into the system from the great disk of planetary matter beyond the farthest giant.

Our astronomers tell us that beliefs about the dwarf companion who shall not be named are ancestral memories of the Sirian system, that the companion went through a normal cycle of expansion and collapse, that its planets, if it had any, were consumed in its red, expansion stage, or expelled into the great darkness. But Sirians have nightmares of being stolen from heaven, never to return, by a powerful blue-white goddess.

Sirians imagine that if they were more powerful, if they could only perfect themselves, they could build a new world around the companion and protect it from the tyranny of their hot blue sun, or liberate Komran itself from the grasp of Sirius as well as Kilran, and rejoin their father. There, on this paradisical dream world, they would shed their fins and live as beings that choose their own fates rather than having them chosen by their solar goddess.

All that is mythology, of course. Sirians know this, but they are dominated by it anyway. I tell you this because these facts control who we are and why we think and behave the way we do, and, ultimately, why I am here, with you, on this ship.

After we have eaten our way out of the father's body, changed, fully developed but still small, often the father dies, having not stored sufficient food for the brood or having a larger brood than customary or not being strong enough. For these reasons families are carefully planned in these days of scientific understanding, and Sirian females choose mates with care. Only one father out of ten dies today, and the death of the father is considered the fault of the female, a crime that is often punished, sometimes up to and including execution. But some fates are worse than death.

Becoming a father, however it turns out, is a life-changing experience ventured into only by the brave and the strong. Even if a father survives, he often is damaged by the experience so that he lives a life shortened by physical debility and an uncertain ability to control internal temperature that itself can be fatal. No male is a father more than once, and used-up males litter the nursing homes and retirement villas. Some philosophers discuss voluntary suicide or euthanasia to clear the scene for greater Sirian accomplishment.

The continual flexing of Komran's surface is a second fact of life. Sirians are born knowing that the land under their appendages is undependable. This understanding gives Sirians an advantage over many species, who have an unreasonable confidence in their physical situations. Sirians know that the unexpected can happen at any moment, that they cannot trust their environment, that they must be ready to adjust to any emergency. This realization made them daring sailors on Komran's tumultuous seas, and, once spaceflight began, sure space voyagers and confident warriors.

And, to say truth, it is safer to be a sailor or a space voyager or a warrior than a nurturing male.

━━

My memories begin when I ate my way through the belly of my father after the food he had stored was consumed by his greedy offspring. My father was a great male. After separating myself from my siblings, I remember seeing my father calmly treating his nurturing pouch with antibiotics and then sewing up the holes we unthinking creatures had chewed. Out of all the others, he picked me as the repository of his wisdom, and we spent many happy hours together as he prepared me to assume the position and power that would have been his if he had not chosen to sacrifice everything for love.

I wish I could say the same for my mother, who ate my father when I was still young and our little piece of Komran was torn apart by quakes. "Do not worry," he told me. "Komran will provide, and the hungry times will pass. Your mother does what she must to keep herself and her children alive, and she will see that you gain the advancement you deserve." But she never did.

I did not eat, having already consumed too much of his substance in my unthinking larval state.

But my father was right. The hungry times passed, and our family grew sound again feasting on my father's memory as we had feasted on his body, and the wise counsel that I passed along in his stead. I became the wise male who served as the head of the family, and part of my wisdom was to reflect that my father did not grow old and feeble like so many males of his generation, sacrifices on the altar of love.

I left home as soon as I could, escaping my mother's ravenous regard and refusal to shield her children from her warmth, and gave myself over to the state, whose concerns, and even its punishments, were blessedly impersonal. Because of my father's once-promising career and the wisdom that he had communicated to me I was appointed to the academy for pre-spacers, where I was educated in the mathematics and the physics of space, astronomy and cosmology, history and practices of spaceflight, Galactic culture, and the preeminence of Sirians among Galactics.

My apologies to fellow Galactics for Sirian parochial attitudes. We teach greatness so that our offspring can rise above the treachery of their biology and so that they will never encounter a Galactic or a situation except on terms of equality. We teach greatness so that we can imagine it, and, having imagined it, achieve it.

I studied hard, though with the skepticism that lies behind every thoughtful Sirians' consciousness of place. We know that the universe is unrelenting and unstable, and so we seek the truth that is unspoken, the reality behind the deception of appearance. And I studied to make my father proud and his sacrifice meaningful. I was passed on to the space college as the most promising academy student of my class.

College was far more demanding, requiring not only the discipline of the mind but the discipline of the body that lies at the heart of the Sirian experience. We must perform not only the exercises that enable Sirians to achieve and to endure but we must learn to control our inner states. Komran provides its offspring with such physical extremes of temperature and Komranology that we must divorce our inner states from our outer existence. Our happiness is dependent not upon events but upon our determination. We will our happiness just as we will our internal temperatures.

In the third cycle of college Sirians are introduced to space, first on a ship manned by experienced crews and then on ships operated by senior cadets. On my first trip I discovered my natural habitat. While my fellow students were panicking, floundering in weightlessness, puking in corners, and, pink with shame, swinging a cloth in an attempt to blot the evidence, I felt as if I had come home, as if I resided once more in my father's belly. It was for this my father had nourished me and shared not only his body but his wisdom. I was a spacer.

Among brighter students now, I was not as successful. My classwork had grown more difficult and my efforts, frantic. Even calmed by the remembered voice of my father, I could not excel as I had been able to do before. But my space skills made up for everything. Where other students had to think before they acted, every decision came to me as if a product of body, not mind. I rose to a position of eminence, what humans would call the captain of cadets, on skill alone—and the attitude of leadership that accompanied it.

By the time my class had reached its final year, I had already been assured of the first place to open on the premiere ship of the Sirian fleet. In response, my intellectual pursuits improved, and once more I began to succeed, sometimes beyond others, in Sirian history, in political science, and, preeminently, in space navigation, engineering, gunnery, and command.

Then I met Romi. She was a first-year student from Komran's other hemisphere. In the ordinary course of life we would never have met. Not only distance but status separated us. I was a commoner, who had survived the hungry times only by reason of my mother's moral turpitude. But here, in the space college, I was the superior, and as captain of cadets able to give orders to first-year students and expect them to be obeyed instantly. Even unreasonable orders—in fact, as tradition and common sense dictate, the more unreasonable the better, for crews must obey without thinking, without considering whether an order is reasonable.

But I could not order Romi. She was the most beautiful Sirian I had ever met, and she was in love with me. I felt stirrings within me, thoughts of storing food within my belly, thoughts of ingesting larval children. And then I remembered my father.

◗━◗

I understand that love takes many forms across the Galaxy, that some is powerful and enduring while some is fleeting and casual. I do not know what love is like for a Sirian female—I think it involves the predatory—but for a Sirian male love is a consuming passion that prepares him for what may be the ultimate sacrifice.

I endured the situation for the rest of the academic cycle, trying to limit my contacts with Romi, but every time she passed I felt the primal urges that I knew my father had felt, the urges that betrayed him. I kept my contacts with Romi to a minimum, even going out of my way to make sure our paths did not cross. But I met her in my dreams.

I understand that some Galactics do not dream; some do not even sleep. The dream life of Sirians, however, is as real as—no, more real than—the waking life. We discuss our dreams as if we had lived them. We analyze them. We write them down. We manage them so that they end satisfactorily, giving us strength or wisdom, or reinforcing our self-images.

But I could not manage my dreams of Romi. They always ended with small Sirians eating their way through my belly while I stared down helpless to control them or my temperature, leaving me helpless and weak, doomed to a lifetime as an invalid. And I told no one.

Finally my ordeal ended. My class completed its class work and we were assigned to ships. Somehow I had managed to retain my status during my inner turmoil, and I joined the *Kilsat* as junior pilot-in-training. I left Romi behind as a second-cycle cadet and put her out of my mind.

I was happy. Space was my environment; Romi no longer frequented my thoughts or controlled my dreams. I was a natural pilot, responding intuitively to subconscious cues, as if my dear father were guiding my actions from his place of honor near the sun that shall not be named. I made friends with my fellow spacers and filled my off-duty moments with good male fellowship. We bonded as Sirian crew members do in the unifying environment of space. We talked of challenges and accomplishments, of ambitions and achievement, and never of family or sacrifice.

The *Kilsat* made its first Jump during my maiden voyage. That took us beyond the narrow limits of our Sirian system. The experience shook many of my crewmates, but I found it exhilarating, not only space but the hidden universes within space were my home. During the second Jump I was at the controls and gloried in the power of transcending time and space. All the universe was mine, I felt, and I dedicated my joy to my father's memory.

By the time we made our third Jump we were in Galactic space, surveying the magnificence of the Galactic Center. Xi told us about meeting with the Galactic Council. What he did not describe was the Center itself—not the center of the Galaxy but Galactic Center, where the representatives of the Great peoples meet and the Galaxy is governed. Galactic Center is an insignificant system of rocky planets orbiting an insignificant sun. No one would think of it as a place of Greatness, as a place of any importance at all. And that, no doubt, is why it was chosen, along with the fact that it was uninhabited, at least by any member species. And although representatives to the Galactic Council and innumerable bureaucrats inhabit those planets, some for their entire lives, its destruction would mean little except to those personally involved.

To look at that impoverished system and realize its importance makes even the most robust Sirian realize the value of inner strength and the pitfalls of appearance. We had learned that principle from the shiftings of Komran beneath our extremities, but here it was brought home to us again.

We looked, we admired from afar, and we departed, learning nothing of the workings inside the capitol of the Galaxy beyond what we had learned in the academy. But it was enough for simple spacers, and we pondered on its meaning as we returned to Sirius and our lives there, now a crew in the true meaning of the word, functioning as the brain and central nervous system of the ship, working as a single entity. For the first time in my life I felt as I had when I was part of my father, at peace with my world, content in my way of life. The *Kilsat* had become my father, or, perhaps more accurately, now the *Kilsat* and my father were one.

But when we returned to Sirius, Romi came back into my life. It was time for the cadet cruises, and, by the evil goddess, she was assigned to the *Kilsat*. When I saw her, I knew my time of greatest temptation had arrived. Without a word to anyone, I went to the nearest two-person fighter craft, crawled through the tunnel that linked it to the ship, detached it from its mooring bolts, turned off the communications gear, and drifted away before I started the propulsion system.

I knew where I was going. I was headed for the nexus point that everyone knows and nobody dares use, the Jump that ends in orbit around the white dwarf without a name.

◆◆◆

To speak truth, my reaction was not the awe and reverence that I expected. During the lengthy trip I had managed to neutralize the panic that had driven me from Romi, but I anticipated a psychic fulfillment that never came. The Companion was an ordinary white dwarf, shining wanly on a ruined desert of orbital space while Sirius burned brighter than any star above the Companion's shawl of night. The Companion had not been stripped of planets, as mythology had told us. Instead, while I watched as if from a height, cinder after cinder swam into view. If they had once been gas giants, the gases had been blown away, leaving only a few charred fragments behind. If they had been habitable worlds like Komran, their atmospheres and seas had been stripped from them, along with all the living things that had evolved there. The Companion had consumed its own children long before life came to sentience on Komran.

My father was not there, nor was any other spirit. The desolation before me was matched by the desolation within.

What was there, as I discovered when my black mood eventually lifted, was a lonely beacon, like the sign of intelligent life in a lonely universe. I tracked it to a location near the Companion. There was no planet, no satellite, no ship, nothing within the discrimination of my sensors that could send a signal.

The passage from the outer reaches to the near-solar space took many periods during which I saw much closer the devastation caused by the Companion's expansion phase. Finally I came upon the source of the signal: a battered escape capsule of an unfamiliar design turning slowly in the Companion's wan radiance, getting just enough energy from its rays to sustain its limited operation.

I connected the capsule to my small ship. I could not decipher the instructions beside the capsule's hatch—they were incised in a cryptic series of lines—but I finally found a button that set off explosive bolts. I sampled the atmosphere, which was within tolerable limits and without apparent toxins. Inside the capsule was a still functioning deep-freeze chamber, and inside the chamber was the ugliest creature I had ever seen—a creature with four weak extremities emerging at awkward angles from a shrunken and fragile central torso and topped by a strange growth dotted with openings and covered in places with threadlike tendrils.

Only later—my apologies to present company—did I discover that this was a human. This was the first human I had ever seen, certainly the first human any Sirian had ever seen except, perhaps, at the highest level of Galactic leadership where, I learned later, human emissaries already were making their demands that soon would result in war.

But all of this was yet to come. Here, now, was this alien creature, and it was dead—or so nearly dead that the difference was imperceptible. If any other Galactic had discovered this castaway, the end would have been certain, but Sirians have such fine control of their temperatures that freezing is not necessarily fatal. Indeed, Sirians have been discovered in hidden glaciers and been revived after being frozen for many hundreds, even thousands, of cycles.

I opened the chamber and set about reviving its occupant, elevating its temperature fraction by fraction, easing the transition from cell to cell, from external to internal, over a period of almost a cycle. Finally the occupant made a sound and shortly thereafter opened what I later learned were its viewing organs.

It made organized sounds that I later learned was something like, "What in the hell are you!"

But we got on and within a cycle, we were able to converse with the aid of my pedia. This human, a male, was part of an expedition to decipher a nexus chart that had been bought from Galactic traders or sold by traitors— he never knew which—and all had gone well until flaws in the coordinates destroyed the ship and all his shipmates, and he launched his escape module through the nexus into the Companion's system. That I should have discovered the module was a chance beyond calculation, depending as it did upon my fleeing Romi and setting my course for the Companion.

The human told me his designation was "Sam." He told me many things about Earth and about humans and their history and literature and art. We had nothing to do but communicate, and Sam loved to talk. He was, he said, making up for his long, silent, frozen cycles. He never realized that his stories about Earth horrified me: the struggles, the competition, the battles, the wars. Even in literature and art these bloody activities were celebrated. I realized that I had to get this information to our leaders, and he—unaware that he had revealed humanity's bloodthirst and its inability to live in a civilized fashion with others—wanted to get back to his leaders with the information gathered about our precious navigation maps.

Of course he had no chance to get back. I did not tell him that when we left the Companion we would return to Sirius and Komran where he would be interrogated at far greater length and in far less pleasant conditions than on my vessel, cramped as it was. I could not let him return with his information, and I had to return with mine. And then, when he was well enough to travel and we were on our way to the nexus point, he sickened and died. The last words he spoke were, "You are an ugly son-of-a-bitch, Kom, but you've been a good friend way out here next to nowhere. It's been great knowing you."

I felt much the same way as when my mother ate my father.

When I got back to Sirian space, I discovered that my information had arrived too late. I had been gone for a dozen cycles, and the war was over. But the rumors of the Transcendental Machine were traveling fast. My leaders were concerned. Because I had spent so many cycles with an alien, and most of all with a human, I was urged to volunteer for this pilgrimage.

I agreed, of course. My experience with the Companion had changed me forever. I was no longer a simple Sirian, bound to myths and biological imperatives. I had experienced both the reality and the unreality of others. I was prepared. And, more important, Romi had chosen another, who already had nurtured her larvae to maturity and suffered the consequences.

Why, you may wonder, did I spend such time and thought with Sam. I wondered myself. And then I began to see that when I reached the Companion I lost the reality of my father's spirit and found Sam. I had begun to think of Sam as my father, and his loss affected me as much.

And he told me, during our long conversations, about the human family and its process of procreation. What if Sirians could procreate as partners, like humans? Could we transcend our biology?

4107's Story

We are called the People, just as species throughout the galaxy call themselves the People. Whatever language we use—the movement of air through passages that restrict its flow in various distinguishable ways, the rubbing of mandibles, the gestures of tentacles, the release of pheromones, or, in our case, the disturbance of air by the movement of fronds—the translation is always the same. We are the People.

Our world is called Earth, as every world is called Earth in its own language. You might call it Flora, because we were a flower people, and for uncounted generations we lived our simple lives of seedlings springing from the soil, growing into maturity and sprouting flowers, enjoying fertilization, dropping our petals and then our seeds upon the soil, and depositing our decaying bodies to nourish the next generation. The generations were uncounted because every day was the same, and every year: we were born, we lived, we reproduced, and we died. Flora was a big world, drawn by its massive gravity into great plains and placid seas, and we thrived in peace and plenty amid mindless warmth and fertile soil. That is the time the People look back upon as Paradise before we were expelled.

True, Flora had grazers, herbivores who lived among us and nourished themselves with our vegetable plenty, and predators who prevented the herbivores from destroying themselves by overgrazing and overpopulation, but the People responded in one of the great breakthroughs of Floran evolution: we made ourselves unpleasant fodder, and when the grazers evolved in response, we developed poisons. The grazers died off, and then the predators, and only weeds remained as competitors. We developed herbicides, and then we were truly supreme and supremely content in our mindless vegetable way. Flora was ours and we were Flora.

Then a passing astronomical body came into our ideal existence like divine punishment for our hubris, showering Flora with devastating radiation that nearly destroyed all life on the planet including the People, stirring Flora's inner fires and releasing continents from their loving embrace. The paradise that Flora had been became the hell that Flora was: eruptions poisoned the air and lava flows covered the plains; the continents crashed together and pushed upward great mountain ranges. The People perished.

Centuries passed and long-buried seeds poked their ways through cracking lava. Among them was a single great Floran, now known as One. Before One, Florans had no separate existence. From One all contemporary Florans trace their origins. Through a process instigated by the destruction caused by the invading astronomical body, perhaps, or more likely by the radiation that showered the planet from the passing cosmic missile or released with magma from Flora's long-sheltered interior, One developed the ability to pull its roots from the soil, an ability it passed along to its descendants. With maneuverable roots, this great Floran no longer had to trust the uncertain breeze to distribute its seeds to suitable soils; it, and its descendants, moved meter by meter and year by year to sheltered valleys where Florans could deposit their seeds in soil prepared to receive them, with more than a hope that chance would alow them to grow and flower.

Each generation took as its designation an ascending number. I am the forty-one hundred and seventh generation since the great One. All the preceding generations have changed, generation by generation, to gain movement, intelligence, and understanding of the world that nurtured and then tried to destroy them, and the uncaring universe that destroys as blindly as it nurtures.

How can I describe the impact of intelligence? Every species represented here has experienced it, but none remembers. Florans remember. The history of their species is recorded in the seeds of their consciousness. At first it was only the memory of process, the irresistible bursting from the seed-pod, the passionate thrusting upward toward the sun and downward toward moisture and food, the satisfying flow of nutrients through capillaries and their cellular transformation into substance, the delightful flowering, the ecstatic fertilizing, and the determined growth of seeds into which all past and future was poured, and the fading sere time that ends in death. But then awareness of environment entered, and from that all else flowed.

We learned that the universe was more than the sun, the soil, and water. The universe held many suns, the Earth held many soils, and the rivers, the lakes, and the seas held many waters, and some of these were nurturing and some were not. We learned that we could manipulate our environment, controlling the fertility of the soil and the rain that fell upon it, and then that we could manipulate ourselves, controlling the patterns of biological inheritance we passed along to our seeds. And we learned to limit our reproduction so as not to exhaust our resources and thus, having postponed our flowering and our going to seed, learned that we could postpone the dying that went with it.

Longevity beyond the season meant an acceleration of the learning process. We learned to develop special breeds, some for greater intelligence to provide more understanding of the universe, some for a new ability you call vision to perceive the world and the universe in new ways, some for manipulative skills to make us independent of our environment, and some for memory to store the wisdom gathered by the others. And finally we learned the terrible truth—that the passing cosmic body that had expelled us from paradise was not some chance interstellar visitor, not some cosmic joke by the cosmic jokester, but a relativistic missile flung across our path by uncaring aliens, envious of our world and eager to reap the benefits of a heavy planet and the mineral wealth that it might vomit from its depths.

We learned all this when the Alpha Centaurans landed in their sterile metal ships.

———

The shining vessels from a world far from Flora descended upon our world, glowing from their passage through an atmosphere thicker than any Centaurans had known but thinner for the passage of the invading missile many thousands of cycles before. They glowed with heat, these vessels, and slowly cooled before the Centaurans emerged like meat asserting its natural dominance over the vegetable world. They wasted no thought or pity on the Florans they had crushed or the paradise they had destroyed. Why should they? They were the gods of the universe.

So we also felt, at first. They had come from the sky like gods, and they came in machines unlike anything ever to touch the soil of Flora, or even imagined among our poets. They destroyed billions in their descents, and billions more as they sent machines to clear the plains, scything us down, trampling us beneath their treads, plowing us under, mindless of our screams and efforts to communicate, to worship their magnificence in our vegetable way. They put alien seeds in our sacred soil, dull, unresponsive cousins from other worlds. We tried to talk to them, but they had nothing but primitive reactions to soil and sun; all awareness had been bred from them, if it ever existed. The Centaurans thought of us, if they thought of us at all, as alien vegetation to be adapted to their purposes or, if that was unsuccessful, eliminated. Finally we despaired and recalled old biological processes. Our herbicides almost succeeded in eliminating the alien vegetation, but the Centaurans responded with even greater destruction, clearing even the few Floran stragglers from their territories, protecting their seedlings with energy walls and developing herbicides of their own.

Finally we realized the terrible truth: they were not gods; they were invaders, and they would destroy the People if we did not find a way to resist. At first we developed sharp leaves stiffened with lignite to kill them when they came among us. You have seen them in action. They are dangerous even to ourselves in a gusty wind. But the Centaurans seldom came into the territories that yet were ours; they preferred to send their machines, against whose metallic hides our weapons slid harmlessly aside. So we developed missiles, poisoned darts that could be expelled by an explosion of stored gas. The Floran that launched such a missile died in the act, but went willingly, for we are all part of the whole. And yet that too failed when our enemies kept us at a distance. We could not use the poison that our ancestors developed to kill the herbivores, because the Centaurans did not eat us, being properly wary of alien evolution. We grew machines like theirs, only with rigid skins of vegetable matter, but they crumpled against the metal of our enemies.

Finally we realized that we could not defeat an enemy using the enemy's weapons, and we moved the battle to our field, the soil and the vegetation that grew from it. If their alien vegetation was moronic, we would elevate it; if it was alien, we would naturalize it. We put our specialized agronomists to work, and within a few generations they infected Centauran seeds with Floran genes subtly inserted to express themselves over the centuries. We took advantage of storms and high winds to scatter the seeds among the Centauran fields and waited while the Centaurans continued their campaign of genocide until only a few remote pockets of Floran civilization remained and our hidden depositories of seeds. Would our tactic succeed before we were destroyed beyond revival?

The memories of Florans are eternal; we can remember the sprouting of the first Floran upon a steaming planet. And the thoughts of Florans are long, long thoughts, suited to the pace of our existence from season to season. But even we began to despair until finally our stunted spies heard the first whispers of intelligence from the Centauran fields. Within a century the whispers grew into a clamor and the Centaurans began to sicken as their sentient food slowly assumed the character of our indigestible Floran genes. More centuries passed before the Centaurans realized that their diminishing vigor and increased disease could be traced to their diet. They wiped out their fields and brought in fresh seed from Centaurus, but it was too late. They could not eliminate all the altered vegetation, and their seeds, bred for dominance and power, soon transformed the new, infecting them with Floran pathogens and Floran intelligence. More Centaurans died.

At last they recognized the inescapable truth: against an entire planet invaders have no chance. They left in their big ships, shining like dwindling spears into the Floran sky, leaving their ruins and their alien vegetation behind.

●─●●

We had Flora to ourselves once more, sharing it now with the uplifted Centauran vegetation. We treated it with the compassion we never received from the Centaurans; we raised it to full sentience and gave it full membership in our community, and it responded by bringing new hybrid vigor to our lives and new memories to share. Those memories, now accessible to rational inspection, included an understanding of Centauran existence that we were never able to reach, and an experience with Centauran technology that we had found alien. For the first time we realized why the Centaurans could not recognize our sentience, and why they had departed, still bewildered by Flora's lethal resistance to their presence.

We also perceived that the galaxy was filled with alien species and that we could never be safe in our splendid isolation, that we had to leave our beloved Flora in order to save it. We took the information on Centauran spaceships buried, unsuspected, in the Centauran seeds of memory and applied it to our own expertise in growing things. We grew our spaceships. At first they were mere decorative shells, but over the centuries they developed internal mechanisms from differentiating vegetable membranes and then movable parts. We grew organic computers operated at the cellular level by selected bacteria. And, finally, we evolved plants capable of producing, storing, and releasing fuel, and the materials able to sustain their fiery expulsion.

Over many generations we tested them and saw them fail, disastrously, one after the other: the hulls failed, the fuel ran out, the liners burned. But we persisted. We knew that the Centaurans, or some other rapacious meat creatures, would return, but we had the vegetable tradition of patience, and we knew that we would persist until at some distant moment we would succeed. And then one of our Centauran sisters produced the answer—the ability to extract metal from the soil and to shape it, molecule by molecule, into support beams and rocket liners. Another, remembering a Centauran model, developed the ability to process internal carbon into a beanstalk extending, atom by atom, into the sky.

Finally we were ready physically if not psychologically. A crew was assembled. Since we share the same heritage and the same memories, though some were specialized in different ways, the selection was easy even if the process was hard. As a species, our dreams were rooted to the soil; our nightmares were filled with the dread of being separated from it. But our will was stronger than our fears, and we launched ourselves into the aching void in which Flora and her sister planets existed, we discovered, as anomalies. The experience was terrifying. Most of us died of shock, a few from madness that our species had never before experienced. But a few survived to return and contribute their seed memories to our gene pool, and from them grew sturdier voyagers. In the long progress of our kind, we persevered, we grew, we became what we needed to become. We explored our solar system.

Our benevolent sun had seeded seven planets and an uncountable number of undeveloped seedlings beyond the farthest aggregation, before they were blasted by the Centauran relativistic missile. The nearest planet was an insignificant rock sterilized by solar radiation; the next had been a gas giant before the missile had stolen much of its atmosphere; the third was a fair world, somewhat smaller than Flora, that had been destroyed by its animal inhabitants; on its overheated soil and evaporated sea bottoms we found evidence of meat-creature buildings like those of the Centaurans and a carbon-dioxide–laden atmosphere that had apparently been a runaway reaction to industrial excess. It would have made a desirable home for Florans but the searing temperature and the absence of water made it a wasteland.

Flora was the fourth planet. Beyond Flora were two more gas giants and a frozen rock. We were the masters of our solar system, though an impoverished one—and poorer for the Centauran violence. Our attackers came from beyond our system. We had to go farther into the unknown, farther then we could imagine.

We found ways to use our sun's energy that surpassed the natural system of converting its rays into stem and leaf and flower. We developed vegetable means of storing these energies. We grew stronger ships, and elevated them up our beanstalks into orbit. We evolved better spaceworthy Florans. And finally we set out for the stars, not knowing where we were going or what we were going to find or what we would do when we got there.

Generations later, as our primitive ships were still only a small way into the vast emptiness that is most of the universe, we were discovered by a Galactic ship that had just emerged from a nexus point. If the Florans aboard our ships had been capable of astonishment, they would have wilted into death; if they had understood the chance of being discovered in this fashion, they would not have believed it.

Fortunately, the ship was Dorian, not Centauran, and even though the Dorians are grazers, they are enlightened grazers. They were as astonished by the Floran crews as the crews should have been astonished by their discovery, and for some cycles the Dorians looked for the meat creatures who must have been the real space voyagers. Finally, because they were enlightened, they came to the realization that we were intelligent, and, through inspiration and dedication, began to decipher our frond-moving communication, just as we began to understand their guttural explosions of air.

The Dorians installed their nexus devices in our Floran ships and took us to the Galactic Council. There they sponsored us, and because we were the first sentient vegetable creatures to be discovered in the galaxy and because we had displayed so much determination in setting out in primitive ships and persisting through unbelievable difficulties, we are admitted into the Council of civilized species.

We had achieved our goal. We now were under the protection of the Galactic Council and all its members.

●●●●

As soon as we understood Council procedures—they are limited in scope but precise in their application—and as soon as we began to acquire minimal insights into animal sentience and motivation (we comprehend concepts outside our own experience only with great difficulty), we filed a genocide complaint against the Centaurans. Council representatives listened with almost vegetable patience, but they ruled against us. We were not sentient, they said, when the Centaurans raped our system with their relativistic missile and the Centaurans, after their later invasion, could not be expected to understand our evolved sentience. Our complaint was dismissed. Indeed, some members of the Council, perhaps with political ties to the Centaurans, suggested that we should be grateful to the Centaurans for the actions that produced our sentience. Florans do not understand gratitude, but they never forget injury.

Admission to the Council brought many benefits and some restrictions. From beneficent members of the Council we got knowledge of metalworking and machines, charts of the nexus points of the Galaxy and the ability to launch our ships through the no-space between them, access to the vast library of information accumulated by a hundred species over the millennia, and the ability to reshape our world and our system's other worlds. We were forbidden, however, to immigrate to worlds beyond our system or to communicate, intellectually or genetically, with vegetable species on Council worlds. This, we were told, would be a capital crime punishable by species extinction. That seemed extreme, but we recognized that we were new and different, and we had the other planets of our system to develop with our new skills, and, when that was complete, other worlds outside the Council jurisdiction.

We called upon our vegetable patience, knowing that, before the end of time, we would succeed. What we did not understand was that other species, under the leadership of the Centaurans, would be launching scientific projects to block our genetic program, that all meat creatures, no matter how seemingly benign, will defend their kind against a threat from our kind. What they did not understand was that animal species have the advantage of speed and quickness but they burn out quickly and decay, while vegetation is slow but persistent. In the end we will win before entropy finally defeats us all.

And yet—all our voyaging beyond the limits of Floran psychology, all our acceptance by the Galactic community, all our new knowledge and confidence in survival, if not as certain, of final dominance was not enough. In order to do these things, we had changed. Vegetable existence distrusts and dislikes change, and accepts it only under duress and through the long, slow swing of the cosmos. We had become great, and we hated it.

And then the humans erupted from Earth—meat inspired by hubris—and, shortly after, war began, and all that we had thought and planned was put aside. We did our part in the war, but mostly in the peace. Animals fight wars; vegetables practice peace. We delighted in the peace and the stasis that followed the war; we might even have become content with our lot, difficult as it was to reconcile with our essential being. And then word came about the Prophet and the Transcendental Machine. More change.

More threat to stasis. More damage to our sense of self. And so, once more, against every instinct, we had to change. Out of this crisis I was grown, against every Floran instinct, to assume the reviled role of individual, to act alone and through my sacrifice find salvation for my sisters. I cannot describe my desolation, my grief, my anguished separation from my fellow Florans as I joined this voyage. I cannot describe, even, what it means to refer to myself as "I."

But I will persevere, because my people demand what only I can provide: a return to paradise. Through me the Transcendental Machine will remove the curse of sapience.

Fred and Me

Fred told me once, "Conventions never end; they just adjourn to another venue." That's the way it was for Fred and me. We met at a convention, the World Science Fiction Convention of 1952, held in the old Morrison Hotel in Chicago. It was my first convention, my first meeting with SF writers and editors, and even readers, of any kind, and it was a wonderful beginning.

I'd been writing science fiction since the spring of 1948 and having my stories published since the fall of 1949. That was my first year as a freelance writer before I went back to the University of Kansas to earn my master's degree in English. During those two years I kept writing, among other things a novella, "Breaking Point," that I adapted from a three-act play I wrote as an Investigation and Conference project. I sent it to Horace Gold, editor of *Galaxy*, and one day I got a telephone call from this clipped New York voice saying he liked "Breaking Point" but it was too long and would I let Ted Sturgeon cut it down.

Horace also suggested my name to Fred Pohl, who was running a literary agency called Dirk Wylie and, I later discovered, was close to Horace, and Fred became my agent. He was a good agent, and he sold a lot of stories for me—some to Horace (though not "Breaking Point," which he sold to Lester del Rey at the new *Space Science Fiction*), some to John Campbell, some to lesser markets, and one wondrous sale to *Argosy*—and a couple of novels. He didn't make much money from all of his efforts: three cents a word didn't add up to much and 10 percent of that was even less; and the novels sold for an advance of $500 each, which meant only $100 for Fred. In fact, Fred was a better agent than a businessman, and the agency went broke.

Which was just as well, because Fred's writing career took off with *Galaxy*'s serialization in 1952 of "Gravy Planet," which became *The Space Merchants* in its Ballantine apotheosis. It was the first of a series of marvelous collaborations with Cyril Kornbluth. That, combined with a series of wittily satirical short stories, made Fred's reputation that he embellished later, after he abandoned his dissection of contemporary culture, with his award-winning novels of the late 1970s, *Man Plus*, *Gateway*, and *Jem*. Those were also his award-winning days as editor of *Galaxy* and *If*.

But this was back in 1952. I'd accepted an editing position with Western Printing & Lithographing Company of Racine, Wisconsin, which then edited and published the Dell line of paperback reprints. Lloyd Smith, an old friend of my uncle John's, from the Haldeman-Julius Little Blue Books era, expected me to create a line of science fiction novels. I did produce a few, but spent much of my time on other editing chores (including a joke book!) until I persuaded Smith to send me to the Worldcon on the pretext that I would make useful contacts.

The contacts were useful enough, though not in the way Smith expected. I met science-fiction writers and editors there: Clifford Simak, Mack Reynolds, Bob Bloch, the just-starting Richard Matheson, Willy Ley, Hugo Gernsback, Tony Boucher, John Campbell, Evelyn Gold (Horace's surrogate), Frank Robinson, Jack Williamson (with whom I would collaborate on *Star Bridge*), and many others, including Fred. There, in a momentous meeting in a corridor, Fred told me he had sold four stories for me. On the strength of that I quit my job and went back to freelance writing!

That was a good period of frequent and good sales with limited income, the publication of two novels that paid almost nothing then but kept getting reprinted later, and the foundation of a later, part-time career, combined with academics, when I returned to Lawrence, Kansas, and took a series of administrative and teaching jobs that allowed me to combine service to the university with my own writing, most of the time. Fred and I met more casually at the convention-that-never-ended—probably in San Francisco in 1953 but certainly in Philadelphia in 1954—but in another year he was out of the agent business and I was represented by others.

Our next fruitful encounter was when Fred was editor of *Galaxy* and, after a half dozen drought years while I was dealing with the student rebels of the 1960s, I was trying to get back in the game with an ambitious novelette called "The Listeners" (which would later turn into a novel). Two agents thought it was overwritten (it contained a bushel of foreign-language quotations), but I noticed that *Galaxy* was going back to monthly publication after a period in the wilderness of being published bimonthly and decided it would need more manuscripts. Fred wrote back that he would be happy to publish "The Listeners" if I would provide translations for the foreign-language parts. I said sure as long as they weren't included as footnotes (they were). That got me an inclusion in a best-of-the-year anthology, a Nebula nomination, and eventually a book contract with Scribner's. Later, when he added *If* to his editorial duties, I sent him the second part of my novel *The Burning*, and he published "Trial by Fire." When I sent him the final part, "Witch Hunt," he wrote back that he'd publish it in *Galaxy* if I could straighten out the beginning (which he figured had been garbled when my typist—I never had one—dropped the manuscript and reassembled it wrong); I told him he could put back in the eight words I'd omitted from the end of the first chapter: "And he remembered how his journey had begun."

When I launched the Intensive English Institute on the Teaching of Science Fiction in 1974, I thought of getting some writers in to help teach the teachers, and in the second year, I brought in three visiting writers, Gordon Dickson, Ted Sturgeon, and Fred. They remained my dependable stalwarts until Gordy and Ted died, and the institute itself ran into enrollment problems. The first year that happened I offered a summer session writers workshop in science fiction. The second year I proposed to Fred that we offer a one-week writers workshop, and that went well and the institute returned—and Fred became a late second-week visiting writer for the two-week intensive writers workshop, with Betty Hull after their marriage in 1984.

In the meantime, however, one of the students in my first institute class invited me to put together a weekend conference about science fiction for a group of teachers meeting in Pueblo, Colorado. That sounded like the beginning of an opportunity to spread the word of science fiction more broadly, and I proposed to Fred that we join forces in what might be a series of such conferences. We put on a show in Pueblo that went over well (although the idea of a continuing project didn't), and it was in Pueblo, over dinner at the Holiday Inn, that Fred told me he knew how he could publish my novel *Kampus*. Fred had become science-fiction editor at Bantam Books after a brief stint with Ace, and I had sent him a couple of chapters. Looking back upon it, I think Fred was the only editor who could have imagined the book *Kampus* became and find a way to publish it. My later attempts to break out of the bubble never met with as much understanding.

We met in other places. In New York, for instance, I was with a group of writers from the annual Nebula Awards who happened, by chance, to come across Fred on Fifth Avenue, and because he was an editor with an expense account we dragooned him to feed us all at Mama Leone's. And we met in Los Angeles at the World Convention of 1972, where Fred was guest of honor and I premiered the series of films on the literature of science fiction for which Fred lectured on "Ideas in Science Fiction."

After a few years as a full-time English teacher, beginning in 1970, I got the idea for a big conference that would bring scientists and science-fiction writers together to discuss the ways in which they interact and together help shape the future. I tried it out on a number of organizations with encouraging comments but no financial support. I turned to Fred, and together we put together a more convincing proposal. But that also got everything but funding—until it got, by chance, into the hands of Dean Joseph Steinmetz of the KU College of Liberal Arts and Sciences, who not only got behind it but raised some money for it. Unfortunately, Steinmetz left to become dean at Ohio State, and his departure, and recession funding cuts, canceled our plans.

There have been others. When Professor Bill Conboy proposed a team-taught course on futurism, Fred Pohl became our outside contributor for a couple of weeks. His wife, Elizabeth Anne Hull, became a member of the Campbell Award jury, where she has served with distinction, often making a graceful announcement of the winner and its merits at the award dinner. And when Orson Scott Card got too busy to organize the Sturgeon Award decision process, I asked Fred if we could do it. Together we recruited Judy Merril and later, after her resignation the year before her death, we got Kij Johnson, a previous winner, as a replacement. I haven't even mentioned Fred's distinguished service as president of the Science Fiction Writers of America (or the irony of his having criticized its value in earlier days), or as president of World SF, or his many invitations to speak as a futurist, or his lecturing on science fiction in Europe for the US Information Agency (he paved the way for my three later trips), or his Grand Master Award from SFWA, or his awards from other groups such as the Science Fiction Research Association, or the trends his stories and novels have anticipated. You can look it up.

We've all grown old together, Fred and me and science fiction, too. Conventions are not what they used to be (neither is the future). I wasn't there at the beginning of the conventions, as Fred was, or of the Futurians, who were banned from the first World Convention but got their revenge by taking over a good part of science fiction in their day. But we've seen a lot of it—Fred for more than seventy years, me for only sixty. Maybe the next convention will convene in an alternate universe.

—James Gunn

Gregory Benford
and Elisabeth Malartre

)(|)(

SHADOWS OF THE LOST

Spen saw the Ugly first. He stopped cutting the sweet meat away from the deer ribs.

"Don't look up," he whispered to his older brother Ourse. "Ugly to the right."

They were kneeling in shadows beside the fallen deer. Spen moved to another rib, setting his knife high and sliding it down to peel the meat away. That gave him a better angle to see the Ugly, who had moved a bit, looking to his left.

"How many?" Ourse whispered.

"One—no, two." Another had moved into view. This one was crouched warily, carrying a spear and looking to his left, as well. "I'd guess there's at least another I can't see."

"If more than three, we run," Ourse said.

The Ugly made a hand gesture to his left and took a cautious step forward. Spen kept his head bent over, looking at the Ugly just past the brim of his straw hat. He put down his knife, slapped the meat slab onto the stack, dropped the knife. Without giving himself away with a false move he felt for his spear by his right hand. Got it, firmly in hand. "They're coming."

Ourse said, "Your call when we get up."

Surprise was essential. The Uglies were inept hunters, slow and dumb. Lately bands of Uglies were robbing the tribe at the kill site. Usually they used a four or five to two or three advantage. The People withdrew then. Uglies didn't have the courage or the numbers to attack a campsite.

Spen judged the distance. His heart leaped, fear shivered through him, but he made himself not move. If there were just two Uglies, then Ourse alone could take them, probably.

Spen turned his head slightly further, masking the move with some cutting at the next rib. A third Ugly appeared just in his field of view. The first two were closer. All of them hairy, short, arms thick with muscle.

Yes, just the three Uglies. They would have to fight, then, not run. Ourse was their best hunter and as an issue of deep pride never gave ground to fewer than four Uglies. Spen had no choice. His breath sang in his nostrils.

"Now." Spen stood, bringing his spear up.

They were squat, on stubby legs. The nearest ran forward with a spear, a short one with a bone point at the tip.

Spen couldn't let the Ugly have the momentum in a fight. He went forward with quick steps, keeping his balance with wide strides, bringing his spear back at the shoulder.

The Ugly held his spear in both hands. But Spen's was longer. Its flint head tapered along two sharp blades.

At the last second Spen dodged sideways and thrust forward. His spear caught the Ugly full in the chest. The tip *thunked* as it plunged into flesh.

A sharp stab jolted his right leg. Spen ignored it, his momentum carrying the spear deeper into the Ugly, who gave a startled yelp of pain. Spen slammed the body down, burying the spear into the body. The Ugly went limp.

Spen jumped back, as he had practiced so many times. His spear came free. He landed in a broad stance and brought the spear point up, ready for the next Ugly.

But there was none. The others were already running away in their sluggish lope. They grunted alarm and fear.

Spen started after them. It should be easy to take one with a throw, into the back—

"Stop!" Ourse called. "Let them go."

Spen whirled. "We can run them down, get—"

"You're hurt."

"But I—"

Ourse brought a reed whistle to his lips and blew a long shrill call. "Wal and Morn can't be far. We'll lug this back together, with one man as a rear guard."

"We could—"

"Cut your losses, keep your gains." Ourse clapped him on the shoulder. "You've got your kill today. Your first!"

●—●—●

The four hunters trekked across the plain, intent on reaching the shelter of the cave before the winter sun dropped behind the distant blue cliffs. They followed the shore of a great shallow lake, turning into the wind as they made their final approach to the bluffs. A cooling breeze rattled the reed stands. Birds flapped to their roosts. They were hunting farther north than ever before, as the shrinking ice bared new pastures for the reindeer herds. The People had sent three men to see the ice again this year and it was farther up the mountains, shedding muddy streams. The world was growing larger, and the People with it.

Even with the sun in his eyes, Spen thought he could pick out the flap of skins they had stretched across the front of the cave to blunt the night wind. He was eager to reach camp and rest, heavily laden as he was with meat. His muscles tightened with the approaching chill, the spear wound in his right leg aching and the battle with the Uglies fresh in his mind.

The small group approached the hunt camp, a thick-lipped cave in the soft gray limestone. Spen could see thin wisps of smoke emerging from behind the skin. He could almost feel the warmth of the fire, a great luxury after a long day hunting. Grandfather Crom would be there, stooped and feeble, tending the fire and knapping new blades from the flint cores. The old man was no good at anything anymore but making tools and tending the fire. As Eldest he had insisted on coming on this hunt, probably his last. Spen feared coming back to camp one day and finding his frail fur-wrapped body stiff by the fire.

Ourse caught up with him, still effortlessly carrying his own pack of meat. He was not called the Bear for nothing. Taller by almost a head than Spen and broad in the shoulders, he was one of the People's great hunters. He knew which way a hunted animal would run, and more often than not his spear brought down the fleeing reindeer.

Spen would think instead of the colors and shapes of the animal. Caught up in a sudden vision of his next painting, he would hesitate, and the prey would slip away. But his back was strong and he could carry most of a reindeer a long way.

Ourse squinted ahead at the smoke. "Unh. The old man still lives, then, painter?"

"This day, yes, but not much longer. I'm afraid our grandfather won't see the new buds break on the willows."

"He's lived longer than anyone else in memory. It's enough."

Spen grunted his assent, always feeling a rush of pride that his grandfather was the last of the First Band, founders of the first tribe of their kind to settle in the valley.

They reached the cave and pushed through the skins. Cozy warmth greeted them, the air acrid with smoke. Crom sat next to the fire, dozing. He started awake when Spen touched him on the shoulder.

"Grandfather," Spen began proudly, "we were successful. Ourse killed a large buck, heavy with fat. We have a lot of meat. Even brought the main bones."

Crom murmured and smiled, his eyes vague. A small pile of freshly flaked flint sat before him.

"Unh." Spen eased the heavy hindquarters and flanks off his shoulders. Fresh washed from the lake nearby, they fell on the reed mat used for food preparation.

Ourse shrugged. "Not truly." As was customary, Ourse demurred. A hunter who boasted of his skill was a threat to the band. One day he'd think he was better than anyone else, and then he'd kill someone. So the successful hunter was expected to minimize his feat. "It was a lucky shot. An old buck that couldn't run fast just happened to pass near me." He unloaded his own pack of deer forequarters and head from his shoulder onto the floor of the cave near the old man. He glanced at it carelessly. "It's not good meat, but it's all I could find."

Wal and Morn entered the cave, each bearing parts of the butchered deer. Morn was tall and rangy with very dark hair, a contrast to Wal's rather light brown hair and short stocky build. Nevertheless, they preferred to hunt together

Crom looked shrewdly at the cut-up carcass, probing the pieces of fat. "It'll do, Ourse, it'll do. We never go hungry when you're hunting." Then he straightened up and pointed to the bloodied packing around Spen's leg. "But what happened to you, painter—daydreaming again? Stick yourself with your spear?"

Spen grimaced; the rebuke stung. He was Crom's favorite grandchild, but that didn't spare him the old man's cutting tongue. "No, Grandfather. Ourse and I were surprised by three Uglies while we were cutting up the buck."

"Where were Wal and Morn?"

"Tracking another deer, out of sight."

"The brutes thought we were only two so they didn't run away," snorted Ourse derisively. "Hah! Spen speared the biggest one first. Good work! The other two ran."

Crom clutched at the fur-covered skin wrapped around his shoulders as though hit by a sudden chill. His eyes widened as he looked at Spen. "You . . . killed him?"

Spen let his pride show a little, grinning. "Sure. They're just animals, and more dangerous when scared. So I stabbed one right away. I wanted to kill them all."

"Spen?" Wal said doubtfully.

Ourse said loudly, "Of course, Spen. You deaf? He got one in the chest, a killing thrust."

The old man sighed.

Spen shivered as he relived the pleasure of killing an Ugly. All his life they had not taken him seriously because of his size. Usually attackers concentrated on Ourse. This time the lead Ugly probably thought Spen would be the easy mark, and then Ourse would run.

This moment, the new looks of respect on the faces of those around him, was well worth a jab in the leg. He liked the memory of his spear sliding into the Ugly. It went in with surprising ease. Then the gush of bright blood . . . Spen felt a warmth sweep over him at the memory, and his hand tightened on his spear.

"Hm. I'm surprised they were so bold. There are so few of them now," said Crom slowly. "They are hungry."

Remembering to not show pride, Spen lost his smile and knelt beside his grandfather. "Did you kill a lot of them in the old time?"

Crom was silent for a moment. "I didn't want to. We used to see them a lot back when I was a young hunter, but we didn't get too close. When we of the First Band came into the valley they were all over, and in great numbers too. But our spears were much better than theirs, and they fought stupidly, and not together, so we always won. After the first few fights we left each other pretty much alone. There was enough game for all."

"You should've wiped them all out," said Ourse. "Stupid useless brutes."

"Yes! But there used to be a lot more Uglies around," said Crom again. "They were in all the caves. They were in this one."

"This one?" Ourse looked around, sat on the damp soil. "How do you know?"

Crom gestured toward the dark back of the cave. "I found a pile of mammoth tusks behind a rock, over there."

"Mammoth? There aren't any mammoth around here. It's just women's tales to frighten children."

"They're real all right. I saw one once, when I was a young hunter, but never since," said the old man. "They like the snow, and it was colder back then."

"What did it look like?" asked Spen.

"Big. A great shaggy beast. Legs like tree trunks and long curved tusks. It was much bigger than the game now."

"Did you kill it?" asked Ourse.

"Kill, kill, that's all you young men are interested in," grumbled Crom.

He rummaged around and pulled out a small deerskin sack. "Here, Spen, clean out your wound and rub this powder in it."

The others turned to the task of cutting up the carcasses with the flint blades Crom had prepared that day. These were new and sharp and made the long work go smoothly as day faded into dark outside. First cutting the hide free, they then sliced out the leg bones so Crom could roast them for the marrow. The flesh itself was cut into pieces small enough to smoke. Dried meat was much lighter and easier to carry back to the village. If the weather held warm, it would take only a day or two to dry and smoke. They joked and laughed as they worked, well pleased with the day's hunt. Finally they stretched the skins along the floor and scraped them of fat and sinew.

As the four hunters worked Crom also cooked the reindeer head, liver, and other organs that could not be dried, and passed around the drinking bowl. It was full dark outside when they finished, their cave a smoky haven of light and warmth in the winter-locked valley.

Before they ate the traditional first piece of liver they paused to consider the spirit of the deer. By honoring it in this way, they induced the spirit to return for the next hunt.

When they had finished the dark, roasted liver, Ourse and Morn smashed the head open with sharp blows to the top of the skull so they could scoop out the warm brains. Lastly, they cracked the roasted leg bones with rocks and sucked out the sweet, fatty marrow.

Later, they sat around the fire, their bellies full of meat and their heads full of the day's hunt.

Spen got up clumsily, favoring his wounded leg, and crossed over to the cave wall, looking for a flat place. His leg ached and the healing plaster he had bound to it did not seem to help. To distract himself he watched the fire glow play on the walls, yellow sprites dancing like living spirits. The rough gray stone of the cave was faintly streaked with vertical bands of lighter and darker gray. The wall protruded into the cave, curving smoothly to the ceiling. In his mind he pictured how he would paint the great herds of reindeer and the hunters. The yellow light from the fire flickered dimly against the wall, caressing it. The herd would be strung out along a horizontal crack just *there*. He had brought the right shade of red ocher to match the color of their hides. Start work when the mist lifted in the morning . . . He half-closed his eyes and squinted to better imagine the painting. His arms moved in short jerks as he sketched in his mind.

"Spen is dream-painting again!" shouted Wal from his place beside the firepit. Morn roared with laughter.

Spen jerked awake. The vision faded. To cover his annoyance, he ignored the taunt and instead turned to face his brother. "How long will we stay here?"

"Not long." Ourse shrugged. "Only until the meat is dry. The herds are restless with the early warmth. They'll be moving north soon."

"There won't be time enough to finish a painting, then."

"There's never enough time for you to finish. You spend so much time on each animal," said Wal, "putting in useless details."

"It's the details that bring the animals to life! The look in the eye, the arch of the back, wind ruffling the coat—"

"Not so," said Wal. "I can catch the spirit of an animal with just a few lines."

"You mean those scratches you make on bones?"

Wal bristled. He was a little younger than Spen, and hadn't been recognized as an artist. His clan name, Wal, meant "carver," but the whittlers who made spears were often called that too. "It's too subtle for you, Spen," he shot back. "You have to have imagination to carve. And it's a lot harder than just slapping colors on a wall."

"Painting is not easy! For one thing, you have to make the right colors. You don't just *find* them, you know."

Wal rolled his eyes. "How hard can that be?"

"I'll tell you. First you have to know what you need, then search out the pigments and prepare them. Blend the colors. Mix them with the right binder so they stick to the wall. And all that time you carry the pictures in your head." Spen was beginning to heat up.

"Mmmm. Messy, maybe, but skill? I don't know."

"All *you* need for carving is a sharp blade like the ones we all carry. Where's the skill in that?"

"Huh. Painting's so easy, even the Uglies do it," said Wal.

"True. I've been in plenty of caves with handprints and dots and black streaks," said Ourse, weighing in.

"That's not painting!" said Spen. "It's . . . scribbling. What children do."

"But Uglies *don't* carve," continued Wal. "You have to have a brain to carve. You have to see the animal in the bone before you start, then make a few good lines to bring it out."

"Even if they were smart enough," said Ourse, "their blades aren't good enough."

Spen touched his bandaged leg gingerly. "Seemed sharp enough to me."

"How could those scavengers do art?" said Wal. "They don't even talk. They're *animals*."

Crom coughed and stirred the ashes in front of him. "Hmmmm . . . I found some things you should see." He pointed to a boulder beyond Spen. "Grandson, as long as you're standing, bring some of those mammoth tusks over here."

Spen limped over and looked behind the boulder. About a dozen very large tusks and a pile of pieces were carefully stacked in the shadow. He picked up several of the pieces and brought them back to Crom.

Crom passed them around to the hunters, giving the biggest piece to Spen. "Now look at these in the light of the fire."

Spen looked down with amazement at the length of huge tusk. Carefully carved into the ivory were about a dozen animals, each sketched with a few lines, but instantly recognizable. Lifelike horse, bison, deer with great branching antlers. And a large animal that could only be the legend, a mammoth. Spen had never seen this style of workmanship before.

"This one is good," said Wal. "It really catches the life of the animals."

"And something else." Spen paused, looking at how the lines seemed to lead his eyes off to things unseen, implied. "It's . . . different."

Wal nodded. "The lines seem to show things that aren't there." He stared at the ivory, frowning.

"Who . . . did this?" demanded Spen.

"I don't know for sure," said Crom. "You saw where they came from. The others are the same."

"Who could do this work?" wondered Wal. "We know all the carvers in the tribe, even the clans from outside the valley. No one does anything like this."

"And . . . why hide it?" asked Ourse.

"Wait a minute," said Morn, weighing in for the first time. "This is the first time we've hunted here on the plain. There are no songs about here."

There was a brief silence. Known as Mouse for his quiet ways, Morn rarely took part in group conversations, preferring to watch and listen. But when he did talk, he often added an interesting new point.

Ourse said slowly, "Yes. The ice has been too close before for the deer to find food."

"You found these just lying behind that rock, Grandfather?" asked Spen.

"They were half buried," said Crom. "I almost didn't see them. There may be more under the sand."

"So they've been here a long time, then," said Wal.

"Looks like it," said Crom.

"It must've been another tribe, then," said Ourse.

"No. We were the First Band," replied Crom firmly. "When we found the valley this cave was at the edge of the ice. None of our kind could've lived here." He hesitated, then said quietly, "But the Uglies were here already."

"Uglies? You think the Uglies could have done this?" demanded Ourse. "They're no more than brutes. Stupid brutes." He spat into the fire.

Spen was stunned. In his mind he saw clearly the Ugly he had killed. Could something more animal than human have carved these wonderful pictures?

"It's impossible," continued Ourse. "They haven't the brains."

"Their tools are too crude," protested Wal.

"They can't even talk," said Ourse disgustedly.

Crom coughed and pulled his fur around his shoulders. "One time when I was a boy," said the old man in a thin voice, "we had a hunting camp by the bluffs, across the big salt pan. It was colder then and the salt pan was a lake, always full of water. We caught small oily fish with a sweet taste there. There were thick banks of reeds around the edges, and flocks of storks fed in the shallows. The storks laid their eggs in nests in the reeds. Good eggs!—tasty. I hurt my foot one day, so my father and uncle left me in camp to collect eggs. I brought the eggs back to the cave and it was still early so I took my spear and followed an old trail at the base of the bluff. After a while I heard wailing coming from a cave nearby. I hid behind a bush and slowly worked my way forward so I could look in without being seen. Some Uglies were putting a mother and baby into a shallow grave in the floor of the cave. They put small objects in with the bodies, maybe they were blades, and then they scattered armloads of flowers on top. There was a lot of wailing and sobbing, and they were saying things that I couldn't understand."

"Uglies can't talk!" broke in Ourse.

"That's what I'd been told, too," said Crom, "but I heard them that day. They were talking, all right. Singing." His voice seemed to fill the cave. "Uglies aren't animals—they're men!"

"We kill them as if they're animals," said Spen. "And we enjoy it."

"If we show people these tusks everyone will know the truth," said Morn.

"What truth? People like us in another band did these. It had to be another band," insisted Wal.

"But that's impossible," said Spen. "You heard the old man. There were no other bands before."

"It's impossible that the Uglies could carve like this!" said Wal. "It's better than anything *we* can do."

"It could only have been the Uglies. The carvings—see how yellow the ivory is? They were in this cave a long time, longer than our kind have been here," said Crom. "That's why I wanted to come on this trip—to see a fresh cave. In the early years some of the young men whispered about seeing ceremonies the Uglies did. Some of us didn't think the Uglies were animals. The Elders told us to stay away or be speared. They were afraid we'd mix with them, and be changed. Maybe even mate! When their women are young they aren't so ugly." He sighed. "We hate them because they're different, and we tell ourselves that they're not human."

"So when we kill them it's okay," said Spen bitterly.

"When people find out the Uglies are human, what'll happen?" asked Morn.

"We'll have to stop killing them, that's sure," said Ourse.

They fell silent, sobered.

"They'll be allowed to stay in the valley," said Spen.

"They'll take our women!" burst out Morn. The others looked at him. In the flickering glow his face was tense and twisted. Shy and taciturn, he'd lost his mate to a brash young hunter from a clan closer to the foothills. He never talked about it.

"That could happen, all right," agreed Crom. "A woman from the forest clan ran off with one of them once. When her relatives finally found her and the Ugly, they were living with some other Uglies, and . . . she was carrying a child."

"Ugh. Half-animal children," said Ourse disgustedly.

"What did they do?" asked Morn.

"They killed her, of course, and her Ugly mate."

Morn leaned forward. "A big fight?"

"They got all the rest of the bunch."

"Good." Morn smiled.

"But two of the People died."

A silence descended over the group. They stared sullenly at the carvings in their lap or into the fire.

"Why do other People have to know?" asked Wal finally. His hands were moving gently over the tusk in his hands.

Spen looked up at him quickly, a faint smile on his face. The artist in Wal was coming out.

"They'll find the tusks, same as we did. There will be more hunting parties around here from now on," said Ourse.

Another silence.

"We could hide them," suggested Wal. "We could just cover them up again . . ."

"We should *burn* them," said Ourse firmly.

The hunters looked at each other, their faces wavering in the dance of the flames. The old man stared at the ground. He seemed suddenly shrunken.

"No one would ever know what we'd found," said Morn, slowly.

"Maybe that would be best," agreed Wal.

"But they're wonderful," said Spen. "We can't just destroy them!"

"You're too soft," growled Ourse, gesturing with a carved tusk. "I'd sooner burn this than admit those brutes are my equals. Wal? Morn? What about it?"

They nodded their assent, faces set.

Spen looked at Crom. The Eldest could stop them. "Grandfather, you know it's *wrong* to destroy these."

The old man sat hunched in his furs, looking small and wizened. "It would be best," he said in a quiet voice. "If we say nothing about this, the Uglies will be gone soon. There are so few of them now. The Elders of the First Band were wise to keep the two kinds apart. Who knows what would have happened otherwise?"

"But what if there are carvings in other caves?" said Spen. "Are we going to destroy everything we find?"

"If we have to," snapped Ourse.

"I wonder if we're the first to find their art?" said Morn, running his fingers over the piece of tusk in his hand.

"If we aren't, what happened to the other pieces?" asked Wal.

"Same thing we're going to do," growled Ourse.

"The Elders of the First Band must've known the truth," mused the old man. "They would've found pieces in many of the caves and destroyed them. They never told any of us young men when we became Elders, though. They thought they were protecting us. They just didn't know the ice would melt and open up more caves."

Ourse stood up. "Enough talk." He threw his carving onto the coals. They all watched, attention riveted, as it began to scorch on the edges, browning, finally catching fire.

Morn scrambled to his feet then and tossed his piece of tusk on top of Ourse's. Then some more branches.

Wal got to his feet slowly, hesitated, then cast his carving into the flames. He looked at his empty hands, snorted, turned and stalked away from the fire.

"Yours too, Spen," ordered Ourse.

Spen looked at Crom, withered and silent. "Grandfather?"

"It is best," said the old man simply. He shared a long look with Spen. "To go forward you must leave some things behind."

Spen looked at the exquisite carving he cradled in his hands, vibrant with the power of the artist's skill. For a moment he could not move. Then he flipped it toward the fire.

The piece of tusk arced out of his hands and landed in the flames in a crunch and a shower of sparks. Today he had killed, not an animal, but another man. Maybe an artist like himself. And now he was destroying the work of such . . . men.

He would carry these regrets the rest of his life. But it had to be if his kind was to continue and prosper.

"Let's get the rest of them," he said.

They worked in silence, moving the cache of carvings from behind the boulder to the firepit. As they dropped tusk pieces into the snapping fire the cave warmed.

"That's all of them," said Ourse finally.

Fed by the ivory, the fire blazed up, became an enormous pyre sending light into every revealed cranny. The hunters moved back from the heat and stared sullenly into the crackling blaze. Light from the flames flickered on their faces and in their eyes. They all shared the gravity of their actions.

Across the walls of the cave leaped huge, vivid shadows. Spen imagined the souls of the artists fleeing from the tusks, into a timeless and eternal darkness.

Afterword

The idea for this story came to me in 1996, triggered by a conversation with Greg, the subject of which is now lost. The story arc came in a flash—a twist on the presumed but still unknown relationship between Neanderthals and modern humans in early postglacial Europe.

As I couldn't sell it, I asked Bob Silverberg for comments, and I'm ashamed to say his detailed response sat in my files for years. When the request for a story for this volume arrived, I asked Greg to consider the suggestions, and to write a new version.

I taught human evolution at University of California, Irvine, some years ago, and have long thought that Neanderthal culture is underestimated. Certainly we cannot know the minds of these early humans, but we do know they had aesthetic abilities, and seem to have envisioned an afterlife for their dead. Their DNA may or may not have mingled with ours, but their culture must have.

Fred has always respected science; following his lead, I was careful to make sure the story violates no paleontological findings. In fact, a few years ago new pieces of Neanderthal art were found that confirm their artistic sophistication and corroborate the story.

—ELISABETH MALARTRE

I first met Fred Pohl at the world SF convention in New York, 1967. I had just finished my doctorate and was about to start a research career, hired by Edward Teller. I had sold a few SF stories, but had stopped writing while I finished my thesis. I wanted to get out of graduate school, after four years in La Jolla, but the SF fire still smoldered, embers glowing.

Fred looked at my youthful, optimistic face and said, "You'll do better spending your time on science." This echoed sage advice I had heard before: if you can be dissuaded from writing, by all means let that happen.

But I couldn't be. He then introduced me to James Blish, the only time I ever saw the man—who then gave me the best advice I ever got about writing stories. "Think of some future innovation, find the person most hurt by it. That person is the center of your story." Fred nodded as Blish said this.

I'm sure Fred has utterly forgotten this little moment in a crowded room party—but I haven't, and can quote from memory. Those two helped me enormously.

Thanks, Fred. Any more advice . . . ?

—GREGORY BENFORD

CONNIE WILLIS

✠

FRED POHL APPRECIATION

If I had never met Fred Pohl, I would still love him for his short stories. And especially for his short story, "Day Million," which I consider to be a perfect science-fiction short story.

Science-fiction short stories are a rare art form. They have to combine complex ideas, a complete world, heart, pyrotechnics, and style, in a field full of literary conventions that must be acknowledged if not followed, and in an incredibly small amount of space. While pretending to be writing commercial fiction.

And if the story's *really* good, it has to resonate long after you've read it, showing up in your thoughts at odd times and in odder places, becoming more relevant and prescient as time goes by, not less. Doing it's sort of like spinning plates while turning somersaults. On the back of a galloping, spitting camel.

Most writers attempt only one or two aspects of perfection. But Pohl stories do them all—and make it look effortless. That may be the best thing of all about "Day Million," that it looks so easy. It's written in a breezy, deceptively simple style that makes you think you're reading something ordinary. Until the last line bursts on you like a fireworks display.

It also—nearly thirty years after it was written—remains a very modern, day-after-tomorrow story about timeless themes, written with humor and an observing eye, and over the years I've found myself reciting its last line when reading about online dating, Twitter, corporations, and countless other nonsensical aspects of modern life. Quite an impact, and all in under six pages.

And it's only one of dozens of wonderful Pohl stories. Some of my favorites are "Fermi and Frost"; "The Midas Plague," which is possibly the truest story every written about our modern consumer culture and should be posted at the front doors of Walmarts everywhere; "The Gold at the Starbow's End"; "Shaffery Among the Immortals"; "We Purchased People";

and "The Quaker Cannon," which I read long before the name Frederik
Pohl meant anything to me and which made my list of best science-fiction
stories ever. And has stayed there ever since.

Frederik Pohl's short stories are literary science fiction at its best—
ironic, funny, often heartbreaking, multilayered, intelligent, subtle, and so
smoothly told that you don't realize you're bleeding till much later.

I said I would have loved Fred Pohl even if I hadn't met him, but luck-
ily, I did get to meet him—I think the first time I got to spend time with
him was at one of James Gunn's writers' conferences in Kansas—and then
got to know him and his wife Betty Anne Hull better at Jack Williamson's
lectureship, and ever since then I've been lucky enough to have both of
them for friends, a friendship enhanced by the fact that all three of us share
the same political passion. (And when we get together we talk politics a
mile a minute and only get to science fiction later.)

Fred is a lovely person, a gentleman and a scholar, a wonderful editor,
and someone who loves science fiction *and* science, and who has helped it
to become the smart, stylish, literary, well-written thing it is today. He's
also a skeptic (a quality growing rarer and rarer in our world and one I've
learned to cherish).

One of my favorite things about Fred is that when he and Jack
Williamson were two young guys and heard about the UFO crash at
Roswell, they both decided to go see for themselves whether there was anything to it—and promptly concluded it was a weather balloon, a conclusion it's taken the rest of the world over fifty years to arrive at (and lots of
them still aren't there yet).

My other favorite thing about Fred is that while he's a skeptic, he's not
a cynic. And he's still as in love with science fiction and as enthusiastic
about it and its future as he was when he started out as a young writer. Listening to him is not only interesting but inspiring. I think that's because in
spite of all the many hats he's worn over the years—book editor, magazine
editor, literary agent—Fred is first and foremost a writer and has always
wanted science fiction to be as well-written as possible.

I've learned something new about science fiction and writing and literature every time I've come anywhere near him, and I recommend to any
beginning writer who wants to learn to write that he or she study Frederik
Pohl's stories. And to anyone else to read them. They're wonderful. But
terrific as they are, Frederik Pohl is more wonderful. I hope all of you have
the chance to get to know him like I have.

VERNOR VINGE

✴

A PRELIMINARY ASSESSMENT
OF THE DRAKE EQUATION, BEING AN
EXCERPT FROM THE MEMOIRS OF
STAR CAPTAIN Y.-T. LEE

At the time of its discovery, Lee's World was the most earthlike exoplanet known. If you are old and naïve, you might think that the second expedition would consist of a fleet of ships, with staff and vehicles to thoroughly explore the place. Alas, even back in '66, that was not practical. The Advanced Projects Agency had too much else to survey. APA paid me and my starship the *Frederik Pohl* to make a return trip, but they eked out the funding with some media-based research folks. And they insisted on renaming the planet. Lee's World became "Paradise."

Ah, the "Voyage to Paradise." That should have given me warning. Over the years, I've had some good experiences with APA (in particular, see chapters 4 and 7), but that name change was a gross misrepresentation. The planet is in the general class of Brin worlds—about the only type of water world that can maintain exposed oceans for a geologically long period of time. Those oceans are extraordinarily deep, almost like an upper layer of mantle, but with no land surface—except in the case of Lee's World, where some kind of core asymmetry forced an unstable supermountain above sea level.

More important than the name change, APA gave the mission's science staff way too much independence. When you are on a starship in the depths of space, there has to be just one boss. If you want to survive, that boss better be someone who knows what she's doing. I have a long-term policy (dating from this very mission as a matter of fact): scientists must be sworn members of the crew. Even a science officer can cause a universe of harm (see chapter 8), but at least I have some control.

In fact, there were some truly excellent scientists on my "Voyage to Paradise," in particular Dae Park. Most legitimate scholars consider Park's discovery as making this expedition the most important of the first twenty years of the interstellar age. On the other hand, several of my so-called scientist passengers were journalists in shallow disguise—and Ron Ohara turned out to be something worse.

•—•—•

We landed near the equator, on the east coast of the world's single landmass, an island almost one hundred kilometers across. It was just after local sunrise. That was the decision of Trevor Dhatri, our webshow producer— excuse me, I mean our mission documentarian. Anyway, I'm sure you've seen the video. It's impressive, even if a bit misleading. I brought the *Frederik Pohl* in from the ocean, along a gentle descent that showed miles and miles of sandy beaches, bordered with rows of glorious surf. The shadows were deep enough that details such as the absence of cities and plant life were not noticeable. In fact, the human eye has this magical ability to take straight lines and shadows and extrapolate them into street plans, forested hills, and colors that aren't really there. Blued by distance, mountains loomed, clouds skirting along the central peaks, and there was a hint of snow on the heights.

I have to admit, the video is a masterpiece. It could be showing a virginal Big Island of Hawaii. In fact, there are no trick effects in these images. They are simply Lee's World shown in its best possible light. The beach temperatures were indeed Riviera mild, and there really was scattered snow high in the far mountains. Of course, this artfully ignored the *minor* differences such as the fact that half the world—all the mid- and high latitudes—was encased in ice, and the fact that there was essentially no free oxygen in the atmosphere. Hey, I'm not being sarcastic; those aren't the big differences.

•—•—•

Fortunately my passengers were not as ignorant of the big differences as the presumed webshow audience. Within an hour of our landing, the geologists were out in the hills, following up on what their probes had reported. Within another hour, Dae Park had her submersible and deep samplers cruising toward the oldest accessible sea floor.

My crew and I had our own agenda. Coming in, my systems chief had been monitoring the seismo probes. Now that we were grounded, we were stuck for a minimum of eight hours before we could boost out. Crew was quietly working at a breakneck speed to get everything ready in case we had to retrieve our passengers and scram.

I did my best to look bored, but once Trevor had taken his media focus off my command deck, I had a serious chat with my systems chief. "Can we get out of here by landing plus eight—and will we need to?"

Jim Russell looked up from his displays. "Yes to the first question, assuming Park and Ohara"—both of whom had insisted on crewing their submersibles—"obey the excursion guidelines. As for the second question . . ." He glanced at the seismic time series scrolling past on his central display. "Well, the problem is that we don't yet have a baseline to make predictions with, but my models show a seismically stable period lasting at least forty hours."

"This is seismically stable, eh?" I was an army brat. I've lived everywhere on Earth from Ankara to Yangon. I was in Turkey after the quake of '47. For weeks, the aftershocks were rattling us. That was nothing compared to this place. The deck beneath our feet had been quivering constantly since we landed.

Jim gave a smile. "Actually, Captain, if we go for more than an hour or two without any perceptible shaking, it would be a very bad sign."

"Um. Thank you so much." But at least that was something definite to watch for.

"I always try to look at the bright side, Captain. You're the one who's paid to worry. And your job could be harder." He waved at a view of the outside. It showed Trevor Dhatri hassling crew and scientists to create the most photogenic base camp possible. Now I saw why our sponsors had paid for state-of-the-art O2 gear. The transparent gadgets barely covered the nose and mouth. Jim continued, "Dhatri is playing the paradise angle as hard as he can. If he ever gets tired of that, I bet he'll go for the high drama of explorers racing the clock to escape destruction."

I nodded. In fact, it was something I had considered. "I welcome the lack of attention. On the other hand, I don't want our passengers to get *too* relaxed. If those subs go beyond the excursion limits, all our diligence is for nothing." It was a delicate balance.

I grabbed one of the toylike oxy masks and went outside. Damn. This was stupid. And dangerous. Explorers on a new world should wear closed suits, with proper-size O2 tanks. But everybody in our glorious base camp was wandering around in shirtsleeves, some in T-shirts and shorts. And barefoot!

I moseyed around the area, discreetly making sure that my crewfolk were aware of the situation and dressed at least sensibly enough to survive a bad fall.

"Hey, Captain Lee! Over here!" It was Trevor Dhatri, waving to me from a little promontory above the camp. I walk up to his position, all the while trying to think what to say that would make him cautious without exciting his melodramatic instincts. "How do you like our view of Paradise, Captain?" Trevor waved at the view. Yes, it was spectular. We were looking down upon a vast jumble of fallen rock, and beyond that the beach. From this angle it looked like some resort back home. Turn just a little bit, and you could see my starship and the busy scientists. I debated warning him about the perils of the view. That talus looked *fresh*.

"Isn't the base camp splendid, Captain?"

"Hm. Looks cool, Trevor. But I thought the big deal of this expedition was the Search for Life." I waved at his bare feet. "Shouldn't your people be more worried about contaminating the real estate?"

"Oh, you mean like the Mars scandal?" Trevor laughed. "No. Near the landing site, it's impossible to avoid contamination. And from the Mars experience, we know there will be low-level global contamination in a matter of years. We're concentrating all our clean efforts on the first sampling of likely spots. For instance, the exterior gear on the submersibles is fully sterile. I daresay you won't find even inorganic contamination." He shrugged. "Later landings, even later runs on this expedition—they'll all be suspect." He turned, looked out to sea. "That's why today is so important, Captain Lee. I don't know what Park or Ohara may bring back, but it should be immune to the complaints that mucked up Mars."

Yeah, so besides their well-known rivalry, Park and Ohara had reason to take chances right out of the starting gate. I glanced at the range traces that Jim Russell was sending me. "I notice Park's submersible is more than sixteen kilometers down, Trevor."

"Sure. I've got a suite of cameras inside it. Don't worry, those boats are rated to twenty kilometers. Dae Park has this theory that fossil evidence will be near the big drop-off."

"Just so she doesn't exceed our excursion agreement."

"Not to worry, ma'am. Of the two, Dae is the rule-follower—and you'll notice that Ron Ohara is still very close to the beach, barely at scuba depth." His gaze hung for a moment, perhaps watching what his cameras were showing from Ohara's dive. "There'll be some important discovery today. I can feel it."

Ha. So while I obsessed about ship, crew, and scientists, Dhatri obsessed on his next big scoop. I messaged Jim Russell to ride herd on the ocean adventurers—and then I let our "mission documentarian" guide me back to the center to the base camp. That was okay. I don't like standing ten meters from a cliff where magnitude seven earthquakes happen every few days.

Back in the camp, I began to see what Dhatri was up to. Of course, it wasn't science and in fact he wasn't doing much with the exploration angle. Dhatri was actually making a case for colonizing the damn place. No wonder he kept calling it "paradise." All this was sufficiently boggling that I let him lead me this way and that, showing off the crusty starship captain working with scientists and crew. My main attention was on the range traces from the submersibles. Besides which, Trevor's video work was really confusing, just little unconnected bits and gobs, all set pieces. It was quite unlike most web videos from my childhood. After a while I realized I was seeing the wave of the future. Trevor Dhatri was a kind of pioneer; he realized that in coming years, the most important videos would never be live. Even the shortest interstellar flights take hours. On this expedition, the *Frederik Pohl* was almost four days out from our home base in Illinois. Dhatri could sew this mishmash into whatever he chose—and not lose a bit of journalism's precious immediacy.

I was still outside when a siren whooped, blasting across the encampment. I got to my system chief while the noise was still ramping up. "What in hell is that?"

Jim's voice came back: "It's not ours, Captain. It's . . . yeah, it's some kind of alarm the scientists set up."

Dhatri seemed to have more precise information. He had dropped his current interview when the siren blared. Now he was scanning his cameras around the camp, capturing the reaction of crew and scientists. His words were an excited blather: "Yes. Yes! We don't know yet what it is, but the first substantive discovery of this expedition has been made." He turned toward me. "Captain Lee is clearly as surprised as we all are."

Yes. Speechless.

I let him chivvy me toward where the scientists were congregating.

Trevor was telling me, "I gave all the away teams hot buttons—you know, linked to our show's Big News feed. That siren is the max level of newsworthiness." His voice was still excited, but less manic than a moment before. He grinned mischievously. "Damn, I love this asynchronous journalism! If I botch up, I can always recover before it goes online." As we got close to the others and the fixed displays, he reverted to something like his official breathlessness. His cameras shifted from faces to displays and then back to faces. "So what do we have?"

An oceanographer glanced in Trevor's direction. "It's from one of the submersibles. Dae Park."

"Dae—?" I swear, Trevor suffered an instant of uncontrived amazement. "Dae Park! Excellent! And her news?"

In my own displays, I was checking out Park's submersible. It was still sixteen kilometers down. Thank goodness the "Big News" did not involve her going deeper. Her boat was either on the bottom or just a few meters up, motionless. Okay, she was within the excursion rules, but near a hillside that could be a serious problem in a big quake. You'd never get me down there. I fly between the stars. Just the idea of being trapped in a tiny cabin under sixteen thousand meters of water makes me queasy.

Around me, I heard a collective indrawing of breath. I glanced back at the fixed displays, seeing what everyone else was seeing—and I got an idea why someone might go to such an extreme: Park's lights showed the hillside towering over her boat. It looked like nondescript mud, but some recent landslide had opened a cleft. The lights shone on something round and hard-looking. The picture's scale bar showed the object was almost forty centimeters across. If you looked carefully, you could see knobbly irregularities.

The oceanographer leaned closer to the display. "By heaven," he said. "It looks like an algae mat."

Everyone was quiet for a moment. Even my crew—well, all but the cook—knew the significance of such a discovery.

"The fossil of one," came Dae Park's voice. She sounded very pleased.

And then everyone was talking except Trevor—who had his cameras soaking it all in. There was significant incredulity, mainly from Ron Ohara's staff: the video showed just the one object. If this was really life—or had been real life—where was the context? Park's guys argued back that this was probably millions of years old, transported by heaven knew what geological cycles to the deep mud. Ohara's people were unimpressed; the rock looked metamorphic to them.

"People, people!" The voice seemed to surround us. It was probably coming from the same sound system that made the siren noise. It took me a second to recognize Ron Ohara's voice behind the mellow loudness. "I for one," Ohara continued, "have no doubt of Dr. Park's outstanding discovery. I'm sure that if she had focused on shallower water, she would have found living instances of communal life."

From her submersible, you could hear Dae Park spluttering, unsure what to do with the simultaneous insult and support. On the other hand, *Park* was the one who had just made the biggest discovery in the history of starflight. So after a moment, she said sweetly, "Thank you so much, Ron, but we've both seen the preliminary genome dredges. If there was significant life here, it was very long ago."

"I disagree. I have a—"

Park interrupted: "You have a theory. We have all heard your theories."

This was true. Ohara had droned on about them at the captain's table every day of the voyage.

"Oh, it's not a theory, not anymore." You could almost hear him gloating, and I guessed what was coming next. After all, Ohara's sub had been scouting around the coast just a few meters down.

"Take a look at what I found." Ohara preempted all the displays with the view from his boat. The light was dim; perhaps it was true sunlight. But it was enough to see that my guess had been a vast underestimate: the creature's thorax was almost fifteen centimeters long, its limbs adding another ten centimeters or so. And those limbs moved, not randomly with the currents, but in clear locomotion. It might have been a terrestrial lobster, except for the number of claws and its greenish coloring.

❦

This was the ninetieth voyage of the Starship *Frederik Pohl*. My ship and crew had visited eighty-seven star systems, all still within a few thousand light-years of Earth. As such, the *Fred Pohl* was one of the most prolific ships of the early years of exploration. My discovery of Lee's World had been one of the high points of that time. This second visit was shaping up to be something even more extraordinary.

By an hour after sundown all the away teams were back—and we were close to having an onboard civil war. I eventually slapped them down: "I swear, if you people don't behave, I'll leave your junk outside and we'll lift off for Chicago this very night!"

For a moment the passengers were united, all against me. "You can't do that!" shouted Ohara and Park and Dhatri, almost in chorus. Dhatri continued: "You have a contract obligation to the Advanced Projects Agency."

I gave them my evil smile. "That's true but not entirely relevant. APA has clear regulations, giving competent ship management—that's me—the authority to terminate missions where said competent ship management determines that the participants' behavior has put the mission at risk."

Some eyes got big with rage, but to be honest that was the minority reaction. Most folks, including Dae Park, looked somewhat ashamed that their behavior had brought them to this. After a moment, Trevor nodded capitulation. Ron Ohara looked around at his faction and saw no support. "Okay," he said, trying for a reasonable tone. "I am always in favor of accomodation. But my discovery beggars the imagination." He waved at the aquarium-sample box that he had set in the middle of my conference table. "We can't afford to postpone the follow-up, no matter what the demands of the other—"

Park cut him off, but with a look in my direction: "So what do you suggest, Captain?"

Ohara wanted all the ship's resources turned toward his discovery, a massive dredge around the edge of the continent, led by his techs and using all our sea gear. Park was defending her own find and implying that Ohara was a monstrous fraud. Right now, my job was to keep them from killing each other. I waved those who were standing to take their seats. We were up on the main conference deck, what doubled as the captain's table at mess. That gave me an idea. "No more fighting about resource allocation," I said. "The latest seismo analysis shows we have at least one hundred hours of safe time here. So take a moment to cool off. In fact, it is just about time for dinner. We'll have some light predinner drinks"— taking a chance there, but I'd make sure Cookie watered the wine—"and discuss, well, things that are not so sensitive. I'll be the umpire, where that's needed." Maybe with a good meal in them, I could get something like an even distribution of resources between Park—who had made an extraordinary discovery—and Ron Ohara's "miracle."

No one was happy, but given my threats, no one complained. On a private channel, I could see Jim Russell's messaging the cook and staff. I passed around a box of Myanmar cigars I'd brought along. Of course no one but me would touch them. I lit up and for a minute or so they stared at each other, silent except for the coughing of wimps. Finally, one of the Japanese contingent said, "So, how about them Dodgers?"

Ohara and Park just looked sullen. Every few seconds the ground somewhere beneath the *Frederik Pohl* gave a wiggle, reminding us all that whatever the seismo estimates, this was a world where evidence could disappear on short notice.

As Cookie had the drinks brought in, Ohara leaned back and said, "Seriously, Captain, we're going to have to settle some of this quite soon." He waved again at the aquarium. Sitting in the middle of it was a greenish critter that looked like a refugee from a very old science fiction video. Ohara's people called it Frito—I have no idea why. In truth, if it were not fraudulent, Frito was the the most extraordinary living thing ever seen by humans. I noticed that the creature was not nearly as lively as it had been in the discovery video. I bet myself that Ron hadn't figured how to keep the poor fake supplied with enough oxygen.

"Just be cool, Ron." If I could get everyone through dinner . . .

Then I noticed Cookie was looking at me nervously. His voice came in my ear, on a private voice channel. "Sorry, Captain, but I can't find any more banquet-class food."

We routinely stocked high-class dinners for passengers, and fresh food for the crew too. Given the short voyage times, there was no need for anything less. I gave Cookie an unbelieving glare.

"The victuals are here someplace, ma'am," continued Cookie's private communication. "It's the new container system that's screwed us."

I gave Cookie another look, and then turned back Ohara: "We'll return to the resource issues right after a good meal. Our staff has planned something special for us tonight. Isn't that right, Cookie?"

Cookie Smith has been with me from the beginning. He doesn't give a damn about starflight or science, but he's a real chef. And he knows how to put on a good front. He gave everybody a big grin. "Yes, ma'am, the very best." He and his white-jacketed assistants made their exit. Cookie's parting comment was private, and it wasn't quite so confident: "I'll keep looking, Captain."

Even if logistics had screwed up the luxuries, Cookie could probably work some kind of miracle with standard rations. The problem was that for now I had to string these guys along with weak wine and sparkling conversation. Actually, that would have been easy on the flight out. Having a captain's table does amazing things for the egos of most passengers. (It also keeps the passengers out of the way of my crew, but that's another story.) This gang of academics was full of theories. Until today their arguments had been in the context of collegial socialization; it's what they got paid to do at their universities, after all. The trick was for me to put them back in that abstract mood, not raging about who was going to get what equipment in the next twelve hours.

"So," I said, looking around the table, "today has truly been a great day for science." I dimmed the lights a bit. Now the window light provided most of the illumination, a panoramic view from the ship's sensor mast. The result was a perfect illusion of looking out glass windows onto the last of the sunset twilight. Not counting my cigar smoke rafting around the table, it was a supernally clear evening. I noticed Trevor Dhatri repositioning his cameras. He had been sucking in the all the Ohara-Park vitriol, but now he was looking outward. And I have to say that this quiet twilight didn't need Trevor's magic touch.

I waved at the sky. "Space, the final frontier." The words will forever send a shiver down my back. "If you look carefully, you can see the stars just coming out." You really could. I was filtering the video stream through an enhancement program—just enough of a boost so you could see the stars as they would appear in the deeper dark, after your eyes adjusted. "We are four hundred light-years from Earth, yet there's not a single recognizable constellation. Unless you're an observational astronomer, you probably couldn't find anything recognizable. Our generation has gone where no one has gone before. Humankind now has answers to questions that have bedeviled us since the beginning of time. We, *here*, *today*, have added immensely to those answers. What would we—who know the answers—say if we could talk to earlier generations?"

One of Park's guys piped up with, "We'd say that we have only partial answers ourselves."

"True," came a voice from the far end of the table, "but we know enough to render a preliminary assessment, real answers after generations of uncertainty." That was Jim Russell, bless him.

I picked up on Jim's point: "We have hard numbers to assess even the uncertainties. Take the central equation that bioscientists have used to summarize the mystery of life in the universe."

"The Venter-Boston relation?"

"No, no. Before that." These guys knew way too much about Venter-Boston. "I'm thinking of the Drake equation—you know, for the number of civilizations with which communication might be possible."

Silence all around.

"Okay," Dae Park finally said, "that's a good question. More general than Venter-Boston."

For a wonder, Ron Ohara seemed to agree: "Yeah. I . . . guess since the stardrive was invented, we scientists have become so focused on the near term that we don't talk about the questions that really drive the whole enterprise."

"Then now might be a good time to see where we stand," said Dhatri. He sounded sincerely interested in pursuing the topic. I could also see that he was rearranging his cameras. "Somebody scare up a definition of the Drake equation and let's supply some answers."

Now if we'd been back on Earth, I'm sure everyone would've had that definition instantly. Groundhogs don't appreciate the solitude of deep space. In deep space, you don't have an instant link to the Internet. It can take hours or days to get home. I take considerable satisfaction from this fact. You don't have to put up with the incessant din of social networking and trivia searches. But some people can't tolerate the isolation. Many cope by hauling around petabytes of crap that they grab from the web before shipping out. On this occasion, I was grateful for their presence. After a moment, one of the Internet cache boobies popped up a definition from Wikipedia:

The Drake Equation (1960):
The number of civilizations in our galaxy with which
communication might be possible can be expressed as
the product of the average rate of star formation times
$$fp*ne*fl*fi*fc*L$$
where
fp is the fraction of those stars that have planets;
ne is the average number of planets that can potentially
    support life per star that has planets;
fl is the fraction of the above that go on to develop life at some point;
fi is the fraction of the above that go on to develop intelligent life;
fc is the fraction of civilizations that develop a technology that releases
    detectable signs of their existence into space;
L is the length of time such civilizations release detectable signals into
    space.

The letters floated silvery in my cigar smoke.

I had not seen the Drake equation in a long time. From the murmuring around the cabin, I could tell that many of the younger folks had never seen it. The equation reached beyond their nearsighted concerns.

Park gave a little laugh. "So how many systems have APA and the other agencies explored?"

That's a question I could answer, since I tracked my ship's standing: "As of this month? Fifteen hundred and two. If you count robot probes"— which I don't since the robots can miss what trained explorers might notice—"maybe four thousand."

Park shrugged. "Four thousand out of hundreds of billions."

"But with the newest versions of the stardrive we can easily reach any point in the galaxy." That was Hugo Mendes, our staff astronomer. We'd need him if there were navigation problems and we wound up someplace *really* far from home. "I agree with Mr. Russell. We've seen enough to make some good estimates . . ." He paused, reading the definitions. "You know, some of those factors aren't very useful."

One of Park's protégés said, "Yes, but that's half the fun, seeing how the truth affects the Old Timers' questions.

And in a few minutes, they were all absorbed by this long-ago vision of our present.

The first factor, "fp," got a big laugh. "Almost every normal star has planets," Mendes said. "Lots of planets. Too many planets, crashing around, with wild-ass orbits and ejections. As stars migrate around the HR diagram, a lot of them even have second and third generations of planets."

Dae Park was nodding. "I remember reading how back in the nineteenth century, the great mathematicians tried to prove the long-term stability of our solar system. They never did, but no one realized that it wasn't a failure in their math. Only one in a hundred planetary systems lucks into stability for even a billion years."

Now in the floating Wiki extract, someone annotated "fp" with a smiley face and the comment "near 1.0, but so what?"

Trevor leaned forward, "That second factor, 'ne,' that's just about zero if you count all the unstable planetary systems that Hugo said."

"Okay, so just count the systems that stay stable long enough to be interesting."

No one said anything for a moment. Then, "Hmm, you know, if you count importing life, like we're trying to do nowadays on our colony worlds, ne might be near one." That was Jim Russell again. I couldn't tell if he was just working to hold up the discussion or if he were seriously intrigued.

"Yeah, with terraforming. That's cheating."

Just then Cookie's voice sounded in my ear. "Captain! I think I found where the logistic jackasses stored our banquet supplies. I've brought the containers up to the galley. It's not everything, but I can put together a nice meal, maybe a little short on dessert."

I leaned back from the table and muttered a response: "Excellent. Go ahead with what you've got." I really didn't care about dessert, that probably being past the time where pacifying distractions would be useful.

I missed whatever the group decided about "ne." They had moved on to "fl," the fraction of habitable worlds that "actually go on to develop life at some point." Oops, was this a problem? Park and Ohara were already growling at each other.

I banged my wineglass on the table. "Ladies and gentlemen! Professors! Isn't factor 'fl' the simplest of all?"

Jim picked up on that. "Well, yes. The interstellar medium—at least where we've been—has enough simple organics that almost any habitable planet evolves bacterial activity. So factor 'fl' is essentially one. Certainty."

"Only technically speaking," that from one of Ohara's techs. "Sure, things like bacteria and archaea pop up very early, but they never go on to anything more. Before Paradise, we never found evidence of a transition to eukaryotes, much less metazoa. But today, all that is changed thanks to

Professor Ohara's magnificent discovery." The tech waved expansively at Frito's vaguely glowing form.

I expected some kind of explosion from the Park camp, but Dae responded almost mildly: "We'll . . . see about Professor Ohara's unbelievable claims, but I agree with the rest. Today we've shown that there are places off Earth where something more advanced than simple bacteria can exist—or has existed. The transition is possible. After today, I would put a meaningful value for factor 'fl' to be at least one in one hundred."

There were nods around the table. Since we had discovered ten Brin worlds and another handful that had had surface water for some time, her numbers made sense.

"Very good," I said, moving right along before Ohara could respond, "that gets us to more interesting territory, namely factor 'fi,' the fraction of life-bearing worlds that develop intelligent life."

Trevor laughed. "I consider Earth to be such a world, but if it's not to be counted in this arithmetic—" He sounded discouraged for a moment. "All the thousands of worlds we've visited the last fifteen years. And yet we've come up with nothing." Strange. Trevor Dhatri had seemed such an unrestrained cheerleader. I hadn't thought he'd take note of failure— though somehow I doubted this little speech would show up in his online show. He paused and sounded a bit more chipper; maybe he'd figured how to spin this. "On the other hand, what we've discovered today gives me faith that the possibility of alien intelligent life is greater than zero. If we can just get a large enough baseline, a large enough sample size, we'll find our peers in the universe."

"It doesn't matter. I think we are effectively alone." This was Hugo Mendes. "You talk about how many worlds we've looked at. Fine. But in fact, we have visual access almost to the cosmological horizon—and nowadays we have observatories that can watch all that, every second. If there were an intelligent civilization anywhere, don't you think it would ask the same questions we do? Wouldn't it make signals we could recognize? But we don't get anything. Whatever the other factors, I don't think there are other civilizations in the observable universe, at least none that make signals." He waved at the silvery formula. Factor "fc" got the annotation: "Zero or as close as makes no difference."

We were getting near the end of the list. I really didn't want to resume the argument about who deserved to hog the research gear. Give them some time to cool off and I could pull a Solomon on them, dividing everything down the middle—which would leave Park with enough to do some real science. I gave Cookie a poke on my private voice channel: "When will you be in with the first course? Appetizers at least?"

"Not more'n five minutes, ma'am! I promise." Cookie sounded breathless.

I turned back to my mob of academics. Some of them looked unhappy with Hugo Mendes. Maybe he had gored their funding opportunities. This could burn up five minutes, but it might also cause real argument. I took a chance and brought them back on topic. "Ladies and gentlemen. We have only one more item on the Drake list, namely the length of time that a civilization might exist in a communicating form."

Ohara laughed. "Well, *we've* lasted. We've got several real colonies. I think factor 'L' could be a very long time."

That seemed hard to dispute.

"Oh, I don't know." This was one of the software jocks, a young fellow with a kind of smart-alecky air. "I think 'L' is as easily zero as any of the other factors."

Trevor Dhatri gave him a look. "Come, come. We're here, aren't we?"

"Are we?" The software guy leaned forward, a wide smile on his face. "Have you ever wondered why computer progress leveled off in the teens, just a few years before the invention of the stardrive?"

Trevor shrugged. "Computers got about as good as they can be."

"Maybe. Or maybe"—the kid paused self-importantly—"maybe the computers *kept* getting better, and became superhumanly intelligent. They didn't need us anymore. Maybe no stardrive was ever invented. Maybe the super AIs shuffled the human race off into a star travel game running on an old hardware rack in some Google server farm."

"Ah, I . . . see," said Trevor. "A novel cosmology indeed." I'll give Trevor this, he didn't roll his eyes the way most did. Me? I thought all the Singularity types had died or been carted off to old folks homes long ago. But here was living example, and not an old fart. I guess like Nostradamus, some notions will never go away.

The embarrassed silence was broken by Cookie, who stuck his head into the room and said, "Captain, dinner is ready at your pleasure."

Bless him, Cookie's timing couldn't have been better. I waved him in. As the mess staff trundled in their silver kettles and table settings, I brought up the lights. I noticed that Frito had hunkered down behind some rocks, no doubt bored by all the chitchat. Hopefully he and Ohara would keep a low profile while we had a good meal.

Whatever Cookie had magicked up, it smelled delicious. As his people set out the plates and silverware, he launched into his grand chef patter.

"Yes, ladies and gentlemen, this dish is one that you might find at the best New York restaurants. I ordered it myself for this mission." That was a lie. Cookie yearned for his days in New York, but I knew that logistics was the responsibility of APA, with Cookie only allowed to state his general wishes. "I do apologize for the delay this evening. The ship's loaders made a major bungle of where they stored what."

"Yes," I said, "but we're just beginning to use the new universal shipping containers. Except for the ID codes, they all look alike." APA had supervised the loading so I didn't want to sound too critical.

Ron Ohara was sniffing suspiciously. He looked pale. "Just where did you find your . . . food supplies?"

Cookie, oh innocent Cookie. Without even trying, he brought down an academic career. "Oh," he said, "they were in Lab Space 14. Stored live." He waved to his servers, and they simultaneously raised the silver lids. "I give you broiled lobster in the shell!"

It smelled like lobster. It even looked like lobster—if you discounted the greenish flesh and the extra claws.

No wonder Frito was trying to hide.

Of course, Ron Ohara was thoroughly screwed. I mean discredited. He tried to claim that the critters had all been brought up during his single dive earlier that day. There were just too many Frito creatures for that explanation to fly. In fact, Ron had intended to plant the others during his later dives—after I gave him both submersibles and clearance to hog all our equipment.

In one grand *coup de cuisine*, Cookie had solved all my problems. Dae Park got the resources to complete her epoch-making survey of Lee's World. In the process, she discovered two more of the famous "Park stromatolites." Analysis back on Earth extended for months and years thereafter. The fossils show signs of metamorphic distortion; the fine detail has been lost. And yet a good argument can be made that they're something like an early eukaryotic form. No doubt they originated several cataclysms earlier in the geological history of Lee's world. Alas, since Park's search, no further examples were found. Some claim this makes her work suspect. Of course this is balderdash. The isotope ratios in Park's fossils are a *perfect* match for the isotopic fingerprint of the crust of Lee's World.

Now thirty years have passed since our voyage to Lee's World and our preliminary assessment of the Drake equation. That equation has crept back into the vernacular of speculation, if only because it captures disappointment and possibility on such a grand scale. In those thirty years we've colonized six of the most terrestrial worlds. A number of others are still in the process of terraforming—teleporting in oceans, for instance. (See chapter 8 for my part in the development of this technique.)

The last thirty years have transformed exploration, but not entirely for the better. Too many people are satisfied with terraforming; they don't expect we can find worlds any better. The massive government funding of the early years has dried up. On the other hand, with the super-scalar extension of the stardrive, now we can go anywhere in less than ten days. Anywhere in the observable universe? Sure, but that's just the beginning. The vast majority of the universe is so far away that its light will never be visible from Earth or from any place you can see from Earth. That's why a system memory failure is so dangerous in modern exploration—you might be so far from home that a lifetime of jumping wouldn't bring you to a recognizable sky. Having a Hugo Mendes on board wouldn't be any help. (If you're a cache booby or have access to a planetary Internet, you can look this up. Search on "cosmological horizon." Or better yet, buy my book, *Beyond this Horizon: Star Captain Y.-T. Lee's Voyage to the Cosmic Antipodes*.)

Nowadays, the best explorers pop out to supra-cosmological distances, survey visually for the one-in-a-million exceptional star—and then home in on that. This strategy has two advantages: first, it may eventually get us to some far corner of the universe where the Drake statistics are improved. Second (a more practical reason), it makes it easier for explorers to keep proprietary control over the location of their discoveries; we're less tied to the capricious funding of APA. Without this innovation, the public could never benefit from our Planets for Sale program.

So what have we found Out There? No little green men (or even little green lobsters). No stable planetary ecology with breathable pressures of free oxygen—i.e., no living eukaryotes or even cyanobacteria. We have seen four planets with fossil algae mats such as Park discovered on Lee's World. Thus, the transition to complex life does happen off the Earth. I think it's just a matter of time before we find such life. I know some folks say we have failed. Some explorers want to shift the focus to hypothetical nonorganic life-forms in Extreme Environments—the surface of neutron stars and black hole accretion disks. This is all very nice, but the Extremists are getting way too much funding for their agenda. There is *no* evidence that Extreme Life is even possible.

Our voyage to Lee's World was full of surprises. Some of them didn't surface till we got back to Chicago: Trevor's webcast was an enormous hit all over Earth—more for the world itself than Park's discovery and the drama of Ohara's fraud. Without actually lying, the videos convinced millions that the place was indeed a paradise. Furthermore, the geologists concluded that although the planet was overdue for a crustal "readjustment" (Krakatoa on a planetary scale), and even though such a catastrophe might come with only a few hours warning, it might not happen for decades.

The Advanced Projects Agency can go nuts when it's hit with a fad. In this case, APA boosted the terraform priority on Lee's World to the max. Planets like Eden and Dorado, stable environments that were already as congenial as Earth's Antarctic and Sahara respectively, just needing a little atmosphere tweaking, these got moved to lower priority. Meantime, fifty million people queued up to homestead Lee's World.

Thirty years later, the place still hasn't blown itself up. A million crazy people live on Paradise. (That's what they call it. Maybe I should be glad my name isn't attached to this incipient disaster. Still, I was the discoverer. What's wrong with "Lee" anyway?)

I actually visited the place last year, at the invitation of the planetary government. Still another surprise is that the planetary president of Paradise is none other than Ron Ohara! I got my own parade and tours all over the hundred-kilometer-wide continent. The towns are beautiful, but with a weirdness you won't find on Earth. Where else will you see architectures designed to survive more rock 'n' roll every week than a *century* of Ankara earthquakes? Where else will you find building codes that require every residence to have an escape-to-orbit vehicle built in? (They look like large-bore fat-ass chimneys.) Anyway, the citizens of Paradise treated me royally. I even got to unveil a discoverer's statue (of me!) in the capital. Maybe my name is okay.

All the while, I was trying to figure who was really behind the hospitality—and if it was Ron, why? Maybe he knew the world was going to blow while I was there. I should stay close to fat chimneys.

The last afternoon of my visit, I had a private lunch with Ron at his presidential lodge at the Place of First Landing. We sat out on the veranda, not more than two hundred meters from the original camp. That ground had long since fallen onto the beach, but the remaining terrace was everything that Trevor's wacky video had implied about this world. We might as well have been at some Mauna Kea resort. And unlike the last time I was on this world, there wasn't even a need for oxy masks!

I hadn't seen Ron in all the years since our expedition returned to Chicago. He's showing his age. But then, I imagine I am too. When his staff had left us alone with our drinks, he raised his beer as if giving a toast to the scenery. "Paradise was the easiest terraform job in the history of starflight. We seeded a few million tonnes of the proper ocean bacteria and now after less than three decades we have breathable levels of free oxygen."

Considering the investment's dubious future, that was only fair. But I didn't say that. I just puffed on my cigar and enjoyed the view. You couldn't see the talus from here, just the sea in the farther distance (complete with some certifiably insane surfers). Closer, above the drop off, there were wide grassy lawns. The planetary flag fluttered on a flagpole between two palm trees.

"Have you seen our flag, Captain?"

"Oh yes." The flag was everywhere: a blue field surmounted by a green lobster with too many claws. "How is Frito, anyway?"

Ron laughed. "Frito, or at least his offspring, are doing great. We tweaked their biology so they're filter feeders. Now they're the most plentiful large animal in the sea, having a feast on the new plankton. But you should know that they're a legally protected species." He smiled. "I don't think I could survive another surprise lobster dinner."

I smiled back. He seemed mellow enough. "There's a question I always wanted to ask you, Mr. President. Did you ever think you could get away with such a transparent hoax?"

"Actually, I thought I had a shot at it. I was betting that Paradise would blow up before any third expedition got here. Meantime, I'd have the subsea videos I intended to make of Frito's siblings—the ones you cooked."

"Yes, but even without Cookie's menu, once we got back to Earth and serious DNA analysis was done on Frito—"

Ron looked embarrassed. "Well, as I'm sure you've read, I rather misrepresented my academic qualifications; my PhD is in sociology. I used a hobby kit to insert the green genes and muck around with a few other things like claw count. Trevor said that would be enough to give us deniability. Actually, I think Trevor was leading me on a bit. He only needed the hoax to last long enough to boost the ratings for his video. In the end, your cook didn't give us even that much time."

He leaned back, looking awfully content for someone who'd had his great hoax blown away. "But that was thirty years ago. Amazing how it all turned out isn't it? I call it the luck of Paradise. You and your cook debunked Frito so fast that no one talked seriously about sending me to jail. And Trevor's video was still a smash hit. We were able to take advantage of all the publicity to become land developers here." He grinned at me. "Life is good."

Hmm. "Paradise could end tomorrow, you know."

"True." Ron set his beer down and clasped his hands across his gut.

"But we Paradiseans are ever alert. Besides," he gave me a sidelong look, "we have you and your fellow explorers working tirelessly on our behalf. I understand you've discovered ten worlds that are a match for Paradise."

We at Planets for Sale don't release the exact totals, but I said, "That's about right. And every one of them is at least as unstable as this world. Are you talking about a culture of throwaway worlds?"

"Sure. If you give us a good enough price. Traditional terraforming also has its place, of course. Both ways, the human race is spreading out." He smiled at the gleaming day. "Up to a few decades ago, we were trapped on one tiny world—and we were getting crowded and deadly. We were close to global catastrophe. That was a very narrow passage. But we got through it. And because of the near-zero values of 'fl' and 'fi' and 'fc,' we've discovered that 'L' may be unbounded. The whole universe is our private playground! We just have to supply the trees and the grass and the pets. I know the biologists are still hunting for higher life. I read how Dae Park is flying around beyond the beyond. She'll be ecstatic if she ever finds a living algae mat. But don't you see? It really doesn't matter anymore. A thousand years from now, we humans will be beyond the reach of any disaster. A hundred thousand years, and the profs will be arguing about whether humans originated on a single world or many. And a million years from now . . . well, by then life will be scattered across the universe and evolved into new species. I'll bet some will be as smart as us. *That* will be the time for a new assessment of the Drake equation!"

➤━ ━➤

Maybe Ron is right about the future; his view is widely held these days. But I can't wait a million years—or even a thousand. And in a way, the spread of Earth's life messes with our learning the truth. It did on Mars. It tried to on Lee's World. I'd like to stay ahead of that, to continue to open up the universe to you, my customers. I remain an explorer, my boots planted in the hard vacuum of reality, my gaze directed beyond this horizon.

Afterword

Frederik Pohl's work came spectacularly into my world circa 1957, when I read *The Space Merchants* (written in collaboration with another of my favorite authors, Cyril M. Kornbluth). I was thirteen.

The Space Merchants stood out from the many wonderful stories I encountered because more than any other, it showed how deeply propaganda and economics affect the fabric of our world. Of course, there are other science-fiction writers who do great things with social issues, but I discovered that Fred was also exploring the technological ideas that the social ideas play out upon. I think the first mind-to-computer upload story that I ever read was by Fred. And then there was *Slave Ship* and "The Tunnel under the World."

These came at a formative time for me, but they are just a tiny fraction of Fred's writing. His later novels have considered the physical limits of the astronomical universe. Both for readers and writers, it has been a marvelous exploration.

Thanks, Fred.

—VERNOR VINGE

GREG BEAR

❧❦❧

WARM SEA

The old man floated in the middle of the warm sea in a tiny sailboat. He dabbled his toes in the gentle swell. He was far from shore. He was home. He doubted anyone would miss him.

The water slapped the hull playfully. The sun, tipping at the horizon, glinted orange in his dark, heavy-lidded eyes. He had made the ocean his family and now that he had just a few months to live, he had come here to think and work up his courage.

His happiest days had been spent sailing back and forth across the Atlantic and the Caribbean on a research ship, making slow sweeps dragging sensors far behind the metal hull, mapping seamounts. He had loved the glowing evening wake that spread aft of the ship, the twin screws tricking microscopic plankton into switching on their lights like sleepless old ladies alarmed by a noise.

Once, the ship's dredge had pulled up a twenty-foot length of squid arm, ruddy orange in color. They had packed the arm in ice and donated it to a museum in Florida. The old man had often dreamed since about netting the whole creature, a forty or fifty foot kraken, or building a robot with a camera that could follow the giant cephalopods into their hunting grounds in the deep offshore canyons.

The ocean was calm, drowsy. He stared into the blue-black depths. Three miles of water fell off below his feet.

The little crab in his groin nudged through the drop of morphine he had tongued half an hour before. He was used to that, he told himself; but he would never get used to it. The old man did not know how to accept the finality of his flesh. When he dreamed, he was young, closer to an angel than to ashes. Age had taught him truths that the mind tried to ignore. But the body knew.

He lay back on the rough fiberglass deck. The first star, Sirius, winked behind the boat's mast. If he lifted his knees, the pain eased back. But it

was getting worse, no doubt about that. In a month he would be unable
to think for more than a few seconds without losing track. The little crab
would gnaw at him bit by bit. He would be crazy with pain, a burden.

Best to get it over with and leave his remains to the real crabs or the
deep-living fishes with their big eyes, honest scavengers. He could become
a true captain's plate, a sea-dweller's feast and delight.

So much better than a coffin.

The pain relented. He felt light-headed with relief. Life had been good
and longer than most.

The old man sat up and again dropped his toes into the water. Swished
them like a boy getting ready for a swim. Even before he knew he would actually do it, he pushed up on trembling arms and slid over the side. The ocean
enveloped him. He expertly blew the water out of his nose with a little puff
and opened his eyes. The salt stung briefly and he saw murky grayness, then
the sunset falling in choppy sparks through the roof of the sea.

He let himself drift. It was peaceful. His lungs would hurt in a minute
or so. The body knew, however, and it was resolved. A chorus of tired little
wills, all the smaller voices below his conscious self, sick of fighting, suddenly made him take the big swallow. He blew out all his air.

For a moment, his arms and legs flailed. It was awful beyond belief, but
short. The little crab in his stomach had eaten away most of his fat. He
sank slowly, arms out, surrounded by wavering lines of silver bubbles.

To his surprise, he could still think. Where am I going? he thought.
What's next? His eyes blinked white in the gloom. He could still see, but
he could not focus. The pain was gone. He did not worry. He felt some curiosity, however. The last emotion, and the first.

He managed to raise his arm and reach out, flex his fingers. He touched
something.

A galaxy exploded, a blurred pinwheel of intense green with a sucking
hole in the center.

The old man's arm dropped. The sunset was gone. The water was
black. His brain filled with salt and cold. One last thing: he saw, far away,
a Christmas tree, waiting for him in his parents' house, blinking green and
yellow.

◄►

It was not the fabled ruddy kraken that found the old man hanging in the
water, but she was of the same family. She, too, had been waiting for the
dark, hovering some distance from the boat, with her short arms and two
long tentacles dangling like a big clump of kelp. Fish rising to the surface
might foolishly dart close and be snared. Most of her time she spent fish-

ing with lazy, looping sweeps that would not alarm the naïve. Whatever was foolish was food.

She had been drawn first by the boat, floating like a log or raft of weed. Then she had heard the splash. Now she could taste the odd creature even at a tentacle's length. It was tangy and oily. It moved and touched her. She flashed in alarm and released a flood of glowing bacteria that sparkled like a thick cloud of stars. Her jet roiled the cloud as she retreated many lengths into the dark.

From the low level of electricity, she quickly observed that she was not being followed. The interloper in the water was not big enough to be dangerous. Muscles were not being engaged to chase her, and the boat did not growl. After a few seconds, she jetted back toward the shape.

She had once before met a creature from the stinging emptiness above the roof of the world. It had drifted with the brackish flow from a river, in an estuary where she had gone to hide from the big-headed whales. It had been brown and white with four kinked limbs and a huge, protruding pink sac. She had felt some curiosity about that thing, but had not thought it would be worth eating, so she had left it to the sharks. They had relished it.

There were so many mysteries, especially above the roof of the world.

The big squid knew how to fish, she knew how to breed, she knew to avoid the big-headed whales that could shatter her insides with an intense pulse of song. To her, during the time of mating, all the world was mystery, either frightening or intriguing, nothing in between. All of her shiniest memories were of puzzlements and impulses, sprinkled with the rich satisfactions of food and mating. Impressions of what she had experienced sparkled in her tiny brain and huge knots of nerves like flitting sardines in a shoal.

She had much time as she fished to contemplate this private album of impressions, paging back and forth in no particular sequence.

The interloper was sinking. With her skin, she could taste the oily slick of it in the water. She lit up along her mantle and on the tips of her tentacles as if signaling a mate, telling the shape to slow down, linger. Somehow she knew that wasn't appropriate, but she had no other response. She rolled her wings in shimmering arcs on both sides of her mantle, adjusting her trim in the slow currents.

The interloper reached a thermocline and paused, caught between warm and cold. Its eyes were so tiny, no bigger than a shark's and much smaller than hers. Strangely, the eyes covered themselves once, then opened wide and stayed that way.

The squid jetted and flowered, then slimmed, flowered again, and slimmed, making a circle. The interloper was neither food nor mate, but it intrigued her. She was disappointed when it finally slipped below the thermocline and continued its fall.

There were males about, and she was hungry and full of eggs. She did not want to waste her strength tonight; she wanted to mate and to fish. Still, the squid followed, adjusting the concentration of ammonia in her tissues to sink in the colder flow. Then, with some alarm, she realized the interloper was dropping to where there would be very few fishes, and at this time of evening, no males.

Regretfully, she hovered, indecisive. Then she reached down with her longest tentacle and touched the flesh below the tiny eyes. Now that they were uncovered, their blank stare seemed familiar, even friendly. She gave the interloper one last taste, one spreading wave of fleshy lights, a salute of red and green along her mantle, as she might touch a friend and tell of the best places to fish and avoid whales.

The body fell deeper. She extended her tentacle, reluctant to give it up even now. Besides, she was proud of her long reach. It was a sign of beauty, to tap a mate from many body lengths away, to touch it below the eyes and then dart off.

The tentacle unwound, straightened, reached down twenty feet, thirty feet, forty feet, fifty, sixty, seventy, ninety.

One hundred.

One hundred and ten. One hundred and twenty.

She knew she was the longest thing in the sea, the brightest, the prettiest, infinitely desirable.

With a will of its own, tired of her curiosity, the long tentacle retracted and recoiled, its swift, springy withdrawal leaving bubbles in the water.

The interloper continued its descent into the dark below where not even her large flat eyes could penetrate. The water spread out its oily taste.

The big squid held her station, trying to be thoughtful, to hold the memory, but the shoals of past flickered and merged so easily with the present.

Pushing her siphon to one side and locking her mantle, she filled with water and jetted to just below the roof of the world. It was night. The fish were coming. The shape had made her uneasy. She wished for males to console her.

She was lonely now, and beautiful, and so full of eggs.

Afterword

While I've always been considered, at first blush, an Arthur C. Clarke kind of writer (and I am), I've said for decades that the two careers and bodies of work I most admire in science fiction are those of Fred Pohl and Brian Aldiss. Fred, chiefly because he writes so well on so many subjects, and can never be pinned down as to what he does best—and Brian for much the same reason. Fred's take on social issues in works as diverse as *Space Merchants* and *Chernobyl* resonate to this day. "Day Million" is a perennial, startling each new generation of readers. I've been haunted by "The Gold at the Starbow's End" for decades. *Man Plus* compels on so many levels. And the Heechee stories are both literature and great fun—a difficult combination in any field of writing.

Fred has been a sparkling, sparking presence in science fiction for at least seventy years now, as fan and editor of both books and magazines, as solo writer and collaborator, as pulp writer and avant-garde experimentalist.

And as inspiration and cattle prod for generations of chronologically younger, but (I hope) no less brash admirers.

—GREG BEAR

Robert J. Sawyer

⊰⊱

FREDERIK POHL

I often get asked what my favorite science fiction book is, and, well, the answer is *Gateway* by Frederik Pohl.

Why is it my favorite? That's hard to answer without spoiling the surprises that are to come, but let me say this: *Gateway* is one of only a handful of novels to have ever won *both* the Hugo *and* the Nebula award for best novel of the year.

The Hugo is science fiction's People's Choice Award, given by the members of the annual World Science Fiction Convention. And the Nebula is the "Academy Award" of the field, given by writers to other writers. As it happens, I myself have been lucky enough to win them both—but each for a *different* book. It's very hard for a single novel to be both a rousing crowd-pleaser as well as being stylistically inventive and rich with touches that might appeal to other professionals. But in *Gateway*, Fred Pohl manages both.

This book has huge, cosmic concepts at its core, as well as a very powerful, heart-wrenching human story. Among other things, it's a novel about artificial intelligence—the computer psychiatrist dubbed Sigfrid Von Shrink is one of the most memorable characters in all of science fiction. It's also a novel about far-out physics. *And* it's a novel about an all-too-human, all-too-fallible man named Robinette Broadhead.

Gateway was originally conceived of as a stand-alone novel, but it's since spawned several sequels, starting with the wonderfully titled *Beyond the Blue Event Horizon*, which was also nominated for both the Hugo and the Nebula.

As I write these words, Frederik Pohl is about to turn ninety years old—and his career as a science fiction professional has spanned over seventy years; his first professional sale came in 1937, when he was just seventeen. His is one of the most remarkable bodies of work in the history of science fiction, and this book is *his*—indeed, as I said, the entire field's—very best.

)●|●(

THE ERRAND BOY

1

By age six, Jason was the ringleader of the other boys in the orphanage. They only lost interest in the new games he invented when he set up the crèche and tried to deliver a sermon, like he'd heard the Reverend Clayton deliver. They were impresed by the way he'd repaired the teddy bear but his sermons bored them.

The Claytons loved him, named him Hendrix after a great aunt, and for a while he thought they might adopt him. When they didn't, he went back to looking for the one family he'd been told would. The other boys were curious as to just who had told him and when he tried to describe what had happened, they stared at him wide-eyed, then silently turned and left, not believing a word he'd said. After that he never mentioned it again. It hadn't made much sense, even to him. It had happened a few months before, just after supper, when he had been alone in the living room playing with the crèche, setting up the figures of Mary and Joseph and the baby Jesus in a row and preaching at them, keeping his voice low so nobody would hear him.

He was waving his arms like he'd seen Mr. Clayton do—it seemed to be part of any sermon—when he was suddenly struck by the silence. He couldn't hear the rattle of pots and pans in the kitchen and the shouts of the boys in the other room building castles with Lego blocks had faded away.

He felt like he was smothering in a big pillow of silence.

Then there was a sudden warmth and a feeling of affection. He had felt like that the day he had been born, a day he remembered distinctly, though when he told the other boys they had hooted and run away to the kitchen to beg the cook for cookies. It had been totally black—he couldn't remember anything before that. Then there had been a sudden flash of light and somebody was holding him and he felt nothing but warmth and reassurance.

He had been wrapped in paper towels and taken to the foundling home, given what felt like a kiss, and then he fell asleep in the blankets of the heated bassinet. He remembered all of it.

This time he felt flashes in his head and once more a wave of reassurance. Nobody spoke but he suddenly knew that within a few weeks somebody would adopt him—somebody he wouldn't like but who would be a great teacher and from whom he would learn a lot. And for a while it would be fun.

Who would it be? He would know when the time came. He would become a very great man and perform great deeds. His life would be hard, but life was hard for everybody and he could always count on the love and protection of . . . somebody.

Then the silence began to fade and little wisps of noise began to seep through the silence. He clutched the baby Jesus to himself and felt a smile and suddenly the baby Jesus turned to gold. It would become his favorite toy; it represented a great man.

How would he know who would adopt him? He would know, he felt, but he musn't let anybody else take him away. Then the room filled with boys and the silence had gone and the baby Jesus had turned back to plaster.

There was a string of would-be adoptive parents after that, almost all of whom loved his red hair and thought he was cute. He coughed in their faces and one time when it looked serious—the wife was fat and pleasant-looking and hugged him until it almost hurt—he stuck a finger down his throat and vomited all over her dress front.

The most dangerous couple after that was a cheerful, middle-aged man and his thin, quiet wife whom Jason could tell the Claytons approved of highly. Their name was Murray and Jason turned them down by saying quietly, "Fuck you, Mr. Murray"—a word he'd heard from the cook when she'd burned herself on the stove.

In one sense, the least likely were the Zions. They were street preachers, Reverend Clayton said, whatever that was. Mr. Zion was rude and loud, although Jason thought his wife looked friendly.

Every third sentence Rudy Zion said was a Biblical quotation, most of which Jason recognized. The silence had told him he would be adopted by a great teacher and while Jason didn't think Rudy Zion was great, there was no doubt he could learn a lot from him.

He found a small, sturdy chair and climbed up on it and quoted the Bible right back at Mr. Zion. The adoption went through within a few weeks. He would miss the Claytons but he had learned as much as he could from them and he knew the voice was right, he could feel it on the inside.

When the time came to leave, he packed his few belongings in a small suitcase, wrapping the plaster Jesus in a worn sweater to protect it. It flashed gold just before he put it in the case. He'd made the right decision, Jesus had been a very great man, there was no one more important.

Until now.

—•—•—

Rudy Zion was middle-aged, getting fat, and had graying red hair that must have been as red as Jason's when he was younger. The first thing he and his wife did when they got home was to give Jason a bath, scrubbing him until it hurt. After that he was measured up for a suit of pure white edged with glitter and he had his hair curled until it was a mass of red ringlets.

When they were through, a puzzled Jason asked, "What am I supposed to do?"

Rudy Zion looked at his creation proudly and said, "We're going to preach on the street and convert the poor and the lonely. I don't preach in the big-box churches—you don't save souls by the thousands, young Jason, you save them one by one. The down and outers who don't have a place to sleep and not much to eat. When those people come to Jesus, they mean it. God lives through them every minute of the day, not just when they let him in the front door on Sunday."

"You can make money that way?" Jason asked.

Rudy looked wise. "When you save a man's soul, he doesn't chintz on you. You've given him the most valuable thing anybody ever gave him in his life and in return it may not be much but he's going to give you everything he's got. When he comes to Jesus, he's going to ask him for salvation every night when he goes to bed and every morning when he gets up."

Jason stared. "What's 'big-box' churches?"

Rudy frowned. "The Costcos and Walmarts of preaching where the choirs number in the hundreds and the congregations in the thousands. But remember what I said—you only save souls one by one."

He was right, Jason thought—already he was learning things. "Are there any boys around here?" He missed the other kids at the orphanage.

"None that I want you to meet. I'll introduce you to the little girl next door and you can be friends with her. Don't want you growing up queer."

After Zion had fallen asleep on the couch—Jason smelled the liquor on his breath and figured he would sleep for a couple of hours—he dressed up in the suit of which he was very proud and hung a gold cross around his

neck, admired himself in the mirror, then went out to meet the boys Rudy
Zion didn't want him to meet.

He didn't find them, they found him. Three of them stared at him for a
long minute, then two of them sauntered over and one of them grabbed at
the gold cross and the other tripped him so he fell on the dirty sidewalk.
Jason was angry and humiliated, rolled over and grabbed one in the crotch
and twisted and sliced at the other with the side of his hand. Within minutes they were limping away with bloody noses and one was holding up his
pants and crying.

The one who had stayed back held out his hand and said, "My name's
Matt. Glad to meet you."

Matthew Shepherd became his best friend.

When Jason got home in his dirty and torn white suit, Rudy Zion took
one look and started whipping him with his belt. "I didn't tell you to go
out and ruin your suit and play with the dirty boys in the neighborhood.
After this, you do what I tell you."

Jason hated him for two days and then his suit was patched and cleaned
and he went out on the street with Zion and his wife. Louise played the
tambourine to attract a crowd and Zion took off his cap and put it on the
sidewalk with a few dollars in it to prime the pump.

Jason was the star of the show. Rudy Zion introduced him as "the little
Jesus on Earth," said a prayer and Jason shouted "Amen!" at the end of it.
Zion looked upset and surprised but a few more dollars and a handful of
coins landed in the hat.

Over the next few years Jason practiced writing short prayers and
speeches. He had a sweet, loud voice and people really listened when he
warned them they'd all go to hell if they didn't come to Jesus right away.

The marks—that's what Zion called them one night after a few bottles
of wine—gave them everything they had and a few of them touched Jason
and shook his hand. They were all true believers, Rudy said with a trace of
cynicism.

Jason was the center of attraction and a huge draw until his voice started
to change when he was twelve. The collections grew thinner and Rudy
looked at him with worry, no longer quite so proud of him.

The blow-off came when Matthew Shepherd found a stream in the woods
with clay banks so they could slide down to the water. It was the most fun
Jason had ever had. He had folded up his suit to keep it dry and when they
were through he washed himself thoroughly to get rid of the clay.

When he got home, Rudy Zion had woken up early and noticed that
while Jason's suit—which had been let out numerous times and now hardly

fit him—was dry, Jason's hair was wet. He took off his belt to whip Jason but Jason had become a very strong twelve. He took away the belt and gave Zion three whacks on his ass, then grabbed up his little case and ran out the door.

He met Matthew Shepherd in the alley and Shepherd gave him some of his old clothes to wear. Jason took off the white suit and spread it out in the alley, Shepherd found a can of gasoline in the garage and they poured it on the suit and set it on fire.

Jason didn't open up the case to look at the plaster Jesus. He was pretty sure it wouldn't be flashing gold. But he had learned a lot, all right—too much.

Matthew Shepherd never saw him again.

But he never forgot Jason, either.

2

Lester Kamps had been making a routing security check of the medical houses in his district when he ran across Blake Pharmaceutical. A pleasant group of whitewashed buildings, neatly landscaped, so it looked more like a college campus than a medical manufacturing site.

The only thing that bothered him was the two-story windlowless building in back that obviously had been thrown up quickly. He leafed through the short description he had in his briefcase and there was no mention of the addition.

He parked his car and stared at the building for a long moment and then the tumblers fell into place and he had a pretty good idea of what he was looking at. A stealth lab. Rumors were a dozen or more were scattered throughout the country. But representatives from the Department of Defense flatly claimed they didn't exist.

Lester arranged lunch with the Blake officers, none of whom was comfortable at the lunch table, and when he asked for a tour of the new addition to check on security, they told him bluntly his security clearance wasn't high enough. The CEO, the chief executive officer, was a thin, elderly man while the chief financial office was a young go-getter who probably played handball without gloves. Henry Ellis, the chief operating officer, was a fleshy man, and Lester guessed he drank too much, was the life of the Christmas party, and knew everybody by their first name.

They had a cover story for the new facility but Lester didn't believe a word of it.

Back at his office, he worked the phones and finally hung up, puzzled. Nobody in Washington knew much about Blake and nothing about any new addition. He finally called in Bailey, the oldest man on staff, one reputed to have been a protégé of J. Edgar Hoover. Lester gave him a list of the three officers at Blake.

"I'd like to know something about their backgrounds." He hesitated. "Personal as well as professional."

Bailey glanced at the list and cracked a thin smile. "There's something on everybody," he murmured. "Start with rumors and then talk to the family, other relatives, friends, and enemies. Find out enough, something's bound to stick. Most people will censor themselves but they seldom censor the same things. Put it all together and you can usually come up with a pretty ugly but accurate picture."

"You learned a lot from working with Hoover, didn't you, Eddie?"

"Mr. Hoover built the Bureau," Bailey said quietly. "He wasn't above blackmail doing it."

●━●●

Bailey announced his visitor at noon a week later. Lester met Henry Ellis at the door, hand outstretched.

"Glad you could make it, Hank—coffee? Cream and sugar, right?"

Ellis smiled nervously and sipped at his cup. "I take it everything at the plant was okay?"

"Everything was fine." Lester glanced at the papers on his desk and shook his head. "That's about it, Hank." He let Ellis get as far as the door then let a note of doubt creep into his voice. "Your daughter, Rachel, still lives in Sebastopol?"

Ellis paled and Lester motioned to the chair. Ellis walked slowly back and sagged into it.

"She happy there?" Lester asked innocently.

Ellis desperately wanted to wipe the sweat from running into his eyes.

"She . . . lives alone, Mr. Kamps. Edna and I send her money every now and then."

"Every month," Lester said, thoughtful. "Something of a remittance lady, isn't she?" His voice now turned official. "You love Rachel, don't you? A little too well," he added dryly. He pulled an eight-by-ten out of an envelope and slid it across the desk. "You remember this, Ellis? Her photograph from the high school yearbook? She was stunning, even when she was fifteen. You were very fond of her—too fond."

Ellis, hoarsely: "What do you want from me?"

Lester rang for his secretary to bring in more coffee and a plate with doughnuts. "You can have the chocolate ones, Ellis—same brand as in the company dining room." Lester waited until the secretary had left the room. "One of your workers—a Valerie Watkins—died recently. Nobody knows what of. Big mystery."

Bailey had been more than thorough in going through the newspaper obits.

"Did she have access to the new addition?" It was just a guess.

Ellis shook his head, the sweat flying off his forehead. "She never went there, her duties didn't take her there."

Lester picked up the papers on his desk and threw them in the air. "You're lying to me. I know fucking well she had access and my guess is that she died of something she found there."

Another guess but a shrewd one.

Ellis hesitated, agonized. "We never gave her access but somebody turned off the cameras and the motion sensors one night and we knew there had been a break-in. We guessed it was her."

"How did you know that?"

"She had wanted to investigate it for a long time. Then we hired a new young security guard . . . and he developed a thing for her."

"And he let her in."

Ellis nodded. "You never met Valerie. She was an incredibly sexy woman." Something showed in his face that made Lester want to throw up. "We couldn't prove anything but then she got sick and we knew for sure it had been her."

"And the guard?"

"Disappeared."

Lester's voice became a gentle purr. "I want to know what's going on in the level-four containment building at the back of Blake."

"I . . . can't tell you."

"Sure you can. This room isn't bugged—everything you say is strictly between you and me."

Ellis sank farther back into his chair. "I . . . really don't know that much."

Lester waited, silent, and Ellis finally said: "We make vaccines."

"Vaccines? As in plural?"

Ellis shook his head. "Just one."

Lester gave him a minute. "Tell me the story, Hank," he said gently.

"World War I—1918." Ellis paused to wet his mouth with cold coffee. "There was a small village in the Alps. It got snowed in, nobody in or out until spring. When the food and mail trucks finally made it up there, they discovered everybody was dead. Their pathologists couldn't find anything and the bodies were buried in a deep mass grave. A few years ago medical men went back to the village—it's a big year-round ski resort now—and took more tissue samples from the bodies in the grave, still frozen."

"The Swiss reconstituted it as a viable virus? Like we've done with the 1918 flu virus?"

Ellis shook his head. "They shipped it to us, we've had more . . . experience in reconstituting viruses. Our scientists took DNA tests and it didn't resemble the 1918 virus at all. It didn't resemble any virus. The only thing they have in commnon is that they're airborne. We suspect this one is a hundred percent fatal."

"But Blake is making a vaccine, right?"

"That's . . . not the first thing we do."

"What is?"

"We tweak it—we make it into the worst possible version of the disease that we can think of." Ellis finally wiped the sweat off his forehead. "We have to do that," he pleaded. "If the other side—any other side—had tissue samples, that's what they'd do. We try to make a vaccine for the worst possible scenario . . ." His voice trailed off. "Human trials should begin in about four years."

It took Lester a moment.

"You've made the worst possible disease," he said slowly. "But you won't . . . have the vaccine for at least another four years."

"That's fast," Ellis said, eager. "Most weeks we work twenty-four-seven."

"How do you detect if somebody's infected?" Lester asked.

Ellis shook his head. "We've done research on mice—it's not detectable by any blood test."

Lester could feel the sweat start to soak his collar.

"What's the incubation period?"

"We're . . . not sure," Ellis said. "Best we could figure out was based on how long it took from the break-in to when Valerie was taken to the hospital. Maybe three weeks, give or take, before the victim becomes . . . infectious."

"And the disease cycle itself once you've become infectious?"

Ellis looked like he was going to be sick. "Judging from Valerie, maybe two or three days. Again, it could be longer—or shorter."

Lester was afraid to ask the next question.

"How is it spread?"

The sweat had started to run down Ellis's forehead.

"I told you it's airborne. Respiratory droplets are probably involved, when people sneeze or cough or even laugh or simply exhale. Some diseases can be spread on dust particles, which means they can travel . . . long distances."

"There's no defense, is there?"

Ellis slowly shook his head. "We don't know of any. It's what we're trying for." There ws a note of pride in his voice.

"Did Miss Watkins steal any of it?"

Ellis looked smug. "We had DOD men check out the plant. Nothing was missing."

DOD had lied, Lester thought, afraid of panic. Something had gotten out. But nobody would use an airborne disease because of the danger of blowback. It would be as dangerous to you as to your enemy—and to all the innocent bystanders.

All Lester could think of then was the World War II training film. *Duck and Cover—What to Do in Case of an Atomic Attack.*

Cynics had made a slight addition.

Bend over, put your head between your knees and kiss your ass goodbye . . .

But this wasn't funny.

"You never found anything in Valerie Watkins's apartment?"

"DOD reported it as clean. They even went through her small basement lab—she did a lot of work at home—and found no trace of it."

"What about the security guard, her boyfriend?"

Ellis shook his head.

"I told you—disappeared."

"What do you know about him?"

"Not much. A few of the people who knew him said he was a 'Jesus freak.'"

"He have a name?"

"Jason," Ellis said, wiping his forehead again. "Jason Hendrix."

3

The locker room in the clubhouse had the same warm, moist feeling that all gyms have. There were the usual metal lockers, wooden benches, posters of tennis greats on the walls and at one end the steam room and at the other a pro shop with new racquets for sale.

The towel boy told Brian that Mr. Shepherd would be coming in from

the courts in a few minutes. There was a wicker chair by a racquet string-
ing machine in one corner and Brian made himself comfortable.

The story he'd gotten from his contact in the FBI was garbled—he
hadn't been far enough up the pecking order to get it straight. A woman
working for a medical lab had died under mysterious circumstances and
her boyfriend had stolen some super-secret material from her. That was it,
except the boyfriend had been named Jason and was a religious type. What
Brian wanted was to unravel the mystery and interview the boyfriend. With
a good videotape, he could be a segment on *The Rachel Maddow Show*.
Maybe.

Matthew Shepherd was a surprise when he walked in. Tall, muscled,
blond, and far too young to be running things. He glanced at Brian, curious, and Brian said: "The towel boy said you were the owner."

Shepherd laughed. "That's Joe, always talking more than he should to
strangers—parents didn't raise him right. My old man died on the courts
and left everything to me." He sat on a bench, untied his tennis shoes, and
pulled off a sock. "Front desk said you're a reporter. Who for and how
can I help?"

Brian handed over his press pass for the *Bulletin*. "Woman working for
a medical lab in Emeryville died under mysterious circumstances and seems
her boyfriend disappeared about the same time."

Shepherd looked surprised. "So where do I come in?"

Brian glanced at his notes. "One of the people I talked to said you
might have known the boyfriend. Jason Hendrix."

"The preacher boy from the Lutheran orphanage? Skinny, redheaded
kid about my age now?" Brian nodded. "Haven't seen him for years. Don't
think there's much I can tell you."

"You grew up with him?" Brian asked.

Shepherd left the other sock dangling. "From when we were six until
he ran away at the age of twelve. We were pretty close."

"Ever see him after he ran away?"

A look of regret flitted across Shepherd's face.

"Never did. We were great friends but when Jason left, he left. No vis-
its, no phone calls, no postcards, nothing. Left me feeling a little used."

"What about the rest of the kids? They like him?"

"For two hours in the afternoon, while Rudy was sleeping it off, Jason
would duck out the back door and us kids would meet him at the end of
the block. He was a natural-born ringleader. Come one Fourth of July he
taught the rest of us how to stick cherry bombs under tin cans, set them
off, and see how high the can would go. Drove our parents wild."

Shepherd slipped off his underwear, slung a towel over his shoulder, and headed for the steam room. "Give me ten minutes to sweat and I'll try and fill you in on anything else I remember."

He came back a little later, toweled off, and starting putting on a new set of whites. "What else you got?"

"Any girls in his life?" Brian asked.

Shepherd laughed. "There weren't many girls in any of our lives, not at that age. One or two tomboys who hung around and then there was always the 'girl next door'—the girl you made fun of but secretly idolized and wouldn't dream of touching."

"In some respects he led a sheltered life then."

Shepherd thought for a moment. "I wouldn't say that. There was a theater in town that showed skin flicks after midnight. Once Rudy and Louise had gone to bed, Jason would sneak out and we'd get in through the side door of the theater."

"Really turn him on?"

"We were around twelve then and I sure got excited. Not Jason. A spirited ten minutes of the old in-and-out but to him it was just an item of curiosity. I think that was the night I got my first boner."

Brian hesitated at the next question.

"What about Jason and religion? A put-on?"

Shepherd shook his head. "The real McCoy. As religious as they come, a lot more real about it than Rudy was. Jason tried to convert us neighborhood kids to saying our prayers before going to bed and paying attention to what the minister had to say in church. But none of us gave a damn about some old man up in the sky."

He was quiet for a moment and Brian said, "He never succeeded then?"

"Shit, no. We used to kid Jason about it before we realized how serious he was. Then we accused him of being too young to have found God." Shepherd paused. "One of the few times he scared us. Said he hadn't found God, that God had found him."

"How did Rudy Zion get into the religion business?"

"According to Louise, he picked up some catchphrases from the Bible and tried the act out on Skid Row. It worked but the money wasn't great. When he ran into Jason, he probably gave thanks to God for the first time in his life—he was stone-cold lucky. I followed them once and caught the act. Louise was good on the tambourine, Rudy was a bore, but Jason was terrific. He had a little sermon worked up that would melt a heart of stone. You'd think maybe Jesus really had to be something like that when he was Jason's age."

"Did he ever mention his parents?"

Shepherd shook his head. "He didn't have any. Part of the romance for us kids was that he'd been found in Paster Clayton's baby barrel. No mama, no papa, no Uncle Sam."

"Not much affection then."

"I think the Claytons loved him a lot. Louise liked him but Rudy was a failure. Jason was his meal ticket but he never loved the kid and when Jason's voice started to change, the meal ticket was gone and Rudy was actually glad when Jason ran away."

Brian frowned. "You were friends and yet you weren't friends, right?"

Shepherd looked at him, surprised. "Brother Brian, you haven't been listening. We were damn good friends but when the lesson was over, it was over. He'd graduated."

"What about the religious part?"

"We were kids—we excused him for that. But I'll admit Jason was a little off the wall about it. He took me to a big cathedral one time and he walked in as if he owned it. We took confession and he shook up the priest by saying he had no sins to confess. I could have lent him half a dozen of mine if he'd needed any."

Brian went over his notes, then glanced up, curious. "What happened to him?"

Shepherd had started for the door, then paused.

"I saw him one more time. I was playing out in the alley when he ran out of the house, carrying a little suitcase. He stripped off his white suit and I gave him an old pair of pants and a jacket of mine to wear. His white suit was dirty and hadn't really fit him for at least two years—Zion was too cheap to buy him a new one and Louise had to keep letting out the arms and legs. He asked me if I could get him some gasoline and I found a can in my dad's garage."

Shepherd stopped for a minute, remembering. "He spread the suit on the ground, poured the gas over it and lit it."

"Why?"

Shepherd shrugged. "Said he didn't want to be a preacher anymore, just a regular kid. He said the bargain hadn't been worth it."

Brian frowned. "What bargain?"

"Got me. He was too young when he first met Zion to have made any kind of a bargain. I never heard from him again. Somebody said he'd moved in with a farm family near Hillcrest and that was it."

"You didn't try to look him up?" Brian asked.

"Sure I did. I hadn't heard anything about him for a few years, went to Hillcrest to find him and talked to some of the people there."

"What did they say?"

"Nobody would talk about him." Shepherd turned back to the door. "Something had happened but nobody would tell me what it was."

4

Nobody in Hillcrest would talk to Brian any more than they had talked to Shepherd. Dry hole, he thought, and started walking back to his car when a man called from a doorway, "Brian?"

The man was in his midfifties. Tweed jacket with leather patches on his elbows, tobacco stains on his teeth, and a craggy, friendly face hiding behind thick horn-rimmed glasses. Brian guessed he was Hillcrest's very own Mr. Chips.

He shook Brian's hand. "Richard Gilly, I teach comparative religion at the high school. I understand you're interested in Jason Hendrix," adding, "Jason was one of my students."

"Good one, I'll bet," Brian said.

Gilly nodded. "He had an edge on me, he had been a street preacher—religious genius when he was younger, I guess. I've never had a congregation."

He paused to light his pipe. "I can drive you to where his farm used to be and tell you something about him, if you'd like." In the car, he added: "Jason showed up at the Scovill's back door one night and they took him in, gave him a bed, and in the morning asked if he'd like to work for them. The Scovills were getting on and he was a godsend."

"Jason was well liked in town?"

Gilly shook his head. "More of an outcast. He was a poor kid in one of the richest towns in the country—the Scovills were truck farmers and the rest of the kids were the sons and daughters of corporate heads and bank presidents. Jason was definitely beneath them and besides, he stank of pigs."

"The farm was close by?"

"Too close. The Scovill family settled here first and the money changers came in later. As the town grew, it crept closer and closer to the farm. Finally you could hear the roosters in the morning and smell the animals on a warm day."

"I take it Jason didn't have many friends."

Gilly took a moment to clean and relight his pipe. "In one sense, he really didn't need any. The animals on the farm were his friends. He'd turned it into a refuge for homeless animals and it grew from pigs and chickens to include a couple of goats, a pair of donkeys, and a dog that Jason had rescued from the pound in Seattle. Jason loved animals and the animals loved him."

"What happened to the Scovills?"

"Killed in an automobile accident. Drunken teenager—but his family had money and he wasn't even fined. Jason was pretty broken up about it but it didn't hold a candle to what happened to him later."

Everybody had their share of bad luck, Brian thought. But Jason's life was becoming a major tragedy. No mother, no father, and then six years as Rudy Zion's meal ticket.

"Jason tried to run the farm by himself," Gilly continued. "He turned out jams and jellies just like Mrs. Scovill did but it wasn't the same. It was one thing to buy jams and jellies from a nice old lady who always had time to gossip. But who wanted to buy anything from a teenage boy?"

He turned off the main road onto a stretch of broken asphalt, then pulled over to the side and stopped. They sat there in silence for a moment. "The animals," Brian said at last. "You said Jason loved them."

Gilly nodded. "The one Jason was closest to was Jasper, a young donkey. It had been a difficult delivery and Jasper almost died but Jason sat up with it around the clock and it pulled through. They bonded immediately. On the farm, Jason and Jasper were a matched pair."

Gilly glanced at Brian. "Ever see a week-old donkey? I was out there when the little thing had just learned to walk. It was before he had any guard hairs and his underfur was fine as silk. Cutest animal I've ever seen."

"Any sports?" Brian asked. Jason must've had some human contact.

Gilly fumbled again with his pipe.

"Jason was skinny as they come but once he learned the holds, he was a really fine wrestler—the best man on the junior varsity. In the senior varsity the top man was Lars Grady, son of the police chief. Jason had it all over the rest of the school in religion, Lars was a genius in biology. Shortly after Jason won top spot among the juniors, there was an intramural contest for best wrestler in the school."

Gilly fell silent and after a moment, Brian said, "And Jason won."

Gilly nodded. "Lars felt a pig farmer representing Hillcrest High was not to be endured. But at the intramurals, it was Jason who challenged Lars, which made it even worse. Nobody had warned Jason that there was such a thing as being too good. Jason should have let Lars win at least one match so he could explain the other two as flukes. Jason won all three matches and if Lars disliked him before, now he hated Jason's guts."

Gilly fell silent again and Brian said, "It didn't stop there, did it?"

Gilly shook his head.

"They had a winner-take-all match for the best high school wrestler in the conference. It came down to a final match between Jason and Lars, and Jason was dumb enough to pin Lars in thirty seconds flat. Lars was destroyed. He was so angry he was crying and some friends had to lead him away. Two weeks later . . ."

Gilly's voice trailed off and he finally said, "It's difficult to talk about this."

"It's important," Brian said gently. He had a hunch whatever it was, it was the keystone to Jason's life.

Gilly started the car. "I can't describe this, you'll have to see it for yourself."

5

It was two weeks after the wrestling match when Jason drove into town to get some feed for the animals. He picked up a new rubber bone for Fritz and a special treat of carrots and apples for Jasper.

A hundred yards from the farm, he slowed the truck and then stopped. It was too quiet, he should at least be hearing the sharp welcoming bark of Fritz. He drove slowly through the gate, then stopped the pickup and stared, his heart beginning to pound.

The three roosters had been strangled and hung over the front door. Of course, he thought, they would be first—they made the most noise in the morning which the people in Hillcrest hated. He got out and walked slowly around the house to the yard in back.

Most of the chickens had their heads twisted off but one clever little bastard had rigged up an amateur guillotine. There was a pile of heads on one side and a small mountain of feathers on the other.

On the other side of the small hill in back of the house, Jason found the remaining goats and the adult donkeys, all of whom had been shot. The president of the archery club had brought his bow and arrows and used Fritz for target practice. Judging from the number of arrows in the body, Fritz was a long time dying.

Almost hidden by a small grove of poplars was a four-by-eight foot sheet of plywood. Jasper had been dissected, the head, skin and organs nailed to the plywood and labeled. It was Lars Grady's graduate test but Jason doubted that Grady's teacher would be very proud.

Jason's mind was blank, it hadn't registered yet. All his friends had been slaughtered and he couldn't quite grasp it. He siphoned the gas from the pickup's tank into a pail he'd gotten from the barn. He made a pile of the bodies, placed the plywood with the remains of Jasper on top, poured the gasoline over it, and set it on fire.

He sat by it until there was nothing left but ash and glowing embers.

It hit him then and he vomited until the vomit ran green. Then the shock and sadness began to fade and was replaced by rage. He ran into the house and found Mr. Scovill's old rifle and a bread knife. He'd drive back to town and kill them all. Men, women, children—he didn't care. None of them deserved to live.

He stopped the pickup at the gate and sat there in growing despair. The gun was old and would probably misfire, the bread knife wouldn't even cut bread.

There was no way he could get even. The town was a small collection of pretty Victorian houses and a scattering of ranch-types plus a steepled church, all surrounded by rolling hills. It was a town that had no use for the too poor, the too smart, the too talented. He had been trapped in a small eddy of time where nothing would ever change and the people who lived there would keep it that way.

It was getting cold and made Jason shiver. He tried to find comfort in religion but couldn't reconcile it with what had happened. He finally decided to pray to God to show him what he should do. He was no longer sure there was a God but if there were, God owed him. He wrapped his arms around himself against the chill; he didn't remember when he fell asleep.

When he woke in the morning, he found that God had sent him a sign after all. For hundreds of yards around him, the ground was salt.

But that was just a down payment.

●●●●

The bargain was sealed once again three weeks later. Lars Grady and Harry Smythe, the mayor's son, had been the ringleaders. The best lawyers in the state were hired to defend them. But trials are decided when they pick the jury and no way was a jury of the townspeople going to send Grady and Smythe to jail. All they needed was a hook on which to hang their hat and the lawyers pointed out that once the Scovills had died, Jason was a squatter and should have been kicked out of town. He was a small-time criminal in their midst.

The jury deliberated for an hour and Lars Grady and Harry Smythe were found guilty of desecrating the morals of the town, fined a thousand dollars each and given six months probation.

Jason disappeared then, living in the woods just beyond the town and stealing blankets and food when he needed them. He had a hunch it wasn't over yet.

Three weeks after the trial, Lars Grady went into the backyard to feed his two pit bulls when they turned on him. One got him in the face, the other in the groin. HIs father heard his screams and ran out and wasted the dogs with his shotgun but the damage was done. The best plastic surgeons in the country wouldn't be able to make Lars handsome again and there was little to be done for the damage below the belt.

The Smythes were great horsemen and Harry was out riding one day when his horse refused to jump a small stream, threw Harry off, then fell on him. Harry drowned in six inches of water.

When he heard about it, Jason said a prayer and sealed the bargain. He would give up his free will and shed his humanity.

He would become God's errand boy.

6

Jason was a young man when he decided to go back to Hillcrest, going by way of the town that boasted one of the largest cathedrals on the West Coast—the same one that he and Matthew Shepherd had once visited.

The interior of the cathedral was a monument to gothic taste with elaborate tapestries on the walls and marble steps leading up to the high altar. A pulpit of carved granite overlooked the congregation below and waves of sunlight through the huge rose window at the rear washed over the pews. Thick granite columns held up the vaulted ceiling and more sunlight poured through the narrow lead glass windows behind the altar.

Shepherd and he had never gotten over their sense of awe and the feeling that the cathedral really was God's house.

Jason glanced around the cavernous space, wondering where the birds would build their nests when the windows had cracked and fallen and the doors had rotted and the cathedral was open to the air and the elements. They'd probably nest high up on the ledges where the pillars met the vault. The mahogany pews, if any still survived, would be stained white with the droppings of pigeons.

There would be no congregations—no people at all.

Jason tried to remember where the confessional had been—then saw it close by one of the pillars on the left hand side. He and Shepherd had once gone to confession there out of curiosity and Shepherd had come out flushed and worried. Jason had asked what he had confessed to and Shepherd wouldn't tell him though Jason had guessed: impious thoughts and too much playing with himself when his hands were in his pockets.

The green light was on, indicating that the priest was present, and Jason stepped in and knelt before the wooden latticework that hid the priest. There was a shuffling and the heavy breathing of a fat man making himself comfortable. Jason could smell his cup of coffee, laced with whiskey as it had been years before.

"Yes, my son?"

"I have no sins to confess, Father."

Jason could sense the sudden nervousness of the man behind the screen. He knew the priest was staring at him through the latticework, trying to remember. It was the first thing he'd said years before in a moment of bravado.

The minutes passed and finally the priest wheezed, "I remember you—the preacher boy." Then a half-drunken, bitter: "The antichrist. The one who is all sins."

"I'm an errand boy," Jason said.

Another long pause. Jason could feel the sudden fear of the priest.

"To tell us about the 'end of days,'" the priest said at last. "Whatever you say, you're lying."

"I don't lie," Jason said.

In a strained, slightly slurred voice: "I believe only in what the prophets say."

"All prophets are errand boys," Jason said. "We all do what God wants us to do."

He felt the priest shiver behind the screen. "And you have come to tell me about the 'end of days,'" he repeated.

"You're living in them," Jason murmured.

Another few moments of silence while the priest shifted uneasily behind the latticework. Jason stood up and quietly left the confessional. It was a hot day outside and he walked over to the shadow of a tree a few hundred yards away and looked back at the cathedral.

Inside, the cathedral had seemed huge, overpowering. But outside, with every step he took it diminished in size. A half mile away, the cathedral looked the size of a dollhouse, lost in the immensity of the world around it. The pigeons would have their way with it and so would the blistering sun

and winds and thunderstorms and someday dogs sniffing through the ruins
would wonder what had stood there.

It hadn't been a wasted day, Jason thought. He had given the priest a
cause and a sense of purpose that he probably hadn't had before. But strong
convictions frequently require little evidence and sometimes none at all.
Most miracles come cheap.

He hadn't lied to the priest. A messenger from God really had appeared
to tell him they were living in the "end of days." The priest would become
one of the anointed who thought they had seen a glimspe of the "end of
days" and could fill it with noble deeds and die happy martyrs.

It would be soon now, Jason thought. But he would have to hurry as
well as watch his back—the men following him were getting closer.

7

Jason was bone-tired and needed to stretch his legs. The highway curved
down close to the beach and he spotted a deserted beach chair on the
sands. He pulled over to the shoulder. He'd spend half an hour just sitting
in the beach chair watching the sun go down—it was warm enough, he
didn't need a jacket. He got out and eased into the chair, took off his shoes
and socks and dug his toes into the sand.

A hundred yards away an SUV was parked on the ocean side of the road
and fifty feet closer to the water was a small tent. A young family camping
out—older and they would've holed up in a motel with running water and
genuine beds.

Jason stretched out and watched the sun sinking toward the horizon. It
was a quiet night except for the squealing of two kids down by the water's
edge. A little boy and girl splashing around in the shallows.

The boy was shouting, the king in their game of Keep Away, the little
girl giggling and making short forays for the red ball the boy held. She
grabbed for it and he threw the ball over her head. A roller caught it
and the ball bounced down the beach and came to a stop a few feet in
front of Jason. The boy ran after it, then spotted Jason and stopped, his
eyes wide.

He stood staring at Jason for a full minute, then said: "What's your
name, mister?"

"Jason—what's yours?"

The boy clutched the ball and walked a few step closer, fascinated by

Jason. After a long moment he said, "My name's Forrest. My parents call me Willow—it's an old Indian name, I guess—after a tree."

Jason shook the boy's hand. "Pleased to meet you, Willow."

"What do you do?" the boy asked.

Jason smiled slightly. "I'm an errand boy."

The boy's sister walked up, equally wary, and they both stared at him. Forrest nodded at her. "My sister's name is Dot."

Jason formally shook her hand; he guessed she was a year younger than her brother.

"Hey, kids, leave the man alone."

Jason hadn't seen him approach; he'd been too intent on making friends with the boy and his sister. The man was tall, a few pounds heavier than Jason, his hair a lighter shade of red. He held out his hand.

"The kids belong to me. Name's Noah, like in the Ark." He glanced around. "You all alone out here?"

"Traveling by myself," Jason said. Friendly, he thought. But danger sometimes came in a friendly disguise.

"Why don't you come down and join us?" Noah said. "We've got a small grill and dinner is corn-in-the-husk, hamburgers, and shrimp—we managed to pick up some genuine ocean-caught shrimp in town. Got plenty enough to go 'round." He smiled. "The kids like you, which means you're not exactly a stranger. They're better than dogs when it comes to sizing up people."

It was tempting, Jason thought. An hour wouldn't hurt and it would take his mind off the men following him, though they were still a day behind. He picked up his shoes and socks, muscled up from the broken beach chair, and followed them. Behind the flap of the tent, a woman was slicing tomatoes for a salad.

"You look beat," Noah said. "Use a pick-me-up?"

"Easy on the booze," Jason said. Middle America, he thought. In a lot of ways they reminded him of the Scovills when he was living on the farm.

"We got company, Emmy." His wife was in her early thirties, a little on the plump side, her brown hair hidden beneath a bandana. She glanced up and smiled. "Nice to meet you—I'd shake your hand but right now I'm up to my elbows in ground beef."

Jason turned away, desperately afraid he was going to be sick. Emmy picked up on it immediately. "I'm sorry—you're a vegetarian, aren't you? You'll have to make do with potato salad, corn on the cob, and some nice greens."

"That'll be fine," Jason said.

There was a camp chair and Emmy nodded toward it. "Take a load off."

"What do you do?" Noah asked.

Jason hesitated. "I told the kids I was an errand boy. Not quite true. I help out the preacher in a Lutheran church in Grove. Maybe have my own church someday."

Their attitudes subtly changed and Jason realized he wasn't just a guest, he was now an honored guest.

"Never met a future minister before," Noah said. He hesitated. "We—ah—we don't call you 'Father' yet, do we?"

There was some splashing and squealing down by the oceanfront and Noah turned and shouted, "Hey, kids, stay away from that pier—probably got iron spikes sticking out and splinters that would cut you in two."

He poured himself two fingers of scotch and relaxed in another chair. "You got any kids, Jason? Don't suppose you do, you being a student preacher and all."

"Not married," Jason said, sipping at his glass. "Found the right girl but she died."

He didn't want to talk about Valerie.

"Sorry," Noah murmured. He glanced at his watch, then yelled: "Willow, Dot—we've just got time for a skinny-dip before dinner!" He turned to his wife. "Leave the food alone for a few minutes, Emmy, let's try the water." He glanced at Jason. "You want to join us, feel free."

Jason shook his head. "Don't have a suit."

"Neither do we," Noah said. "Go skinny-dipping every so often so the kids get used to seeing naked bodies and won't have any hang-ups about them."

Jason thought: Why not? He stripped down and a few minutes later was in the water, playing a game of water polo with the kids. He lost sight of Forrest and Dot for a moment, then felt Forrest squirming up his bare back shouting "Chickenfight! Chickenfight!" A little farther out, Dot had climbed up on Noah's shoulders and hooked her feet under his arms.

"Come and get me!" Forrest shouted. Jason and Noah obligingly waded a few feet closer to each other, making sure they didn't go too deep. When they got close enough, Forrest and Dot started grabbing for each other. Noah winked at Jason, they ducked suddenly and Willow and Dot ended up in the water at the same time, both giggling and splashing toward the beach. Noah laughed, picked up Dot and waded toward shore. Forrest was tugging at Jason so he bent down and carried the boy piggy-back.

They spent a few minutes drying off and snapping towels at each other.

It all felt good, Jason thought. Too good. Even better than at the farm where the Scovills were lovely people but he had no friends of his own. Human friends. He put on his clothes and folded himself into the spare camp chair.

Noah hadn't bothered to dress, just placed a towel across his groin and balanced a plate on top. He liked his hamburgers rare and Jason did his best to avoid looking at the blood.

"Emmy will have some coffee ready in a minute. Coffee okay?" Jason nodded and Noah let out a contented sign. "Weekends like this don't come often enough."

Lights had started to appear a good mile down the beach and light laughter and shouts floated over the water.

"I hope they don't come too close to us," Emmy said.

Noah sniffed. "Not likely. Smells like it might rain in another hour or so and then they'll hole up inside." He glanced at Jason, curious. "How'd you ever get into the religion business?"

"My stepfather was a street preacher."

"And you helped him out?" Noah was fascinated. Emmy looked more than interested and the two kids stared at him openmouthed. "You pass the hat?" Noah asked. "Beat on a drum to gather a crowd?"

"My stepmother did that," Jason said. He was easy with it now, there was nothing incriminating about it.

"You ever get to do any preaching?" Forrest asked, once again googgle-eyed.

"Sometimes," Jason said.

"What are you doing out here?" Noah asked.

Jason smiled. "I came out here for the same reason you did. Get away from things for a while."

Noah nodded. "You came to the right spot. We try and hit it twice a year—like to think it's our private beach."

Forrest had been rooting around in the picnic hamper and cried, "You forgot to bring any ice cream!"

"It'd be soup by now if I had," Noah said. He stood up and put on his pants. "I'll drive down to the 7-Eleven and get some."

"Chunky Monkey!" Dot insisted.

"Strawberry cheesecake!" Forrest added.

Jason pushed out of beach chair and said, "Let me go—I owe you something for the food."

Noah was tempted. "Hell, you're the guest but if you want to go . . ."

Jason's Honda coughed once but wouldn't start. Jason walked back to

Noah and said, "I'm not going anyplace after all. The Honda just crapped out."

Noah fished in his pocket and pulled out a key fob. "Take the SUV, I'll give you a jump in the morning. No problem—we've got a spare sleeping bag and another air mattress." He grinned. "Always bring along spares for strangers who might show up."

Jason climbed into Noah's car, put the keys in the ignition, then hesitated. He walked back to the Honda and grabbed his backpack off the front seat. He'd come this far babysitting it, he wasn't going to leave it now . . .

Once inside the crowded 7-Eleven, he couldn't remember the flavors that Dot and Forrest had wanted. Not that it made any difference, all that was left was old-fashioned strawberry and butter pecan. He bought a pint of each, then started back in the SUV. The meeting with Noah and his family was . . . pure pleasure.

Then Jason began to feel uneasy. Liking them was too dangerous for him . . . When he got back he'd give them the ice cream, then ask Noah for a jump start and get the hell out of there. When he got a hundred yards away and turned to look back, would they still be there? Or would they have vanished, like some sort of mirage? Maybe the whole encounter had been a test, like the Third Temptation of Christ . . .

He rolled the windows down to catch any errant breeze. When he was still a quarter mile away, he heard a muffled sound like small firecrackers going off. He'd heard it often enough in the Middle East training camps and in the action that followed.

He cut the motor and drifted to a stop just behind his Honda. There was another car on the shoulder, parked a hundred yards farther down.

Noah and his family had visitors.

The popping sound had cut off abruptly and he sat in the car for a long moment, smelling the night air. Mixed in with the faint nauseating stink of frying hamburgers and the smells of beer and spilled wine from the beach parties down the road was the faint, acrid odor of human blood. A lot of it.

He got out of the SUV, careful not to slam the door, and walked silently over to the other car. The empty car was unlocked but on the backseat were two styrofoam containers of half-eaten dinners. He wrinkled his nose, the usual menu at the camps.

Nothing else was in the car or in the glove compartment. Somebody else had to be in charge.

He found the other car around a bend in the road, where it couldn't be seen. Clean interior, the keys still in the ignition. A small plastic ID tag hanging from them was stamped USDC—M. MELLORS. #35. The number had to be the number of the car in the company fleet.

He studied it for a long moment. Contractor group, action agency. He remembered them vaguely from Iraq. Somebody stateside had hired them and now they were local, operating in the United States.

Looking for him.

No surprise, every security agency in the country was probably looking for him by now.

He walked back and looked down at Noah's tent. There was a lantern on the inside and he could see the shadow of somebody moving around. One person.

He opened the door of his Honda, loosened his belt and placed it on the backseat. He took off his shirt and pants and when he was naked, folded his clothes neatly and placed them on the seat with his belt. They were his only clothes and didn't want to get them bloody.

He looked again at the tent below, then opened the Honda's glove compartment, took out a small roll of fine nylon twine and slipped it over his arm. The bread knife he took from beneath the front seat and strapped to his bare leg.

He was now ready for wet work.

8

It was a long time since Mellors had hid in a ditch—not since Iraq. But it was a warm night and he didn't have to worry about roadside bombs or ragheads crawling up behind him, though two domesticated ones had been assigned to him.

He'd watched the movement around the little tent close to the ocean for an hour. Two men, a woman, and a couple of kids. One of the men had to be Hendrix; for sure it was his Honda parked this side of the road.

He had been lucky as shit. The FBI guys would never have found Hendrix and his Honda. Too little money to work with. They tried to appeal to the patriotism of the people they talked to but money always spoke louder than words.

He had finally tailed Hendrix to this neck of the woods but this "neck of the woods" wasn't small. The dirtbag who ran a used car lot had said yes, the FBI photograph of Hendrix looked like the guy who'd just bought an old blue Honda.

Where was he going? The owner shrugged. "He didn't tell me. Last I saw of him he was taking the beach road up north."

Mellors copied down the license number and he and the Arabs trolled along the road for an hour looking for an old blue Honda. Just as he was driving out of a Denny's lot, Mellors got lucky. An old blue Honda was leaving and turning out on the coast road heading north. Mellors followed, staying a few hundred yards behind. He was surprised when Hendrix—he was absolutely sure it was him, the car matched and so did the plates—pulled over and stopped on the shoulder. Then Hendrix got out to walk down to the beach and crap out in a battered beach chair.

There was a bend in the road and Mellors parked several hundred feet up where he couldn't be seen from the Honda. It was dusk and clouds and fog were rolling in, which was as much cover as he would have unless he waited until midnight.

He finally noticed what he should have seen immediately—an SUV parked on the sand a few hundred feet down from the road. It was dark-colored and blended in with the drifting shadows. A little ways away was a small, khaki-colored tent. Mellors lay flat on the road and watched the people around it. A man and his wife and two kids. The boy hit a ball toward the seated Hendrix, then he and a little girl—his sister?—walked up and started talking. A moment later the man joined them and they all walked over to the tent. Mellors swore to himself. Father, mother, two kids, and now they had a houseguest.

It was going to be a long night. The clouds were thicker now and it was getting a little chilly. Mellors pulled his jacket up around his face and watched the tent in disgust. Five million Euros of bounty money, dead or alive, was down there and he couldn't touch it. What was Hendrix going to do—spend the night?

Mellors huddled in the shadows of the ditch and yawned once, then again. He woke suddenly when he heard a car start and looked up to see the SUV pull over on the road and head north toward the next town. The family had left, probably to see a movie. But the Honda was still there and there was still a light on in the tent.

Hendrix was all alone.

Mellors was wide awake now. He nudged the two Arabs and told them to go down to the beach and if they saw any college kids walking along the oceanfront with their girlfriends and a case of beer to chase them away. A mile up the beach, the parties were in full swing and the college types who didn't have a room would be looking for a spot on the sands to shed their

Speedos and ball their brains out. The Arabs would look like two body-guards for some rich bastard who'd claimed a chunk of the beach for his own.

The Arabs squirmed down the ditch for a hundred yards, then padded quickly across the road to disappear into the shadows from the clouds scudding across the moon. Mellors wasn't even sure they had actually been in the Pakistan camps with Hendrix, they'd probably heard about the reward money and would have sworn they'd spent months trekking across the sands with Muhammad.

Mellors give them time enough to get to the beach, then figured this was it. The SUV hadn't returned. He took his automatic and a duffel bag full of camera equipment and walked silently across the sands. He stopped a few feet away from the tent, watching the moving shadow within.

He was ready to crash through the tent flap when it occurred to him there was an easier way to do this. He lifted his pistol, got off one shot and watched the shadow fall. Anybody hear anything in the parties down the beach, it was just an early Fourth of July firecracker.

He waited a moment but the shadow didn't move. He whistled to himself, pushed the tent flap to one side and walked in. The body was lying on its side, a pool of red flowing around its face. Damn good shot, one bullet through the tent wall and he'd caught Hendrix right in the temple. He hadn't lost his touch; his years in Iraq had been great training.

He put down the bag and pulled out the camera equipment so he could take photographs to confirm the kill. A battery lantern to highlight the face, a Nikon with a tripod and zoom lens for a sharp-focus head shot. Hendrix's hair was a little lighter and he looked several pounds heavier than in the FBI photograph but hell, the photograph was a couple of years old by now. Mellors was sweating and took off his jacket and gunbelt and tossed them to the side of the tent. He finished setting up for the shot and moved the body so its face was turned toward the camera, then took a rag and wiped away some of the blood.

Oh, Jesus . . .

He crouched on one knee for a good minute, trying to catch his breath and control his heartbeat.

He'd just killed a stranger.

He was still staring at the body when he heard a soft, *"Oh, my God . . ."*

He whirled. The rest of the family. The wife and the two kids, both about six years old, both of them staring first at him and then down at the body and both of them peeing in their shorts.

It was a thirty-second tableau, then the little girl started to scream. They were witnesses, Mellors thought, and scrambled for his gunbelt.

He'd have to cover, he thought a few moments later, he had to think of something . . . And then: who the hell were these people?

He rummaged through the tent and found a purse and a man's fanny pack. The purse held a driver's license—Emmy Weinberg. The man's pack had a matching license for her husband, Noah. The kids. He didn't know their names, then spotted a small pile of children's dirty underwear in the corner. Name tags were stitched into the waistbands. Willow and Dot. Cute.

Hendrix had gone swimming with them, he'd eaten dinner with them. Since he wasn't there and the family was, chances were he had taken the SUV into town—probably because his junker of a Honda had coughed its last. Pick up some marshmallows for roasting in a campfire, something like that.

And there he was, sitting in a tent in the middle of a circle of bodies like he'd never left Iraq. How could he explain what happened?

Then he decided it was really simple.

Tell the USDC and the DOD the truth. He'd had every reason to think that the family had taken the SUV into town and Hendrix had been left behind alone. Mellors had seen somebody moving around in the tent and fired through the tent wall, shooting Noah Weinberg by mistake. What was he supposed to do, walk up and introduce himself? Hendrix was a homicidal maniac, you took as few risks as possible.

He'd shot Weinberg in error and when the rest of the family showed up a few moments later, he'd panicked and shot them as well.

Murder one.

But Hendrix was probably due to return any moment, Mellors thought. He'd call the two Arabs back and wait. When Hendrix walked in, he'd terminate him and become a hero in the eyes of the USDC and the DOD. Plus he'd be five million euros richer.

The Weinbergs?

Collateral damage. It happened in every war.

He was intent on his camera work and never heard the SUV coast to a stop on the road above.

9

Jason walked along the shoulder of the road nearest the ocean—the sandy side—searching for where Mellors and the two Arabs must have crossed.

Almost directly opposite the small tent, he found three sets of footprints in the sand. A hundred feet farther down, the footprints diverged and headed for the beach, flanking the tent. There were none returning.

The third set of footprints led directly to the tent. Again, there were none returning. Mellors. The man from USDC, the man in charge.

Jason felt the cold growing in his chest again. Emmy and the two kids had been treasure-hunting on the beach and Noah had been in the tent arranging the sleeping bags.

How many shots had he heard? First one muffled shot, followed a few minutes later by three more.

While Jason was watching, a camera flash went off in the tent. Then another. Mellors taking photographs of the scene to back up whatever story he offered later.

Mellors would be there awhile but Jason didn't want the two Arabs to show up as reinforcements. He walked quietly down to the beach where the Arabs would be playing at being guards. It was a training exercise—how many times had he practiced it in the camps? Sneak up on the enemy encampment but take care of the guards first.

He kept to the shadows of the old pier, watching the beach as brief patches of moonlight moved along it. He paused when he saw a darker shadow sitting on a driftwood log, staring out at the ocean.

Jason swung up to the top of the pier and inched his way toward the end. He wondered if he knew the guard, if they had met at the camps. Maybe they had been friends—except nobody at the camps had any friends. They came from different countries, spoke different languages, had their own interpretation of the Qur'an.

The guard was a few yards from the end of the rotting pier and Jason hid in the shadows as he crept along. When he ran out of pier, he loosened the roll of nylon twine from around his wrist and cupped the pebbles he'd picked up in his other hand.

Another patch of moonlight and he tossed a pebble so it landed between the pier and the guard. The Arab lurched to his feet and turned to face the shadowy pier. He took his long knife out of its sheath and warily approached the rotting wooden supports, crying "Who is there?" in broken English.

Jason froze as the guard poked around the garbage and the driftwood below. Just in time he stretched on his side along one of the pier's surface planks when the guard flashed his lantern at the pier bottom. After a few moments, the guard grunted and turned to leave.

Now!

Jason stood up and dropped a noose of nylon cord around the Arab's neck, threw another loop around what was left of a nearby bollard, and yanked.

The guard's feet flew out from under him and he dropped his lantern and knife to try and pull the noose away from his throat. He kicked at the air and tried to scream but the fine twine had already cut halfway through his windpipe.

Jason gave a final yank and twisted the line tight around the bollard. In a moment the guard was dangling there, his feet free of the sand, still staring at the ocean.

Jason slipped down from the pier just as a patch of moonlight lit the Arab's face. The executioner's apprentice, the one who wielded the sword in the beheadings that were filmed at the camps. There was a fading light of recognition in his eyes and Jason said, "Good-bye, Selim," and continued down the beach.

One down, two to go.

The other Arab was taking his job seriously, holding his lantern with one hand and his knife with the other, turning to the north for a minute, then looking south, and finally staring up toward the road to catch anybody walking down to the beach.

Jason could see patches of moonlight coming and when they got closer, flattened himself on the sand. What you looked for was movement, when a rock that had been forty feet away was now only twenty.

The moment came almost as quick as Jason thought about it. He caught a frown on the Arab's face, then was caught in the dazzling beam of light from his lantern. Jason was already on his feet. He ran toward the Arab, hit him in the midsection, and both knife and lantern went flying. The Arab tried to shout for help, then started coughing when Jason threw a handful of sand in his face.

Jason grabbed the Arab around the waist to throw him down on the sand and realized his mistake as soon as he attempted it. The Arab was a stocky man, with thick strong legs. He wasn't going to go down easily.

Jason slid down his thighs and grabbed his ankles and rolled. Another mistake. The Arab fell on top of him and momentarily had the advantage. Jason buried a stiff two fingers in the Arab's stomach and twisted and the man grunted and let go, then tried to run up the sand toward the tent. There was a small sewer stream running from the road down to the ocean; the Arab didn't see it, slipped on a rock and Jason leaped on top of him.

The holds he'd learned in wrestling came back with a rush. He hooked an arm behind the Arab's right arm and cupped his hand around the head and straightened up. You could break a neck that way but again, too thick a neck.

The Arab broke the grip, staggered back a foot, and Jason hit him in the stomach with his shoulder. The Arab went down, landing in the stream. Jason flipped him in the water, wrapping his legs around the Arab's waist and holding him facedown in the sewage.

The Arab swallowed and water flooded his lungs. He heaved convulsively and in a moment was still, facedown in the water.

Jason started to walk away, then noticed a lump in the Arab's rear pocket. A tiny gun, useless at any distance but deadly for short range. The USDC had failed to check its mercenaries for small arms. Jason held the gun in one hand, the Arab's battery lantern, turned off, in the other and started up the sand.

There was no longer a light inside the tent.

Mellors was through taking photographs but Jason had heard no car start from the road above. Mellors had probably left his camera equipment behind and walked down to the beach to get his Arabs.

Jason slipped into the tent, shielding the light from his lantern with a jacket hanging from the tent pole. Mellors hadn't moved the bodies nor bothered to cover their faces. A look of despair was etched on Emmy's, fear on Willow's and Dot's.

Jason killed the lantern and started walking down the sandy slope outside. Both he and Mellors had to be on the same stretch of sand between the ocean and the tent. Bad news, Jason thought, but not for him. His time in the camps had taught him how to maneuver in complete darkness.

He stood stock-still and listened for minutes, figuring that Mellors was doing the same. But he could stand like that until morning and he was willing to bet that Mellors couldn't.

It was half an hour before he picked up the sound of feet trying to shuffle noiselessly through the sand. Not that far away and to his left.

Jason abruptly turned on his lantern and lobbed it to his right at shoulder height. It never hit the ground. Mellors shot at it several times, then flicked on his own lantern to see what he'd hit.

Jason shot him then, once in the arm so he couldn't fire his automatic again, and once in his lower leg so he couldn't run. Mellors dropped his lantern and Jason walked over and picked it up, kicking Mellors's hand away when he grabbed at him. He turned the lantern on so it shone directly into Mellors's eyes.

"You're blinding me," Mellors said.

"The better to see you with," Jason said. Then: "How much did they pay you?"

"I don't have to tell you anything," Mellors said, his eyes following Jason, looking for an opening if only he could move.

Jason took his knife and slit Mellors's shirt, leaving a thin red line on his chest.

"I'm curious," Jason said.

Mellors hesitated and Jason waved his bread knife again, now lightly streaked wiith blood.

"Five million," Mellors grunted. "In euros."

One and a quarter million euros each for Noah and Emmy, Willow and Dot.

Jason glanced at the ocean. It would be easy to wash up.

He looked back at Mellors and thought of the Scovills, Jasper, and Paul—his best friend from Reno, when he had finally left Hillcrest. Paul had gone to fight in Iraq and came back a month later in a pine box. Then of Valerie and the needle-stick injury that had killed her. She had been going to blow the whistle on Blake Pharmaceutical, to warn the world. He'd wanted to tell her she was too smart to be that naïve.

He had wanted to give up the bargain when he'd met Noah and Emmy, Willow and Dot. But two hours after meeting them, he knew it would have been a mistake. His life had been full of lessons. That was the last one.

He took a step toward Mellors, holding the bread knife out and to his right.

"This won't be quick," he said.

He was still human enough to take pleasure in revenge.

10

It was a warm Sunday morning in Hillcrest and Jason had chosen a spot on the wooden bench where the sunlight would hit his face. He was wearing shades and had on his backpack; he doubted anybody would recognize him. He ran a hand over the cloth of the pack and could feel the small vial that Valerie had given him. She had been very angry—her life for the world's, she'd said.

He hooked his arms over the back of the bench and watched the congregation as it straggled into the white-steepled church. The parishoners were mostly middle-aged and older, many with children—he was sorry about that. There were very few young singles.

It was a wealthy congregation, the kind that went to white steepled churches in this country and huge granite monuments overseas. The men wore linen suits and you could see your face in their shoes. The women favored print dresses with high necklines. They would smell of various lotions and perfumes—one of the many things that set them apart from other animals. The kids were dressed to the nines, the boys in miniature suits, the girls in starched dresses and white shoes. All of them looked uncomfortable and probably wished they were somewhere else.

Those who had showed up for the services would sit well forward and most of the pews in back would be empty—it was a beautiful summer day and God had too much competition. Who wanted to listen to somebody's droning interpretation of the Bible when they could be at a picnic or playing tennis or swimming at the beach?

Something was tugging at his pants leg and he glanced down. A squirrel was chittering up at him. He draped his jacket over his arm and the squirrel ran up it and sat on his shoulder, nuzzling against his neck.

"Got nothing for you, little beast—left all the nuts at home." He touched it lightly behind the ears, then under the chin. It preened up at him, rolling over so he could stroke its belly.

"Same to you, little brother."

Several pigeons fluttered overhead, finally sitting on the top of the bench next to him.

Some of the parishoners looked at him, curious, then continued into the church. The minister had been greeting them at the door and occasionally glanced his way. When everybody was inside, he walked over and smiled at Jason.

"You coming in, son?"

"Maybe a little later."

The minister looked disappointed but managed another smile. "I've never seen any of the squirrels so friendly before. You're a regular Saint Francis of Assisi, aren't you?"

"Never met the man," Jason said.

The minister's smile faded. He turned and continued into the church. The doors closed behind him and a moment later Jason heard the swelling tones of the organ and the congregation singing the doxology. He muttered the words to himself and shook his head in wonder. In a few weeks it would all be over but none of them would be able to figure out why it was happening. Perhaps a few of the truly religious would connect the dots but it was much too late to do anything about it. Generations too late.

An hour slowly passed. The occasional bird landed on Jason's shoulder, pecked at his ear, then flew off. Inside the church there was the subdued murmur of the minister's voice and from time to time the response of the congregation. After the final "hallelujah" the doors swung open and people started to leave. Most of them paused to shake the hand of the minister, who had stationed himself just outside the door, and tell him what a wonderful sermon he'd given. Jason wondered how many of them had slept through it.

The minister looked his way once, went back inside and the doors were closed. They wouldn't be locked, Jason thought. There were always those who wanted to stay and pray in solitude. He gave the squirrel a final stroke and stood up. It was time.

The inside of the church looked like a small, decorated cave. The high vaulted ceiling, the wooden pews with hymnals stuck in the railings in back, the carpet down the center aisle . . . He liked the silence, the emptiness, the aloneness. There was even the standard old lady close to the front and a middle-aged couple halfway back, on their knees in the pew and praying quietly.

Jason walked up the center aisle until he stood in front of the altar and a large statue of Jesus on the cross. He looked at it for a long time. Jesus had been the first of the errand boys, followed by a steady stream of saints and prophets.

He would be the last one.

He stared a moment longer at the wooden Jesus, then turned to leave. *Now it's my turn.*

*Author's note: This story, extensively rewritten, is based on material in an unpublished novel with the same title—*The Errand Boy.

Afterword

Freddy Pohl was my first agent and sold my first dozen or so short stories, cementing my opinion of myself as a "writer." (Excuse the affectionate diminutive but we go back more than fifty years and I think I'm entitled. He can call me "Frankie" any time he wants to.)

Fond memories include the time at a convention when Fred, who owed me for a story, pulled out two hundred-dollar bills from his wallet. It was the very first time I had ever seen a Franklin. Another fond memory is when I brainstormed a story for Bill Hamling, then editor of *Amazing Stories*. Knowing the editors there always changed the titles of stories they bought, I simply called it "Untitled Story" and let it go at that.

Some time later, on leave from the navy, I picked up the latest issue of *Astounding* and there it was—"Untitled Story." (John W. Campbell Jr., the editor, hadn't bothered to change the title either.) Campbell had needed a twelve-thousand-word short badly and Fred saw the hole and promptly filled it—at three times what *Amazing* would have paid.

But my memories and respect for Fred go far beyond the commercial. At the age of twenty-one, he became the editor of *Astonishing Stories* and *Super Science*, the youngest editor in the science fiction field since Charles D. Hornig ascended to the throne at *Wonder Stories* at the age of seventeen. After the war, Fred edited several other science fiction magazines (*Galaxy, Worlds of If*, et cetera), collaborated with almost every science fiction writer of the period, including his friend Cyril Kornbluth (*Gravy Planet*, et cetera) and Jack Williamson (*Undersea Quest* and other juveniles) and hit the really big time with his solo efforts of the Heechee novels, the first of which—*Gateway*—won the Hugo, the Nebula, and the John W. Campbell Memorial (thus tying Lance Black for his screenplay for *Milk*, which won every award out there).

Somehow he found the time to be president of the Science Fiction Writers of America. And did I mention that he wrote the definitive article on the Roman emperor Tiberius for . . . the *Encyclopedia Britannica*?

Freddy's an easy man for me to envy—if I'd had his energy and talent, I wouldn't have needed mine.

—FRANK M. ROBINSON

GENE WOLFE

❎

KING RAT

Well, honey, I saw the elephants and that was the start of it. I'd heard about them only I'd never seen any before, so I hid and watched them swinging along the street. I counted them, too, counting with chunks of cement when I ran out of fingers. Two tens and three was what it was, only after the first ten there started to be people, too, keeping in their shadows, just one here and one there and staying down so you knew they didn't want the spiders to see them.

No, they weren't walking fast at all. They had to step over things all the time, and go around them, too, and hold on to the tail of the one in front, you know how they do, and all that slowed them down. It wasn't hard for the people to keep up at all.

Well, honey, I should've gone with the last elephant, and I knew it, only I was scared and it took me a time to get my guts up. Then I ran from one place to the next one, keeping to the shadows as much as I could. That's how you do. I know I've told you before, but it's how you do and don't you never forget it.

It took me a long time to catch up, but I did because they went clear out of the city. That was where we lived then, in the city. There had been buildings and houses for us there once, only the spiders broke it, I don't know why, and smashed everything down flat after. Edwards, he knew the name of it and told me one time, only I don't remember it. It never seemed right to me that the city should have a name like it was a woman. Only Edwards, he had known it when it was still alive, see? So what was just the city to me was Minny or whatever the name was to Edwards, only she was dead.

Well, honey, I'd never been out of the city before and it scared the shit out of me. I wanted to go back and go back quick, only there were two or three reasons not to. One was that there was so much to see out there, like great big bushes that grew on top of big tall posts. You know what a bush is?

That's right, like a broom upside down only green. A bush is alive, too, like grass, only it can't move—just stay right where it is and grow. I used to cut sticks off them to clean my teeth. Quite a few of us did that.

The other one was that the shadows were getting long, you know, honey? Like when lights are turned down and there is only this one light a long ways away. Back then all of us had just the one light, really. The sun was what everybody called it, and it was way up overhead, way too far for anybody to touch, ever.

No, not even if I climbed up on something. It was big and bright and we couldn't turn it off. Or turn it on, either. Back before the spiders, people had made these little lights you could shake. That was the way you fed them, and when you'd shaken them enough you could turn them on to see things, and turn them off, too, when you didn't want the things to see you. I used to have one, only it broke.

Well, honey, the sun wasn't like that. Not at all. It turned itself on and it rolled across the dome so the spiders could see into all the dark places and look for us. Only when it got to the other side it went out, and then it was our turn. We could go all around and they couldn't see us hardly at all unless we lit cook fires. Which we had to do, you see, when we had something that had to be cooked. Mostly that was one of us. We killed each other and ate the meat a lot more there than we do here, because there wasn't as much to eat there. Nowhere near like here. If you went out looking when there was lots of sunshine—that was light from the big light way up—the spiders would get you, probably. Only if you went out looking when it was dark, somebody else would.

If you went out by yourself, it was really, really tough, because it could be five or six of them, sometimes a family or just friends. I got away from that many two or three times, but it was never easy.

So that was another reason not to go back. I'd be in strange parts after dark, and it was the way lots of people got jumped.

Only the main thing was I was hungry. It was going to be poison hard to get something to eat back in the city and probably I wouldn't. And I figured that there had to be food where the elephants were going or the others wouldn't be following them. I was right, too.

Out there past where the city had been, there was a spider boat. It was this one we're on right now, only you can't ever understand how big it was. It was bigger than the whole city and higher than the dome, and it sparkled everywhere just like broken glass in the sun.

Well, sure, honey. If I'd have thought, I would've known you'd never seen broken glass. Only I've seen a lot of it, and it was the thing I thought of when I saw that spider boat. Ever since then, I've been wondering how it looks at night, because it wasn't night yet when I saw it. I bet it looks the way the stars do, only you've never seen them either. There's a place where you can see them. I'll show it to you as soon as I've got the time.

Say you and me were out in the grass country, and we went to the river, up toward the clean part where there aren't any lizards, or not many, anyhow. And say you dipped up some water and threw it in the air so the light hit it. On the outside, this spider boat looks like that only a million million times bigger and more sparkly. It seemed like it went up forever, and spread out bigger than the city, like I said, and the bottom of it was sunk down into the dirt by the weight of the top, so I couldn't really see how big it was.

And the elephants went in there, up a big bridge that hadn't been smashed at all, still holding each other's tails. You know how they do. They walked so far through the boat that I was ready to quit, and I saw a lot of stuff that looked good anyway. Some did quit—

Yeah, elephants will do anything the spiders tell them to do. They're only animals, honey, but they're not just animals either. The river lizards are just animals and they don't hear the spiders. Neither do the dogs.

Back in the city we had dogs and they could be bad. But we'd catch them and eat them whenever we could, so there wasn't hardly any left. The grass-country dogs are bigger and meaner than ours ever were, and trying to kill them is a real good way to get hurt. I saw one bite right through a spear once.

That's right, I went in with the elephants and so did the other people. We went quite a ways inside the boat, then through a big door into the grass country. It was dark in there, and I'll tell you I didn't like that one bit. It wasn't because I was scared of the dogs or the lions. I didn't know about either one yet. I wasn't scared of the elephants either. They'd let us walk real close, keeping in their shadows, so it didn't seem likely they were going to do anything much to me. No, it was the people that scared me. See, I figured they'd be hungry.

That was pretty much how it was, too. I came on three of them, and started talking like I was one of them, hoping they'd be friends, that we could all go looking through the grass for something to eat, and water, too.

It was a man and two women, and when they saw me and saw the shine of my knife—it wasn't as dark as this in there then, and their eyes had got used to it—they went right along. Not saying we were all together, but talking like it. Then two more came up, and I wasn't too sure, so I backed off a little. After that, the biggest man you ever saw came, and more with him. They hadn't hardly gotten there when they tried to get behind me, and I ran.

Two were after me just like a couple of arrows, only we didn't have arrows then. Here I've got to stop and go back and tell you about the big man. His name was Kazi, only I never found it out until after I killed him. When I was talking to him, I told him what a nice place I thought he had here and how I'd bring him three more, all women, from the city tomorrow. It was the sort of stuff I always said when I was trying to get away, only I could make a real good pitch for it, make it sound like these women were real and they'd come if I said everything was cool. I didn't think it would go over with him, only it seemed like I ought to try it.

Yeah, that's right. Mostly right, anyway.

Only when I saw those guys slipping off I knew it was time to go. What I didn't know was how fast two of them were—first thing I knew, they were so close I could hear them sucking air.

Then I tripped. It was lucky, I guess, because both of them fell over me, only I'd lost my knife when I fell. One stabbed the other one thinking he was me, and I hid in the grass. Pretty soon the third one came, and they helped the stabbed man up and promised him they wouldn't eat him unless he died. I don't know if he believed them, but I didn't.

I hunted around through the grass after that looking for my knife. It took me a long, long time and I kept thinking that pretty soon it would be light again. Only it wasn't, and I finally found it. Just before that, I heard a lion roar. He was still roaring off and on when I found it.

Sure I do—Hack drew it there for me. Lions have always been lucky for me. Sometimes I think maybe it's lions and me like it's elephants and spiders. You remember when there was this one lioness that was killing us? I said all right we've gotta kill her and I want five men brave enough to help me. I sort of hoped all the men would volunteer, you know? But I only got four.

The five of us went off anyway, and when we were alone I told them, okay, we're the Lion Friends. You're special, all four of you. Stick with me and nothing bad is going to happen to you, ever. We did the handgrip thing and swore, and off we went.

Yeah, you're right, honey. I told you about running away from Kazi, right. And finding my knife in the grass, right? Well, I felt pretty good about things then, only I was still hungry and it seemed like it would be light soon and I wouldn't be the only one in sight. Night is worse than day out there in the grass country, only I didn't know that yet.

I was sort of cussing my knife inside for being lost so long and making me waste all that time when I heard something moving through the grass. I stopped right where I was and listened, and after a while I sort of crouched down. For a long, long time I didn't hear it again. Then I did. It was big, I could tell that, and moving really, really slow. Only it was so big it couldn't help making some noise when it moved.

No, not its feet. It was just pushing the grass to one side that I heard. The grass whispered every time it did that, and there wasn't any way to stop it.

At first I thought it was probably an elephant. Only by that time I had a pretty good idea of where it was—what direction, I mean. I knew it was close, too. I just didn't know how close. But when I looked in that direction I couldn't see a thing. Even little elephants are really big, and the dome was getting light by then. I was pretty sure I'd be able to see an elephant, even a little one quite a ways off.

After a while I got a good fix on how far it was, too, and it was close. Really, really close. So I thought it was probably good to eat, and if it came close enough for me to see it I'd kill it and have something to eat.

The big round snout of it came first, and it was just light enough by then for me to see the teeth. Their lips don't cover their teeth right. I hope you don't ever see one so close you can notice that.

I jumped and it charged. It knocked me off my jump so I fell in the grass, but I bounced up quick and ran before it figured out where I was.

That's right, it was a river lizard. The big ones come up out of the water when it gets dark and hunt along the shore if they're real hungry. The little ones don't do it, because they know the big ones will eat them if they catch them. They're a lot like people, those river lizards.

The thing was, I was close to the river, and I hadn't even known it. That's not a good place to be any time, but when it's dark it's the worst place in the boat. Well, honey, I wanted a drink of water almost as much as I wanted something to eat, but that river water looked dirty and stunk, so I just backtracked it instead. I'd like to say here how smart I was, but the truth was that the thing I was most afraid of was going in circles. If I did that, I'd find myself back with Kazi and those guys. Only I figured that if I followed the river it would never circle back.

What I hadn't figured on, was that the water would clear up, but I sure was glad to see it. When I thought about it, I saw that the spiders must pump it out up there in the hills, and filter it when it gets where it's going, and maybe even boil it or something. Anyway, I had a drink and it was pretty good. After a while, when I'd walked quite a bit and was getting hot, I had another one that was even cooler and better than the first one. By that time the water was so clear I could see there weren't any river lizards hanging around in it. There weren't any on the bank either.

So I got in and had a nice swim, like I used to swim in the lake back home when it was summer and the weather got hot. That could be pretty dangerous back home, and probably it was dangerous where I was, too, only I didn't see any dogs or anything.

Those dogs are worse than lions, and don't you forget it. If a lion decides to go for you, she'll come right at you. But—

Well, I said *she* because it's nearly always the girl lions that do it. Like that one I was telling you about that me and my Lion Friends hunted. We found her, too, and some younger females with her, and cubs, and one big black-maned male. He just stared at us, but I knew what he was saying. I always do, nearly, with lions. He said, *I don't want any trouble, but if you start some I'll finish it.* So I told him we didn't want any either, but one of his girls had killed three of us, and that was the trouble. The other guys, my Lion Friends, looked at me like I was crazy. But I knew the big male had understood me. He had blinked, and I know what that means when a lion does it.

The females were snarling a little, and those that had cubs were trying to get them out of way. I went up to the one we were hunting then and told her she had to stop killing us or we'd have to kill her. I said I knew it made her feel young again. I understood that, but it had to stop just the same. So what was it? Stop killing us or die today?

She stared at me, and then she nodded and turned away. That meant it was over. I relaxed, and so did the lions. My friends had their spears and shields up, though. I had to tell them it was over and we could relax and go home. After a while one said I had talked to the lioness only she hadn't never talked to me. I said yes she did, she promised to stop killing people. That shut them up for a while, then one said how do we know she'll keep her promise? And I explained that she was bound to keep it, she was a lion. And she did, too.

Fine, let's get back to that. I wasn't trying to get out, just trying to find something to eat. You know about the deer and goats, and the striped ones that are sort of like horses, and they're all good to eat. Only I didn't see any then, and I don't think I could have gotten one if I had.

What happened was that the hills got bigger, and there were cliffs, and after I'd walked a long, long way, I came to the end, the place where the river started. It ran out of a cliff there, and if you looked careful you could see a door beside it, a great big door big enough for a spider. It was painted to look like rock, and a good job too. Only it wasn't really rock, it was metal, and the spider that had gone through it last hadn't closed it all the way. There was a little crack, like, that I could squeeze through.

So I did, and when I had I was in a tunnel, like underground, only it was in the boat. I knew there'd be spiders and they'd get me if they could, so I went fast until it opened out, and when it opened out it was a food place with the boxes and things hung up where you couldn't get at them. You know how they do. It smelled good in there, so I cut open a few boxes. I think it was three, but it was a long time ago and I can't be sure. Could have been four or even five. Finally I found one that had food in it, the kind we call "meal" because we pretty often make a meal of it.

I was hungry and ate a lot, and then I was thirsty. I thought I'd run back along that tunnel and go out into the grass country and drink from the river. Only that time I noticed something I had been too scared to see before. You could turn off into a place where a lot of noise was, and see the river getting born right there. Big pipes, you know, and water running out of them and all running together until all the water ran out through a hole that I knew had to go out into the grass country. So I could get a drink right there and I did.

I slept and ate some more, and it took me a long time to find my way out of the boat, but I did that, too. And when I did, I went back inside and got some really good food to take with me.

Why? Well, honey, you'd know if you'd just think about it. I was all alone in there, but I had friends back in the city. You're always a lot safer if there's people around you that know you. I had some friends, and there was this girl, and I figured I'd bring them all in. So back I went, with the food wrapped up in a kind of paper the spiders have that you can eat.

Everybody was gone. Irene, Edwards, all of them. I looked and looked and about got myself killed, only I never did find them—or find out what had happened to them, either. Then I found another girl, really young and about starved. I was hungry again myself by then, so I said, hey look at all this good stuff I got here. You give me what I want and I'll give you as much of this as you can eat. Naturally she said I had to give her some food first, and that was when I surprised her. I said, sure, sit down. Here it is, only I get some, too.

So she did and ate until I thought she'd bust, and didn't stop until everything was gone. Only I'd been eating, too, and I was bigger. I didn't eat as much as she did, but I ate one hell of a lot. There's nothing like sharing with somebody who's about starved to make you eat everything in sight.

So then she lay down and everything, and that decided me. I had about decided already, but that nailed it down. I said, you stand up and come with me. I said you had to give me what I wanted, and what I want is for you to come along with me to a place I'm going to show you where you won't ever be hungry again. That last wasn't quite true, we've been hungry a time or three, only I thought it was true when I said it so I wasn't lying.

Sure, I took her back to the spider boat, and brought her in with me. I showed her some food, and told her she could stick with me or split. I couldn't watch her all the time and I wasn't going to try. If she split, that was okay, I'd said she could. Only I knew my way around, she'd seen that a couple times on the way to the boat, and even if she did (because she'd said she did, too) a friend with a knife never hurts.

She said she'd stick, so then I said, "Fine. I'm all for that. Now if we stay here where the food is, pretty soon a spider is going to come along and see we've been eating it and start looking for us. Moving the big boxes and the round things and all this stuff. Maybe he doesn't find us the first time, okay? But the next time he might bring somebody to help. We'd have to get out, or we're meat. So what I say is, I'm going where the water is. I know where there's plenty of water, good clean cool water that's good for drinking and swimming, too. I don't think they come there a lot, and there's no way they could tell we were drinking their water because it's running downhill anyhow. So that's where I'm going. If you're really going to stick, just come along."

She did, so I took her out to the grass country, down the river just far enough that we were out of sight of the door. Spiders walk quiet, but I had the notion that the door opening was bound to make a noise, and shutting a lot more. I wanted to be close enough to hear them both, but not so close that a spider would see us as soon as it stuck its eyes out. They've got eight eyes. I know you've never been close enough to count them, but I have. It's eight, just like the legs, only some little and some big.

Maybe you saw this one coming, but I didn't. Somebody closed that door. We'd found a hole in the rocks that made us pretty safe. If anything wanted to get at us, there was only one way it could. We'd collect dry stuff, dead grass and bushes, and make a fire at the opening. Not a big one, a little one that didn't smoke. It gave us light to see anything trying to get in, and it was something anything that tried to get in had to dodge to do it.

So we were pretty safe in there, only we didn't have a lot of food. We'd got some while the door was still open and piled it in back. That was good, but it didn't last. We tried to find something else, and did sometimes, but what we needed was another way to get back to where the meal was and the rest of it. We looked and looked, but we didn't have any luck with it.

Getting in where the water came out would have been great, but it goes too fast.

Finally I told her there had been other people on the grass, lower down where things flattened out. They had come in the way the elephants did, and it was how I'd come in, too. Maybe that was still open, or maybe they'd found another way out. So the thing for us to do was find them, stay out of sight, and see what they were doing.

She said no. She'd stay right where she was, and I could go scouting like I said. There were long-legged bugs you could eat if you picked the legs off first and toasted the rest in the fire, and she'd catch them and eat them and maybe find something else.

We argued about it for a couple of days, but pretty soon I saw it was no go. If I made her come when she didn't want to, she'd give us away sure. Or else she'd split when my back was turned. Either one would be a lot worse than leaving her behind, so I said okay.

Then she surprised me again. She made me promise that if something got her or she starved, I'd bury anything that was left and not eat it. I said have you got a sickness or something? She said no, she just didn't want anybody to eat her.

Have you got that one figured yet, honey? Well, don't feel bad. It took me most of the first day, but I got it eventually. We were both hungry, and she was afraid I'd off her and eat her. Only if I went away by myself it'd have to be somebody else. I hadn't even been thinking about that, only about finding some way to trap the little deer or goats or whatever they were that were about the only animals we saw there. Maybe after a few more days, it would've been different, though. I don't know.

If anything more happened the day I left, I don't remember what it was. But something pretty big happened the next day. I was up on a rock, and I saw a herd of striped horses running like crazy. There might have been twenty of them, but I couldn't see what was scaring them.

Then one went down, and I did. It was a lion and she'd got one and so she quit chasing the rest. I went there. You probably think it was a damned fool thing to do, but here's how I figured. She had the horse, and the hungrier she was the more likely she'd eat that and not chase me. Besides, she couldn't possibly eat the whole thing. She was bound to leave some, and just a little piece of it would hold me for a day or so. Maybe I'd get killed, but it seemed like I was bound to starve if I didn't do something and this was something.

The problem was that I wasn't the only one. Some big birds had seen her kill the striped horse, too. Pretty soon six or eight were circling high up, waiting for a turn at the meat.

They weren't the worst. Not at all! A dog showed up, and pretty soon two more. They were thinking about the striped horse, sure. But they were thinking about me, too. I could see it in the way they looked at me and the way they acted. There weren't nearly as many rocks there as I wanted—it was most dirt and grass—but I found a few, and every time I found one I pegged it at one of those dogs. They didn't have the guts to rush me from in front, but they kept trying to get around behind. Pretty soon I found the thing to do was to get close to the lion and her dead horse, only keep my back to them. She didn't want to jump me, she was too busy eating. And she'd start getting nasty any time one of those dogs got close.

Finally I stunned one with a rock. It fell down, and when it did, I ran up and stabbed it in the neck. The other two tore into it, which didn't surprise me at all.

Pretty soon the lion finished eating and started dragging her horse away. I followed her, not getting too close and watching behind me a lot more than ahead. She dragged it down a rocky slope to a little place where there were slopes or little cliffs all around, and bushes a lot bigger than grass. There were weeds there way higher than my head, weeds that rattled together. You probably don't believe it, honey, and I don't blame you. But there were. They came in handy, too.

When the lion got her horse there, she covered it up with bushes and grass. Some of it was dead stuff she raked together, and some was stuff she tore up herself, not using her paws but biting the stems.

When she finished, she went off into the rocks and drank. I couldn't see what she was doing, but I could hear her and felt like I'd found a new knife. I wanted water at least as much as I wanted food, and I knew that where I was now the river water was bound to be bad.

Probably I should've gone for the striped horse then, but I didn't. I waited for her to come up. She was as pretty a lion as I've ever seen, maybe as pretty as anybody ever has, darker than most of them with the little black marks on her face you see sometimes. It was a good face, too—good bone under the skin, and she moved sort of like one of those spotted cats. Her feet never made a sound, and it seemed like nothing she did took extra effort.

Well, honey, I told her I just wanted one little piece off her horse, and I showed her how big I meant with my hands. I said I'd run off the dogs, which was kind of true, and they'd have taken it all. She agreed with that, so after that I knew I had a good chance and I tried even harder. I said I only wanted a piece like I'd showed her, and I'd cut it off and not ruin any more while I was doing it. She could stay and watch if she wanted. Only she wouldn't have to, because I'd be just as honest with her gone. After I got my piece I'd cover up her horse just like she had it, and add more cover I'd cut myself. She could stay and watch that, too, if she wanted.

She said no. It was her kill and I couldn't have any.

I said, you could kill me if you wanted to. Both of us know that. You're stronger than I am, and you can run faster. So why don't you kill me?

She said she didn't need to. She never killed more meat than she could eat. Killing too much meat just meant more dogs and more birds. I knew then that she hated the dogs. I could tell from the way she talked about them. So I said I'd killed a dog today.

She had seen it, so she had to agree with that.

Isn't somebody who kills dogs better than the dogs?

She said she didn't know, but I knew how she felt. So I said I wouldn't ask a reward for what I'd done, but if she gave me the meat I asked for I'd kill another one for her. I'd been looking at the tall weeds, you see, and I'd had an idea.

She stared at me for a long time after that, trying to decide if I was honest. Finally I said I'd be her friend if I could, and I was starving. Wouldn't it make sense to help me? That did it. She let me cut myself a piece and I did, no bigger than I had told her I'd take. I ate about half of it then and there.

No, I didn't cook it. Cooking it would have made it easier to chew— that's the big advantage of cooking as far as I can see—but making a fire would have taken half a day. After that I went down in the rocks like she had, and found a little spring down there. It was good water, and I drank all I could hold. When I came back up, I put the grass and bushes back that I had taken off, and cut some more and piled them on, too. Sometimes she watched me, and sometimes she closed her eyes and lay down her head.

Do you wonder why I am telling you all these things, honey? It's not because I like reliving the old days. It's not to entertain you, either. This history's yours, and you've got to know it and teach it to your kids. You think that kids are way far away. I hear their footsteps, many feet, closer all the time.

Yeah, I found the door the elephants had used. It wasn't hard—I'll get to that in a minute. First I've got to tell you that while I piled up brush, I heard a fight behind me. Turning quick, I saw a dog die in the jaws of a young lion.

When it was dead, I nodded and thanked him and said it had been a good job.

He licked the blood from his lips. Only birds eat dead dogs. Give me that meat, he said. I nodded again, saying he'd earned it, and I gave it to him. He'd never been able to kill a man, he told me as soon as he'd eaten it. You won't kill me either, I told him, but why should you want to? I'll be a friend. We'll have lots of kills.

His eyes said he didn't believe me.

There's something I got to do first, I told him. It won't take long, and when I finish it I'll show you a man twice as big as me and give him to you.

His eyes got big and I knew I had him. I cut down a tall weed then and lopped it—it was hard and hollow, and cutting it slantwise made a point.

We found Kazi and his people after dark on the second day. They'd made a fire, and we saw it a long way across the level grass. They saw me and my lion and backed off, all but Kazi. I told the lion that was him. He should've jumped him then, but he hung back and Kazi went for his knife. I hit his wrist with my spear before I drove it in his belly because I was scared it wouldn't work. It worked great, and my lion jumped him.

You take him, I told my lion. He's all yours. I'll eat somebody else. Only I didn't have to and I knew it. They had a little deer on the fire, and I got all I wanted. They didn't have the guts to come close until I told them they could.

Well, honey, that's how I got to be king, and it's probably more than a little head like yours can remember.

Oh, sure. We found the elephant door like I said, and it wasn't hard. What I did was keep after this one young one, giving her a bad time. She wasn't big and didn't have the guts of a bull, so I'd hit her with rocks or stick a spear in her. Or shoot an arrow after we got those. Keep her miserable, you know. So pretty soon she went back to the door. Elephants aren't like people. They don't ever forget, and she wanted to go home.

No, of course not. Once she'd showed us, we killed her and ate her, what did you think? After, we got it open and that's how we got back in here. The grass country's a good place when the spiders get to putting out traps, though—safer for you kids.

Sure I did. Kazi'd had two wives and I took them over, only a river lizard got one by the leg and drowned her. It's how they do. The other one got to giving me a hard time, so we ate her. After that I remembered your mom and went back for her. Now I want you to remember all this stuff and think about it before you sleep. You're going to have to teach your own kids how I got to be king and why you're queen, see? I know you think your kids are way far away, but guys see your tits already. You pick a good one. He doesn't have to be big, but he's got to be tough, and he's got to be somebody who'll stick by you. If he isn't I'll off him if I'm still around. If I'm not, you'll have to off him yourself. Quick.

Now you lie down and think about all this before you go to sleep, honey.

Out Beyond the Stars

For years and years now I have been accustomed to say that I knew Frederik Pohl. It is true only conventionally. Let me tell you a story.

When I was very much younger, Frederik Pohl bought a story from me. It was my second sale, and it meant a lot to me. One waits and hopes and prays for the first sale; but when it comes, there is a suspicious look of tinsel, and a faint odor. Could that be cardboard?

The first sale may be a fluke. The world is full of people who sold a short story once. *Is this for real? Am I a real writer? If so, why do I feel just the same?*

The second sale confirms and convinces. One knows then that one can do this marvelous thing. One can sit in one's basement, type away and have fun doing it, and send off the result to some magical address that will provide (a little) money and (a little) fame.

Neat!

Frederik Pohl (whom I knew even then was a famous SF writer) had given me my second sale. Have I said that? I may say it a third time. It made me feel wonderful and I was deeply grateful.

Soon I went to my first SF convention, a Worldcon in St. Louis. (This was in the days when Worldcons drew fewer than a thousand people.) In the lobby of the con hotel, I found a guy whose badge was festooned with ribbons and asked whether Frederik Pohl was at the con. Beaming, he assured me that he was.

I explained that I had never seen Frederik Pohl. Could he describe him?

"You can see him for yourself." The beribboned guy pointed. "That's him, right over there."

It was a group of four or five men chatting. When they broke up, I introduced myself and said, "Mr. Pohl, you bought a story from me, and selling to you gave me the confidence I needed to keep writing. I want to thank you. I owe you much more than I can ever repay."

He smiled. "You don't owe me a damned thing, Gene. You sent me a good story and I bought it. That's my job. If you'd sent a bad one, I would've rejected it. I'm the one who owes you. I get a lot of stories, and very few of them are good enough to publish. Whenever somebody sends me a good, publishable story, he's doing me a big, big favor."

I left thinking, "Wow! That Frederik Pohl is a great human being!" The next day I found out I had been talking to Lester del Rey.

So now I know Frederik Pohl. I could never mistake him for Lester del Rey again. For one thing, Fred is taller. For another, his face is not as hairy. Now I'm acquainted with this great human being, who now lives only five or six miles from my front door.

But I do not KNOW him. I mean really know him. It may be that Betty does, but if she does she's the entire membership of a set of one.

Things I do know about Fred Pohl:

He is a high-school dropout.
He's the best-educated dropout in America.
Maybe the world.
He was in the army in World War II.
He was a sergeant.
He hated the army.

He married a second lieutenant. (There may be a connection here to the fact above.)

He has attended every Worldcon, beginning two years before they did.

He knows everybody in science fiction; he knows them because they are proud to know him.

He has been an agent and an editor (which is what he was when he bought my story).

He has been a leading science fiction writer ever since the publication of *The Space Merchants* in 1952. (In 1952 I went from college student to dropout to soldier.)

Fantasy makes him break out in hives and swear.

He destroyed the SF club I joined when we moved into the area by marrying our club's president, Elizabeth Anne Hull.

They are national treasures.

•—•—•

Read that list carefully, and you will find that I do not really know Fred Pohl at all. I don't know what makes him write so well, and I don't know what lets him keep writing whole decades beyond the age at which most writers fall silent. I don't know what makes him rove the world so tirelessly, writing all the time and going to places too remote for the average stamp collection. I don't know what it is that permits him to send his mind out beyond the stars—not once, but over and over again. And I don't know why he tolerates me.

But I'm certainly glad he does.

—GENE WOLFE

ROBERT SILVERBERG

FRED

I don't remember when we first met—perhaps it was at the Milford Writers' Conference in September 1956, or else at the New York Worldcon a week or so earlier, or maybe it was a year before at the Cleveland convention; who knows, after so many years?—but of course I had known *about* him long before we ever said a word to each other, because when I came into the science fiction field as a reader in 1948 I quickly discovered that he was a conspicuous figure in any number of ways. I knew that he had edited a couple of the prewar pulp magazines (*Astonishing Stories* and *Super Science Stories*) that I had found in back-number shops, that in his fan days he had been a charter member of the amateur publishing group (Fantasy Amateur Press Association) that I had just joined, that he had been the literary agent for a lot of the most famous SF writers, that he was the book reviewer for the postwar incarnation of *Super Science Stories*. The one thing I didn't know about him, for a while, was that he had also written some science fiction, because until around 1952 his stories had appeared only under pseudonyms, James MacCreigh and Warren F. Howard and such. I found out about Fred the writer later on, of course.

He began to loom larger in my life in 1952—a big year for me, because that was when I entered college and very tentatively decided that I was going to try to write science fiction professionally. That was the year that Fred finally put his own name on a story—the serialized novel *Gravy Planet*, written in collaboration with Cyril Kornbluth—and on a superb anthology, *Beyond the End of Time*. Soon afterward came the first volume of his paperback series *Star Science Fiction*, a collection of new stories so good that it served me for many years as a model of the kind of science fiction I wanted to write and the kind of anthology I wanted to edit.

Frederik Pohl the writer became a favorite of mine right away. But it was Pohl the editor with whom I formed a friendship, early in my career, that now has lasted more than half a century.

I wanted to write for the anthologies (and, later, the magazines) that he edited. And he saw, back there when I was a twenty-one-year-old beginner, that I had talent. But he also saw that I was writing too much too quickly, frittering away my obvious abilities doing hasty hackwork, and otherwise generally sending my career, which had begun while I was still an undergraduate at Columbia, off in directions that he thought were mistaken ones. Since he had made some of the same mistakes himself when he was my age, he knew whereof he spoke, and he didn't hesitate to let me know where and how I was going astray.

My Fred Pohl correspondence file is a couple of inches thick, and it starts with a bunch of rejection slips from 1957 and 1958, when he was editing a magazine version of *Star*. They are courteous, thoughtful rejection slips, and they keep urging me to send him more stories, but they also point out the flaws in the rejected ones very clearly, even bluntly. (This at a time when I was selling stories to other editors by the bucketful, and had even won a Hugo as the best new author of the year.) He saw my virtues as a writer, but he saw my flaws, too, and he let me know, sometimes gently, sometimes not, that regardless of what I might be selling elsewhere he wasn't going to buy anything from me that didn't come up to the level he felt I *should* be reaching.

Eventually he did buy a story or two from me, and then (he was editing *Galaxy* and *If* by then) he bought some more, and finally he was buying everything I sent him, though not always graciously. Sometimes he would tell me, even as he bought a story of mine, that he had reservations about it. ("I'm buying it, of course. I much admire your colorful touches and free-swinging style. Yet I found it hard to know just what the hell was going on in some parts of it. Do you think there is anything you can do about this?") Apparently I could, because not only did Fred buy the story, he passed it along to Betty Ballantine of Ballantine Books with a recommendation that she sign it up to be turned into a novel, thus opening the door for one of the happiest publishing relationships of my career. (Of a later story in the same series, where I mistook a critical comment from him for a rewrite request when what he really hoped I would do was throw the story away altogether, he wrote, "Considering that tinkering 'Where the Changed Ones Go' into some improved form was not what I wanted you to do, I must all the same concede that you did it well. . . . I will enter into your delusion that it is a story and print it that way." He continued to buy my work—and continued to nag me onward to a higher level of achievement, even as he had been doing a decade before. ("I hope you understand that when I talk to you candidly it is not because I want to put you down but because I think you are competent enough and talented enough to stand candor.")

I was no longer a novice by this time, of course, and, despite the sixteen-year gulf in our ages, Fred and I had developed not just a business relationship but a warm social one, going out to dinner together frequently, exchanging letters and phone calls. When some bad things happened in my life in 1967 and 1968—a devastating fire in my New York house, and other ugly stuff—Fred, who had been through experiences of much the same sort ahead of me, offered the consolation of one who had survived similar catastrophes. (He also, in his Fred-like way, asked if I wanted to know what the likely next catastrophe would be if I kept on following his path. I thanked him and declined.)

In the turbulent decade of the 1970s our lives both changed radically—I moved to California, and Fred's marriage broke up, and my marriage broke up, and we both had some career problems; and so, when we saw each other at conventions or when he visited the West Coast, we had plenty to talk about. Sometimes we snarled at each other. He was, it seemed to me, getting very touchy. He thought the same of me. (March 30, 1976, Pohl to Silverberg: "Yes, in my opinion, you are getting too touchy.") But we always snarled in a loving way. (He told me that he had torn up the first draft of his March 30 letter to write a gentler version. Looking at what he did send, I am grateful even after all these years that he did.) When I was editing an anthology and Fred missed a deadline, causing me enough of a problem so that I yelled at him, I felt an odd reversal of roles: he was supposed to be the old pro, I was the unruly kid, and what was happening here? (He yelled right back, of course.) We got past it. We always remained on cordial terms when we met. We did professional favors for each other. We offered advice to each other, sometimes unasked advice. He and I both traveled widely, and we arranged to meet for dinners in odd places of the world, and traded travel notes about trips we had taken, recommending hotels and sights to each other. And the years went by, big handfuls of them, and suddenly here we are in the twenty-first century, and Fred is very old and I'm no youngster myself, and it has been a wonderful friendship all the way, one of the central ones in my long career in science fiction, and, I think, something of the same for him. "We are of one blood, you and I," he wrote, in 1996, when I was going through one of my periodic disillusionments with writing and he was urging me to ignore the flaws in the publishing world and go on writing anyway. "You need to write, because that's what you are," he said.

I suppose so. Here I am, almost a decade and a half later, still at it. And so is he. It is hard to imagine what my life as a writer would have been without Fred Pohl. Or what it would have been without his friendship, too. We have had our differences over this and that—oh, Lord, have we had our differences!—but we are of one blood, Fred and I. And what a long, strange trip we have had together.

Harry Harrison

THE STAINLESS STEEL RAT AND THE PERNICIOUS PORCUSWINE

1

It was that time of day that should be inviolate, one of the rare moments in life when everything is going perfectly. I leaned back in the armchair and turned on the room-sized stereo—woofers the size of locomotives, tweeters that vibrated the teeth in your head—and J. S. Bach's toccata and fugue saturated the air with beauty.

In my hand was a glass of just-poured three-hundred-year-old treasured bourbon, chilled with million-year-old ice brought from one of the outer planets. How perfect! I smiled benignly and raised the glass to my lips.

Like a throbbing toothache, or a mosquito's distant whine, something penetrated paradise. A *tinkle-tinkle* that clashed with mighty Bach. I felt a snarl twist my lips as I touched the volume control and the great organ throbbed unhappily into silence. The front doorbell could be clearly heard again.

Tinkle tinkle . . .

I punched an angry thumb at the button and the viewscreen came to life. A smiling, sun-darkened face leered out at me; broken teeth—and was that a straw hanging limply from his lips?

"You in there, Jimmy? Can't see nothing . . ."

A wispy white beard, a battered cap, an accent horribly familiar: I felt the hairs stirring on the back of his neck.

"You . . . you . . . !" I gurgled hoarsely.

"Guess you can see me allrighty! I'm your long-lost cousin Elmo come all the way from Bit O' Heaven."

It was like waking from a nightmare—and discovering the terrible dream had been true. A name I thought I would never hear again. The planet of my birth that I had fled so many years ago. Unwelcome memories flooded my brain while my teeth grated together with a grinding screech.

"Go away . . . ," I muttered through the gnashing.

"Yep—a long way to come. Though I can't see you I can tell yore glad to see me . . ." The imbecilic smile, the bobbing stalk of straw.

Glad! Elmo was as welcome as a plague of boils, a poison chalice, a raging tsunami . . . Why hadn't I installed door-mounted guns? . . . I thumbed the volume control viciously, which only amplified his hoarse breathing, the straw-chomping lips. I hit the weapons detector, which flashed green. If only he had been armed, a reason to destroy . . .

"Let me in Jimmy, I got some great news for you."

There was a sound now along with his voice—I high-pitched squeal I thought that I would never hear again . . . Trancelike I rose, stumbled to the front door, unlocked it . . .

"Why Little Jimmy—you shore growed . . ."

A sirenlike squeal drowned out his words as a small black body shot between my legs, quills rattling, heading straight for the kitchen.

"A porcuswine!" I gurgled.

"Shore is. Names Pinky. Brought her along to remind you of the good old days!"

I was reminded, all right! Dull, depressing, stupid, stifling, claustrophobic—yes indeed, I did have memories of Bit O' Heaven! A loud crashing and even louder squealing came from the kitchen and I staggered in that direction.

Destruction! Pinky had overturned the garbage can and was rooting in it happily as she pushed it crashing around the kitchen. Elmo stumbled by me holding out a leather leash.

"Come on, Pinky, be a good li'l swine!"

Pinky had other ideas. She drove the bin around the kitchen, crashing into the walls, knocking over the table, squealing like a siren with Elmo in hot pursuit. He eventually cornered her, dragged her out by the hind leg, wrassled her to a fall—at full scream—and finally got the leash on her.

Garbage covered the floor, mixed with broken crockery. As I looked down, horrified, I saw that I was still holding my brimming glass. I drained it and my coughing joined the angry squeals.

"Shore nice to see you, Jim. Mighty fine place you got here . . ."

I stumbled from the room—aiming for the bourbon bottle.

Elmo and companion followed me with grunting companionship. I poured myself a drink with shaking hand, so shocked by this encounter that

I actually filled a glass for him. He glugged it down and smacked his lips—then held out his empty glass. I sealed the bottle. That single drink probably cost more than he earned in a year from his porcuswinery. I sipped at my own while his bucolic voice washed over me with stunning boredom.

". . . seems there has been a kind of interplanetary secession out our way, futures in porcuswine shares is drying up . . ."

With good reason, I muttered to myself—and drank deep.

". . . then Li'l Abner diGriz, yore forty-eighth cousin on yore papa's side, said he saw you on the TV, he did. We was all talking and Abercrombie diGriz, been to a big school, cousin on your mama's side, he looked it up somehow on the computer and said you was in great shape, a millionaire somehow . . ."

Somehow I would like to throttle Abercrombie slowly and painfully to death.

". . . so we all kind of chipped in and rented this old spacer, loaded her with porcuswine and here we are. Broke but happy, you betcha! We knew once we got here that you would take care of yore own kin!"

I drank deep, thought wildly.

"Yes, ahh . . . some merit in what you say. Porcuswine ranching, fine future. On a suitable planet. Not here of course, this planet Moolaplenty, being a holiday world. I would hazard a guess that farming isn't even allowed here. But a little research, another agrarian planet, write a check . . ."

"Might I interrupt for a moment—and ask just *what* is going on here?"

Innocent words spoken in a tone of voice of a temperature approaching absolute zero.

My darling Angelina stood in the kitchen door, holding out a broken teacup. I visualized the kitchen—*her* kitchen—from her point of view and my blood temperature dropped by ten degrees.

"I can explain, my love . . ."

"You certainly can. You might also introduce me to the person sitting on my couch."

Elmo may have been a rural idiot but he was no fool. He scrambled to his feet, his battered cap twisting in his hands.

"Name's Elmo, ma'am, I'm Jimmy's kin . . ."

"Indeed . . ." A single word, two syllables, yet spoken in a manner to strike terror into the hearts of men. Elmo swayed, almost collapsed, could only gurgle incoherently.

"And I presume that you brought that . . . creature with you?" The broken teacup pointed at Pinky who was stretched out and burbling gently in her garbage-stuffed sleep.

"That ain't no critter, Miz diGriz—that's Pinky. She's a porcuswine."

My darling's nose wrinkled slightly. I realized that many years had passed since her last encounter with these animals. Elmo babbled on.

"From my home planet, you understand, a cross between wild pigs and porcupines. Bred there to defend the first settlers against the terrible native animals. But the porcuswine done licked them all! Defended the settlers, good to eat, great friends."

"Indeed they are!" I chortled hollowly. "As I recall during our magical engagement on Cliaand, that you were very taken by a piglet porcuswine named Gloriana . . ."

A single icy glance in my direction shut me up with a snap of my jaw. "That was different. A civilized beast. Unlike this uncouth creature that is responsible for the wholesale destruction of my kitchen?"

"Pinky's sorry, ma'am. Just hungry. I bet she would apologize iffen she knew how." He nudged the guilty porker with his toe.

She opened a serene red eye, clambered to her feet and yawned, shook her spines with a rattling rustle. Looked up at Angelina and squealed a tiny squeal.

I waited for the skies to part and a lightning bolt strike the swinish miscreant dead on the spot.

Angelina discarded the shard of pottery, dropped to her knees.

"What a darling she is! Such lovely eyes!"

I swear Pinky smiled a beguiling smile. As from a great distance I heard my hoarse whisper. "Remember how porcuswine love to be scratched behind their ear-quills . . ."

Pinky certainly did; she grunted with porcine pleasure. Other than this happy swinish chuckle, silence filled the room. Elmo smiled moronically and nodded. I realized that my mouth was hanging open. I shut it on a slug of bourbon and reached for the bottle.

Swathed in gloom I saw only trouble ahead. All my dreams of swinicide and mass murder vanished with my darling's newfound amour.

"So Elmo—you must tell me all about your travels with this adorable swinelet."

"Her name's Pinky, Miz diGriz."

"How charming—and of course I'm Angelina to family." A chill look in my direction informed me that all was still not forgiven. "While we're chatting, Jim, will pick up a bit in the kitchen before he brings in the drinks trolley—so we can join him in celebration . . ."

"Just going, great idea, drinks, munchies, yes!"

I made my escape as Elmo's nasal drone hurried me on my way.

I shoveled all the crockery—broken and unbroken—into the disposal and ordered a new set from Kitchgoods. I could hear its clunking arrival in the cabinet as I stepped out of the kitchen and hit the nuclear unbinder in the floor. The binding energy that held the molecules together lessened just enough so that the spilled garbage sank out of sight; there was a satisfying crunch as it became one with the floor when the binding energy was restored.

A sherry for Angelina, a medium-dry one that she enjoyed. I rooted deep in the drinks closet until I found a bottle of Old Overcoat coal-distilled whiskey—proudly displaying in illiterate lettering, AGED REELY OVER TWO HOURS! Elmo would love it.

I added a bowl of puffed coconuts and wheeled my chariot of delight into the family room.

". . . and that's how we done ended up here at yore place, Miz Angelina."

The nasal phonemes died away into blessed silence.

"That is quite an adventure, Elmo. I think you are all so brave. Thank you, Jim." She smiled as took the glass of sherry.

The room temperature rose to normal. The sun emerged from behind the clouds. All had been forgiven! I poured a tumbler of Old Paint Remover for Elmo who glugged it—then gasped as his mucous membranes were destroyed on contact. I sipped happily until the voice I loved spoke the words that sealed my doom.

"We must make plans at once to see that your relatives and friends— and their sweet companions—are well taken care of."

A shipload of refugee rubes and their companion swine well taken care of . . .

I could see my bank balance depleting at lightning speed with nothing but zeroes looming on the horizon.

2

Most of my attention was on my drink when the nasal whine of Elmo's voice cut through the dark thoughts of my coming fiscal failure.

"The captain said *what*?" I broke in.

"Just that we was longer getting here than he thought so we owe him eighteen thousand an' thirteen credits. He ain't letting any more critters— human or swine—offen the ship until we pay up . . ."

"That's called kidnapping—and pignapping—and is against the law," I growled. Cheered to have a target for my growing anger. "The name of this miscreant?"

"Rifuti. His first name is Cap'n. Cap'n Rifuti."

"And the ship is called . . . ?"

"Rose of Rifuti."

I shuddered.

"Don't you think it's past time we paid the captain a visit?" Angelina said. She smiled down at the snoring Pinky—but the chill of death was in her words as she thought of the crooked captain.

"We shall—but in some style," I said, turning to the viewscreen and punching in a number. The screen instantly lit up with image of a robot— apparently constructed out of groundcar parts.

"Moolaplenty Motors at your service Sire diGriz—how may we aid you this lovely summer's day?" it said in a sultry soprano voice.

"A rental. Your best eight-seat vehicle . . ."

"A Rolls-Sabertooth, gold-plated, satellite-guided with real diamond headlights. It will be in your drive in . . . thirty-six seconds. Your first day's rental has been debited to your account. Have a good one."

"We leave," I announced. Leaning over and scratching Pinky under her ear-quills. She grunted happily, stretched, climbed to her trotters and gave herself a good rustling shake.

The groundcar was waiting for us, humming with barely restrained power; the robot chauffeur nodded and smiled mechanically. The albedo was so high, with the sun glinting off the gold plating, that I had to squint against the glare. I handed Angelina into her seat, waited until the porcuswinette curled up at her feet, and joined her. After Elmo clambered aboard I pressed the pearl-studded GO button on the armrest.

"To the spaceport."

"Arrival time three minutes and twelve seconds, Sire Jim and noble passengers." The robot chauffeur had obviously not looked too closely at Elmo. "And welcome as well to their pet dog . . . errr . . . cat . . . pszip—" It's voice chuntered to a halt, its computational software undoubtedly un-acquainted with porcuswine.

For a few moments I was cheered by the gold-and-diamond luxury; then deeply depressed when I thought of the coming assault on my bank balance.

Moolaplenty was a holiday world and catered to the very rich and even richer. The glint of the diamond headlights drew a salute from the space-port gate guard as that portal swung wide.

"We're going to the *Rose of Rifuti*," I said. His nostrils flared at the name; unflared when I slipped a gold cinque coin into his tip pocket.

"You jest, sire."

"Alas—it is our destination."

"If it is, I suggest that you stay upwind. Row nine, pad sixty-nine."

The carputer beeped as the driver heard the location and we surged forward.

While all about me the riders smiled, laughed, grunted porcinely—I was struck down and immersed in the darkness of gloom. I hated the fact that Elmo had ever been born and grown up to invade my happiness. I was cheered that Angelina was cheered—but I had the depressing feeling that all was not going too well.

I was right. Our magic motor stopped, the doors swung open—and we must have been downwind because a certain effluvia crept over us. The eau de barnyard flashed me back to my youth.

"Porcuswine . . . ," I muttered darkly.

"Not the most welcome reception," Angelina said, frowning at the spacer.

An understatement if there ever was one. Each of the landing fins of the battered, rusted spaceship was attached to a thick chain, which in turn was bolted to the ground. A heavy chain-link fence circled the pad. There was a single large gate in the fence, that was just closing behind an official-looking vehicle. A dozen armed guards scowled at our arrival while a grizzled sergeant stepped forward and jerked his thumb over his shoulder.

"No visitors. All inquiries at the guardhouse."

"But that car just went in!"

"Officials only. They're an inspection team from Customs and Quarantine."

"Understandable. Now, sergeant—would you be kind enough to do me a favor? See that this donation reaches the Old Sergeants' Rest Home and Bar."

The thousand-credit note vanished as swiftly as it had appeared. It tempered our conversation.

"The ship's quarantined. Just those medical officers allowed inside now."

But it wasn't quite working out that way. A gangway had been run out from the lower spacelock. The officials had just started up it when loud cries and a fearful squealing sounded from the open lock. An instant later there was a thunderous pounding as a black horde of quill-shaking, galloping porcuswine poured out of the ship. The officials dived for safety as the stampede swept by. The thundering herd headed for the gate, which was now closed and locked. The lead boars snorted with porcine rage and turned, leading the pack around the circumference of the fence.

Then, waving shovels and prods, the angry farmers poured down the gangway and ran after them in hot pursuit. 'Round and 'round the fenced enclosure they rushed. I leaned back against our groundcar and beamed happily.

"Beautiful!" I said. Angelina frowned at me.

"The swinelets might get hurt . . ."

"Never! The sows are the best mothers in the known universe!"

Eventually the great beasts tired of their circular performance and were hurried back aboard the ship. I resisted the urge to clap in appreciation of the performance. The sergeant waited until the clatter of hooves had died away and considered his litany of woe.

"Quarantined with good reason, I would say, sir. In addition to these sanitary problems there are financial ones. Landing fees, rubbish removal, and site-rental charges have not been paid. If you wait here I'll send for an officer to give you the gen."

Then he moved like a striking adder. Kicking the gate open, grabbing the yiping Elmo by the collar and hurling him through it, he hauled a squealing Pinky by the leash right after him. The gate slammed shut behind him and he dusted off his hands.

"This guy and that thing got out before the quarantine came down. Somebody is in very bad trouble."

I sighed tremulously and suspected that that person would surely turn out to be me. I dug deep into my wallet again. All I could ahead see was my bank balance spiraling downward, ever downward. I also saw that one of the guards was hauling Elmo and the loudly protesting Pinky to the spacer. They went up the elevator in the access gantry. Their arrival in the ship provoked almost instant results. Short moments later a uniformed figure emerged and retraced their footsteps.

As he came toward me I saw the wrinkled uniform, battered cap, and even more battered, unshaven face. I turned away from the sergeant and looked coldly at the approaching figure. This repellent creature had to be Captain Rifuti.

"I want to talk to you!" he shouted.

"Shut up," I suggested. "I'm the only chance you have of getting out of this mess. I talk and you answer? Understand?" My patience was wearing thin.

His face was twisted and dark with anger. He took a deep breath and, before he could say anything, I made a preemptive strike.

"Sergeant—this officer appears to have violated quarantine procedures. He is commander of an unsafe ship, has kidnapped his passengers, as well as committing a number of other crimes. Can you put him behind bars—at once?"

"Good as done." He reached out, then stopped; no moron the sergeant, and he quickly twigged as to what was going on, then added in a growling voice, "Unless he shuts his cakehole and follows your instructions." For punctuation he grabbed the protesting captain and gave him a quick shake that rattled the teeth in his head.

Crooked he certainly was—but stupid he was not. His face darkened and I thought he was going to burst a blood vessel. "What you want?" he asked, albeit with great reluctance.

"Slightly better. You have told your passengers that they have additional fees to pay. You will produce records justifying these payments. Only then will I pay these and the spaceport charges that you have incurred. After that we will discuss what is going to be your next port of call, to which you will transport your passengers and their cargo . . ." This last was a feeble attempt to get rid of my friends and neighbors—not to mention their porcine companions.

"No way! I gotta contract that says I bring 'em here and here they stay!"

"We'll see what the quarantine authorities have to say about that." Grasping for straws, aren't you, Jim?

Sometime later—and a good deal lighter in the bank account—I sat in the base commander's office sipping at a very fair domestic brandy that he had been kind enough to open for us. And the mayor's first assistant who had joined us. They smiled—as well they might with all my money in their coffers—but they were firm.

Elmo's pilgrims and their quilly creatures were not welcome on the holiday world of Moolaplenty. This was a vacation planet for tourists—as well as home for well-heeled residents like me. And all the food was imported. Not a single farm or tilled field sullied the well-manicured countryside. Dreadfully sorry—but this policy was entrenched in their constitution, pinned down in the law books, inviolate and unchangeable. We are desolate, Sire Jim—but do have another bit of brandy, the base commander smarmed. With no reluctance whatsoever I accepted. All I could see was gloom and unhappiness and a prevailing blackness in my future.

Blackness—the color of porcuswine quills . . .

3

Lighter in bank balance and heavier in heart, I led the way to the gantry elevator and thence into the welcoming airlock of the *Rose of Rifuti*. My Angelina smiled, then laughed aloud when she heard the distant squeals and grunts of a porcuswine herd. My bucolic youth down on the farm flashed before my eyes—with concomitant black depression. I had fled the agrarian cesspit of Bit O' Heaven for a successful—and happy—life of crime. Now I felt myself retrogressing through time, returning to a life-choking farming fate that I thought I had left far behind me. I went down the entrance corridor, staggering under a dark cloud of gloom.

I was jarred back to the present by sudden loud squealing that assaulted my ears—accompanied by shouts of pain and picturesque cursing. More crashing and the sound of mighty hoofbeats sounded down the corridor. Then, squealing and grunting, a porcuswine thundered around a bend in the corridor and galloped toward us.

Angelina, no coward, gave a little shriek at the sight. Who could blame her?

One tonne of outraged boar rushed directly at us. Sharp tushes sprayed saliva, tiny red eyes glared.

Sudden death was but meters away.

Salvation rose reluctantly from the dark depths of my memory and I heard my voice, calm and relaxed, gently beguiling in a swinish way.

"Sooo-eee . . . sooo-eee . . . here swine, swine swine!"

With skidding hooves a tonne of outraged pork skidded to a halt before me. Sinister red eyes rolled up to look at me; the razor teeth chomped and drooled. I reached out, gently lifting the creature's meter-long quills with my left hand, reached under with my right and scratched vigorously behind the beast's ears.

It shivered with pleasure and burbled happily.

Angelina clapped her hands with joy.

"My hero!"

"A humble childhood skill that proved most useful," I said, scratching away to the accompaniment of blissful swinish grunting.

Crisis averted I became aware of a tumult of shouting—plus some screaming—that grew louder. Then two of the crewmen came into view, running toward us carrying a stretcher with a recumbent figure. Close behind them a galloping crowd of angry farmers, waving pitchforks and clubs—very much like the last scene in a vampire film. Leading them, his face red with rage, was the normally placid Elmo.

"And iffen he comes on this deck again he won't leave it alive!"

The subject of his wrath appeared to be Captain Rifuti himself. He moaned theatrically as he was carried past, with his good hand clutching his obviously broken arm.

"We caught him sneaking into the sty deck!" Elmo stopped and smiled down at the happy boar, then got in a quick quill-scratch of his own. "Crusher here knocked the cap'n over. Was going to eat him if we hadn't got there in time. Swineknapping, that's what it was—he was after one of our porcuswinelets! And we know WHY!" Even Angelina joined in with the horrified gasps.

"You mean he . . . wanted to . . . ?"

"That's right, Miz Angelina." He nodded grimly and everyone gasped again. Except me; it was a little too hypocritical since I did enjoy my breakfast bacon now and then.

Angelina's horror turned quickly to cold anger. Unhappily aimed at me since I was the nearest target.

"Well, former farmer diGriz—what do you mean to do about this?" Her tone of voice lowered the air temperature by ten degrees. I groped for an answer.

"Well—first I'll turn this fine tonne of porcuswine over to his owners. And then I'll take care of the rapacious Rifuti."

"And what will that cataclysmic action be?"

I looked around, then whispered, "I'll tell you in private since there are other ladies present." Desperately buying some time—since my mind was emphatically empty of any inspiration. "Stay with Elmo and I'll find you later. I don't want you to see what happens next for I am mighty in my wrath!"

I shouted the last, turned, and stamped down the corridor after the miscreant.

But what could I possibly do? Rifuti had paid quite a price already for his attempt to supplement the ship's undoubtedly rotten rations. Plus—I had a lot more important things to think about besides his failed swineknapping. This little contretemps had already cost me a small fortune with no end in sight.

I was on the bridge deck now with most official nameplates on the doors in some ancient language—from the captain's home world presumably. UFFICIALE, CAPITANO, COMUNICAZIONE and OBITORIO.

I didn't want to see the capitano just yet, but the entrance next to his held more promise—since it sounded very much like the Esperanto *komu-nikoj*. I knocked and opened the door.

Lights flickered on a U-shaped control board, a speaker crackled with static.

"We're closed," the man at the control console said, not glancing up from the 3D comic he was reading; a tiny scream rose from its pages. "Open at fifteen-hundred."

"I want to send a warpdrive interstellargram—and pay cash."

The scream was cut off in mid-gurgle as he slammed the magazine shut and spun about in his chair.

"We're open. What you got?"

The lure of lucre, the call of cash—it never failed. I had been mulling my problem over and the answer seemed obvious. Money means banks and banks means bankers. And my son James was now a most successful banker. I scratched out a brief cry for help.

I soon had my answer and sent a return communication answering his relevant questions. The operator's eyes glowed warmly as the cash-on-the-line pile of credits grew.

"Will the captain see any of this?" I asked.

"You just out of the funny farm?" he sneered. Hard to do when you are biting down on a silver credit: it joined the others in the desk drawer.

My wallet contained just dust when the last communication from James arrived.

BE THERE SOONEST WITH SINGH.

I was broke so would have to wait until soonest to see who or what this was.

"Come back any time!" the operator chuckled. My snarl and the slamming door his only answer. I was now in the right mood to see the captain. I threw open the door of his cabin and was instantly cheered.

He was screaming and writhing on the top of a hard desk while green-clad demons held on to his limbs and tortured him. I did not interrupt. Particularly when I saw that they were medics who were setting his broken bones. Reducing his fracture—a most painful procedure.

Once the cast was in place the needles came out and I interrupted.

"Painkillers, yes—but I want him conscious to answer a few questions."

"Why?" the doctor asked, his occupation now revealed by the stethoscope around his neck.

"Because I must find out some most important facts."

As I spoke I groped through all my pockets until, fortuitously I found a single coin, dredged it out, and passed it over.

"A hundred credits donation for the charity of your choice for your assistance in this important matter."

"Thank you. For the Children's Aid Society. Plus I didn't really appreciate some of the curses he laid on us. A painkiller and a stimulant."

Needles flashed. Then they bundled up their equipment and were gone. The red-eyed Rifuti turned his wrath on me but I got in a snarled preemptive strike before he could speak.

"You're in big trouble, Rifuti. The police are on the way to charge you with attempted swinicide, assault and battery, kidnapping, grievous bodily harm, and barratry." He gurgled incoherently, but I drove on mercilessly.

"But you are lucky that I am here to save you. I will have the police drop the charges. I will pay all the debts of your passengers, both two- and four-legged. I will pay all port charges accrued here. And—wait for it!—I will pay a fair price to buy this decrepit excuse for a spaceship."

He gurgled again and his eyeballs bulged at this last and I nodded and smiled benignly.

"Because if you don't agree you will be dead within twenty-four hours." I husked this in a venom-dripping voice.

His face turned dark with anger and he opened his mouth to speak. Then bulged his eyes even bulgier and gasped.

Because a scalpel had appeared in my hand—liberated from the doctor's bag—and was rock-steady just millimeters before his eyes. With a quick flip it neatly punctured the tip of his prominent nose and was still again—with a glistening drop of blood on its tip.

"Say yes . . . ," I whispered.

I stayed silent, cold, counting upon his undoubtedly dicey history to put the frighteners on him.

"Yes . . . ," he whispered back.

The scalpel vanished and I stepped back. "I'll be back to you with my offer. Of course if you talk to anyone about this you won't live until morning."

I exited. I didn't know if my threat would work or not. If he did complain to the authorities I would see to it that he was sneered at—and a lot of official charges would be dropped on him. At the very least my nebulous threats could only help the financial negotiations to come. I returned happily to face my dear wife. As I strolled I was already embroidering and improving on the story of my success.

I tracked Angelina down to the mess hall where she was having a bucolic tea with the lady farmers from Bit O' Heaven. The men had been dismissed as redundant and sent back to work. Angelina smiled when I gave her a thumbs-up sign and a big nod. She bit daintily into a wurflecake and slipped a bit to Pinky who—just as daintily—snuffled it down.

"Ladies," I called out, "if I might have your attention. The forces of evil laid low, the captain—very painfully—bandaged and repaired. And made to see the light."

"And which light would that be?" Angelina asked.

I smiled and bowed to my attentive female audience.

"All debts will be paid. These kind people, and their porcine charges, will find a new home on a sunlit paradise planet. The good guys win!"

I pumped my fist over my head in a victory salute in answer to their joyous cries of happiness. Angelina started to speak but I beat her to it.

"Not only that but our good son James is on his way here at this very moment—to handle the finances and mechanics of the agreement!"

"Jim—you don't mean it?"

"I do my love—I most certainly do!"

She leaned over and gave me a most inspiring buss on my cheek, radiant with joy, while the audience applauded. But, happily, she did not lean so far over that she could see that the fingers of both my hands were crossed behind my back.

Oh let it happen, oh powers that rule the odds of seeing that white lies come true.

Oh *please* let it happen—or Slippery Jim diGriz is really in the deep, deep cagle.

Angelina's brow furrowed with thought. With good reasons—my pep talk had more holes in it than a *truo* cheese. I chuckled and turned away, speaking over my shoulder.

"Sorry—no time for tea. James asked me to do an inventory of the ship for him. I'll be back soonest."

If I had a conscience I would be staggering under the weight of all my white lies. But I had happily laid that burden down when I opted for a life of crime.

But I did want to see what shape the ship was in. I started my survey on the bridge deck and worked my way down to the engine room. With each noisome compartment entered, each scuffed door opened, my depression grew. Firstly—no one seemed to be on duty. None of the stations was manned; lights were turned low or burnt out. Filth everywhere. The *Rose of Rifuti* was a spacegoing slum. It was only when I reached the dorm deck that I found any trace of the crew. I pushed open the door labeled TRESPASSERS WILL BE SHOT and fought my way in against a miasma of old food, stale sweat, and dope fumes. I kicked my way through the discarded trays and crushed drink containers, to reach the bunk where a scruffy man lay smoking a green joint and listening to a scratchy recording of some coal-mining and steel-mill music. I knocked the music player to the deck and crushed it under my boot heel. The unshaven music lover looked up and snarled an oath.

"Ekmortu stultulo!"

Drop dead stupid! My temper—by this time held in place by only a slender thread—cracked. In an instant I dragged him from the bunk by the collar of his soiled jumpsuit, shook him teeth-rattlingly, cursed a mighty oath and—if this wasn't enough—the scalpel, appeared large before his popping eyes.

"Take a breath and you're a dead man," I growled with the voice of doom.

Only when his face began to grow blue with incipient cyanosis did I hurl him, gasping for breath, back onto his bunk.

I glared around at the terrified men who lolled on the other sordid bunks.

"Now hear this! I have just bought this ruin of a spaceship and am the new owner. You will obey my orders or—" My wrist twitched and the scalpel sped the length of the room and thudded into a distant pillow—a scant millimeter from the shocked face of a crewman.

I spun on my heel, dropped into a karate killing position and glared at the now terrorized crewmen. "Anyone disagree with that . . . ?"

Of course none of them did. Nostrils flaring I turned slowly, facing them down one by one. Stalked the length of the bunkroom and retrieved my scalpel.

"My name is James diGriz. You may call me 'master'—LET'S HEAR IT!"

"Yes . . . master . . . ," the ragged response came.

"Good. I will now inspect the rest of the ship and will return in precisely one hour. By that time you will have cleared up this swinesty, washed and shaved, be prepared to be loyal crewmen—or die . . ."

The last words were spoken so coldly that they breathed a mutual moan and swayed like trees in the wind. On this high note I exited and continued my depressing inspection of the specious spacer.

The engine room was last and the unoiled door hinges squealed like all the others. The shouted voice rattled off my eardrums.

"You are a mechanical moron! Don't you know which end of a screw-driver goes into the slot of a screw? Come closer and I will demonstrate on your . . ."

There was a pained shriek and a crewman fled by me, followed by a veritable hail of screwdrivers. His pained moans died away down the corridor. I nodded approval; at least someone was working on this garbage scow.

He was gray-haired and as solidly built as one of his engines, bent over the guts of one of them, probing in the recesses behind an open panel. As I approached I heard him mutter imprecations.

And I understood them! A language I had learned painfully on a very painful planet. Cliaand.

"Well done, oh mighty engineer, very well done!" I said in the same tongue. He straightened, spun about, jaw dropping.

"You are speaking Cliaand . . . ," he said.

"I'm glad you noticed."

Then his eyes widened and he pointed a greasy finger at me.

"And I know you—you were the pilot of my ship during the Final War. In fact, I even remember your name—Lieutenant Vaska Hulja."

"What a memory! Whereas I have completely forgotten yours."

"Stramm, Lieutenant Hulja."

"Lieutenant Hulja is gone with the war! My name is Jim. It is a pleasure, good Stramm. I was indeed your pilot. And, sadly, your saboteur. Let me apologize at last for blowing up your fine engines."

He waved away the words and smiled broadly. "I should thank you, Jim. Ended the war and got me out of the navy and back to work as a civilian." His smile turned swiftly to a depressed frown. "Not your fault that I signed on to this bucket of rusty bolts."

"Soon to change," I said and shook his oily hand, then wiped my hand on the rag he passed over. "You'll never guess who the new owner is."

"Make my day! It isn't . . . you . . . ?"

I lowered my head and nodded slowly. He chortled with joy and we pumped a greasy handshake again.

"Can I ask you a few questions about this ship?"

His smile vanished and he growled deep in his throat. "Ask—but you won't like the answers."

"I agree in advance."

"The captain's a crook and a smuggler. The crew are alcoholic villains. They were only hired because by interplanetary law a crew this size is required. They do nothing. Their work is done by robotic controls, which are slowly deteriorating. I'm surprised we made planetfall at all. I've already quit this job. But I want to adjust the atomic generator before it goes into meltdown. My engines are sound—but nothing else on the ship is. All patched up and jury-rigged and decaying while you watch. I've already quit and I have sabotaged the engines. I'll put them right—when I get my overdue salary. Welcome, Jim, welcome to the *Rose of Rifuti.*"

I sighed a tremulous sigh. "I had a feeling that's what you would say, oh honest engineer Stramm. At least things can't get worse."

Even as I spoke these words aloud my mother's oft-repeated dictum whispered in my ear. *Bite your tongue.*

Firmly superstitious, she believed you were tempting fate to say this. Ha-ha—so much for superstition . . .

There was a crash as the door burst open and Elmo staggered in, red-faced and clutching his chest.

"Jim . . . ," he gasped. "Come quick! The worst has happened!"

He drew in a tortured breath and spoke in a doom-laden voice.

"They are here now—hundreds maybe!" Shouted aloud dark with despair.

"Men with guns! They want to kill all the porcuswine!!"

Knowing Fred

If Fred and I didn't meet in 1939, I know that we were at least in the same room together. This was at the first ever World Science Fiction Convention held in New York in 1939. (The world of fandom then consisted of New York and New Jersey.) By the time we had ceased being teenagers the war was on and the army grabbed us. After the war we were both working in the publishing world and crossed trails in the Hydra Club in New York. The rest, as they say, is history.

Though we had known each other for a few years, we had no professional contact—though we were both in publishing. My work was in comics, drawing, writing, and editing them. We got together when I began to dip a toe into science fiction. I did illustrations for a number of magazines, while Fred had become an agent. I was soon doing illustrations for Damon Knight's magazine *Worlds Beyond.* At five dollars each.

I wrote a science fiction story at the same time. It was titled "I Walk Through Rocks" and I submitted it to Damon. Who changed the title to "Rock Diver" and bought it—for fifty dollars. Better rates than drawing. I now needed a literary agent. I asked Fred, who said sure, read the story, and bought it for fifty dollars for an anthology he was editing. Writing at a hundred dollars a story or art at five dollars a pop . . . I changed jobs.

The more I wrote, the more our professional careers crossed. As an editor Fred was more than helpful. He stepped in with many a bacon-saving purchase. Highlighted in memory was my novel *Bill, the Galactic Hero*. Admittedly it was a surrealistic, humorous, out-of-category story. Damon had very avant-garde tastes so I submitted an outline of the proposed book to him; he was now reading for Berkley Books. He had advanced ideas about fiction and even signed himself "d. knight" in the manner of e.e. cummings.

He liked it, bought it—and got me a tiny advance from the publisher. Wonderful! My parody and hatred of the military would see the light of day!

Maybe. When I turned in the final manuscript Damon bounced the book, saying it was an army novel and I should go through it and take out all the jokes. . . . I of course refused. No sale. And no income for almost the year that I had worked on the book. I must have moaned to Fred about it—he was then editing *Galaxy* magazine.

He looked at the book and bought the magazine rights. In those days Fred was a great retitler. He called it *Starsloggers*, which I could bear. Except for a typo in the magazine when he mentioned the story would start in the next issue. This was fine—other than the fact that there was a massive typo in the plug and it came out as *Starloggers* . . . A sort of interstellar lumberjacks I imagine.

This was the time of the war in Vietnam. The war impacted on science fiction when some of the more military-minded writers paid for a full-page ad in *Galaxy* supporting the war.

This would not do. Fred contacted the rest of the writers who, being more intelligent—or at least of more liberal tendencies—published an ad decrying our involvement in the war. I like to think we helped the cause in some small way.

By this time I was living in Denmark with my family, writing and publishing novels and short stories. At least once a year I would visit New York and touch base with the editors; this was most important for a freelancer. Fred was editing *Galaxy* and *If* and I used to visit him in his office. Not to touch editorial base but to possibly pick up an assignment. Since he worked from home a good part of the time, his publisher had the habit of meeting some of the artists who came around looking for assignments. Many times they would bring samples with them. All too often it was cover art of varying quality. Some of these the publisher liked and he would buy them on the spot.

For Fred to muse over when he was next in the office.

Most were dreadful. A few were possible—but what were they illustrating?

Fred would offer them to visiting authors to look at. The deal was if you wrote a story that the cover could illustrate you got a sale. And a cover credit!

Great. I would mutter over a possible story that had to explain every cover detail. This was a teasing problem—and occasionally I would come up with a decent story that Fred could use.

Life was simpler then.

Just once I reversed our roles.

An SF writer of prominently conservative views was editing a series of anthologies with the endearing title of *There Will Be War*. I looked at this as an insult to the intelligence of mankind. Surely, in the fullness of time, we could rise above this invidious practice. Bruce McAllister agreed to coedit a book of original short stories with me. We suggested to the same publisher that he let us edit a volume to be titled *There Won't Be War* to take a look at the better alternative. He agreed and I solicited stories from SF writers. Starting with those who had supported the good-guys *Galaxy* ad about Vietnam.

The response was tremendous. Nineteen of the top writers came through with amazingly good stories. Fred was among the first with "The Rocky Python Christmas Video Show." A fine story—with a glorious future. It kept gnawing at Fred, until he finally turned the idea into a novel, *Mining the Oort*. Which he dedicated to me, saying ". . . he made me do it."

This despite the fact I had submitted a story to *If* magazine—that he was editing—my story titled "If." He bought it and, quite correctly, changed the title.

A few years later, when I was living in Ireland, I had the germ of an idea that was to grow into a worldwide enterprise. Living in Europe I had personal contact with writers and publishers from many countries. But not the Russians. We corresponded but that was it. This was during the height of the Cold War and none of them could travel abroad without an official government invitation. Which meant there was plenty of to-ing and fro-ing between the Soviet Union and what were called the satellite countries. But no farther. Almost all of the western countries were out of bounds.

But where did this leave Ireland? It was not a member of NATO, which would have made contact impossible. Would the Russian writers be able to visit Eire's green and pleasant shores?

I had to find out. I phoned the Russian embassy in Dublin and made an appointment to see the cultural attaché. He was named Romanoff—the same as the last czar—which I thought might be a hopeful sign.

He was a pleasant man who held out little hope. "We try for years to get cultural agreement with Ireland. We say you send us Irish harp player—we send you Bolshoi Ballet. But this country is, as you surely know, very anticommunist."

"Let me get back to you," I said.

For I had made some valuable Irish contacts. At that time—well before the Celtic Tiger roared—Ireland was not in good economic shape. Because there were no jobs, most university graduates sought work abroad. Only tourism was a booming industry. I had discussed with the tourist board and the government travel authorities the possibility of holding an international writers SF conference with attendees from many countries. They were very interested. If I could get the Russians to attend, success could be guaranteed. They grew grim when I mentioned the lack of a cultural agreement with the Soviets. Politics was one thing—tourism was another. They approached the Irish Arts Council about this matter. Pressure was applied; the Arts Council caved in. As long as it didn't cost them any money. I assured them if they issued an official invitation to the USSR writers, I would handle printing up copies and sending them off. Agreement was reached and the first-ever international writers' conference was on.

(This is the way it happened. Catholic Ireland and Communist Russia agreed to full cultural exchange. I don't think that science fiction writers have ever received credit for this major cultural accomplishment.)

The conference was a roaring success. There were calls to have more conferences like this first and World SF was founded. I was elected president. We held another Irish conference before fatigue overwhelmed me. The international SF community, one after another, stepped in. Fred Pohl became president and carried the organizational ball. As did Sam Lundwall of Sweden. As president he held a conference in Stockholm. Brian Aldiss from England was the also president. As well as Gianfranco Viviani from Italy. These four had supported World SF from the first days in Ireland. And had happily volunteered for this arduous position. They did a wonderful job and World SF went from strength to strength. We established contact with all the Eastern European countries and before we were through we held a conference in China. It was a most worth-while endeavor that died a natural death when the organizing pioneers ran out.

Now I sit back and marvel. Fred and I have been friends now for close to sixty years. Both still working, still writing. So it was with great pleasure that I seized the opportunity to join with my fellow writers in this Festschrift volume.

I can only join the other contributors in saying—well done, Fred—well done.

—HARRY HARRISON

JODY LYNN NYE

)x(•)x(

VIRTUALLY, A CAT

The burly male technician loomed over the smaller man in engineer's orange coveralls as if by sheer size he would drive home his message.

"I swear, Ardway, if you tell me one more cat story, I'm going to kayo you and put you out the airlock!"

"I thought you liked hearing them, Callan," Benny Ardway said, wondering if he could wriggle his skinny frame any farther into the bulkhead of the forward engineering compartment to escape his shipmate's wrath. He lifted apologetic, round blue eyes to the engineer. "You laughed. I thought you enjoyed hearing about Parky and Blivit."

"Once, on the way out of orbit, was okay. Twice, while we were waiting for the calculations to jumpspace. But you have to have told the same damned stories a million times since we broke atmosphere," Callan said, sticking a furious finger in his shipmate's face, "and enough's enough!"

"All right," Ardway said, meekly. Callan gave him one more glower, then kicked off the wall to continue replacing modules in the astrogation console. Ardway handed himself down to his keyboard and looked out at the blackness of nonspace, wishing he could swim all the way back to Earth. He felt bereft. No one on board the ship felt the way he did about cats. No one understood what it was costing him to make this long trip, knowing that back on Earth his pets were missing him. No, not his pets: his *family*.

When he'd been assigned to the *Calliope*, the station quartermaster had told him that he was entitled to bring with him twenty kilograms of personal gear. *Perfect*, he had thought. Both of his cats together didn't weigh more than ten. Add to that their food dishes, maybe one more kilo. The corps supplied his uniforms, his tools, dishes, food, and bunk space. He could use a discarded cabinet casing for the cats' litter pan. That left him nine kilograms for bookcubes and personal items. The cats would sleep with him. No bunk had ever been too small to contain all three of them. He had even asked his assigned bunkmate, the communications officer named Polson, if he liked cats, and Polson had said he did. It was going to be great.

Ardway had weighed everything several times to make certain everything he was bringing fell under the allowable limit. He even had half a kilo to spare. He had been devastated when, upon reaching the launch center with his luggage, he learned that his cats wouldn't be allowed to come with him.

"We can't have animals in deep space," the mission commander said, as if shocked that Ardway would even consider such a thing. He regarded the cats in their carrier with horror. Ardway recalled having moved between Captain Thurston and the cats to protect them in case the officer went crazy. The way his nostrils puffed out reminded Ardway of Parky about to have a fit. "They could panic! Destroy precious equipment! Er, soil, er, the environment."

"Sir, they're very clean animals," Ardway had protested. "They're both neutered shorthairs. They won't cause any kind of fuss."

"You must be out of your mind!" Captain Thurston said, crossing his arms. He was the poster-boy type for the deep space program, tall, handsome, muscular, and crew cut, the physical opposite of Ardway, who was hollow-chested and mousy-haired. "Get those animals out of here, and I mean *stat*!"

There was nothing Ardway could do. He'd signed an ironclad contract, and he really did want to be in on this project. Who wouldn't want a crack at being astronavigator on the first team to use the new jump technology for a long-range jaunt outside the solar system? NASA had wanted him, too. He was the lead software designer who had come up with the format for the benchmark system that kept the ship on beam. The program ran like a top, but NASA thought it would be better to have him out there with them in case something went wrong on a long test, after the eighteenth century custom of sending the engineer to sea with the ship he'd designed. Ardway thought he could leverage his desirability into making them agree to let the cats come, but they waved his signature in front of him, and told him to get over it. He'd only be gone two years. Two years! Ardway felt as if his heart would be torn apart.

The only way Ardway could cope was to have lots of reminders of the cats with him. With ten kilos of his personal allowance freed up, he was able to pack in a personal viewer and hundreds of videos of the cats playing and sleeping. He enlisted a trusted friend to watch over his pets, set up a mail account between his apartment and the communication station at

Canaveral so he could get updates on his pets, and shared stories about Parky and Blivit with his new shipmates. Alas, the first wasn't satisfying enough, and the last endured only as long as the patience of the final person on board the *Calliope* who would listen to him. That had been Callan.

Ardway watched the technician's orange-clad legs floating weightlessly under the console. The flutter kick Callan made to keep himself in place reminded him of his orange tiger cat, Parky, lying on his side in the sun batting idly at a ribbon. He opened his mouth to say so, and very quickly closed it again. Callan might really put him outside in nonspace. Ardway glanced at the clock and decided to take a break. The program didn't need him at that moment. No one did. His job had really been done the day he finished debugging the system, more than a month ago, and wouldn't begin again unless something went wrong. In the meantime, he was useless baggage. He slid out of his chair, nodded to the helm officer, Frida Lawes, and handwalked out of the forward engineering compartment and made for the break room.

The *Calliope* had been designed to support up to fifteen crew members for a period of at least three years for her mission to Gliese 86. The ship's complement was ten crew members, and the mission was intended to run only twenty-two months. If the bounce technology worked as planned, they would break space periodically, once just outside Sol's heliopause, then enter the tunnel under normal space for approximately five months, surfacing occasionally to make sure they were still on beam, and emerge on the edge of the heliopause of Gliese, counting on Ardway's program and his skill to get them there safely. The crew would undertake as much exploration of the star system as they could manage in their time frame, followed by the turnaround journey. All the crew cabins except the mission commander's were doubles. The break room, the mess hall, and the exercise center were common areas. Six private one-man carrels were available when the pressures of the mission and communal living got to be too much for human nature. That wasn't Ardway's problem. He wanted company. They just didn't want him.

"Coffee," he told the wall in the break room. A hatch slid open in the mural, and Ardway took the insulated bulb. The food service system made pretty good coffee, scrambled eggs, oatmeal, and spaghetti sauce—anything soft. Any food with texture kind of suffered in processing. He floated over to an outer bulkhead where he secured himself on a loop to watch the entertainment hologram in the center of the room. It showed a couple of earnest men in surgical greens leaning over a patient and calling for tests.

Reruns already? Who cared? He wondered if he had time to go back to his cabin and watch one of his personal tapes. Maybe the one of black-and-white Blivit washing herself.

"Hey, Benny!" Cora Handley, the ship's blue-suited medical officer, swung into the room and noticed him hanging there all by himself. The oldest member of the crew, she'd been on more long-range flights than anyone else in the service. She was only around fifty, but her hair was almost pure white. Except for that and the "spaceman's squint," she looked thirty. "What's the word from your cat sitter? How are the Terrible Two?"

Ardway perked up. "You won't believe it, Doc," he said, delighted to expand upon his favorite subject. "Melanie said that she showed them my message tape, and they both sat in front of the screen watching me. She said Blivit reached up to touch me through the screen. She couldn't, of course," Ardway said, sinking into depression again. If only it was that simple. His hands ached for the stroke of fur, to feel that soft vibration of a deep, throaty purr. "She said they are eating well, but I had to remind her to give Parky his vitamins where Blivit can't see it, because she thinks they're a treat, and she gets jealous . . ."

"Later, honey," Handley said, hastily, her pleasant face contorting. "I'm running a stress test on the commander. Look, twenty-two months isn't that long a time. You'll be back there before you notice." Handley ordered herself a coffee, and somersaulted out of the room with the bulb bobbing beside her.

Ardway appreciated her kind words. She was very sweet, but she was a 100 percent wrong. He noticed, all right. He noticed at the beginning of every sleep shift when no firm, furry bodies snuggled in with him, pushing him away from his pillow. He noticed at every mealtime when there were no sets of green or gold eyes looking up at him, hoping for the choicest morsels. He noticed when no friendly shoulders bumped into his legs while he sat at his console. And the worst was that no one wanted to hear about his troubles. Ardway blamed the space program for being shortsighted. If they'd let him have his little friends, he wouldn't have to talk about them all the time. They'd even be good for crew morale. He drank his coffee and went back to his station. Just like the state of warp, the outlook for him looked black.

● ━ ●

The *Calliope* broke space on schedule, and exactly where Ardway's computer told them they'd be: on the very edge of the Sol system, in among the junk in the Oort cloud that surrounded the open space. The sun was a tiny dot at the edge of the astrogation screen. Ardway's loneliness was put on hold for a time while the ship went on manual helm to explore the belt. Everyone got excited, as they were able to employ their specialities for the first time in the mission.

Spinning frozen boulders the size of small moons danced in the giant circle that surrounded his home system like a ring of mountains. Ardway enjoyed the narrow squeaks as he steered the ship close to chunks of space debris, fascinated by the largest amount of solid matter that existed any-where but a planet. The geophysics team, Johnson and Mackay, gathered samples using both the ship's grappling arms, and a short-range small re-trieval unit that, like Ardway's nav system, was on its shakedown cruise. The retrieval unit was nothing more or less than an empty spacesuit that went on tethered spacewalks by itself. Unmanned spacewalks were another of the service's bright ideas to protect the fragile human beings in the crew from being exposed to radiation or accidents. The retrieval suit went out the airlock and acted as a kind of waldo while someone in the ship wearing the corresponding receptor-motivator unit felt everything the suit did, and saw everything the camera in the helmet did. The system was terrifically flexible and adaptable. When the suit successfully collected an interesting chunk of rock, Johnson made it do an end-zone disco boogie as the crew cheered.

The fun was short-lived. Once they reentered the blackness of warp space, an idled Ardway became morose, and simply didn't talk to people for a while. He holed up in the privacy cubicles with his collection of home videos and his thoughts. Unable actually to be with his precious cats he spent a lot of time imagining himself home with them, in his personal heaven-on-earth. All right, so his bachelor flat was small and about twenty floors up with an unreliable lift; it had a great view to the south that allowed his pets to have sunlight all day, most suitable for naps and stretching. He had had so many happy days, playing with Parky and Blivit, reading with them on his lap, talking to them, and just enjoying the companionship.

He knew the others in the crew watched him and worried. Every so of-ten he'd leave the privacy cubicle grinning over a particularly cute video or picture and catch the eye of one or another of his fellows, who would hastily look away. Ardway wondered if he could be dropped out of the ser-vice for cat addiction. But it'd be worth it. The cats were his companions, his friends, his comfort. Life like this wasn't the life he wanted to lead. It was great during the big moments, the discoveries, but enduring the long stretches without his little friends was devastating. The view out the ports was an unchanging black, but he knew, intellectually as well as emotion-ally, that he was flying farther and farther away from his cats. He lived for the moments when they broke out of jump and received beamed messages from Earth. New video from Melanie of Parky and Blivit lifted his spirits like nothing else. He ached for them, and the longing got worse and worse as time went by. No one on the ship understood. No one wanted to hear about it.

With little to do and an indifferent company to keep, Ardway began to be lax about shift times, showing up when he felt like it. Who cared? Not the other people in the crew. His program didn't need him. He started to go without shaving, and occasionally without bathing. By the twelfth week he sometimes wouldn't even bother to get out of his bunk unless he was hungry or had to use the head. Ardway knew his behavior was unhealthy, but he simply could not motivate himself. He began to spend his break times in his privacy cubicle, screening videos, and coming out only when he was called. No one seemed to miss him. Except his cats.

Late one evening shift in the third month of the mission, Ardway heard a tap on the cubicle door. On the little viewscreen, Parky had just jumped out from behind the couch and assaulted Blivit, who'd just been having a drink, and was minding her own business as she walked back to her favorite sprawl spot. The two of them rolled together, rabbit-kicking at one another's bellies. The tap sounded again.

"Just a minute," Ardway called. He didn't want to miss the best part. Here it came: Parky and Blivit rolled into the couch. The contact surprised them. They jumped apart, and sat at opposite ends of the open area washing themselves to cover their discomfiture. Ardway laughed and shook his head. He unlocked the door.

"Benny?" It was Mel Johnson, the junior geophysicist, a large, dark-skinned, friendly man with big hands. "Hey, buddy, we don't see a lot of you anymore."

"I'm there when you need me," Ardway said, defensively. He popped the cartridge out of the video reader and prepared to load another one.

"Yeah, but you're not *there*, man. You haven't been yourself since about four weeks ago." Johnson looked at the recorder and met Ardway's eyes with sympathy. "You miss 'em that much, huh? No"—he held up a hand as Ardway took a deep breath—"don't tell me your stories again, man. Tell them to your diary. I'm tired of 'em, too."

"I think even the computer is tired of them," Ardway said, with rueful humor. "I do miss them. I can't even *tell* you how much. I'd give everything for a cat. I can't last two years like this. I'm going to go crazy!"

"Well, what is it you really miss?" Johnson asked, propping himself in the door frame so Ardway couldn't shut him out. "You've got one of those virtual pets on your screen, right? Feed me, clean me, scold me . . . ?"

Ardway dismissed the idea with a wave of his hand. "It's not the same. Feeling Parky rub against my leg in the morning when I'm getting his breakfast. That's after Blivit has woken me up by jumping on my . . . my bladder to make sure I'm awake. The way they cuddle into my arm or my lap when I'm reading, even the way they run across me when they're fighting!"

"Yes, yes," Johnson said hastily, throwing his hands up, and Ardway remembered Johnson had been very patient about listening for weeks even when it was clear he'd had it up to his neck with Ardway's favorite topic. "Let me think about it."

"You think you can convince the brass to bring me a cat? Way out here?" Ardway was full of hope. Maybe Johnson, a disinterested party, could succeed where he had failed.

●—●●

Not even for the finest astrogator in the service, which Ardway was proving to be. No living animals would be put into danger, or be able to put the crew of the deep-space mission into danger. Besides, as the message from NASA said tartly, nothing in the space program existed that could catch up with the *Calliope* in less time than it would take to return to Earth on their normal schedule. Ardway read a copy of the reply Johnson received. There had been half a dozen attachments, but Ardway didn't read those. All he was interested in was the denial. He fell into a real depression, refusing to come out of his quarters or the privacy cubicle, sometimes not even for meals.

A couple of weeks later, Johnson's voice came again outside the privacy cubicle, tried to persuade him to open up the enamel box. Ardway sat with his arms folded, refusing to budge. Eventually, he heard fumbling on the bulkhead and swearing. Callan's sweating red face appeared as the door slid open.

"I'm taking the locks off all these doors," Callan said, and turned to Johnson. "He's all yours."

"C'mon, buddy," Johnson said, bravely ignoring the stink of unwashed and unshaved crewman as he took Ardway's arm and pulling him toward the geophysics lab. "I've got a surprise for you."

In the white-enameled room, all the samples the crew had gathered on their stops were in clear, vacuum-sealed cases to prevent direct human exposure. Against one wall was the lightweight waldo-suit Johnson wore to gather specimens.

"You know what this does, right?" Johnson said, pointing to the suit. "It's a remote-control unit for the one outside. The suit that corresponds to the motions made by this one was in a compartment behind a panel on the skin of the ship."

"I know all that," Ardway said, waving it away.

"But do you know how it gets its feedback? On the inside, it's got a fine mesh suit of two kinds of sensors fused together, receivers and responders. Together, they're only about a micron thick, like a second skin. The cloth is thinner than nylon stockings. If the suit picks up a rock, I can feel the shape of it in my hand as if I'd picked it up myself. If the suit takes a knock from a meteor, I get knocked ass over teakettle. Of course, the responses are toned down so that I can take it without getting hurt. I can feel that the rock is cold, but not the burning cold of deep space. I get pushed around by the responders, but not enough to do more than bruise me a little."

"So?" Ardway said.

"So I made you a suit, man," Johnson said, opening a compartment and taking out a wad of tan cloth about the size of his fist. "Instead of getting real output from out there, I've used your home movies to program the computer for sufficient characteristic behavior. I'm plotting the right size, shape, and motion in three points in space, which the suit will respond to."

"So what?"

"So when you wear the suit," Johnson said, smiling broadly, "you'll have your own virtual cat around you. No one will be able to see it, or hear it, including you, but you'll be able to feel it."

Ardway let hope gleam in his eyes. "That'd save my life, Mel."

"And our sanity," Johnson said.

◆━◆

The sensor suit worked exactly as Johnson had said it would. When hooked up to the central computer, Ardway could feel subtle motions against his arms and legs. Nothing like a cat, yet, but it was promising. The program Johnson adapted needed to be debugged first, and Ardway jumped in to help. He pored over the code for days on end, motivated for the first time since he had left home. He gave Johnson his best videos and pictures, along with precise measurements of the two animals that he had made when he thought they would be coming along on the mission. Johnson devoted his spare shifts for a week helping him to fine-tune the responders so they would push against Ardway's skin in the right sequence and at the right amount of pressure. The testing had to be done during the gravity periods each day so the plotting for ship placement would be accurate. Not unlike the benchmarking program, Ardway thought.

"Okay," Johnson said, kneeling at Ardway's side to adjust the flat control box in the middle of his back. Ardway wore nothing but the suit and a pair of boxer shorts over it. The suit itself was of pale tan filaments, not all that much darker than his skin, and was so fine he felt the cold of the floor through the feet, and the breeze from the ventilation fan. "You know, you can shower in this. And should. The sensors work best when they're kept clean. Okay, try it. The cat ought to be right about there." Johnson stood up and pointed to a spot approximately three feet up over a white dot painted on the floor.

Ardway put out a hand in space, and was surprised as it ran into an obstruction. He couldn't see it, but his body told him it was there. His hand insisted there was something solid in the way. He ran a hand over the form. It was shaped approximately like a cat. The soft ears bent under the pressure of his glove, but the hard round skull resisted the downward motion. Encouraged, Ardway stroked his hand down its back. The spine arched upward to meet his caress. The edges were very rough, but Johnson tweaked the programming until the sawtooth spine under his palm melted into a surface like silken fur. Ardway felt the body shift. A rough tongue, at first limp as corduroy but stiffened with a little help into wet sandpaper, occasionally licked the back of his hand.

"It's wonderful, Mel," Ardway said, feeling a lump rise in his throat. "I don't know how to thank you." Then it disappeared. Ardway felt around with both hands.

"Where did it go?" he asked.

"On the floor, man," Johnson said, consulting the monitor. "Wait." In a moment, the firm body reasserted itself, rubbing against Ardway's calf. It was such a real sensation, he could almost picture himself home again.

"It's wonderful," Ardway said again, shaking his head in wonder. "You're a true friend, Mel."

Johnson stood away from his screen and stretched his long back. "I'm starved. Let's stop for a while and get something to eat." For the first time in weeks, Ardway felt as if he had an appetite. He followed eagerly.

The two of them headed for the mess room. Ardway walked along, feeling the occasional sensation of the pressure against his leg as the programming caused the "cat" to bump into him impatiently.

"It's following me," Ardway said, with delight.

"It's yours."

If the rest of the crew was surprised to see Ardway in his underwear, they didn't say anything as he and Johnson sat down to a meal. He tucked into his dinner as though he hadn't eaten since he'd left Earth. Then, suddenly, he felt sharp pain in his knee.

"Ow! The damned suit attacked me!"

"It's in the programming, man," Johnson said. "It just scratched you. What's it want?"

"It's hungry," Ardway said, after a moment's thought. "That's what Parky always does. What do I do?"

"What you would do at home. Pretend to throw him something. Or try to teach him not to beg at the table. Maybe it'll learn. Maybe it won't. It's a cat. It'll act like one."

With an incredulous glance at his friend, Ardway reached into his plate-bowl, a clear globe with a gasket to admit his hand or fork but to keep the rest of his food from floating away in zero-gee, picked up an imaginary morsel between thumb and forefinger, and tossed it onto the floor. Instantly, the invisible presence left his side. Ardway could imagine the cat chomping and chewing at his offering, or maybe symbolically burying it in the floor the way Blivit always did. He hoped the bit had been something the cat considered good. In a moment, he felt a light touch on his kneecap, a little paw, beseeching and thanking in one soundless motion. He reached down toward the invisible presence, felt his palm stopped by a hard, round object, the cat's head. It shifted, maneuvering his hand downward a couple of inches to a softer surface that must be its throat. Automatically, his fingers curved and began scratching lightly against the presence the glove told him was there. Incredibly, a gentle vibration came through his fingertips. The cat was *purring*. His heart melted. He looked up at Johnson. "Thank you, Mel. I owe you."

Johnson held up his hands. "Hey, it's a challenge. I'm enjoying it. Really. Just do us a favor and keep your clothes on over the suit."

From that moment on Ardway was a new man. He wore his mesh of sensors under his uniform all of the time. Most of the time the invisible cat, whom he'd named Boojum, stayed in his cabin. Ardway leaped back into his work, becoming the most willing of the crew, working long shifts, never complaining, cheerful all day long, because he knew that at break times and meal times and rest periods, he could go back to his quarters and play with his very own cat. He rejoiced in the marvel as if he had never had a pet before. He could pick it up and put it on his shoulder, feeling a several-kilos weight there. He could sit and read, feeling a sprawled figure across his lap and a whiskery chin on his wrist. Boojum would even come to him when he called. He could play fight-games using an old sock as a glove. The mesh calculated a compensation for the padding, lessening the force of the cat's nips or scratches. The best part was sitting in the mess, or in the break room, or floating at his station feeling a small, rumbling body cuddle up against his. He pictured Boojum as a solid, mackerel-striped tabby with black mascara markings around the eyes. A bit of a bruiser, but loving and devoted. Ardway loved him back without reservation.

The crew referred to the program as Ardway's "imaginary playmate," but they didn't knock something that had solved the morale problem so neatly. Ardway still enjoyed receiving his updates from his cat sitter on Earth, but he could see the cats were well and content, now that he was not reading extra angst into their responses. All that had come from him, and he was cured. Polson moved into a spare bunk room, so Ardway wouldn't be embarrassed to talk to his cat in the middle of the night. The cat proved to be a good listener. The sensor receptors responded to the vibration of his voice, creating a response in the cat's programming. Ardway talked, and the cat sat with him and purred. Ardway was happy.

When he had a chance, Mel Johnson made him a hood to go with the suit, for Ardway to wear in the privacy of his cabin, so he could be awakened by cheek rubbings and roundhouse paws to the ear, and so he could enjoy again for the first time in five months the sensation of a cat asleep, curled up in the hollow of his neck and shoulder.

Johnson had gotten interested in the Boojum project in spite of himself. To the captain, he'd argued that such a refinement of the retrieval-suit technology could be a useful side product of the space program, one with applications in industry as well as the military, which kept Thurston from complaining about misused resources. Johnson had incorporated plenty of Ardway's personal stories about his cats as well as the videos into the programming. One shift while Ardway drowsed over his control board thinking in three dimensions, he fell asleep. Suddenly, he woke with a start. There was something slimy in his hand. No! He jumped up out of the seat, batting at his palm, and looked down. There was nothing there. What could it be? Gingerly, he felt for it, and read the shape with his sensor-covered fingers. With a smile, he remembered. Johnson had worked into the cat's repertoire the actions from the time Blivit had decided to help feed her poor stupid human. She had brought him one of the goldfish from his apartment tank. Ardway reached down, knowing that Boojum was there, waiting for approval.

"Thanks, kitty," he said, petting the hard little head that was under his hand, whether he could see it or not. He threw the imaginary morsel toward the disposer bin, and hoped the cat wouldn't try to go after it and retrieve it for him.

But, Johnson had done more than invest Boojum with the characteristics of either Ardway's stories or his home videos. He'd asked other people on board for their own cat stories, and put them into the database. And he'd added random factors, with his own sense of humor. In the mesh, the program treated Ardway as though he was barefoot all the time. Early one morning, Boojum left him a "present," just inside the door to the head. Ardway hopped around for a moment on one foot, feeling the mushy, wet coldness on the sole of his foot. He limped over and pulled a towel out of the dispenser and wiped off his ship-boot. The pressure against the receptors caused the sensation to abate.

"Thanks a lot, you silly animal," Ardway said to the air, and caught Captain Thurston coming out of a stall. The commander gave him a strange look, and edged out of the room, giving him a wide berth.

The cat's existence was plotted within the relative points of the spaceship for all the empty internal spaces that existed, so he was never to be found sticking half in and half out of a wall, unless there was a door or a duct, and he became more real by the day to Ardway.

The sullen, unshaven Benjamin M. was gone. In its place, the crew got to enjoy a productive, happy, whistling astrogator, who could listen to other people, and felt content enough in his own happiness not to inflict innumerable stories on anyone. They grew to like him, didn't care about his computer-generated security blanket, so long as it worked, and they stopped noticing that he was clad in tan nylon to the neck under his orange jumpsuit. Ardway was proving the recruiters right to have brought him aboard, and whatever made him functional, so long as it didn't cross space agency policy, was fine with them.

By month ten it became more necessary by the day for Ardway to be actively involved in the mission. Space near the Gliese system was riddled with anomalies that NASA had not detected or even suspected. Odd gravitational fields suggesting minute quantities of black matter invisible from many light-years' distance exerted gravitational pull on the ship, yanking them slightly off course and sending the instrument readings whirling. Ardway adjusted his program as needed, and was keeping up just fine in plotting new courses, assigning benchmarks to the area of space. Data came in by the terabyte, and they hadn't even begun the exploration of the system itself.

On the fourteenth day of month eleven, they broke out of jump and passed within the heliopause of the Gliese 86 system, seeing it clearly for the first time. The geophysics and astrogation departments went crazy with delight. Johnson, Mackay, and Ardway took scans, analyses, visual images of the star and its attendant pair of gas giant planets. Mackay declared them the most important satellites since human beings first looked up and saw the moon. They toasted the planets with champagne and coffee, and promptly went back to work. No one could keep away from the viewscreens, drinking in the sight no other human eyes had ever beheld.

What could not be seen from Earth but merely suspected were the huge asteroid belts situated in two places within the system. While life as they knew it was unlikely to exist on either giant planet, they held out hope for some of the moons they could now see circling Gliese A, the inner planet. The xenobiologist, Carmen Hosteen, felt her palms itching every time she saw the spectrum analysis of the second largest of the moons and crowed over the large bands in the scan that showed the presence of nitrogen, hydrogen, and oxygen.

Every department began to hoard its supply of available memory space as their databanks started to fill up. There was a general fear that Mission Control had grossly underestimated their needs, and might leave them out there scrambling for anything that would hold programming.

Suspicion of a coming storage crunch gradually became a reality. The crew simply needed more file room than they had. By month thirteen they started blanking anything that wasn't absolutely needed for day to day operation. First, backup system files went. The technicians complained bitterly, worrying about what to do in case of a system crash, and started arguing among themselves over room. Eventually the captain stepped in and issued a fiat: any nonunique file and swap space was sacrificed to contain the incoming images, facts, and figures pouring into their sensors from the two planets. Ardway and his colleagues reconfigured and reformed every possible hard drive, chip, crystal, and disk on the ship to make more room, including rewritables in their personal possession. All entertainment videos were taken out of the ship banks and reused. Then, as the ship went into orbit around Gliese B, audio entertainment. Everyone's music disks went, too, because they were rerecordable. Vital files were backed up on those, and they were put into cold storage for safety. Then, around Gli A, text went. Ardway had to upload his book disks one at a time, instead of being able to leave them in memory. One at a time, he sacrificed the disks themselves to his department. Far be it from him to lose precious navigational information because he didn't want to do without *A Tale of Two Cities*.

Next went personal correspondence. The crew was given one shift to

download all personal mail onto primitive cold cubes before that compartment of ship storage went, too. There was a lot of protest. The crew went
in a body to confront the captain in the mess room.

"With respect, sir," Callan said, "we don't need *all* this crap. I've checked
the files. We have hundreds of identical scans of the system! Plenty of them
are redundant copies."

"We can do without a lot of stuff, Lieutenant," the captain said imper-
turbably. "I don't want to ditch my letters from home, either, but it's a sacrifice for the job. Should I write home and tell them we're coming back
early because you want to keep your photo collection? Put what you can
on datacubes, and I promise you when we get within sending distance of
home I'll notify NASA to instruct the server to resend all of it. We'll triage
the raw information later, people. For now, we can't be discriminatory. We
need all the space there is!"

Callan, Ardway, and the others went along with the program, however
reluctantly. Ardway felt he could cope without letters from home, or even
his precious videos. Then, nine days before they were to depart the system,
the evil day came.

Ardway, coming out a self-induced fog at the beginning of his shift, realized that Boojum wasn't at his knee begging for an imaginary scrap from
his breakfast. No little paw touched his knee; no back rubbed against his
calf. He looked around to see if anyone else had noticed. Long ago, he'd
stopped thinking of the cat as a programming construct, and felt as though
other people could see him. Ardway unhooked himself from the grapples
holding him to the table, and felt around the floor area, wondering if the
cat was lying on his side, waiting to trap his hand when he reached for him.

"Boojum," he called softly. "Where are you, baby?"

"What's the matter, Benny?" asked Cora Handley, the medic.

"My cat is gone," he said, now beginning to panic. He got down on
hands and knees and felt out farther. "Maybe my power pack is out of
whack. Will you check it?" He undid the zipper on his coverall and pulled it
down to show her the middle of his back. She swam over through the air.

"Nope," she said, unhooking the flat box to show him. "It's on green.
How many bytes did the program take?"

"What program?" Ardway asked.

"Your cat," said Handley. "Everything nonessential has been yanked
out of the system. I guess they finally had to reach for everybody's personal files. I'm really sorry about that. We'd all given up a little of our per
areas for you. In a way, seeing you so happy lifted everybody's morale."

Ardway was touched by the crew's generosity, even as he felt dismay rising in him. "He's gone?"

"Until we hit sending distance of home again, it looks that way," Handley said, with real sympathy in her blue eyes. "Don't worry. I'm sure Johnson put it on a disk somewhere. He wasn't about to lose all the complicated programming the two of you have done on Boojum. He even thinks he'd like to market it when he gets home. You couldn't be an isolated case, though I'm thankful you're the only one on this mission. No offense, honey." She tilted her head toward her office. "Come and see me if you need to talk. I promise I'll listen."

Ardway felt like mourning, even though Boojum wasn't really dead. He had come to enjoy it, to believe in it as if it was real. The loss twisted his heart until he could hardly breathe. Cats helped provide him with a sense of identity, and he had almost nothing left. He had given up the vids he'd taken of his cats to store navigational data. Oh, the videos were just copies, but the originals, like the cats, were trillions of miles away. Home. On Earth. Boojum had made the separation bearable, and now he was backed up on disk somewhere, just as if he wasn't real.

Of course he wasn't real, Ardway scolded himself. But it'd felt that way. The complex programming Johnson had given him had taken on a personality so he was virtually a real cat.

"I can handle this," Ardway said, firmly. He went about his shifts, ate his meals, and did his job, but all the time half hoping that the loss of the cat was a glitch, and that he would be back soon. He started to get edgy and snappish again. The techs on caffeine or alcohol rations or nicotine patches were starting to give him dirty looks. He was an addict of a different kind, and his fix had been withdrawn from him. He missed Boojum. He went to appeal to Captain Thurston.

"No, you can't have your cat back. The damned thing isn't real!" the captain roared.

"He's real to me, sir," Ardway said humbly. "Please. I'll sacrifice any of my personal files you want."

"They're all gone anyhow, Lieutenant," the captain said impatiently. "So are all of mine."

It was true, but Ardway was desperate. "There must be something, sir. I'm begging you!"

Thurston snapped, and stood up, glaring. Rumor had it he was wearing a sedative patch, too. "There's nothing, dammit. This project must be accomplished. Go back to your station. Now, spaceman!"

Glumly, Ardway went back to his station. His hands kept doing the work, but neither his mind nor his heart were in it.

Without his program he started to withdraw into himself again. It wasn't the sight of cats he missed. He had permanent 3D images of Parky and Blivit. Those couldn't be rerecorded, so they'd been spared in the data crunch. It was the physical contact, the constant checking in that cats did, the "Hi, how are you?" touches that he missed. Captain Thurston avoided him, and rumor had it that he would cheerfully have spaced him if he could have found an excuse. Ardway didn't care about his own well-being anymore. He took to shutting himself in the cubicles again.

But he was not alone in isolating himself. Other members of the crew were now suffering from detachment as much as he was. Without entertainment media to keep their minds busy, they were becoming touchy and sniping at one another. He hadn't realized it had gone so far until the day he saw the unflappable Cora Handley haul herself into the carrel next to his and slam the door.

Benny Ardway was grateful for all the kindness his crewmates had shown him over the past months. At that moment he determined to pay it back as much as he could.

He floated over to bang on the cubicle door.

"Hey, Handley!" he shouted. "Did you ever hear the one about the computer programmer and the cow?"

❧

From that decisive moment onward, Ardway became everyone's court jester. Whenever he had an audience of even a single person in the mess hall or the break room, he sang songs, told every joke he knew, and made up silly games to involve the bored crew. He even oversaw a card tournament.

"The first card party in space," he insisted. Neither he nor anyone else on board knew how to play bridge, and no books remained to teach them how, so he taught them Crazy Eights. He told stories.

"And not one word about a cat," Callan marveled at the end of an evening. It was praise, however offhand, and Ardway glowed. In hopes of soothing everyone else's misery, he had forgotten about his own. Though the mesh suit no longer worked he continued to wear it. He slept in it, showered in it, did his shifts in it. He considered it a kind of amulet. It was his physical contact, as much as anything else, to help keep him sane. With that to bolster him, he gave all he had to planning entertainment for his companions.

Three months passed that felt like three years. Half the crew was overweight from eating out of boredom; the other half was musclebound from intensive bodybuilding for the same reason. But they were all in better spirits than might have been expected, thanks to Ardway's evening antics.

Having something else to concentrate on also kept him more alert at his job. As the ship's navigator he was the first to know the moment they arrived back within hailing distance of Earth. Ardway saw the readings come up on the astrogation console. He looked up at the viewscreen. There was nothing to see, but the computers confirmed the good news. Yes! He bounced up, straining against the straps holding him in his seat during zero-gee. Whirling his arms he spun around to face the center seat, where Thurston sat rotating a couple of ball bearings in his palm. "Captain, we've just entered line of sight to Earth!"

"Thank God," the captain said, showing animation for the first time in weeks. His smile wrapped clear around his handsome, strong-jawed face. "Helm!"

"Sir!" Lawes exclaimed, the force of her salute throwing her to the end of her restraint straps.

"Drop us out of warp. Communications, send a tachyon squirt to Mission Control, my dictation begins now. This is Captain Thurston on the *Calliope*. We're about halfway home from Gliese. We've got data for you beyond your wildest dreams, folks. We're going to start sending you digital squirts on this beam. In return, we need a few things. Attached to this transmission is a list of personal comm numbers for my crew. Do me a favor: check those out and send whatever's in the servers. There's a lot of lonely people here who need a word from home." Ardway and the others in the control room broke into cheers. The captain raised his voice over the din. "Plus some good music. And a few new vids wouldn't hurt. We've been reduced to watching *Attack of the Killer Tomatoes* almost every night after chow."

After some days had passed, a message came back from Mission Control. The sound of the controller's voice was punctuated with hoots of hysterical laughter, the response of the ground crew hearing the captain's plea.

"Roger that, *Calliope*. Entertainment on the way. Can't wait to see the vacation photos, folks! Welcome back to Sol!" A steady stream of digital data came in the wake of the reply.

A few weeks after the first message, another squirt from Mission Control came through, and there was awe in the communication officer's voice. "First sixty terabytes of data received! You've got a wow coming from the big brass, *Calliope*. We're proud of you. I don't frigging *believe* what you're sending back!"

"It took sacrifices from whole crew," Captain Thurston said, and he looked straight at Ardway when he said it. "Okay," he said to the waiting crew. "You saw the receipt. You can dump the redundant scans from the first 60T." The crew started cheering wildly.

"Mail call," Polson, the communications officer said, with a grin on his face. "I feel like Santa Claus." Anyone who was not on duty kicked off for their cabins to hear their messages. Ardway had to wait until shift's end to download his mail, but he was pleased to see he had received three new uploads, audio and video, from his cat sitter. He thought both Melanie and the cats looked a little older, but they all seemed healthy and happy. A big knot rose in his chest. He missed them so much. And, though he'd never seen it, he missed Boojum. Ardway chose a frame of his cat sitter holding Parky and Blivit on her lap, and left it glowing on the face of his reader beside his bunk when he went to sleep.

●—●●

Ardway drifted drowsily halfway between sleep and waking, batting at the buzzing alarm in the bed head. The astrogation program was due for a check-over, although it had been ticking along the whole mission without hiccuping once. He glanced over at the picture on his viewer and smiled.

"Be seeing you soon, kids," he said. Suddenly, something hard stabbed him in the bladder twice, then struck him in the leg as if it was rolling off the end of his bunk heading toward the door. Ardway threw off the covers and looked around. There was nothing there, but he knew what had happened. Boojum was back!

"Hey, kitty!" he cried. "Wait for me." He started to roll over to unfasten his net, starting to swim toward the door, when he felt the pounding sensations again, knocking him back against the padded wall. Those footsteps were going in the same direction as the previous ones. Ardway shook his head. There must be a hiccup from the program being downloaded and uploaded again. It was repeating actions. He was going to have to help Johnson to fix it as soon as he had a break. But his virtual cat was back. He was delighted. He couldn't wait to pet Boojum and welcome him home.

Ardway clambered out of his net, and pulled himself down to his clothing locker. Something thumped against his leg, struggling, and sharp pains lacerated his calf and knee.

"Boojum, stop that!" He bent down to feel what was going on, and his hand was captured and severely beaten up. Ardway swore, hopping around as he pulled on sweatpants while the cannoning body floated around, banging into him occasionally. "Knock it off!"

The familiar shape thudded into his chest. Ardway reached out automatically to catch him, and was rewarded with the deep vibration as the
cat's head scraped against his neck and chest. He stroked the soft, furry
body. "Oh, baby, I have missed you!" The purr resonated through the receptors, vibrating deeply. Ardway sighed with delight.

Plaintive stropping at his ankles surprised him so much he flutter-kicked
away in the air. He reached out a tentative hand, and felt another feline
body, programmed into space just like the first. This one was smaller and
slimmer, with shorter fur and larger ears.

Another cat?

It was! Completely at home in zero gravity, the newcomer walked up his
body and snuggled into his arms, shoving Boojum to one side. Ardway felt
the contented rumble turn to a growl deep in the first construct's chest, but
it quickly turned to a resigned purr. Two cats! He had *two* cats!

He kicked across space and hit the intercom.

"Johnson!"

"Hey, Ardway, good morning," the hearty voice said.

"The program's back, but it's got a hiccup. There's a second cat walking around in here."

Johnson sounded smug. "Yep, I know. It's a surprise, kind of a thank-
you from the crew for pulling so hard when we knew it was killing you.
You did good, boy. Even the captain approves. He gave the go-ahead for
the extra data space. We've been calling the second kitty cat Snark. Enjoy." The intercom clicked off.

"Snark, huh?" Ardway said, bringing his hand around the bulge in his
arms to scratch the top of the smaller cat's head. "Hey, baby, nice to meet
you." An approving rumble said he had found just the right spot. The head
tilted under his hand until he was massaging a tufted ear and a sharp slash
of cheekbone. He wished he could see it, but he imagined Snark to be a female. Maybe a Jellicle cat, with black and white fur and big gold eyes. Boojum wriggled, trying to get at the petting hand, and captured it between two
big paws. Ardway shifted so he could stroke both of them at the same time.
They all floated in the middle of the cabin, Snark massaging his side with
her small paws, and Boojum lying with his head on Ardway's shoulder.

Two cats! He had never been so happy. There might have been a couple
of gas giants circling Gliese 86, but as far as Benny Ardway was concerned,
the most important pair of satellites in space was right here.

Afterword

I offer this story in tribute to Fred because one of the facets of his work that I always appreciated was how his characters struggled to remain human while confronting the strangeness of the universe around them. I admire the scope of his imagination. His stories postulate the large changes of which we human beings are capable when called upon to make them.

"Virtually, A Cat" is a small story by comparison, but my main character, Benny, also has to reach deep inside himself to cope with the effects of living in deep space without one's usual defining comforts.

—JODY LYNN NYE

David Marusek

FREDERIK POHL: AN APPRECIATION

Fred came into my career at an important turning point. I had just begun to publish short stories when in 2000 he judged the Sturgeon Award and awarded it to my novella, "The Wedding Album." I was very disappointed that illness prevented Fred from attending the award ceremony in Kansas, but I was delighted to meet him not long after at a Worldcon. The attention the award brought me has helped me clamber one or two rungs up the endless ladder of literary success.

BRIAN W. ALDISS

THE FIRST-BORN

This week marks the first fifty years of humanity walking on the planet Mars. As yet, a better and more peaceful culture has to establish itself, but that the settlements still exist is a matter for congratulation.

Fadrum and his buddy Reet were kicking a ball against the alley wall, Fadrum to Reet, Reet back to Fadrum. *Thud bump thud bump*, went the echoing ball, in terms of complaint. They seemed never to tire, those two bored boys, but suddenly ceased their game.

Reet made off, ball under arm.

"You don't say much these days," he shouted back at Fadrum.

"Gotta study," was his response.

Fadrum, before heading for his house, launched a jet of urine against the wall, that wall like most others made of processed rock and fabric-blend.

He trotted right, right again, then left, into a small courtyard. Blind eyes of windows faced each other, dung-colored.

He entered the block, where Gadramm, his father, sat with others watching *Three Down, One to Go* on his tiny screen. "Hello, lad," said Gadramm, cheerfully, keeping his gaze on the screen.

"Ho," Fadrum replied. There were sixteen other men in the room.

A square electralite on the table served to illuminate photocuts on one wall.

OFF-PLANET POPPET DOING GREAT
FIRST EVER MARTIAN MUM!
MIRACLE BIRTH BOOSTS BUM WORLD
BABY BURSTS FROM THE BARRENS

And so forth.

The mother of this headline-grabbing child was Cauley Gore. She sat upstairs in a hard-backed chair, unmoving hands folded on her lap. Cauley was alone in the room.

That in itself was remarkable. This building was crowded with people, mainly men. Certainly, they understood that the birth of a living baby on Mars was a noteworthy event, unique, almost a miracle. But all of them had practical work to do, whereas looking after a baby—even this marvelous baby—was regarded as woman's work.

Fadrum kept out of the way of both his father and his mother. He had not seen Cauley, his mother, for some days: not since that day, now a week past, when the baby—that most famous baby on the planet—the baby whose birth had been announced all 'round the Earth—had died. Then Fadrum had wept secretly.

They had called this amazing baby Snooks during its brief life. Drina, its sister, had liked to cuddle it. The little baby whimpered and never smiled.

Snooks had lived only for eight days—just long enough to hit the world's headlines.

Directly it had shown symptoms of illness, the doctor had come in his crawler. He was a doctor of works, still in his overalls.

"Congenital heart disease," he said. He hardly made an examination of the little body. "Epstein's anomaly. All too common on Mars." He shook his head. "Hard luck on the mothers . . ."

"Is that all you got to say?" Gadramm demanded. "This is my kid that's died!"

"No, it is or was my '*kid*,'" said Cauley, and was ignored as the two men confronted each other.

The doctor backed away. "Look, it's the lighter gravity. Bones don't build up like they should. Heart don't kick in like it should. Pregnancy has got big problems on this planet."

"Oh, shit," said Gadramm, and to his wife, "Stow that crying, will you, girl? We already got three kids and that will have to be enough for anyone . . ."

Cauley already had three children, born on Earth before the family took the subsidized trip to Mars. They were Drina, the oldest and a girl, Leen, a boy, eighteen months younger, and Fadrum, the youngest, fifteen years old. They were all in the little tinpot room, standing upright and silent.

●━●━

Fadrum followed the doctor from the house. As the latter climbed into his crawler, Fadrum asked him hesitantly, "So was this death of the kid anything to do with the—well, let's say the guy who humped her?"

"*Her? Your mother?* You heard what I said. It's a gravity problem, okay?"

"Couldn't be a problem with—for instance, the immaturity of the donor semen?"

The doctor scowled down at him. "Did you hear what I just said? We aren't adapted. The womb is not adapted. It don't properly realize there's a fetus in it needing support. Not that I know much about it. I ain't that kind of a doctor." He revved the electric engine and the crawler crawled off down the street.

Building was in progress. Fadrum stuck hands in pockets and stared at the dreary scene. This was the city. Their block was finished and had the sign saying TAMPA over the door. Most of the blocks were unfinished. It was this that caused Tampa, Gadramm's block, to be so overcrowded. Gadramm was i/c Diggers and had been forced to house all his team until they set off on their next operation.

The Chinese block opposite Tampa was finished. Fadrum envied the Chinese expeditionaries. They were financed by the Chinese government back on Earth, making them comparatively wealthy. And they concentrated mainly on developing soils and growing things that passed for food—even occasionally sending over edible dishes to Tampa, as a token of goodwill.

Fadrum went back into his own building. It was full of clatter. Another Digger expedition was getting underway. The amalgamation of North Florida universities going under the name of Tampa subsidized everything in this block they liked to call their Mars extension. But a new American/world recession had hit their generosity; now they needed results to perk up funding contributions.

Gadramm was in the forum with other men, struggling into his exoboots, looking angry.

"Where you been?" he asked his son.

"Where do you think? Jupiter?"

"Look, I don't want no lip from you. I need your help. Come nearer, will you?"

Fadrun moved two inches nearer to his father and to those boots, designed to act not only as footwear but as containers for bodily excretions.

"Pa, why you always so angry with me?"

Angrily, Gadramm explained that the Tampa sentry had died. It was up to him as leader to act as guard and sleep by the door, armed, to prevent anyone trying to escape in the night. His men had been known to sneak out and take refuge in the European or Chinese outposts, where life was supposedly more easy.

"We'll be away two weeks, maybe more. Your brother Leen is coming with us. I want to toughen him up. There will be about fifteen guys and the women left here. The rest will be with me in the Hecates Tholus region. That's our instructions from Tampa . . ."

"You go on about Tampa. I reckon they're a stingy bunch," said Syril, who often sat chatting with Gadramm through the long evenings.

"Tampa saved me," said Gadramm. "I used to be a regular boozer. It was my brother. I blame him. He introduced me to the hard stuff. He's dead now, God rot his soul. We stowed away on a trade ship and ended up in a place called Jamaica. It's an island. Tropical. An island. We slept on the beach."

"We've heard all this before. You seem to think it's to your credit," said a tall man by name of Dak Doran. He got up and walked away.

Gadramm pointed a thick finger at the retreating back. "I heard he was a schoolteacher. A superior sort, yet they still gave him the push. That's where we end up, on this miserable dump of a world. You can't get booze on Mars . . . Sounds like a line from a tourist attraction; 'You Can't Get Booze on Mars.' Well, there's this weak piss Tampa occasionally ships in. Hardly worth drinking. 'You Can't Get Booze on Mars'!" He roared with laughter at his own joke.

"Jamaica . . . That was where I picked up Cauley. How she put up with me I don't know."

"It's a woman's job," said Syril. He and Gadramm chuckled about that. "They're a different species."

"I was born on Jamaica," said Leen. Leen was Gadramm's eldest son. "Good swimming there. I could swim before I could walk."

"Try and find a place to swim here," said his father sarcastically. "Anyhow, you was more trouble than you was worth."

"Fadrum and me looked after Ma this time, when she was in labor—more than you ever did."

Gadramm gave a snarl. "I was busy down here, wasn't I? No more lip from you, boy. You never been through what I been through. I'm reformed. That's what I owe the Tampa guys . . ."

—•—

Other men were laughing, shouting, trying on equipment. Gadramm went on talking but Fadrum could hardly hear what he was saying. Gadramm swore he would kill the man who had seduced his wife and made her pregnant. His violence was frightening.

"You should have got someone else to guard the door," Fadrum said. "You shouldn't have left your wife alone in bed."

Gadramm went on about Cauley having the only proper bed in Tampa. He had made it himself from the wooden packing cases dispatched from Earth.

His son was frightened. "Yes, yes, it's a good bed, but I can't help it . . ."

"This swine got your ma pregnant and then the bastard child makes news all over Earth! How you think I feel about that? I'll suss him out, I'll cut his motherfucking throat. You understand that, boy?"

He thrust his big enflamed face at Fadrum. Fadrum ran off.

⚫━⚫

Earth. USA. Florida. Daytona. A big white building slumped not far from the shoreline. Administration Center for MSS, Martian Settlement Scheme.

Chancellor Professor Eddie Skelton arrived early on his cyclemotor, clipped it into a rack along with other bicycles, many with the motorized rear wheel. The uniformed lackey who used to check identities and welcome visitors was long gone in these recessional days. Skelton punched in his code and entered the building . . . Many people of all races were lingering here, or walking about. There was much consultation of watches and whispering into mobiles. This was the day of the International Consultation of Martian Mortality, called because of the death of Snooks Cauley Gore, many thousands of miles away.

The elevators had long been closed. Skelton made his way slowly up the great curving stair. Aware that he was dragging his feet, he recalled his wife's sneer that he was just an old crock. He diverted his mind to the forthcoming debate; his advisory team had reached no conclusion as to what damage light gravity did to the fetus, and how it could be remedied. Somehow he must put a positive sheen on the failure.

He would speak of a mother's grief when her son dies, and of scientific research regarding strengthening bone structure.

Skelton entered the offices allotted to the US delegation. The windows looked out across the celebrated beach to the ocean.

"The oceans of ignorance man has to fight against. After the triumph of men reaching Mars and establishing themselves there, who would have suspected this wretched womb-predicament would confront us?" So ran his thought—but then his second secretary, Niccola Bell, was smilingly coming to him. Had he ever known anyone so gorgeous, so kempt, so becoming?

"The Chinese and European delegations are already beginning to assemble," Niccola said. "Our two colleagues have already gone ahead. May I escort you in? I have a note from the president for you."

"I'll love to have you with me," he said.

━ ━

Fadrum was in hiding when the Hecates expedition set off the next day. With an enormous clatter the men left, loading food and equipment into the exo-crawler, hauling themselves aboard the tracked bus, laughing, jeering, some coughing. Despite the electrosealing overhead, the atmosphere contained beneath it was thin.

It took over an hour before the expedition was ready to move. It went at a walking pace over the regolith, throwing up grit behind it, and dust that was slow to settle.

The team fell silent. Several preferred to walk beside and slightly ahead of the vehicle, since walking was not demanding in the lighter Martian gravity. Hecates Tholus was a distorted region, where ancient impact craters were often linked by fretted fault lines. There were channels, some as much as thirty kilometers across. The vehicles used them as roads, engine noise being thrown back at them by crumbling walls. Ice debris formed a kind of rock.

They moved along an incline to a site Tampa HQ had designated, following an old Viking Orbiter photograph. What the photograph did not show was the severely ravaged desolation of the area.

A section of three men worked by one of the natural walls, where there were indications of water having run at some period in the distant past. This section was led by Dak Doran, a loud hot-tempered man in his early thirties.

"If Tampa says do, so we sodding do," he said. "Anyone'd think we was archaeologists, not just a bunch of down-and-outs."

A short distance farther on, where a narrow stretch of ground was choked between two close-lying mesas, the other section went to work.

━ ━

Gadramm was in charge here. Presently, he was back at the crawler, looking for a lever stowed in the rear locker. He needed it to split open an obstructing boulder. The other two members of his section were painstakingly sorting and dusting slices of shalelike rock when a call came from the opposite party.

"Hey, you suckers!," shouted Dak Doran, "Come here see what we found! This will really make our names—or mine, at least!"

━ ━

Directly the team had set off for Hecates Tholus, Drina and her boyfriend started to tease Fadrum. Fadrum was working at his computer on Twister, concentrating on "Space Birth," an article full of technical and medical jargon.

"Why don't you live, you weed?" Drina said. "Always got your nose on that screen . . ."

"Get lost, you dreary thing!" he said, wearily.

"You're the dreary one," said Brunce, the boyfriend. "Show your sister some respect."

"You keep out of this," shouted Fadrum, jumping up, ready to fight. But Brunce got in first and gave Fadrum a hearty push. Caught off balance, Fadrum fell back over his stool, to sprawl on the floor.

"Serve you right!" exclaimed Drina, laughing.

"Cow!" he yelled at her.

Brunce blew on his nails and polished them on his uniform. "Now those guys are away, we two are going to have a nice bit of nooky some place. You're too joov for that kinda stuff, I guess!"

Fadrum gave a bitter laugh. "Little you know about it, big head!"

Brunce grabbed Drina's arm and pulled her away.

Later, when Drina was alone, she bumped into Fadrum. "You oughtn't to annoy Brunce, you know," she told him. "He's a bit hot-tempered."

◆━◆

Dak Doran's section were clapping their gloved hands. "Radio our find to Tampa HQ right now," one man suggested. But his mate knew that the Martian orbit was such that the bulk of the planet was between them and Earth, making contact temporarily impossible.

Gadramm came over, clutching his lever, followed by his two workers. "What you found?" he asked Doran.

"I hear you're a Christian," Doran said, by way of reply. "Then you're gonna like this. It's a Christian sign." He went to the patch they had cleared by the ice wall and flashed his torch.

"Look at this, boyo!"

Gadramm went closer and squatted. The ground was as full of wrinkles as a creased sheet. He stared and shook his head.

"For God's sake!" exclaimed Dan Doran. "Show him, will you, Chez?"

The member of the team, Chez, squatted by Gadramm and pointed with a gloved finger to the outline of what appeared to be a fish.

"It's a fish, clear enough. Can't you see that, Gad?" said Doran impatiently. "Fish—a Christian symbol." He gave a curt laugh. "Maybe Christ walked here in better days. Maybe he came over in a spacesuit . . ."

Gadramm said, "It's not a fossil. It's just a random shape in the rock. This whole patch is full of striations. Sure it looks a bit like a fish but it's nothing. Just a pattern, Dak, sorry."

"Look. It's a fish. I'm the guy who has found there was life on Mars. When the news gets out, maybe they'll take us off of this dump and back to Earth. If I turn up more fish, will you see sense then?"

"Of course not. It's a common enough pattern. We can check with the instruments. Forget it." He kicked the rock with his heavy boot.

Doran seized his arm and tried to drag him away. "Destroy the evidence? You jealous bastard!"

Gadramm swung the lever and caught his opponent in the ribs. Doran doubled up.

Krike, one of his team, intervened. "Give me that lever, Gad. You must be goddamn crazy!"

"Stand back or you'll get it too . . ."

They stood there in that alien place, the only life on Mars, hating each other.

◂▸ ◂▸

Fadrum sat by himself in the galley, a bowl of lentil soup in front of him. He had felt lonely before. He was wondering if it was possible to feel more lonely on Mars than on Earth. Maybe he could invent an instrument to gauge the volume of loneliness suffered by individuals.

He thought of Snooks. That pitiable little body was tightly sealed in a plastic box, ready for shipment back to Earth for medical examination.

He thought too of Cauley—his mother lonely in her room. Longing overcame him.

He left the soup and began cautiously up the flights of stairs. Somewhere, a small group of men left behind from the Hecades expedition were singing in chorus an old traditional song:

. . . why did I decide to roam?
gonna take a sennimental journey . . .

The song covered the creak of the stairs.

Reaching his mother's room at the top of the house, Fadrum crept in without knocking.

The room was pitch dark.

"Mother?" said in a whisper.

"Faddy?" A whisper in response. "You naughty boy! Come here to mumma . . ."

"Where are you?"

"In bed, of course. Come to me and let me comfort you."

He did not hesitate. He knew no pleasure as great as his mother's kind of comfort . . .

• •••

Night on Mars held majesty. Unimpeded by atmosphere, the stars took on brilliance and the great drifts of nebulae took on color, eclipsed only by the mighty shingles of the Milky Way. No intelligent creature gazing outward at the spectacle of the universe could help feeling himself or herself dwarfed by its immensity, and yet also exhilarated by the sensation of being part of it.

So thought Gadramm, lying only half-asleep in his tent. He regretted that, in taking command of the human outpost, he had neglected his wife, just to guard the exit. So it was that among that lawless group of men someone had seized the opportunity to cuckold him.

And so he had not been the father of the famous baby. That would surely have ensured his fame. And now that baby was one with all the other dead things on this dead planet. Of course there had been no fish. Or had there once been stone fish?—A different course sentience had taken?

Such matters troubled his sleep. And now came another intrusion. Gadramm propped himself up on one elbow. It was no illusion. He could hear a stealthy noise.

He slept in his clothes and kept his lever by him. Clutching it, he unzipped his tent flap and stared out. Torchlight flashed nearby. He could make out figures of men. It could only be Dak Doran and his team. Up to no good.

In a fury, Gadramm climbed out of his tent. He ran forward, shouting.

Doran's voice returned to him. "Keep your hair on, buster! We're off back to barracks."

"No, you're not. We're under Tampa orders to explore this region. Get back in your tents, you men!"

Doran came up to him, shining his torch in the other's face. "You stay here if you flaming well want. We're going back. No sense in hanging 'round here when you deny the evidence of your eyes."

"Will you get that cocksucking light out my face!" He strove to keep his temper. "Look. Come daylight, we'll get an analysis on your so-called fish and then you'll see. Meantime, we have to go along with Tampa's instructions. Doran, try to figure it out. I'm as keen as you to find traces of life. It will mean cash in the bank for us. To give up now . . ."

Doran interrupted with a roar. "Fer Chris' sake! Tell Tampa what you like. Make up what lies you like. We don't give a toss for you."

"Tha's right," said a man standing by Doran. "We don't give a toss. It's back to barracks for us." He sniggered. "Home comforts . . ."

"We have to draw up a map," said Leen, rather feebly, to defy Doran's man. Despite his anger, Gadramm could see no way of stopping them. And then Doran said, slyly, almost coaxingly, "And if you stay put here then one of us might get the idea of having it off with your missus, like they done before . . ."

The lever came swinging up to catch Doran under his jaw. It swung a second time, across the skull as Doran fell. He flung up his arms with a choked cry and fell backward, his body hitting rock.

"Oh jasers," cried Doran's man. "You've done for him!" He turned and ran, his companions with him.

Gadramm had dropped his lever. His group dragged him away, cursing.

"It was him bonked my wife," gasped Gadramm. "It was him—him— him . . . I didn't mean . . ."

They pulled him back to his tent, Leen and Syril and the others, leaving Doran's body where it lay on the lifeless rock.

◆◆◆◆

The conference on Martian Mortality was in session. The American delegates had opened the occasion, to be followed by the Chinese and Asian delegates, and then the English and European delegates.

There was now a brief discussion concerning the nature of the Martian colonists and their remuneration.

Eddie Skelton explained that the prevailing recession, reinforced by the uncertain climatic changes, had increased the numbers of the unemployed. Studies by an independent body showed that a number of men and some women would volunteer to live on Mars if a certain wage were paid into an American bank account. This wage was provided by various universities provided the new Martians were set a program of scrutinizing the red planet's surface. The scheme was satisfactory to all parties until the question of infant mortality had arisen.

The Chinese minister, Lee Quang Ju, claimed they had the better system, in that their explorers (to use his word) did not pioneer for monetary reasons, as under the capitalist system. Instead, brave pioneers of both sexes traveled for reasons of patriotism and the greater glory of the human race. The scheme was working well, despite the handicap of infant mortality.

Roger Stillby Hayes, speaking for the European contingent, said that their Martian pioneers combined elements of both systems as so far explained. Volunteers had been sought from explorers and scientists, and these were reinforced by the unemployed who had graduated at the postprimary stage. Questions of expense bore heavily on the Exchequer but, he admitted, Martian infant mortality was a problem of a different order.

•◦•◦

While these speeches were in progress, Skelton found his mind wandering
to the question of intimacy with Niccola Bell, his second secretary, who
sat close to him in the great hall. She was dressed in a one-piece black cos-
tume, which concealed but emphasized her figure. As for her beautiful
face, that cute little chin—

•◦•◦

But now there was a brief break in proceedings. Candidates circulated.
Skelton found himself next to Lee Quang Ju, whom Skelton knew of old,
and knew to be a genial individual. Between them they agreed to an-
nounce for the first time the number of deaths caused by lighter gravity on
fetal bone structure.

This proposal was agreed upon.

The European secretary said that as far as they knew deaths of this kind
numbered seventy-one, of which possibly sixty had been stillborn.

The Chinese gave the number as forty-seven. The number was low because there were few women who saw it as their patriotic duty to go to
Mars.

Skelton's team put the number at about sixty. Not all premature deaths
had been announced and, despite the birth of Snooks, and the excitement
he had briefly caused worldwide, women had become increasingly reluctant to undergo pregnancy.

•◦•◦

Next came the question of what should be done to halt this virtual epidemic. Unless the problem was solved, all agreed that permanent settlements on Mars were out of the question.

As had been stated, women were increasingly reluctant to risk pregnancy if the result was to be only death and sorrow. It could be anticipated
that shortly no women would wish to visit Mars under any circumstances.

"In which case," said a voice from the American contingent, "men will
be equally unlikely to want to visit Mars!"

Laughter came mainly from American and European contingents.

•◦•◦

The next subject to be dealt with was the obvious question of what could
be done to ameliorate or entirely cure Martian postfetal mortality.

First to speak on the subject was a well-known American surgeon and
proctologist, Dr. Susan Khashaba.

"Supposing the precipitating weakness to be due to fetal bone mal-
function in continuous lighter gravity, we have to remember that bone is a

living organ, which responds to external influences. It acts as a reservoir for phosphate and calcium. If the fetal bones fail to develop strongly, then a failure of phosphate and calcium may result.

"We should therefore make sure that a supply of these chemicals is available.

"This is my supposition. Unfortunately we can come to no clear conclusion until we are able to examine an infant corpse or, better still, a fetus almost ready for its ejection. Osteomyelitis maybe a different or a concurrent cause, where bacteria lying dormant in the bone may erupt into septicaemia.

"It's a pity that no trained surgeons were ever dispatched to Mars. Our governments have all been negligent."

꘎꘎꘎

Next came a German speaker from the European contingent.

"I do not like to hear what we may call unspoken allegations. It is bold that we attempt colonization of another planet when the world is beset with financial difficulties. We tried to look ahead when dispatching our pioneers and, in fact, wondered if the Martian environment might have bad effects on pregnant women.

"Our plan was that every pregnant woman should be brought back to Earth in her fourth or fifth month to give birth here, being returned to Mars only when the baby achieved its twelfth month of life.

"You will agree, I'm sure, that this was farsighted. Unfortunately, the expenses of such an operation were too great. We approached both of you two august bodies but no agreement could be secured. So the prospect had to be dropped."

Niccola Bell passed Skelton a note, which he read hurriedly. He announced that the European scheme had been deemed impractical, not merely on financial grounds but because the shipping of women to and fro between planets would have proved worse than their remaining peacefully on Mars.

꘎꘎꘎

Lee Quang Ju said they should not bring up minor quibbles between themselves when they were here to establish a solution to this unexpected problem.

"Our methods may not be yours. All the same, we are now arranging for a number of lead platforms to be sent to Mars. On these platforms, with artificial gravity, pregnant women will be able to live more or less normal lives—and so will their fetuses.

"We respect the suggestion of the well-known surgeon Kashaba, but we suggest strongly that she should be accompanied by our leading specialist in acupuncture anaesthesia. He can save much pain, also the considerable expense of relaying old-fashioned Western apparatuses across space."

There followed a period of whispered consultations between the members of the three contingents.

●—●—

Finally, a member of the European group spoke up. "We cannot at present see any reasonable method in which Mars could be settled and become a comfortable second home as we had once wished and tried to plan for. Perhaps there is no way."

Eddie Skelton remarked with a smile that that sounded like a slice of British pessimism.

"Maybe," was the retort, "but you offer us only American optimism and no solution."

●—●—

The conference cheered up at this bit of banter. At which juncture, an old bearded man by the name Angus Campbell rose from the European ranks.

"It could be that, delving into the realms of surgery, or what was that other word? 'Practocology,' was it?—we may find a patch to this wound in the heel of progress. Yet I hear almost no expression of sorrow for these children who have died in the unnatural conditions of a foreign planet, or for their mothers who mourn them. Indeed, I hear next to nothing of a feel for women themselves—women, the better part of the human race . . .

"I take it upon myself—and you must call out to stop me if you cannot bear it—to read you just a paragraph from an old book, first published in 1872, by a man called Winwood Reade, much derided in its time. It's called, *The Martyrdom of Man.* Here goes. Mr. Reade is speaking of a woman who protests against her sex's subordinate role in society.

" 'It is forbidden to receive her; it is an insult to women to allude to her existence, to pronounce her name. She is condemned without inquiry, as the officer is condemned who has shown cowardice before the foe.

" 'For the life of women is a battlefield: virtue is their courage and peace of mind is their reward. It is certainly an extraordinary fact that women should be subjected to a severe social discipline from which men are almost entirely exempt . . . it is due to the ancient subjection of women to the man.

" 'But it is not the women who should be pitied; it is they who alone are free . . . Men? What miseries they cause, how many intellects they paralyze, how many families they ruin, how many innocent hearts they—' "

"Okay, that's entirely enough!" someone called.

Angus Campbell shrugged, ceased reading, and sat down.

Shortly after that, the meeting broke up, after proposing to meet again in a month's time.

▬▪ ▪▬

Eddie Skelton turned to his second secretary. "Well, we did air the subject . . . Now, dear Niccola, if we can find a secluded nook, come and have a drink with me."

Afterword

There are many reasons for liking Fred Pohl—and for liking his work. He is a man of fine discrimination and determination. For instance, at the Brighton Worldcon in '87, he and Betty stayed at a hotel on the seafront, where the nearby restaurant Wheelers served an excellent Dover sole dish. Moreover, they served it in seventeen different ways. So every evening Fred and his lady ate their way steadily down the menu, until they had pretty well taken all that sole had to offer. . . .

Abandoning gastronomy for literature, I recall sitting on the dais with Fred in Cambridge (U.K.). In those distant days, Fred was against the New Wave—which was exciting British writers. To put it briefly, the writers here seemed more keen to get to bed than to Mars. Fred and I both had a word on the subject. Afterward, he told me he had changed his mind and henceforth would be pro–New Wave. It must have been something I said. We should always respect a man who can change his mind—and admits it. You remember such things. Good for you, Fred! Some of us still read *Space Merchants* once every year. It helps us stay modest . . .

—BRIAN W. ALDISS

BEN BOVA

SCHEHERAZADE AND THE STORYTELLERS

"I need a new story!" exclaimed Scheherazade, her lovely almond eyes betraying a rising terror. "By tonight!"

"Daughter of my heart," said her father, the grand vizier, "I have related to you every tale that I know. Some of them, best beloved, were even true!"

"But, most respected father, I am summoned to the sultan again tonight. If I have not a new tale with which to beguile him, he will cut off my head in the morning!"

The grand vizier chewed his beard and raised his eyes to Allah in supplication. He could not help but notice that the gold leaf adorning the ceiling is his chamber was peeling once more. I must call the workmen again, he thought, his heart sinking.

For although the grand vizier and his family resided in a splendid wing of the sultan's magnificent palace, the grand vizier was responsible for the upkeep of his quarters. The sultan was no fool.

"Father!" Scheherazade screeched. "Help me!"

"What can I do?" asked the grand vizier. He expected no answer.

Yet his beautiful, slim-waisted daughter immediately replied, "You must allow me to go to the Street of the Storytellers."

"The daughter of the grand vizier going into the city! Into the bazaar! To the street of those loathesome storytellers? Commoners! Little better than beggars! Never! It is impossible! The sultan would never permit you to leave the palace."

"I could go in disguise," Scheherazade suggested.

"And how could anyone disguise those ravishing eyes of yours, my darling child? How could anyone disguise your angelic grace, your delicate form? No, it is impossible. You must remain in the palace."

Scheherazade threw herself onto the pillows next to her father and sobbed desperately, "Then bid your darling daughter farewell, most noble father. By tomorrow's sun I will be slain."

The grand vizier gazed upon his daughter with true tenderness, even as her sobs turned to shrieks of despair. He tried to think of some way to ease her fears, but he knew that he could never take the risk of smuggling his daughter out of the palace. They would both lose their heads if the sultan discovered it.

Growing weary of his daughter's wailing, the grand vizier suddenly had the flash of an idea. He cried out, "I have it, my best beloved daughter!"

Scheherazade lifted her tear-streaked face.

"If the Prophet—blessed be his name—cannot go to the mountain, then the mountain will come to the Prophet!"

The grand vizier raised his eyes to Allah in thanksgiving for his revelation and he saw once again the peeling gold leaf of the ceiling. His heart hardened with anger against all slipshod workmen, including (of course) storytellers.

◆━◆

And so it was arranged that a quartet of burly guards was dispatched that very morning from the sultan's palace to the street of the storytellers, with orders to bring a storyteller to the grand vizier without fail. This they did, although the grand vizier's hopes fell once he beheld the storyteller the guards had dragged in.

He was short and round, round of face and belly, with big round eyes that seemed about to pop out of his head. His beard was ragged, his clothes tattered and tarnished from long wear. The guards hustled him into the grand vizier's private chamber and threw him roughly onto the mosaic floor before the grand vizier's high-backed, elaborately carved chair of sandalwood inlaid with ivory and filigrees of gold.

For long moments the grand vizier studied the storyteller, who knelt trembling on the patched knees of his pantaloons, his nose pressed to the tiles of the floor. Scheherazade watched from the veiled gallery of the women's quarters, high above, unseen by her father or his visitor.

"You may look upon me," said the grand vizier.

The storyteller raised his head, but remained kneeling. His eyes went huge as he took in the splendor of the sumptuously appointed chamber. Don't you dare look up at the ceiling, the grand vizier thought.

"You are a storyteller?" he asked, his voice stern.

The storyteller seemed to gather himself and replied with a surprisingly strong voice, "Not merely *a* storyteller, oh mighty one. I am *the* storyteller of storytellers. The best of all those who—"

The grand vizier cut him short with, "Your name?"

"Hari-ibn-Hari, eminence." Without taking a breath, the storyteller continued, "My stories are known throughout the world. As far as distant Cathay and the misty isles of the Celts, my stories are beloved by all men."

"Tell me one," said the grand vizier. "If I like it you will be rewarded. If not, your tongue will be cut from your boastful throat."

Hari-ibn-Hari clutched at his throat with both hands.

"Well?" demanded the grand vizier. "Where's your story?"

"Now, your puissance?"

"Now."

●━●━●

Nearly an hour later, the grand vizier had to admit that Hari-ibn-Hari's tale of the sailor Sinbad was not without merit.

"An interesting fable, storyteller. Have you any others?"

"Hundreds, oh protector of the poor!" exclaimed the storyteller. "Thousands!"

"Very well," said the grand vizier. "Each day you will come to me and relate to me one of your tales."

"Gladly," said Hari-ibn-Hari. But then, his round eyes narrowing slightly, he dared to ask, "And what payment will I receive?"

"Payment?" thundered the grand vizier. "You keep your tongue! That is your reward!"

The storyteller hardly blinked at that. "Blessings upon you, most merciful one. But a storyteller must eat. A storyteller must drink, as well."

The grand vizier thought that perhaps drink was more important than food to this miserable wretch.

"How can I continue to relate my tales to you, oh magnificent one, if I faint from hunger and thirst?"

"You expect payment for your tales?"

"It would seem just."

After a moment's consideration, the grand vizier said magnanimously, "Very well. You will be paid one copper for each story you relate."

"One copper?" squeaked the storyteller, crestfallen. "Only one?"

"Do not presume upon my generosity," the grand vizier warned. "You are not the only storyteller in Baghdad."

Hari-ibn-Hari looked disappointed, but he meekly agreed, "One copper, oh guardian of the people."

●━●━●

Six weeks later, Hari-ibn-Hari sat in his miserable little hovel on the Street of the Storytellers and spoke thusly to several other storytellers sitting around him on the packed-earth floor.

"The situation is this, my fellows: the sultan believes that all women are faithless and untrustworthy."

"Many are," muttered Fareed-al-Shaffa, glancing at the only female storyteller among the men, who sat next to him, her face boldly unveiled, her hawk's eyes glittering with unyielding determination.

"Because of the sultan's belief, he takes a new bride to his bed each night and has her beheaded the next morning."

"We know all this," cried the youngest among them, Haroun-el-Ahson, with obvious impatience.

Hari-ibn-Hari glared at the upstart, who was always seeking attention for himself, and continued, "But Scheherazade, daughter of the grand vizier, has survived more than two months now by telling the sultan a beguiling story each night."

"A story stays the sultan's bloody hand?" asked another storyteller, Jamil-abu-Blissa. Lean and learned, he was sharing a hookah water pipe with Fareed-al-Shaffa. Between them, they blew clouds of soft gray smoke that wafted through the crowded little room.

With a rasping cough, Hari-ibn-Hari explained, "Scheherazade does not finish her story by the time dawn arises. She leaves the sultan in such suspense that he allows her to live to the next night, so he can hear the conclusion of her story."

"I see!" exclaimed the young Haroun-el-Ahson. "Cliff-hangers! Very clever of her."

Hari-ibn-Hari frowned at the upstart's vulgar phrase, but went on to the heart of the problem.

"I have told the grand vizier every story I can think of," he said, his voice sinking with woe, "and still he demands more."

"Of course. He doesn't want his daughter to be slaughtered."

"Now I must turn to you, my friends and colleagues. Please tell me your stories, new stories, fresh stories. Otherwise the lady Scheherazade will perish." Hari-ibn-Hari did not mention that the grand vizier would take the tongue from his head if his daughter was killed.

Fareed-al-Shaffa raised his hands to Allah and pronounced, "We will be honored to assist a fellow storyteller in such a noble pursuit."

Before Hari-ibn-Hari could express his undying thanks, the bearded, gnomish storyteller who was known throughout the bazaar as the Daemon of the Night, asked coldly, "How much does the sultan pay you for these stories?"

‐‐‐

Thus it came to pass that Hari-ibn-Hari, accompanied by Fareed-al-Shaffa and the gray-bearded Daemon of the Night, knelt before the grand vizier. The workmen refurbishing the golden ceiling of the grand vizier's chamber were dismissed from their scaffolds before the grand vizier asked, from his chair of authority:

"Why have you asked to meet with me this day?"

The three storytellers, on their knees, glanced questioningly at one another. At length, Hari-ibn-Hari dared to speak.

"Oh, magnificent one, we have provided you with a myriad of stories so that your beautiful and virtuous daughter, on whom Allah has bestowed much grace and wisdom, may continue to delight the sultan."

"May he live in glory," exclaimed Fareed-al-Shaffa in his reedy voice.

The grand vizier eyed them impatiently, waiting for the next slipper to drop.

"We have spared no effort to provide you with new stories, father of all joys," said Hari-ibn-Hari, his voice quaking only slightly. "Almost every storyteller in Baghdad has contributed to the effort."

"What of it?" the grand vizier snapped. "You should be happy to be of such use to me—and my daughter."

"Just so," Hari-ibn-Hari agreed. But then he added, "However, hunger is stalking the Street of the Storytellers. Starvation is on its way."

"Hunger?" the grand vizier snapped. "Starvation?"

Hari-ibn-Hari explained, "We storytellers have bent every thought we have to creating new stories for your lovely daughter—blessings upon her. We don't have time to tell stories in the bazaar anymore—"

"You'd better not!" the grand vizier warned sternly. "The sultan must hear only new stories, stories that no one else has heard before. Otherwise he would not be intrigued by them and my dearly loved daughter would lose her head."

"But, most munificent one," cried Hari-ibn-Hari, "by devoting ourselves completely to your needs, we are neglecting our own. Since we no longer have the time to tell stories in the bazaar, we have no other source of income except the coppers you pay us for our tales."

The grand vizier at last saw where they were heading. "You want more? Outrageous!"

"But, oh farseeing one, a single copper for each story is not enough to keep us alive!"

Fareed-al-Shaffa added, "We have families to feed. I myself have four wives and many children."

"What is that to me?" the grand vizier shouted. He thought that these pitiful storytellers were just like workmen everywhere, trying to extort higher wages for their meager efforts.

"We cannot continue to give you stories for a single copper apiece," Fareed-al-Shaffa said flatly.

"Then I will have your tongues taken from your throats. How many stories will you be able to tell then?"

The three storytellers went pale. But the Daemon of the Night, small and frail though he was in body, straightened his spine and found the strength to say, "If you do that, most noble one, you will get no more stories and your daughter will lose her life."

The grand vizier glared angrily at the storytellers. From her hidden post in the veiled gallery, Scheherazade felt her heart sink. Oh father! she begged silently. Be generous. Open your heart.

At length the grand vizier muttered darkly, "There are many story-tellers in Baghdad. If you three refuse me I will find others who will gladly serve. And, of course, the three of you will lose your tongues. Consider carefully. Produce stories for me at one copper apiece, or be silenced for-ever."

"Our children will starve!" cried Fareed-al-Shaffa.

"Our wives will have to take to the streets to feed themselves," wailed Hari-ibn-Hari.

The Daemon of the Night said nothing.

"That is your choice," said the grand vizier, as cold and unyielding as a steel blade. "Stories at one copper apiece or I go to other storytellers. And you lose your tongues."

"But magnificent one—"

"That is your choice," the grand vizier repeated sternly. "You have un-til noon tomorrow to decide."

●—●●

It was a gloomy trio of storytellers who wended their way back to the bazaar that day.

"He is unyielding," Fareed-al-Shaffa said. "Too bad. I have been think-ing of a new story about a band of thieves and a young adventurer. I think I'll call him Ali Baba."

"A silly name," Hari-ibn-Hari rejoined. "Who could take seriously a story where the hero's name is so silly?"

"I don't think the name is silly," Fareed-al-Shaffa maintained. "I rather like it."

As they turned in to the Street of the Storytellers, with ragged, lean, and hungry men at every door pleading with passersby to listen to their tales, the Daemon of the Night said softly, "Arguing over a name is not going to solve our problem. By tomorrow noon we could lose our tongues."

Hari-ibn-Hari touched reflexively at his throat. "But to continue to sell our tales for one single copper is driving us into starvation."

"We will starve much faster if our tongues are cut out," said Fareed-al-Shaffa.

The others nodded unhappily as they plodded up the street and stopped at al-Shaffa's hovel.

"Come in and have coffee with me," he said to his companions. "We must think of a way out of this problem."

All four of Fareed-al-Shaffa's wives were home, and all four of them asked the storyteller how they were expected to feed their many children if he did not bring in more coins.

"Begone," he commanded them—after they had served the coffee. "Back to the women's quarters."

The women's quarters was nothing more than a squalid room in the rear of the hovel, teeming with noisy children.

Once the women had left, the three storytellers squatted on the threadbare carpet and sipped at their coffee cups.

"Suppose this carpet could fly," mused Hari-ibn-Hari.

Fareed-al-Shaffa humphed. "Suppose a genie appeared and gave us riches beyond imagining."

The Daemon of the Night fixed them both with a somber gaze. "Suppose you both stop toying with new story ideas and turn your attention to our problem."

"Starve from low wages or lose our tongues," sighed Hari-ibn-Hari.

"And once our tongues have been cut out the grand vizier goes to other storytellers to take our place," said the Daemon of the Night.

Fareed-al-Shaffa said slowly, "The grand vizier assumes the other storytellers will be too terrified by our example to refuse his starvation wage."

"He's right," Hari-ibn-Hari said bitterly.

"Is he?" mused Fareed. "Perhaps not."

"What do you mean?" his two companions asked in unison.

Stroking his beard thoughtfully, Fareed-al-Shaffa said, "What if all the storytellers refused to work for a single copper per tale?"

Hari-ibn-Hari asked cynically, "Would they refuse before or after our tongues have been taken out?"

"Before, of course."

The Daemon of the Night stared at his fellow storyteller. "Are you suggesting what I think you're suggesting?"

"I am."

Hari-ibn-Hari gaped at the two of them. "No, it would never work. It's impossible!"

"Is it?" asked Fareed-al-Shaffa. "Perhaps not."

◆—◆—

The next morning the three bleary-eyed storytellers were brought before the grand vizier. Once again Scheherazade watched and listened from her veiled gallery. She herself was bleary-eyed as well, having spent all night telling the sultan the tale of Ala-al-Din and his magic lamp. As usual, she had left the tale unfinished as the dawn brightened the sky.

This night she must finish the tale and begin another. But she had no other to tell! Her father had to get the storytellers to bring her fresh material. If not, she would lose her head with tomorrow's dawn.

"Well?" demanded the grand vizier as the three storytellers knelt trembling before him. "What is your decision?"

The three of them had chosen the Daemon of the Night to be their spokesperson. But as he gazed up at the fierce countenance of the grand vizier, his voice choked in his throat.

Fareed-al-Shaffa nudged him, gently at first, then more firmly.

At last the Daemon said, "Oh, magnificent one, we cannot continue to supply your stories for a miserable one copper per tale."

"Then you will lose your tongues!"

"And your daughter will lose her head, most considerate of fathers."

"Bah! There are plenty of other storytellers in Baghdad. I'll have a new story for my daughter before the sun goes down."

Before the Daemon of the Night could reply, Fareed-al-Shaffa spoke thusly, "Not so, sir. No storyteller will work for you for a single copper per tale."

"Nonsense!" snapped the grand vizier.

"It is true," said the Daemon of the Night. "All the storytellers have agreed. We have sworn a mighty oath. None of us will give you a story unless you raise your rates."

"Extortion!" cried the grand vizier.

Hari-ibn-Hari found his voice. "If you take our tongues, oh most merciful of men, none of the other storytellers will deal with you at all."

Before the astounded grand vizier could reply to that, Fareed-al-Shaffa explained, "We have formed a guild, your magnificence, a storyteller's guild. What you do to one of us you do to us all."

"You can't do that!" the grand vizier sputtered.

"It is done," said the Daemon of the Night. He said it softly, almost in a whisper, but with great finality.

The grand vizier sat on his chair of authority getting redder and redder in the face, his chest heaving, his fists clenching. He looked like a volcano about to erupt.

When, from the veiled gallery above them, Scheherazade cried out, "I think it's wonderful! A storyteller's guild. And you created it just for me!"

The three storytellers raised their widening eyes to the balcony of the gallery, where they could make out the slim and graceful form of a young woman, suitably gowned and veiled, who stepped forth for them all to see. The grand vizier twisted around in his chair and nearly choked with fury.

"Father," Scheherazade called sweetly, "is it not wonderful that the storytellers have banded together so that they can provide stories for me to tell the sultan night after night?"

The grand vizier started to reply once, twice, three times. Each time no words escaped his lips. The three storytellers knelt before him, staring up at the gallery where Scheherazade stood openly before them—suitably gowned and veiled.

Before the grand vizier could find his voice, Scheherazade said, "I welcome you, storytellers, and your guild. The grand vizier, the most munificent of fathers, will gladly pay you ten coppers for each story you relate to me. May you bring me a thousand of them!"

Before the grand vizier could figure how much a thousand stories would cost, at ten coppers per story, Fareed-al-Shaffa smiled up at Scheherazade and murmured, "A thousand and one, oh gracious one."

◄•►•

The grand vizier was unhappy with the new arrangement, although he had to admit that the storyteller's newly founded guild provided stories that kept the sultan bemused and his daughter alive.

The storytellers were pleased, of course. Not only did they keep their tongues in their heads and earn a decent income from their stories, but they shared the subsidiary rights to the stories with the grand vizier once Scheherazade had told them to the sultan and they could then be related to the general public.

Ten coppers per story was extortionate, in the grand vizier's opinion, but the storyteller's guild agreed to share the income from the stories once they were told in the bazaar. There was even talk of an invention from far-off Cathay, where stories could be printed on vellum and sold throughout the kingdom. The grand vizier consoled himself with the thought that if sales were good enough, the income could pay for regilding his ceiling.

The sultan eventually learned of the arrangement, of course. Being no fool, he demanded that he be cut in on the profits. Reluctantly, the grand vizier complied.

Scheherazade was the happiest of all. She kept telling stories to the sultan until he relented of his murderous ways and eventually married her, much to the joy of all Baghdad.

She thought of the storyteller's guild as her own personal creation, and called it Scheherazade's Fables and Wonders Association.

That slightly ponderous name was soon abbreviated to SFWA.

Afterword

Beneath the whimsy of "Scheherazade and the Storytellers" lies a hard, bitter fact: publishers have often treated writers with bleak disdain, and even contempt.

In addition to being a brilliant writer and one of the best editors the field of science fiction has ever seen, Frederik Pohl has also worked tirelessly to help writers achieve their deserved rights in the hard business of publishing. He has been a major force in establishing and maintaining both the Science Fiction Writers of America and World SF, organizations that protect and advance the writer's position.

For this, writers everywhere owe an enormous debt to Fred Pohl. Perhaps the most rational man I've ever met, Fred has done as much as any person, and more than most, to help writers earn a decent living and the respect they deserve.

The grand vizier of my story is not entirely a figment of my imagination. There was a time when writers toiled for a penny a word, and even less. Fred Pohl was one of them, and clearly one of the best. Today writers are much better off financially and in terms of esteem from both the publishers and the reading audience. For this, we writers owe an everlasting debt to Frederik Pohl.

—BEN BOVA

JOAN SLONCZEWSKI

※|※

APPRECIATION OF FRED POHL

Fred's work has long appealed to me for its satirical and farsighted depictions of commercial dominance of the future. From *Space Merchants* to the Heechee, I knew of Fred Pohl as a towering presence in the science fiction universe. It came as a total surprise when I heard that Betty and Fred had nominated my book, *A Door into Ocean*, for the Campbell Award. When I visited the University of Kansas to receive the award, it was an amazing experience to actually meet Fred, someone of whom I'd heard so much.

Since then, over the years, I've enjoyed seeing Fred at many meetings of the Science Fiction Research Association. Fred has always inspired me as the model of a professional writer and mentor in the science fiction community. He exemplifies the ability to live in two worlds at once—the world of science fiction, and the world of so-called reality. Those who truly understand the implications of science fiction know how challenging that is. One incident I recall, years ago at a SFRA meeting in Reno, brought this home to me. At the meeting, Fred and I were invited to be interviewed by a local television station. I was glad Fred came along because I had no idea what to say and I knew Fred would be a good guide.

When we arrived at the station, we discovered that our interview was to be the second act following the station's weekly dog adoption. The dog to be adopted was placed in the seat of honor, right next to Fred. My seat of course came a distant third. The dog went first, getting its pitch for adoption broadcast to the Reno audience. After that, the announcer asked Fred to explain the significance of science fiction. Fred did so, creditably explaining how science fiction explores the nature of society. After his response, the announcer observed, "My, these science fiction writers use long words." So then it was up to me. I did my best to follow Fred's example of grace under pressure, with the hope that someone out there in Reno TV land might catch a spark from our long words.

I think our experience in Reno would fit just fine into one of Fred's books, or for that matter into *Brain Plague*, a book I dedicated to Betty and Fred because it would never have been written without their support and inspiration. I look forward to exploring the universe with the Heechee for many years to come.

SHERI S. TEPPER

THE FLIGHT OF THE
DENARTESESTEL RADICHAN

The Pronunchumniak Institute of Moral Zoology (PIMZ) in Sector ORV 254 was directed by its board of ethicists to conduct a biological assay of certain planets in Thrasbol sector. It was decided to lease the Thwartian charter ship, *Sprot*, together with a good part of its crew, as the *Sprot* was already equipped for multiple environmental containments. While in Thwartian the word *Sprot* conveyed intrepidity, a mindless adherence to arbitrary rules of honor, and a complete willingness to maim/kill/destroy any being, thing, or place that got in its way, the Pronunchumniaks used the same auditory label to identify a certain bit of personal equipment used rarely and only under conditions of extreme embarrassment. The Pronunchumniaks (Pronun-CHUM-nee-aks; Chums or Chummys, as the Thwartians called them), did not consider a ship named *Sprot* appropriate to be cited in dignified academic documents or be identified with the Institute's research. *Denartesestel Radichan*, on the other hand, meant "words of high praise for worthy endeavors," a much more suitable label. The ship was promptly, though temporarily, given that name. It is probably unnecessary to remark that the Thwartians, though excellent space-farers, are a people of few words. The Pronunchumniaks are, on the other hand, academics.

Thrasbol sector, the Institute's target area, contained five suns, twenty inhabited planets, and, as it turned out, a few previously unknown and quite dangerous space dwelling organisms. The first inkling of the existence of these organisms occurred when the *Denart Sp**t*—pronounced "spbleept" by the largely Thwartian crew—left its last scheduled survey site to return to Sector ORV 254, home base, as it were. Methane cargo holds one through four were wall to wall with creature-containers; aquatic hold five was about half full; oxygen holds six and seven were chock-a-block; and the smaller, exotic holds (offering extremes of pressure, temperature, and radiation) held numerous specimens that the Pronunchumniaks believed to be not only totally new to scholarship but capable of opening many new areas of academic specialization, a greatly felt need on their home planet, where one could not go to a gathering of anyone who was anyone without bumping into several someones looking for a thesis topic that had not already been worn tissue thin by repeated elaboration. The mood aboard ship was celebratory, even ebullient, except among those highly trained Moral Zoologists who were serving as PECSNIFs, that is Professional Ethical Calculators and Special Native Intelligence Functionaries, as their arduous work always began after everyone else's had been completed. Even they, however, admitted to being glad the long voyage was over and resigned to beginning their work in oxygen hold six, where a particular omnivorous, bisexual, bipedal, unarmored race of creatures (OBBUs) required immediate final classification.

"Not understand need for hurry," the Thwartian captain said.

"The race is curiously repellent," said the PECSNIF-in-chief. "We are afraid it may be so far gone in moral degeneracy that we would be prohibited from bringing any sample of it into that space which we hold in sentimental partiality."

"Race is OBU," the captain said. "Omniv, biped, unarmored. Not dangerous."

"The race in question is not OBU, Most High Up of All Those Aboard with the Exception of the Professional Ethical Calculators. The race is OBBU!"

"Yes. Omnivorous. Bipedal. Unarmored . . ."

"And bisexual," said the PECSNIF, with unusual brevity.

"No!" cried the captain with an aversive gesture, his bud pores flushing with embarrassment. "Then assess at once. Assess. Do what is needed."

While the Care and Cleanliness Androids (CACAs) continued their care of the other specimens, the PECSNIFS drew a small sample population from the appropriate oxygen hold and set about their investigation. They had barely begun, however, when the first of the previously unknown space-dwelling predators was spotted by one of the Chummies, a Worm Hole Officer, Acting (WHOA). As that operator was entering the calibrations necessary for the first jump and as the jump-field expanded to the diameter necessary to encompass the ship—the *Denart Sp**t* being, as may be imagined, sizable—the officer was surprised to see several large instabilities entering the field from widely separated points. The expansion process could not, unfortunately, be discontinued at that stage of operation, though the WHOA resolved to mention the instabilities as soon as the *Denart Sp**t* had entered the wormhole.

When the WHOA did so, both Pronunchumniak and Thwartian bridge officers examined the readings with interest. The instabilities were certifiably present in the jump-field, but they were maintaining a constant distance from the *Denart Sp**t*, making no threatening movements. Since the instabilities were an unknown, the PECSNIFs were also alerted and brought to the bridge.

"First transit where?" the Thwartian captain asked the WHOA.

"Deep space, Most High Up and Worthy of Respect of All Persons Aboard," said the WHOA. "Second transit is some remote and quite insignificant system on a trailing edge."

"First transit, lose instabilities?"

"It is feared by myself as Wormhole Officer, Acting, there would be insufficient distance to maneuver, Most High Up of and Worthy of All Persons Aboard," replied the WHOA. "The nexus postulated presents the complication of being virtually an adjacency to our arrival point."

"Second transit?"

"We will in all probability find we have sufficient maneuvering space, there, Most High Up of All—"

"Captain!" bellowed the Thwartian captain. "Just say 'Captain.'"

"We have spacial sufficien . . . room there, ah, Captain."

"Very well. Keep oglers ready while in hole. Set long-range oglers for closer look. If things alive, MZ people will want look."

"Yes, Most High . . . Captain."

The wormhole was a complicated one, of extensive duration. The oglers were set to record and the Moral Zoology people serving as PECs, SNIFs, or both stood around the screens gazing at the things and debating whether they were alive or not. Certainly they did not look alive, but then, they didn't look like rocks, either. Or ice. Or clotted space fume. Or impacted gravitic nodules, which would have made the expedition members very rich if the *Denart Sp**t* could have snagged them without getting crushed in the process. All the PECSNIFs agreed that some possessed a certain repetitive and segmentary appearance, while others showed an erratic and nonfractal crystallinity. There were five of them in total, and no two were alike.

"What are they?" the captain asked the Moral Zoologists.

The Moral Zoologists performed a concerted shrug followed by a lengthy and complicated tentacular twiddle, meaning they had no idea. One of them suggested that at the next nexus, they attempt to get a closer look before making the succeeding transit. The WHOA was consulted about the advisability of such an action.

"If you believe ourselves so lacking in prudence as to take such a not inconsiderable leap in abysmal ignorance of consequences, certainly," said the WHOA. "If you believe moral correctness requires approaching an unknown quantity or quality, which may prove to be antithetical or even fatal in nature."

The argument concerning this observation occupied the Chummy contingent during the remainder of the transit, with the majority still in favor of approach. True scholarship, as the dean of Spatio-Temporal Studies was fond of pointing out, required intrepidity.

When the *Denart Sp**t* emerged, and after the momentary crew disorientation passed, the MZ contingent gathered around the screens as the ship turned toward one of the instabilities, which immediately coiled up and extended several large claw-shaped energy fields.

"I cannot but believe it would be acceptable to reconfigure our approach toward one of the other instabilities," suggested the WHOA in an unhurried but impassioned tone.

Accordingly, two more instabilities were approached in turn, only to have each respond with a movement that, while not immediately destructive, was menacing enough to be considered an aversive response. When the *Denart Sp**t* pulled back, each instability took its former shape.

"Machines," said one of the MZs. "That's my opinion."

"Life-forms," said another. "What would machines be doing out here?"

"We conveyed them to this location," said the WHOA with unusual brevity. "They were at the time colocated within the expansion field."

"Sprot-burricles!" said the captain, at which all Chummys within hearing turned their ashen budstalks downward in shame. "At next nexus we lose or destroy them! Be ready."

All the MZs flushed a vivid puce and began to discuss the order with great vehemence. The discussion went on for some time without arriving at a conclusion. The next nexus was reached and the *Denart Sp**t* emerged into a small system at the back end of nowhere. The moment the oglers were refocused, the WHOA screamed at the top of his gas sacs, "Antithetical approach! Antithetical approach."

Without taking time to discuss the matter, the captain armed the ship's cannons and turned the ship directly toward the system star, barely visible in a wide gap between two of the threatening creatures. The *Denart Sp**t* picked up speed and fled between the two at a considerable distance, receiving a punishing blow from one or possibly both of them.

"What happened?" cried the captain. "Damage report!"

"Energy field, Most High Up and Worthy Though Perhaps Somewhat Precipitous of All Those Aboard Ship," cried a Pronunchumniak damage control officer. "Engines one and five of the ship *Denartesestel Radichan* have been effectively nullified for purposes of directional propulsive activity.

All five instability creatures are currently manifesting activities indicating possible intensively antipathetic approach."

"Weapons Officer," cried the captain. "Get rid of those things!"

"Greatly regretful, Most High Up of All Those Aboard Ship Except the Moral Zoologists," cried the Chummy weapons officer. "No MZ rating on the attackers is currently available. Offensive weapons may not be used on those rating six or above . . ." On any ship occupied by Pronunchumniaks, the weapons officer was Pronunchumniak, as no other races could be trusted to be consistently moral when they had itchy trigger fingers.

"This is emergency," shouted the captain. "Another hit like that, we all dead, you all dead, Thwart will sue hind tentacles off every Chummy still living!"

A rapid though lengthy discussion ensued, after which the WO was allowed to fire warning shots across what were assumed to be the frontal areas of the instabilities. One stopped, two withdrew, and the last two, which were also the largest, continued to follow the *Denart Sp**t*, though at greater distance.

"I am of the opinion it would not be totally inappropriate to assume a manifestation of both animosity and aggression," said one MZ to another.

"Though one must take into consideration that they were, perhaps, provoked," replied the other. "I think we should maintain course, swing around that little star and see if the things don't give up." It shrugged one tentacle, tentatively. "They might."

"Such a course of action would require that we gain a great deal of velocity," said the WHOA. "I will accordingly compute an orbit that will result in our arriving back at the proper nexus which is, at this juncture, a relatively great distance behind us. We will, however, expend an enormous amount of time in the endeavor."

"That's all right," said the chief MZ. "There's a marvelously complicated gas giant very near, which bears a huge roseate vacuity upon it. We can take this opportunity to do a survey. Also, no doubt the crew needs some time to repair the engines."

The damage control officer snarled. "Engines one and five of the ship *Denartesestel Radichan* are unfortunately in no condition to be considered repairable. The aforementioned engines are not even salvageable, being in a condition of total absence."

"Oh, my gracious," said the chief MZ. "Will we be able to return to the locus considered by most of us to be one of sentimental partiality?"

"It may be possible to get home given a little luck," replied the WHOA, with such Thwartian brevity as to sound positively rude. "If nothing else happens."

The two persistent instabilities continued to follow the *Denart Sp**t*. The one instability that had remained in place moved toward the gas giant. The two that had withdrawn moved slowly toward another gas giant, far-ther out, which was haloed with several debris rings. The MZs watched with great interest as the two instabilities approached the rings, abruptly broke up into a multitude of small, fractal subunits, and joined the rings of debris. Long-range scanners showed the smaller units happily munching on ring debris and building others of their kind.

"Machines," said one MZ. "That's what I thought."

The third instability approached the largest gas giant and plunged into it without a moment's pause. Some time later, a huge, brilliant green plume of gas came up from the place it had entered. All this was recorded by the MZs, as were the two instabilities that were still following the ship. Noth-ing else happened for some little time.

Then: "It is with deep regret and reluctance that I acknowledge the ex-istence of a problem of some considerable dimension," said the WHOA to no one in particular. "It seems the *Denartesestel Radichan* is currently of too great a mass for us to make the required orbit with only four engines."

"Make it how?" asked the captain.

The WHOA sighed and condensed what it had been going to say. "Make it back to the nexus, so we can go home."

"What can we do?"

"Jettison cargo," said the WHOA.

"Jettison cargo," cried the chief MZ. "We've only partially classified one section of oxygen hold six. There's no morally acceptable way we can jettison an unclassified cargo!"

The WHOA composed itself and said in a tightly controlled voice, "If the cargo classifies as type five or below, you could jettison it, right?"

"Quite correct."

"If the cargo classified above a five, you could jettison it in order to save our lives, right?"

"That is true."

"Since there is no other classification than that included in the afore-mentioned categories, I suggest you jettison the entire cargo under either or both of the classifications I have mentioned."

"But we don't know which is which," cried the chief MZ. "The rec-ords would need . . ."

"Since the end result will be the same in either case, I would suggest an arbitrary classification," cried the WHOA.

The Moral Zoologists spent the next six waking periods discussing this, at the end of which time they had agreed upon a course of action. There would be a valid but preliminary classification based on survival characteristics, after which some creatures would be jettisoned onto the rocky planet inside the orbit of the big gas planet. Some creatures would be jettisoned back toward the big gas planet itself. Some creatures would be jettisoned on each of the subsequent inner planets: a watery one, a very cloudy hot one, and an even hotter one close in. In each case, the creatures having the best chance of survival in that location would be jettisoned.

Each creature container was, in fact, a self-contained environment, provided with appropriate life support, including soft landing and automatic-release systems. The Moral Zoological Institute had ruled long ago that organisms might be collected only if such safeguards were provided in case of shipwreck. As the *Denart Sp**t* plunged sunward, therefore, the cargo holds were gradually purged of their contents, escape environments hastening away toward planets where they would land after only several revolutions. The ship was able to make an appropriate swing around the sun, which headed it back to the nexus that would take it home. The two instabilities that had pursued it as far as the orbit of the hot cloudy planet had entered that planet's atmosphere and had later been seen disporting themselves in the sulphurous cloud layers that masked its surface.

Having jettisoned sufficient cargo, the Thwartians and the Pronunchumniaks returned to Sector ORV 254 without further incident. The Moral Zoological Institute thereupon began hearings as to what, if anything, should be done to recover the specimens jettisoned in that far-off, lonely corner of the galaxy. Reports and recommendations on this subject were heard at each annual meeting for the next fifty-three revolutions, at which time it was determined that retrieval was a moral necessity if for only one reason: in their haste to return from their unfortunate voyage, the Moral Zoologists aboard the survey ship had neglected to find out if there were life-forms on any of the planets toward which they had released their cargo. This fact had already resulted in the commission of grave ethical errors, which might, on further study, turn out to be irreparably indicative of the necessity for ritual suicide. This was particularly true in the case of the suspected OBBU race, the bisexual one. While the depravity of bisexuality was not totally unknown in Sector ORV 254, virtually all practitioners of it had been sought out and destroyed during periodic ritual cleansings of the sector.

A multispecies committee was formed to consider this subject, and was ordered to do a prompt and thorough feasibility study of various rescue methods. It was determined that special, small, disk-shaped retrieval ships should be sent to the various planets to locate the surviving creatures and extract them, particularly the creatures that had been dropped on the watery planet third from the sun, as they were considered to be so morally reprehensible that any native population they had encountered might already have been eradicated. The Moral Zoologists ruled that immediate extraction of these castaways had first priority, as the creatures had the disgusting habit, among many others, of taking the shape of whatever race might be numerous in any given ecosystem and preying upon that race from within.

The extraction ships that approached the third planet, which was called *Urth* by many of its inhabitants, found that it was completely occupied by an omnivorous, bipedal, bisexual, unarmored race calling itself *peepul*. The castaway creatures had had quite a lengthy time in *Urth* years in which to become well established. The Moral Zoologists estimated that inasmuch as the castaways could no doubt have taken the form of the *peepul*, one in ten of the OBBUs on *Urth* might actually be a castaway. Still, the Moral Zoologists did not consider that the problem was beyond solution. Since they had previously determined that the OBBUs picked up during the survey used a consistent and unique form of predation, the MZs felt it would be relatively easy to determine which of the OBBUs were the products of native evolution and which had been cast away upon the planet.

The unique form of predation commonly used by the castaways began with the subversion of the brains of their prey, starting with the younger ones, by sensory assault, largely sonic. This short-circuited the victim's not-yet-developed "ugmomfit," or "common sense," so called because it was common to all speaking races in the universe, as well as a good many non-speaking ones. The vacuum resulting from the extraction of common sense was then replaced by a set of "wish images" tailored to the basic yens of the various subsets of native creatures. These "wish images" were then used to weld the native creatures into subgroups that could be relied upon to provide their "leaders"—the castaways—with whatever needs and pleasures were wanted: food, drink, sensory stimulation, accommodations, all in return for having their "wish images" repeatedly confirmed. The "wish image confirmations" took the form of, 1. *Definition* (You love woggle fruit! Yes you do!!) 2. *Affirmation* (Everybody who is anybody loves woggle fruit and Mumdah knows you do too!!) 3. *Purchase price* (Well, you work real hard for Mumdah) and, finally, 4. *The promise* (Mumdah will see that when you get old you'll go to a wonderful world that is just full of woggle fruit, and you can eat it forever). Or, 1. "You hate those nasty old other-politicals/other-believers/other-skinned people/other-haired people. 2, "Everybody who is anybody hates those other people." 3. "Well, you just give lots and lots of money to Mumdah and help Mumdah throw a few bombs." 4. "We'll get rid of every one of them!" This latter wish system had often been used on the castaway's native planet to decrease population density in certain areas. The castaways called their method of predation "economics."

As has been mentioned, PECSNIF statistics indicated that one out of every ten of the OBBUs should be a castaway. Imagine, then, the dilemma presented to the Moral Zoologists when their retrieval ships returned with tests of the population showing that only a few of the creatures could be identified as native born. Virtually all OBBUs were either leading wish groups or members of them. The entire planet was filled by swarms of OBBUs inventing wish images, advertising wish images, and desiring wish images. Meantime, the basic bisexual genetic depravity with which they were burdened, constantly stimulated by wish images into repeated and needless sexual activity, had resulted in overpopulating their world and driving virtually all other living creatures into extinction. As had been true in ORV 254 before bisexuality was declared depraved and subject to immediate eradication, all planets so occupied inevitably destroyed themselves. This process was so well known and recognized that bisexuality was no longer tolerated in any civilized sector. Only calm and rational budding, as needed for population balance, was approved.

The leaders of the retrieval expedition turned the matter over to the PECSNIFs who would make the final determination. That was, after all, why the Professional Ethical Calculators and Special Native Intelligence Functionaries got the big bucks!

PECSNIF declared as follows:

A: If we assume there had never been a native OBBU population, merely a very fast population explosion of castaways, then all the OBBUs on *Urth* would need to be eradicated because they threatened the native biome and had predated upon all living things including their own kind. In that case, no fault would be assigned nor would there be any remediation except fixing the local ecology ruined by the castaways.

B: If, however, we assume there had been a sensible, non–wish image native population that, in its entirety, had been subverted by the castaways, then the fault lay with the members of the original expedition including the PECSNIFians among them, all of whom would be expected to commit ritual suicide out of shame.

C: If, however, an existing native population of OBBUs had *always* been as it was now, then no fault extended to either the Thwartians or the Pronunchumniaks, not even remediation of the environment.

In order to ascertain which of these possibilities was true, a significant body of *Urth* history and literature extending back to precastaway times was borrowed from the libraries of the *Urth* and translated into both Thwartian (one slim volume) and Pronunchumniaknius (one newly built orbiting library including all resultant theses).

After much discussion—of which meticulous minutes were kept by the Chummies in order to prove beyond controversy that all sides of every argument had been considered—it was determined that the *Urth* creatures had always been mostly that way—with a few unisexual exceptions—that the castaways had had, in fact, no discernible effect and therefore, no guilt was assigned to either Thwart or Pronunchumniak. Since no one could tell the difference between castaway or native bisexual groups, reliable extermination would simply include every member of the population in any way connected to a bisexual wish image group or activity. After extermination, a team of Budding Coaches would be sent to the planet to adapt the remaining unisexual *peepul* so they could bud rationally.

The Professional Ethical Calculators required that the usual warning be prepared and delivered to the planet in question. The planet would be watched for at least one hundred of its solar orbits to assure the warning had been continuously visible and to allow the creatures there to correct themselves if they would, though, as one PECSNIF said to another at the time, *"Do not feel it necessary or appropriate at any point during the next hundred years to restrain the continued and usual functions of your aspirating organs."* At the end of that time, any corrected OBBUs would be spared, while all the uncorrected, filthy, depraved bisexuals on the planet would simply . . . go.

●—●●

It was later recalled among amused PECSNIFs who viewed the oglers left upon *Urth* that for decades afterward, OBBUs on *Urth* sniggered at or ignored the bearded old creatures walking through their cities with their signs: THE END IS NEAR. REPENT. THE WORLD IS COMING TO AN END. Because the sign carriers offered no wish images at all, not a single OBBU during the entire century bothered to ask who sent them or what it all meant.

Afterword

During the long years between knowing I "wanted to write," and finally, "ended up writing," I occasionally accomplished something on paper, prose or rhymes (from Bad to Verse). Sometimes I sent them off to no purpose and little encouragement. One exception was a verse concerning interstellar transport (can't remember the title) in which each item discarded as useless by one planet ended up being purchased for some interestingly nefarious purpose on another. It ended up on Fred's desk. He published it, and then, as I recall (it was a very long time ago) another one later on.

Many of my books have silly verses in them, including the "Hay Wainer's Song" in *The Margarets*, and the "Horse's Song," which both begins and ends *The Waters' Rising*. Each time one pops into my head (which is what they do, probably from some other dimension), I think fondly of Fred. His enjoyment of that silliness and the encouragement of publication kept me aimed at writing, one way or another for many, many years. I wish him a happy ninetieth birthday and send sincere hope that he will celebrate his hundredth with continued enjoyment of the profound silliness that seems to be our world.

—SHERI S. TEPPER

NEIL GAIMAN

✖⬧✖

THE [BACKSPACE] MERCHANTS

The [backspace] merchants sell deletions and removals,
masters of the world (or so they claim)
they go by
many hundred different names
and live inside a giant block of Spam.

It quivers, as if alive, is fed
by tubes and tendrils, and is inhabited.
Portions are cut from it continually to feed the people.
Insidious, invidious,
(occasionally in videos),
the [backspace] merchants seek to sell you:
V1agRa and all its magical cousins
(*If you had a larger thing in your pants your life would have been better!!*)
(*MAGIC PENIS ENLARGEMENT PILLS*)
(*She'll love the new growth!*)
(*Make nights turbulent.*)
Also, designer watches, diplomas,
diplomats who will entrust you with their missing millions.
There are girls in your town who want to
meet you.

The [backspace] merchants want so to delete you.

The [backspace] merchants click and they erase
our faces, so we keep on losing face.
The [backspace] merchants
offer relief from their own excesses:
The products will not work as advertised
The Spam is vast and must be satisfied.

In the old days of the future
our freedom fighters lived deep inside the chicken meat
Their coffee was the coffiest, their dreams the dreamiest.
The rest of us craved and grazed our lives away
and wondered if we should emigrate to Venus.

These are the poles we navigate between:
Yesterday's futures now reshape our days
into futures past, somewhere between last week and day million
as ancient as a black and white TV show, watched so late
and all the names we conjured with appeared to us in monochrome
with their faces, such young faces,
to those of us who would learn to be plugged in at all times,
they told us of the future, that it was what they saw
a Game of If when they opened wide their eyes.

So we avoided all their awful warnings,
ignored the minefields as the klaxons sounded
played "Cheat the Prophet" just as Gilbert said,
we sidestepped cacatopias unbounded
and built ourselves this gorgeous mess instead

I wish we could still emigrate to Venus.

Sometimes I wonder what the Spam makes of us:
does it define us by our base desires,
or hope we can transcend them? Like small gods,
the [backspace] merchants offer us all choices
and each day
we can be tempted
or delete.
They lay their traps ineptly at our feet.

The present moves so quick we can't describe it,
so Science Fiction limns the recent past.
We future folk are just another tribe who
hyperlinked our colors to the mast,
When *now* is always *then* and never *soon*.
Our freak flags will not fly upon the moon.

Our prophets opened gateways, showed us pitfalls
gave us worlds of if and galaxies uncountable.
They made us think then take the other road.
But future yesterdays are growing cold.
The [backspace] merchants huddle in their meat
while we demand a finer, nobler future:
It waits for us beyond the blue horizon.
Our future will be glorious and gold.

If it lasts more than four hours
consult your physician.

For Fred Pohl, with infinite admiration.

Afterword

When I was little more than a boy, I stayed up after my bedtime to watch a TV documentary on SF writers on British TV. I was thrilled to get to see people who had hitherto only been names—Isaac Asimov, Arthur C. Clarke, and, most excitingly of all for me, Fred Pohl. The idea that these people walked, had faces, were human-size, seemed astonishing to me. I had read all of Pohl, and Pohl-Kornbluth, I could get my hands on.

A few years later, the history of SF creeping into my head via osmosis and white knowledge, I bought old SF magazines in dirty secondhand bookshops because Fred Pohl had edited them; was impressed that Fred Pohl presented Samuel R. Delany's *Dhalgren* and was uncertain which of them gained more credit from the presentation.

Time passed. I stopped reading a lot of SF writers whom I loved when I was young. I didn't stop reading Fred Pohl.

This should have been a story, but it never coagulated, and seemed more comfortable as a poem: it's about *The Space Merchants*, and what we ask of our science fiction, I think. And it's a small and extremely heartfelt thank-you.

—Neil Gaiman

EMILY POHL-WEARY

)•(|)•(

APPRECIATING FRED, AKA GRANDDAD

There are grandfathers, and then there are grandfathers like Frederik Pohl. I've loved him dearly all my life—he's my oldest blood relative, as he reminded me while I was writing this *very* slowly—and he's been our family's benevolent patriarch since I was born. In a family of activists and feminists and artists and politicos and writers and weirdos, that's a messy, complicated role to play.

He's never just been my granddad, though. A huge part of Fred, possibly the biggest chunk of him, is reserved for his made-up worlds. The lies (as I've come to think of them) that writers spin from truths we witness are as important as the real world around us. At a young age, I also got used to him being in the public eye. You can't help but recognize a certain startled look on your friends' parents' faces when you confess that you're related to a famous author.

Even though he spends most of his time hiding out in an overcrowded, until recently smoky little grotto of an office, his unusually athletic imagination has meant that people all over the world felt like they knew him. Some part of Fred was theirs. I share my grandfather with the entire planet—possibly with several planets, if there's truth to some of his speculative predictions.

So I've loved him as family, but I've also looked up to him as a role model. Fred, and my writer grandmother Judith Merril, were my homegrown examples of how to develop successful careers. Both sides of him were equally important. The professional Fred proves over and over that it takes hard work to become successful in this industry, just like any other. Being a writer is more than just indulging the rush to write down some new idea in your head. It's rewriting and tweaking and pushing past the feeling of being creatively tapped. For so many years, I watched him write four pages a day, no matter where he was in the world. I still aspire to gain that kind of self-discipline . . .

Fred's shown me that being a gentleman—in the sense of being some-one who always tries to treat others with decency and respect—is impor-tant. He's always been a loving man who takes care of his family, holds up to his responsibilities, tries to do right, and lives by a strict moral code about how to treat other human beings. Despite the fact that authors have these unusual brains that allow us to see the world in caricatures and tragedies and silly little plot twists, we must never forget to leave our sto-ries long enough to be kind and grateful to those around us.

My memories of him begin before my brain could focus on anything other than the fuzzy excitement that came with a visit: presents! grandfa-ther! chocolate! Later, the images are more clear: a dapper, whip-smart man who could charm and surprise anyone he was introduced to and managed to turn some otherwise intelligent adults into starstruck, blathering idiots.

While I was touring with my first books or visiting for his birthday, he and Betty Anne provided me a home away from home. Sometimes I brought a motley crew of punks, queer activists, academics, and others through their house. Far from the usual grumpy-old-man reaction to my friends, he seemed genuinely interested in debating current affairs with them and find-ing out what made them tick. Being able to explain to people that my grand-parents are some of the most radical, strange, and wild people they'll ever meet is a matter of pride for me.

As the patriarch of a family in which patriarchs aren't recognized and instead are frequently treated like they need to be taken down a notch (yeah, we're a fiery, independent lot), he walks a very fine line that involves a lot of diplomacy. Whenever he crosses it, don't worry, we're all there to point that out. Lucky guy continues to learn from mistakes even at the age of ninety. But honestly, we keep him on his toes. And for the most part, because he treats us with respect and kindness, we accept that since he *has* gathered nearly a century-worth of life experience, whatever he says might be worthy of attention.

Mike Resnick

)✕|✕(

ON SAFARI

It was a sunny summer day on Selous, as it always was. The sky was a perfect blue, the grass was green, and you could smell excitement in the air.

"Just think," said Anthony Tarica, as he and his companion stepped through the hatch of the ship and began walking down the ramp to the ground. "We might have won a negatronic washer and dryer instead."

"Poor Roberts," agreed Linwood Donahue, following him down the ramp. "If he'd sold just three more units, he'd have replaced one of us here." He snickered. "I hope the poor sonuvabitch has a lot of laundry."

"I can't believe we're really here!" enthused Tarica. "All my life I've wanted to go on a real safari."

"I wonder how they could afford it," said Donahue. "I mean, a safari has to cost a lot more than a washer and dryer."

"Why worry about it?" said Tarica, taking a deep breath and scenting adventure. "We're here for the next five days, and that's all that matters."

They cleared customs and walked out of the tiny spaceport. They looked around, but there were no people in sight, just a few parked vehicles.

"That's funny," said Tarica. "I'd have thought there'd be someone from the safari company here to meet us."

"Yeah," said Donahue. "What do we do now?"

"If you gentlemen will step this way," said a cultured masculine voice, "I will attend to all your needs."

Tarica looked around. "Who said that?"

"I did."

Tarica and Donahue exchanged looks. "Am I going crazy, or did that safari vehicle just speak to us?" asked Donahue.

"I most certainly did," said the vehicle.

"I never saw a talking car before," said Tarica. "Oh, back home mine reminds me to fasten my seatbelt and take the keys out of the ignition and not to try to beat the yellow light, and it castigates me when I go over the speed limit, but I've never actually had a conversation with one."

"I am Quatermain, your fully-equipped safari car and guide, trained in every aspect of safaris and safari life. I have an encyclopedic knowledge of the flora and fauna of Selous, I know every watering hole, every secret trail, every hidden hazard. I come equipped with a minikitchen in my trunk, an auxiliary trunk for your luggage, and a supply of water that will last for the duration of your safari. Furthermore, I am capable of erecting your rustic tent at day's end, and of protecting your safety at all times. I run on a small plutonium chip, and will not run out of energy for another 27.348 Earth years." One of the trunks popped open. "If you gentlemen will please deposit your luggage in here, we can begin our exotic adventure."

"Right now?" asked Tarica, surprised.

"Have you a problem with that?" responded Quatermain.

"No," said Tarica hastily. "I just expected that we'd spend a day unwinding in some luxury lodge before we set out on the actual safari."

"Luxury lodges are incompatible with safari experience," replied Quatermain. "If you gentlemen will climb into my backseat, we can be off on the adventure of a lifetime."

"Do you do this every day?" asked Donahue, as he joined Tarica on the backseat and the door automatically shut and locked.

"Yes, sir," responded the car. "This is old hat to me, but each excursion is still thrilling, because each is unique."

"Have you ever lost a client?"

"No, sir," said Quatermain. "I always know right where they are."

Tarica pulled out a cigar. "Well, I can't tell you how much I'm looking forward to this."

"I'd prefer that you didn't smoke, sir."

"But you've got an ashtray built into the armrest here, and I assure you my friend here doesn't object."

"It's bad for your health, sir."

"I've been smoking for thirty-five years," said Tarica, "and I'm in perfect health."

There was a brief humming sound.

"I have just given you a level three scan, sir," said Quatermain, "and you have incipient emphysema, an eight percent blockage of the arteries leading to your heart, adult-onset diabetes, and an undefined gum disease. You really must take better care of yourself, sir."

"I feel fine," said Tarica.

"I could give you a printout of the scan, sir."

"All right, I'll take better care of myself."

"You could begin by not lighting that cigar, sir," said Quatermain. "I notice you're still holding it."

"Aren't you supposed to be looking for animals?" complained Tarica.

"I can see in every direction at once, sir."

Tarica sighed and put the cigar back in his pocket.

"I'm sure you'll be much happier for doing that, sir."

"You have two more guesses," growled Tarica.

They rode in silence for a few minutes. Then Donahue asked Quatermain how to open the windows.

"Why bother, sir?" replied the car. "I am equipped with the most modern climate-control system. You name the conditions and I will accommodate you."

"But I'd like to feel the wind in my face," said Donahue.

Suddenly a blast of cold air hit his face.

"Simulated wind at thirty-two miles per hour, eighty-two degrees Fahrenheit, seven percent humidity," announced Quatermain. "Would you like any adjustment, sir?"

"I'd just like some fresh air," complained Donahue.

"All right," said Quatermain. "Just let me slow down first."

"Why?"

"Even a small insect could damage your eye at the speed I was going," answered Quatermain. "It will take us an extra hour to reach the closest of the great herds, but your comfort is more important than an extra hour of daylight."

"All right, forget it," said Donahue. "Close the windows and get back up to speed."

"You're sure?" asked the car.

"I'm sure."

"You're not just doing it to make me feel better?"

"Just speed up, goddammit!"

They drove for twenty minutes in absolute silence. Then Quatermain slowed down to a crawl. "Bluebucks at nine o'clock," it announced.

"It's three thirty," said Tarica. "Do you expect to wait five and a half hours for them to show up?"

" 'Nine o'clock' means to your left, sir," explained Quatermain. "Three o'clock is to your right, twelve o'clock is straight ahead, and six o'clock is straight behind us."

"And I suppose twenty o'clock is some bird that's directly overhead?" asked Donahue with a smug smile.

"I don't call that by an o'clock, sir."

"Oh? What *do* you call it?"

"Up, sir." A brief pause. "Daggerhorns at two o'clock."

"There must be a thousand of 'em!" said Tarica enthusiastically.

"1,276 by my count, sir," said the car.

"Drive a little closer. I'd like to get a good look at them."

"I think this is as close as we should go, sir."

"But we're still half a mile away from them!" complained Tarica.

"783 yards from the nearest, to be exact, sir—or 722.77 meters, if you prefer."

"Well, then?"

"Well what, sir?"

"Drive closer."

"My job is to protect you from danger, sir."

"They're grass-eaters, for God's sake!"

"There are two cases on record of tourists being killed by daggerhorns," said Quatermain.

"Out of how many?" demanded Tarica.

"There have been 21,843 safaris on Selous, comprised of 36,218 tourists, sir."

"So the odds are 18,000 to 1 against our being killed," said Tarica.

"Actually, the odds are 18,109 to 1, sir."

"Big difference," snorted Tarica. "Drive closer."

"I really advise against it, sir."

"Then take us back to the spaceport and we'll get a vehicle that caters to our needs."

"You don't *need* to see a daggerhorn close up, sir," noted Quatermain reasonably. "You merely *want* to."

"The spaceport or the daggerhorns," insisted Tarica. "Make your decision before they all move away."

"You are adamant?"

"I am."

"Very well," said Quatermain. "Shields up! Screens up! Laser canon at the ready!" It began playing a male chorus singing an invigorating martial song.

Tarica and Donahue peered out through a suddenly raised titanium grid that covered the windows. The daggerhorns continued their grazing, paying no attention to the approaching vehicle.

Suddenly Quatermain's voice blasted out at three hundred decibels through the external speakers. "I warn you: I am fully armed and will not let any harm come to my passengers. Go about your business peacefully and make no attempt to molest them."

The second they heard the speakers all grazing stopped, and the entire herd suddenly decided it had urgent business elsewhere. A moment later Quatermain and its passengers were all alone on the savanna.

"Invigorating, wasn't it?" said Quatermain in satisfied tones.

"I'm starting to understand why the corporation could afford this particular safari company," muttered Tarica.

"Tailswinger at nine o'clock," announced Quatermain.

"Where?" said Donahue, who was on the left side of the vehicle.

"Well, actually it's about 1,400 yards away, and is totally obscured by branches, but my sensors detect its body heat."

"Well, let's go over and look at it."

"I can't, sir."

"Why not?"

"There is a female tailswinger in an adjacent tree, and she's nursing an infant."

"We're not going to steal it," said Donahue. "We're just going to look at it."

"I really can't disturb a nursing mother, sir," said Quatermain.

"But you had no problem disturbing twelve hundred daggerhorns," complained Donahue.

"None of *them* were nursing, sir."

"Fine," muttered Donahue. He tested the door handle. "Oh, well, as long as you're stopped, unlock this thing."

"Why, sir?"

"We left the spaceport before I could stop by a bathroom and I've got to pee." He tried the door again. "What's the problem? Is the door stuck?"

"Certainly not, sir," said Quatermain. "I am in perfect repair."

"Then let me out."

"I can't, sir."

"Nothing's going to attack me," said Donahue. "You scared all the animals away, in case you don't remember."

"I agree, sir. There are no potentially dangerous animals within striking distance."

"So why won't you open the goddamned door?"

"Uric acid can do untold harm to any vegetation it comes in contact with, sir," said Quatermain. "We must keep the planet pristine for future adventurers. Surely you can see that, sir."

"Are you telling me that all those daggerhorns we saw never take a piss?"

"Certainly they do, sir."

"Well, then?"

"Unlike yourself, *they* are part of the ecosystem."

"I don't believe this!" yelled Donahue. "Are you telling me no one you ever took out had to relieve himself?"

"If you will check the pouch just ahead of you, sir," said Quatermain, "you will find a small plastic bag."

"What if he needs a big one?" asked Tarica.

Another humming sound.

"I have just scanned his bladder, sir, and it contains only thirteen fluid ounces." A brief pause. "You really should cut down on your sugars and carbohydrates, Mr. Donahue."

Donahue muttered an obscenity and reached for the bag.

It was ten minutes later that Quatermain announced that they had come to a small herd of six-legged woolies.

"They look just like sheep," observed Tarica.

"They are identical to Earth sheep in almost every way," agreed Quatermain. "Except, of course, for the extra legs, and the heart, lungs, spleen, pancreas, kidneys, jaw structure, and genitalia."

"But besides that . . . ," said Donahue sardonically.

"Note the billpecker perched on the nearest one's head," said Quatermain. "It forms a symbiosis with the wooly. It keeps the wooly's ears clean of parasites, and the wooly provides it with an endless supply of food." Suddenly the wooly bellowed and shook its head, sending the billpecker shooting off into the air before the shocked bird could spread its wings.

"Its ear is bleeding," noted Donahue.

"Very nearsighted billpecker," said Quatermain knowingly. "It is my opinion, not yet codified in the textbooks, that this is actually a triple symbiosis. The billpecker is a bird with notoriously poor vision, and the blood it inadvertently draws due to this shortcoming actually attracts bloodsucking parasites. Without the blood, no parasites. Without the parasites, no billpecker. It works out very neatly."

"Without the parasites there's no need for billpeckers," said Tarica.

"All the more reason for parasites," answered Quatermain, leaving Tarica certain that there was something missing from the equation but unable to put his finger on it.

"It will be dark in another forty-five minutes," announced the vehicle. "I think it's time to choose a place to set up the tent."

"How about right here?" said Donahue.

"No," said Quatermain thoughtfully. "I think seventy-five feet to the left would be better."

"We're in the middle of an open plain. What the hell's the difference?"

"A meteor fragment landed there 120,427 years ago. One has never landed here. The odds of a second fragment landing in the very same spot are—"

"Never mind," said Donahue wearily. "Set it up where you want."

Quatermain drove seventy-five feet to the left, and the tent constructed itself as if by magic. "I will be the fourth wall," announced the vehicle. "That way I can continue seeing to your comfort."

The two men exited through the right-hand door and found themselves in a rustic but spotless tent that possessed two cots, plus a table and two chairs.

"Not bad," commented Tarica.

"There is also a portable bathroom just behind this door," said Quatermain as a small door began flashing.

"When's dinner?" asked Tarica. "I'm starving."

"I shall prepare a gourmet dinner, specially adjusted to your individual needs. It will be ready in approximately two minutes."

"Now *that's* service," said Donahue. "Maybe we misjudged you."

"Thank you, sir," said Quatermain. "I do my best."

"Yeah, it was probably just a matter of getting used to each other," added Tarica. "But what the hell—a gourmet dinner on our first night on the trail!"

"We are not on a trail, sir. We are on the Maraguni Plains."

"Same thing."

"No, sir," said Quatermain. "A trail is a—"

"Forget it," said Donahue.

"I'm sorry, sir, but it is embedded in my language banks. I cannot forget it."

"Then stop talking about it."

"Yes, sir." A brief pause. "Please take your seats at the table. Dinner is ready."

The two men sat down, and a moment later a long mechanical arm extended from the vehicle and deposited two plates.

Tarica looked at his dish. "That's an awfully big salad," he remarked. "I'll never have room for the main course."

"Not to worry, sir," said Quatermain soothingly. "This *is* your main course."

"I thought we were having a gourmet dinner!"

"You are, sir. On your plate is lettuce from Antares III, tomatoes from Greenveldt, radishes from far Draksa VII, mushrooms from—"

"There's no meat!" thundered Tarica.

"Your cholesterol reading is 243," answered Quatermain. "I would be ignoring my responsibilities if I were to prepare a meal that would add to it."

"Your responsibilities are to take us to animals, damnit!"

"No, sir. My contract stipulates a total experience. Clearly that includes nourishment."

"What about me?" said Donahue. "There's nothing wrong with *my* cholesterol."

"You are friends with Mr. Tarica, are you not?" asked Quatermain.

"So what?"

"Clearly you would not want to cause your friend emotional distress by consuming an eighteen-ounce steak smothered in caramelized onions while he was obligated to eat a salad with fat-free dressing."

"It wouldn't bother me a bit," said Donahue.

"This false bravado cannot fool me, sir," said Quatermain. "I know you do not want your friend to suffer."

Donahue saw that it was an unwinnable argument and took a bite of his salad.

"That washer and dryer is looking mighty good to me," said Tarica. "Hey, Quatermain—are there any animals around?"

"No, sir, not at this moment."

Tarica got to his feet. "I think I'll take a walk. Maybe I can work up an appetite for this junk." He walked to the doorway and fiddled with it for a moment. "How the hell do you open this thing?"

"I'm sorry, sir," said Quatermain. "But it is not safe for you to go out."

"I thought you said there weren't any animals in the vicinity."

"That is correct, sir. There are no animals in the vicinity."

"Then why isn't it safe?"

"There is a six percent chance of rain, sir."

"So what?"

"The last ninety-four times there was a six percent chance of rain, my clients left the tent and came back totally dry," explained Quatermain. "That means statistically you are almost certain to be rained on."

"I'll take my chances."

"I cannot permit that, sir. If you get rained upon, there is a 1.023 percent chance that a man of your age and with your physical liabilities could come down with pneumonia, and our company could be held legally culpable, since our contract states that we will protect your health and well-being to the best of our ability."

"So you won't let me out under any circumstances?" demanded Tarica.

"Certainly I will, sir," said Quatermain. "If the chance of rain drops to four percent, I will happily open the door to the tent."

"Happily?"

"Yes, sir."

"You have emotions?"

"I have been programmed to use that word, sir," responded Quatermain. "Actually, I don't believe that I have any emotions, hopes, fears, or perverse sexual desires, though of course I could be mistaken."

"Can you at least pull back the roof so we can enjoy the sounds and smells of the wild?" asked Donahue. "You can put it back up if it starts raining."

"I wish I could accommodate you, sir," said Quatermain.

"But?"

"But flocks of goldenbeaks are constantly flying overhead."

"So what?"

"You force me to be indelicate, sir," said the vehicle. "But when you stand beneath an avian . . ."

"Never mind."

The two men finished their salads in grumpy silence, and went to sleep shortly thereafter. Twice Quatermain woke Donahue and told him to turn over because his snoring was so loud it was likely to wake his friend, and once Tarica got up and trudged to the bathroom, which he used only after demanding that Quatermain avert its eyes or whatever it used to see inside itself.

Morning came, the two men had coffee (black) and low-calorie cheese Danishes (minus the cheese and the frosting), and then climbed back into the vehicle. The tent was disassembled and packed in less than twenty seconds, furniture included, and then they were driving across the plains toward a water hole where Quatermain assured them they were likely to encounter at least a dozen different species of game.

"We're in luck, sirs," announced Quatermain when it was still half a mile away.

"We are?"

"Yes, indeed," the vehicle assured them. "There are silverstripes, spiral-horns, six-legged woolies, Galler-Smith's gazelles, and even a pair of treetoppers, those fellows with the long necks."

"Can you get us any closer?" asked Tarica without much hope.

"Yes," answered Quatermain. "They are all on the far side of the water hole. I foresee no danger whatsoever. In fact, with no avians in the area, I feel I can finally accommodate your wishes and put my top down."

The vehicle drove closer, finally stopping about one hundred feet from the edge of the small water hole. The two men spent the next twenty minutes watching as a seemingly endless parade of exotic animals came down to drink.

Suddenly Quatermain shook slightly.

"Did you backfire or something?" asked Donahue.

"No," answered the vehicle. "I am in perfect working order."

"There it is again," noted Donahue.

"Yeah, I feel it too," said Tarica. "A kind of *thump-thump-thump*."

Suddenly there was an ear-shattering roar. Most of the animals raced away from the water hole. A few froze momentarily in terror.

"What is it?" asked Tarica nervously.

"This is your lucky day, sirs!" enthused Quatermain. "You are about to see a *Gigantosaurus Selous*."

As the vehicle spoke, a huge creature, twenty-five feet at the shoulder, eighty feet in length, with canines as long as a tall man, raced up to the water hole, killing two silverstripes with a swipe of its enormous foreleg, and biting a treetopper in half.

"My God, he's awesome!" breathed Donahue.

"Maybe we should put the top back up," said Tarica.

"Unnecessary," said Quatermain. "He's made his kill. Now he'll stop and eat it."

"What if he wants to eat *us*?" whispered Tarica.

"Calm yourself, sir. He is hardwired to attack his species' prey animals, into which category safari cars and humans from Earth do not fall."

The gigantosaur glared across the water hole with hate-filled red eyes, and emitted a frightening roar.

"I'd back up if I were you," urged Tarica.

"He's just warning us off his kill," explained Quatermain.

"He's not eating," said Donahue. "He's just looking at us."

"Hungrily," added Tarica.

"I assure you this is all in keeping with his behavior patterns," said Quatermain.

"Uh . . . he's just put his front feet in the water."

"He has no sweat glands," said the vehicle. "This is how he cools his blood."

"He's halfway across the water hole!" said Tarica.

"He has a long neck," answered Quatermain. "Wading into the water makes it easier for him to drink."

"He's not drinking!" said Donahue. "He's coming straight for us!"

"It's a bluff," said Quatermain.

The gigantosaur emitted a roar that was so loud the entire vehicle shook.

"What if it's not?" screamed Tarica.

"Just a moment while I compute the odds of your survival."

"We haven't *got* a moment!" yelled Donahue.

"Checking . . . ," said Quatermain calmly. "Ah! I see. The shaking of the ground dislodged a small transistor in my data banks. Actually, the odds are 9,438 to 1 that he *is* attacking us. That's very strange. I've never had a transistor dislodged before. The odds of it happening are—"

"Shut up and get us out of here!" hollered Tarica as the gigantosaur reached their side of the water hole, leaned forward, and bared its fighting fangs.

"Shall I back up first or put up the top first?" mused Quatermain. "Ah, decisions, decisions!"

Tarica felt something hit the top of his head. He looked up and found himself staring into the hungry eyes of the gigantosaur, who was drooling on him. It opened its enormous mouth, lowered its head—

—and the top of the vehicle slammed shut. There was a bone-jarring shock as the gigantosaur's jaws closed on Quatermain. Three teeth were broken off, and the creature roared in rage, releasing its grip. Quatermain backed up quickly, spun around, and raced off in the opposite direction.

"Well, that's that!" said Tarica, pulling out a handkerchief and wiping the drool from his face and head.

"Not quite," noted Quatermain. "The gigantosaur is in full pursuit."

"You've already told us you won't run out of fuel for decades," said Donahue.

"That is true."

"Then there's no problem."

"Well, there is one little problem," said Quatermain. "My right rear tire is dangerously low, and of course if it goes flat I will have to stop to change it."

"Why did I work Super Bowl Sunday?" moaned Tarica. "I sold five units during the game. Why didn't I stay home and watch like any normal man?"

"I didn't have to sell at nights," added Donahue. "I could have sneaked off to the waterbed motel with that sexy little blonde from the billing department who was always giving me the eye. She was worth at least four sales."

"Relax, sirs," said Quatermain. "The gigantosaur has stopped to kill and devour a purplebeest. We are totally safe." There was an explosion as the tire burst. "Well, 13.27 percent safe, anyway."

"I'm starting to hate mathematics," said Tarica.

"I don't suppose one of you gentlemen would like to help?" suggested Quatermain.

"I thought you could change it yourself," said Tarica.

"I can. But when unassisted, it takes me four hours and seventeen minutes. The gigantosaur, should he choose to take up the pursuit again, can reach us in three minutes and twenty-two seconds."

"Why would he?" asked Donahue. "I mean, he just made a kill, didn't he?"

"He made some kills as the water hole," said Tarica. "Maybe he's not hungry at all. Maybe he just likes killing things."

"Open the door and tell me where the jack, wrench, and spare are."

"Those are obsolete," said Quatermain. "Get outside and I will instruct you. My tool case is in the trunk."

Donahue and Tarica were outside, standing before the remains of the back tire, tool kit in hand, half a minute later.

"All ready?" asked Quatermain. "Good. Now, which of you is better versed in quantum mechanics?"

The two men exchanged looks.

"Neither of us."

"Oh, dear," said Quatermain. "You're quite sure?"

"Quite," said Tarica.

"How about non-Euclidian mathematics?"

"No."

"Are you certain? I don't mean to distress you, but the gigantosaur has finished his meal—I believe it took three bites, though there is a 14.2 percent chance that it took four, given his missing teeth—and he will be upon you in approximately fifty-three seconds."

"Oh, shit!" said Donahue. "Let us back in. At least you're armored."

"Please replace the tool kit first," said Quatermain. "We can't leave it here for some unsuspecting animal to injure itself on it."

Tarica raced to the back of the vehicle.

"Open the goddamned trunk!" he bellowed.

"Sorry," said Quatermain. The trunk opened, Tarica hurled the tool kit into it, and it slammed shut.

"You shouldn't have yelled so loud," said Quatermain, as the ground began to shake. "The sound of the human voice seems to enrage the gigantosaur. He will be here in nineteen seconds."

"Let us in, damn it!" yelled Donahue, tugging at the door.

"I am afraid I can't, sir," said Quatermain. "I am obligated to protect the company's property, which is to say: myself. And the odds are 28.45 to one that you both can't enter me and close the door before he reaches us."

Tarica looked behind him. It seemed that the entire world consisted of one gaping gigantosaur mouth.

"I hate safaris!" he yelled, diving under the vehicle.

"I hate safari cars!" screamed Donahue, joining him as the gigantosaur's jaws snapped shut on empty air, sounding like a clap of thunder.

"What are we going to do?" whispered Tarica.

"I'll tell you what we're *not* going to do," replied Donahue. "We're not going to crawl out from under this thing."

They lay there, tense and silent, for half a minute. Then, suddenly, they became aware of a change in their surroundings.

"Do you notice it getting lighter?" asked Tarica.

"Yeah," said Donahue, frowning. "What's going on?"

"Do not worry about me, sirs," said a voice high above them. "I am virtually indestructible when my doors and trunk are locked. Well, 93.872 percent indestructable, anyway. Besides, it is a far better thing I do today than I have ever done."

They looked up and saw Quatermain sticking out of both sides of the monster's jaws. The gigantosaur tensed and tried to bring his jaws together with full force. Six more teeth broke, he dropped the vehicle (which missed Tarica and Donahue by less than two feet), and raced off, yelping like a puppy that had just encountered a porcupine.

"If you gentlemen will lift me off my side," said Quatermain, "I will change my tire and we will continue the safari as if nothing happened."

The men put their shoulders into the task, and a few moments later Quatermain was upright again.

"Thank you," said the vehicle. "Please reenter me now, while I go to work on the tire."

They climbed into the car, and the door closed and locked behind them.

"Four hours and seventeen minutes and I'll be as good as new," said

Quartermain. "Then we'll travel to the Marisula Delta and explore an entirely different ecosystem."

"Let's just travel back to the safari office," said Tarica. "I've had enough."

"Me, too," added Donahue.

"You want to end your safari four days early?" asked Quatermain.

"You got it."

"I am afraid I cannot accommodate you, sirs," said Quatermain.

"What the hell are you talking about?"

"Your company paid for five full days," explained Quatermain. "If you do not experience all five days, we could be sued for breach of contract."

"We've experienced five days' worth," said Tarica. "We just want to go home."

"Clearly your travel has left you mentally confused, sir. You have actually experienced only twenty-one hours and forty-nine minutes. I am not aware of confusion taking this form before, but I suppose it can happen."

"I know how long we've been here, and I'm *not* confused," said Donahue. "Take us back."

"Yes, sir."

"Good."

"As soon as the safari is over. My tire will be ready in four hours and thirteen minutes, and then we will proceed to the Marisula Delta."

Tarica tried the door. "Let me out!"

"I am afraid I cannot, sir," said Quatermain. "You might try to find your way back to the spaceport. If you do, there is a 97.328 percent likelihood that you will be killed and eaten, and should you make it back intact, there is a 95.673 percent chance that a breach of contract suit will be brought against my owners. Therefore, I feel I must fulfill our contract. Sit back and try to relax, sir."

"We'll starve."

"Not to worry, sir. I will be able to feed you right where you are."

"We can't sleep in this thing," complained Donahue.

"My understanding of human physiology, which I should note is encyclopedic, is that when you get tired enough you can sleep anywhere." A brief pause. "All your needs will be provided for, sir. I even have a one-month supply of plastic bags."

◄─ ─►

It was five days later that Quatermain pulled up to the spaceport.

"Serving you has been a true pleasure, sirs," it intoned as Tarica and

Donahue wearily opened the door, raced around to the back, and grabbed their luggage. "I hope to see you again in the near future."

"In your dreams!" growled Tarica.

"I do not dream, sir."

"*I* do," muttered Donahue. "And I'm going to have nightmares about this safari for the rest of my life."

A squat robot, looking for all the world like a fire hydrant on wheels, rolled up, took their bags from them, and led them to a small waiting spaceship.

"This isn't the same spaceliner we took here," said Tarica dubiously. "It looks like a small private ship."

"Your Stellar Voyages ship is not available, sir," said the robot, as it placed their luggage in the cargo hold "This ship was supplied, gratis, by the safari company as a sign of their appreciation."

"And to dissuade us from suing?" asked Donahue.

"That, too," agreed the robot.

The two men climbed into the ship and strapped themselves into the only two seats provided.

"Welcome, gentlemen," said the ship as the hatch closed and it began elevating. "I trust you enjoyed your once-in-a-lifetime safari experience on the planet Selous. I will be returning you to Earth. I come equipped with all creature comforts except sexual consorts"—it uttered an emotionless mechanical chuckle—"and have a gourmet kitchen at your disposal."

"What happened to the ship we were supposed to be on?" asked Tarica.

"I regret to inform you that it was destroyed in an ion storm just as it was entering the system," answered the ship.

"Uh . . . we're not going through that same storm on the way out, are we?" asked Donahue.

"Yes, sir," said the ship. "But there is no need for concern, sir. I am a new model, equipped with every conceivable safety device. I am far more maneuverable than a—" The ship shuddered for just an instant. "Just some minor space debris. Nothing to worry about. As I was saying, I am far more maneuverable than a spaceliner, and besides, this is my home system. Every ion storm during the past ten years has been charted and placed in my data banks."

"So you've flown through them before?" said Tarica.

"Actually, no," said the ship. "This is my first flight. But as I say, I am fully equipped and programmed. What *could* go wrong?"

Tarica cursed under his breath. Donahue merely checked to make sure there was a small paper bag near his seat.

"I am sure we're going to get along splendidly together," continued the ship. "You are Mr. Tarica and Mr. Donahue, am I correct?"

"Right," said Tarica.

"And my name was clearly discernible in bold letters on my nose as you entered me," said the ship proudly.

"I must have missed it," said Tarica. "What was it?"

"I am the *Pequod*."

Donahue reached for the bag.

Flavors of Fred

Fred Pohl was editing *Astonishing Stories* a year before I was born. He was a giant in the field by the time I started reading science fiction. He won a shelf of Hugos for editing, and another shelf for writing.

I've probably read 80 percent of the words he's written, which is one hell of a lot, and I subscribed to *Galaxy* and *If*, and I read most of the Bantam books he edited, plus those early *Star* anthologies. But when I think of Fred, those aren't the memories that pop to mind first.

I think of Fred, and I instantly smell cigarette smoke. I was a heavy smoker when we were both hitting a lot of Midwestern conventions, so was he, and we seemed to always find ourselves in each other's company, sneaking out of some boring banquet for a smoke, sitting in splendid and befogged isolation in the smoking suite, or otherwise polluting the convention.

I also remember a Windycon where there was a Fred Pohl roast, and the committee asked me to be the roastmaster because no one else would say anything nasty/funny about him. I pored through his wonderful autobiography, *The Way the Future Was*, and found a most interesting fact hidden away in the middle of it. Once, when (like so many writers) Fred needed a little salaried income, he took a job at a racetrack as the guy who irritates the winning horse's genitalia with an electric prod to get urine samples for the track vet. I built an entire routine about how after years of causing the same reaction in editors and readers, he'd finally found his calling. Just before the roast a couple of panelists insisted I couldn't say those things about an icon, but I did—and no one laughed louder than Fred.

When our mutual friend Algis Budrys died, it was Fred who contacted me and suggested we put together a collection of his very best works before they were forgotten—but only on the condition that we take, at most, an absolutely minimal fee, and that the bulk of the advance and all of the royalties go to Ajay's widow. I accepted instantly. Why? Partially because Ajay was a friend . . . but my main reason was that after well over half a century of reading him, and smoking with him, and appearing on panels with him, and roasting him, I was finally offered the opportunity to work with one of my heroes. Health considerations have slowed the project down, but it'll still come to fruition one of these days.

Everyone knows what a fine writer and editor Fred is, but he also has some accomplishments that have gone relatively unheralded. For example: a lot of writers have found one teammate and turned out a series of fine collaborations. L. Sprague de Camp and Fletcher Pratt come to mind, or Henry Kuttner and C. L. Moore, or Larry Niven and Jerry Pournelle. But no one's ever been part of two long-lived, stellar, wildly successful teams—except Fred, who did it with Cyril Kornbluth, and then, just to prove it wasn't a fluke, did it all over again with Jack Williamson.

He also wrote the single best article on self-promotion to appear in the past fifty years: "The Science Fiction Professional," which appeared in Reginald Bretnor's *The Craft of Science Fiction* back in 1976, and so impressed me that when I collected seven years of my "how-to" columns from *Speculations* in book form, I titled it *The Science Fiction Professional*. (Holster that lawsuit, Fred; the statute of limitations ran out in 2007.)

Science fiction doesn't have many renaissance men, no matter how much we like to believe we do. Fred's been an authentic one for damned near three-quarters of a century, and has improved his art with almost every passing decade. We're not going to see too many men like that, and I'm proud to know him.

—MIKE RESNICK

CORY DOCTOROW

※※※

CHICKEN LITTLE

The first lesson Leon learned at the ad agency was: nobody is your friend at the ad agency.

Take today: Brautigan was going to see an actual vat, at an actual clinic, which housed an actual target consumer, and he wasn't taking Leon.

"Don't sulk, it's unbecoming," Brautigan said, giving him one of those tight-lipped smiles where he barely got his mouth over those big, horsey, comical teeth of his. They were disarming, those pearly whites. "It's out of the question. Getting clearance to visit a vat in person, that's a one-month, two-month process. Background checks. Biometrics. Interviews with their psych staff. The physicals: they have to take a census of your microbial nation. It takes time, Leon. You might be a mayfly in a mayfly hurry, but the man in the vat, he's got a lot of time on his hands. No skin off his dick if you get held up for a month or two."

"Bullshit," Leon said. "It's all a show. They've got a brick wall a hundred miles high around the front, and a sliding door around the back. There's always an exception in these protocols. There has to be."

"When you're 180 years old and confined to a vat, you don't make exceptions. Not if you want to go on to 181."

"You're telling me that if the old monster suddenly developed a rare, fast-moving liver cancer and there was only one oncologist in the whole god-damned world who could make it better, you're telling me that guy would be sent home to France or whatever, 'No thanks, we're OK, you don't have clearance to see the patient'?"

"I'm telling you the monster *doesn't have a liver*. What that man has, he has *machines* and *nutrients* and *systems*."

"And if a machine breaks down?"

"The man who invented that machine works for the monster. He lives on the monster's private estate, with his family. *Their* microbial nations are identical to the monster's. He is not only the emperor of their lives, he is the emperor of the lives of their intestinal flora. If the machine that man invented stopped working, he would be standing by the vat in less than two minutes, with his staff, all in disposable, sterile bunny suits, murmuring reassuring noises as he calmly, expertly fitted one of the ten replacements he has standing by, the ten replacements he checks, *personally*, every single day, to make sure that they are working."

Leon opened his mouth, closed it. He couldn't help himself, he snorted a laugh. "Really?"

Brautigan nodded.

"And what if none of the machines worked?"

"If that man couldn't do it, then his rival, who *also* lives on the monster's estate, who has developed the second-most-exciting liver replacement technology in the history of the world, who burns to try it on the man in the vat—*that* man would be there in ten minutes, and the first man, and his family—"

"Executed?"

Brautigan made a disappointed noise. "Come on, he's a quadrillionaire, not a Bond villain. No, that man would be demoted to nearly nothing, but given one tiny chance to redeem himself: invent a technology better than the one that's currently running in place of the vat-man's liver, and you will be restored to your fine place with your fine clothes and your wealth and your privilege."

"And if he fails?"

Brautigan shrugged. "Then the man in the vat is out an unmeasurably minuscule fraction of his personal fortune. He takes the loss, applies for a research tax credit for it, and deducts it from the pittance he deigns to send to the IRS every year."

"Shit."

Brautigan slapped his hands together. "It's wicked, isn't it? All that money and power and money and money?"

Leon tried to remember that Brautigan wasn't his friend. It was those teeth, they were so *disarming*. Who could be suspicious of a man who was so horsey you wanted to feed him sugar cubes? "It's something else."

"You now know about ten thousand times more about the people in the vats than your average cit. But you haven't got even the shadow of the picture yet, buddy. It took *decades* of relationship-building for Ate to sell its first product to a vat-person."

And we haven't sold anything else since, Leon thought, but he didn't say it. No one would say it at Ate. The agency pitched itself as a powerhouse, a success in a field full of successes. It was *the* go-to agency for servicing the "ultra-high-net-worth individual," and yet . . .

One sale.

"And we haven't sold anything since." Brautigan said it without a hint of shame. "And yet, this entire building, this entire agency, the salaries and the designers and the consultants: all of it paid for by clipping the toenails of that fortune. Which means that one *more* sale—"

He gestured around. The offices were sumptuous, designed to impress the functionaries of the fortunes in the vats. A trick of light and scent and wind made you feel as though you were in an ancient forest glade as soon as you came through the door, though no forest was in evidence. The reception desktop was a sheet of pitted tombstone granite, the unreadable smooth epitaph peeking around the edges of the old-fashioned typewriter that had been cunningly reworked to serve as a slightly less old-fashioned keyboard. The receptionist—presently ignoring them with professional verisimilitude—conveyed beauty, intelligence, and motherly concern, all by means of dress, bearing, and makeup. Ate employed a small team of stylists that worked on all public-facing employees; Leon had endured a just-so rumpling of his sandy hair and some carefully applied fraying at the cuffs and elbows of his jacket that morning.

"So no, Leon, buddy, I am *not* taking you down to meet my vat-person. But I *will* get you started on a path that may take you there, someday, if you're very good and prove yourself out here. Once you've paid your dues."

Leon had paid plenty of dues—more than this blow-dried turd ever did. But he smiled and snuffled it up like a good little worm, hating himself. "Hit me."

"Look, we've been pitching vat-products for six years now without a single hit. Plenty of people have come through that door and stepped into the job you've got now, and they've all thrown a million ideas in the air, and every one came smashing to earth. We've never systematically cataloged those ideas, never got them in any kind of grid that will let us see what kind of territory we've already explored, where the holes are . . ." He looked meaningfully at Leon.

"You want me to catalog every failed pitch in the agency's history." Leon didn't hide his disappointment. That was the kind of job you gave to an intern, not a junior account exec.

Brautigan clicked his horsey teeth together, gave a laugh like a whinny, and left Ate's offices, admitting a breath of the boring air that circulated out there in the real world. The receptionist radiated matronly care in Leon's direction. He leaned her way and her fingers thunked on the mechanical keys of her converted Underwood Noiseless, a machine-gun rattle. He waited until she was done, then she turned that caring, loving smile back on him.

"It's all in your work space, Leon—good luck with it."

●━ ●━

It seemed to Leon that the problems faced by immortal quadrillionaires in vats wouldn't be that different from those facing mere mortals. Once practically anything could be made for practically nothing, everything was practically worthless. No one needed to discover anymore—just *combine*, just *invent*. Then you could either hit a button and print it out on your desktop fab or down at the local depot for bigger jobs, or if you needed the kind of fabrication a printer couldn't handle, there were plenty of on-demand jobbers who'd have some worker in a distant country knock it out overnight and you'd have it in hermetic FedEx packaging on your desktop by the morning.

Looking through the Ate files, he could see that he wasn't the last one to follow this line of reasoning. Every account exec had come up with pitches that involved things that *couldn't* be fabbed—precious gewgaws that needed a trained master to produce—or things that *hadn't* been fabbed—antiques, one-of-a-kinds, fetish objects from history. And all of it had met with crashing indifference from the vat-people, who could hire any master they wanted, who could buy entire warehouses full of antiques.

The normal megarich got offered experiences: a ticket to space, a chance to hunt the last member of an endangered species, the opportunity to kill a man and get away with it, a deep-ocean sub to the bottom of the Marianas Trench. The people in the vat had done plenty of those things before they'd ended up in the vats. Now they were metastatic, these hyperrich, lumps of curdling meat in the pickling solution of a hundred vast machines that laboriously kept them alive amid their cancer blooms and myriad failures. Somewhere in that tangle of hoses and wires was something that was technically a person, and also technically a corporation, and, in many cases, technically a sovereign state.

Each concentration of wealth was an efficient machine, meshed in a million ways with the mortal economy. You interacted with the vats when you bought hamburgers, Internet connections, movies, music, books, electronics, games, transportation—the money left your hands and was sieved through their hoses and tubes, flushed back out into the world where other mortals would touch it.

But there was no easy way to touch the money at its most concentrated, purest form. It was like a theoretical superdense element from the first instant of the universe's creation, money so dense it stopped acting like money; money so dense it changed state when you chipped a piece of it off.

Leon's predecessors had been shrewd and clever. They had walked the length and breadth of the problem space of providing services and products to a person who was money who was a state who was a vat. Many of the nicer grace notes in the office came from those failed pitches—the business with the lights and the air, for example.

Leon had a good education, the kind that came with the mathematics of multidimensional space. He kept throwing axes at his chart of the failed inventions of Ate, Inc., mapping out the many ways in which they were similar and dissimilar. The pattern that emerged was easy to understand.

They'd tried *everything*.

— —

Brautigan's whinny was the most humiliating sound Leon had ever heard, in all his working life.

"No, of course you can't know what got sold to the vat-person! That was part of the deal—it was why the payoff was so large. *No one* knows what we sold to the vat-person. Not me, not the old woman. The man who sold it? He cashed out years ago, and hasn't been seen or heard from since. Silent partner, preferred shares, controlling interest—but he's the invisible man. We talk to him through lawyers who talk to lawyers who, it is rumored, communicate by means of notes left under a tombstone in a tiny cemetery on Pitcairn Island, and row in and out in longboats to get his instruction."

The hyperbole was grating on Leon. Third day on the job, and the sundappled, ozonated pseudoforested environment felt as stale as an old gym bag (there was, in fact, an old gym bag under his desk, waiting for the day he finally pulled himself off the job in time to hit the complimentary gym). Brautigan was grating on him more than the hyperbole.

"I'm not an asshole, Brautigan, so stop treating me like one. You hired me to do a job, but all I'm getting from you is shitwork, sarcasm, and secrecy." The alliteration came out without his intending it to, but he was good at that sort of thing. "So here's what I want to know: is there any single solitary reason for me to come to work tomorrow, or should I just sit at home, drawing a salary until you get bored of having me on the payroll and can my ass?"

It wasn't entirely spontaneous. Leon's industrial psychology background was pretty good—he'd gotten straight As and an offer of a postdoc, none of which had interested him nearly so much as the practical

applications of the sweet science of persuasion. He understood that Brautigan had been pushing him around to see how far he could be pushed. No
one pushed like an ad guy—if you could sweet-talk someone into craving
something, it followed that you could goad him into hating something just
as much. Two faces of a coin and all that.

Brautigan faked anger, but Leon had spent three days studying his tells,
and Leon could see that the emotion was no more sincere than anything
else about the man. Carefully, Leon flared his nostrils, brought his chest up,
inched his chin higher. He *sold* his outrage, sold it like it was potato chips,
over-the-counter securities, or under-the-counter diet pills. Brautigan tried
to sell his anger in return. Leon was a no sale. Brautigan bought.

"There's a new one," he said, in a conspiratorial whisper.

"A new what?" Leon whispered. They were still chest to chest, quivering with angry body language, but Leon let another part of his mind deal
with that.

"A new monster," Brautigan said. "Gone to his vat at a mere 103.
Youngest ever. Unplanned." He looked up, down, left, right. "An accident.
Impossible accident. Impossible, but he had it, which means?"

"It was no accident," Leon said. "Police?" It was impossible not to fall
into Brautigan's telegraphed speech style. That was a persuasion thing,
too, he knew. Once you talked like him, you'd sympathize with him. And
vice versa, of course. They were converging on a single identity. Bonding.
It was intense, like make-up sex for coworkers. "He's a sovereign three
ways. An African republic, an island, one of those little Baltic countries.
On the other side of the international vowel line. Mxlplx or something.
They swung for him at the WTO, the UN—whole bodies of international
trade law for this one. So no regular cops; this is diplomatic corps stuff.
And, of course, he's not dead, so that makes it more complicated."

"How?"

"Dead people become corporations. They get managed by boards of di-
rectors who act predictably, if not rationally. Living people, they're *flam-
boyant*. Seismic. Unpredictable. But. On the other hand." He waggled his
eyebrows.

"On the other hand, they buy things."

"Once in a very long while, they do."

◗◗

Leon's life was all about discipline. He'd heard a weight-loss guru once explain that the key to maintaining a slim figure was to really "listen to your
body" and only eat until it signaled that it was full. Leon had listened to his
body. It wanted three entire pepperoni and mushroom pizzas every single

day, plus a rather large cake. And malted milkshakes, the old-fashioned kind you could make in your kitchen with an antique Hamilton Beach machine in avocado-colored plastic, served up in a tall red anodized aluminum cup. Leon's body was extremely verbose on what it wanted him to shovel into it.

So Leon ignored his body. He ignored his mind when it told him that what it wanted to do was fall asleep on the sofa with the video following his eyes around the room, one of those shows that followed your neural activity and tried to tune the drama to maximize your engrossment. Instead, he made his mind sit up in bed, absorbing many improving books from the mountain he'd printed out and stacked there.

Leon ignored his limbic system when it told him to stay in bed for an extra hour every morning when his alarm detonated. He ignored the fatigue messages he got while he worked through an hour of yoga and meditation before breakfast.

He wound himself up tight with will and it was will that made him stoop to pick up the laundry on the stairs while he was headed up and neatly fold it away when he got to the spacious walk-in dressing room attached to the master bedroom. (The apartment had been a good way to absorb his Ate signing bonus—safer than keeping the money in cash, with the currency fluctuations and all. Manhattan real estate was a century-long good buy and was more stable than bonds, derivatives or funds.) It was discipline that made him pay every bill as it came in. It was all that which made him wash every dish when he was done with it and assiduously stop at the grocer's every night on the way home to buy anything that had run out the previous day.

His parents came to visit from Anguilla and they teased him about how *organized* he was, so unlike the fat little boy who'd been awarded the "Hansel and Gretel prize" by his sixth-grade teacher for leaving a trail behind him everywhere he went. What they didn't know was that he was still that kid, and every act of conscientious, precise, buttoned-down finicky habit was, in fact, the product of relentless, iron determination not to be that kid again. He not only ignored that inner voice of his that called out for pizzas and told him to sleep in, take a cab instead of walking, lie down and let the video soar and dip with his moods, a drip-feed of null and nothing to while away the hours—he actively denied it, shouted it into submission, locked it up, and never let it free.

And that—*that*—that was why he was going to figure out how to sell something new to the man in the vat: because anyone who could amass that sort of fortune and go down to life eternal in an ever-expanding kingdom of machines would be the sort of person who had spent a life denying himself, and Leon knew *just* what that felt like.

•—•—••

The Lower East Side had ebbed and flowed over the years: poor, rich, middle-class, superrich, poor. One year the buildings were funky and reminiscent of the romantic squalor that had preceded this era of light-speed buckchasing. The next year, the buildings were merely squalorous, the landlords busted and the receivers in bankruptcy slapping up paper-thin walls to convert giant airy lofts into rooming houses. The corner stores sold blunt skins to trustafarian hipsters with a bag of something gengineered to disrupt some extremely specific brain structures; then they sold food-stamp milk to desperate mothers who wouldn't meet their eyes. The shopkeepers had the knack of sensing changes in the wind and adjusting their stock accordingly.

Walking around his neighborhood, Leon sniffed change in the wind. The shopkeepers seemed to have more discount, high-calorie wino-drink; less designer low-carb energy food with FDA-mandated booklets explaining their nutritional claims. A sprinkling of FOR RENT signs. A construction site that hadn't had anyone working on it for a week now, the padlocked foreman's shed growing a mossy coat of graffiti.

Leon didn't mind. He'd lived rough—not just student-rough, either. His parents had gone to Anguilla from Romania, chasing the tax-haven set, dreaming of making a killing working as bookkeepers, security guards. They'd mistimed the trip, arrived in the middle of an econopocalytpic collapse and ended up living in a vertical slum that had once been a luxury hotel. The sole Romanians among the smuggled Mexicans who were de facto slaves, they'd traded their ability to write desperate letters to the Mexican consulate for Spanish lessons for Leon. The Mexicans dwindled away—the advantage of de facto slaves over de jure slaves is that you can just send the de facto slaves away when the economy tanks, taking their feed and care off your books—until it was just them there, and without the safety of the crowd, they'd been spotted by local authorities and had to go underground. Going back to Bucharest was out of the question—the airfare was as far out of reach as one of the private jets the tax-evaders and high-rolling gamblers flew in and out of Wallblake Airport.

From rough to rougher. Leon's family spent three years underground, living as roadside hawkers, letting the sun bake them to an ethnically indeterminate brown. A decade later, when his father had successfully built up his little bookkeeping business and his mother was running a smart dress shop for the cruise ship day-trippers, those days seemed like a dream. But once he left for stateside university and found himself amid the soft, rich children of the fortunes his father had tabulated, it all came back to him, and he wondered if any of these children in carefully disheveled rags would ever be able to pick through the garbage for their meals.

The rough edge on the LES put him at his ease, made him feel like he was still ahead of the game, in possession of something his neighbors could never have—the ability to move fluidly between the worlds of the rich and the poor. Somewhere in those worlds, he was sure, was the secret to chipping a crumb off one of the great fortunes of the world.

◆—▶◆

"Visitor for you," Carmela said. Carmela, that was the receptionist's name. She was Puerto Rican, but so many generations in that he spoke better Spanish than she did. "I put him in the Living Room." That was one of the three boardrooms at Ate, the name a bad pun, every stick of furniture in it an elaborate topiary sculpture of living wood and shrubbery. It was surprisingly comfortable, and the very subtle breeze had an even more subtle breath of honeysuckle that was so real he suspected it was piped in from a nursery on another level. That's how he would have done it: the best fake was no fake at all.

"Who?" He liked Carmela. She was all business, but her business was compassion, a shoulder to cry on and an absolutely discreet gossip repository for the whole firm. "Envoy," she said. "His name's Buhle. I ran his face and name against our dossiers and came up with practically nothing. He's from Montenegro, originally, I have that much."

"Envoy from whom?" She didn't answer, just looked very meaningfully at him.

The new vat-person had sent him an envoy. His heart began to thump and his cuffs suddenly felt tight at his wrists. "Thanks, Carmela." He shot his cuffs.

"You look fine," she said. "I've got the kitchen on standby, and the intercom's listening for my voice. Just let me know what I can do for you."

He gave her a weak smile. This was why she was the center of the whole business, the soul of Ate. *Thank you*, he mouthed, and she ticked a smart salute off her temple with one finger.

◆—▶◆

The envoy was out of place in Ate, but she didn't hold it against them. This he knew within seconds of setting food into the Living Room. She got up, wiped her hands on her sensible jeans, brushed some iron-gray hair off her face, and smiled at him, an expression that seemed to say, "Well, this is a funny thing, the two of us, meeting here, like this." He'd put her age at around forty, and she was hippy and a little wrinkled and didn't seem to care at all.

"You must be Leon," she said, and took his hand. Short fingernails, warm, dry palm, firm handshake. "I *love* this room!" She waved her arm around in an all-encompassing circle. "Fantastic."

He found himself half in love with her and he hadn't said a word. "It's nice to meet you, Ms.—"

"Ria," she said. "Call me Ria." She sat down on one of the topiary chairs, kicking off her comfortable Hush Puppies and pulling her legs up to sit cross-legged.

"I've never gone barefoot in this room," he said, looking at her cal-loused feet—feet that did a lot of barefooting.

"Do it," she said, making scooting gestures. "I insist. Do it!"

He kicked off the handmade shoes—designed by an architect who'd given up on literary criticism to pursue cobblery—and used his toes to peel off his socks. Under his feet, the floor was—warm? cool?—it was *perfect*. He couldn't pin down the texture, but it made every nerve ending on the sensitive soles of his feet tingle pleasantly.

"I'm thinking something that goes straight into the nerves," she said. "It has to be. Extraordinary."

"You know your way around this place better than I do," he said.

She shrugged. "This room was clearly designed to impress. It would be stupid to be so cool-obsessed that I failed to let it impress me. I'm im-pressed. Also," she dropped her voice, "also, I'm wondering if anyone's ever snuck in here and screwed on that stuff." She looked seriously at him and he tried to keep a straight face, but the chuckle wouldn't stay put in his chest, and it broke loose, and a laugh followed it, and she whooped and they both laughed, hard, until their stomachs hurt.

He moved toward another topiary easy chair, then stopped, bent down, and sat on the mossy floor, letting it brush against his feet, his ankles, the palms of his hands and his wrists. "If no one ever has, it's a damned shame," he said, with mock gravity. She smiled, and she had dimples and wrinkles and crow's-feet, so her whole face smiled. "Do you want some-thing to eat? Drink? We can get pretty much anything here—"

"Let's get to it," she said. "I don't want to be rude, but the good part isn't the food. I get all the food I need. I'm here for something else. The good part, Leon."

He drew in a deep breath. "The good part," he said. "Okay, let's get to it. I want to meet your—" What? Employer? Patron? Owner? He waved his hand.

"You can call him Buhle," she said. "That's the name of the parent company, anyway. Of course you do. We have an entire corporate intelligence arm that knew you'd want to meet with Buhle before you did." Leon had always assumed that his work spaces and communications were monitored by his employer, but now it occurred to him that any system designed from the ground up to subject its users to scrutiny without their knowledge would be a bonanza for anyone *else* who wanted to sniff them, since they could use the system's own capabilities to hide their snooping from the victims.

"That's impressive," he said. "Do you monitor everyone who might want to pitch something to Buhle, or . . ." He let the thought hang out there.

"Oh, a little of this and a little of that. We've got a competitive intelligence subdepartment that monitors everyone who might want to sell us something or sell something that might compete with us. It comes out to a pretty wide net. Add to that the people who might personally be a threat or opportunity for Buhle and you've got, well, let's say an appreciable slice of human activity under close observation."

"How close can it be? Sounds like you've got some big haystacks."

"We're good at finding the needles," she said. "But we're always looking for new ways to find them. That's something you could sell us, you know."

He shrugged. "If we had a better way of finding relevance in mountains of data, we'd be using it ourselves to figure out what to sell you."

"Good point. Let's turn this around. Why should Buhle meet with you?"

He was ready for this one. "We have a track record of designing products that suit people in his . . ." Talking about the vat-born lent itself to elliptical statements. Maybe that's why Brautigan had developed that annoying telegraph talk.

"You've designed one such product," she said.

"That's one more than almost anyone else can claim." There were two other firms like Ate. He thought of them in his head as Sefen and Nein, as though invoking their real names might cause them to appear. "I'm new here, but I'm not alone. We're tied in with some of the finest designers, engineers, research scientists . . ." Again with the ellipsis. "You wanted to get to the good part. This isn't the good part, Ria. You've got smart people. We've got smart people. What we have, what you don't have, is smart people who are impedance-mismatched to your organization. Every organization has quirks that make it unsuited to working with some good people and good ideas. You've got your no-go areas, just like anyone else. We're good at mining that space, the no-go space, the mote in your eye, for things that you need."

She nodded and slapped her hands together like someone about to start a carpentry project. "That's a great spiel," she said.

He felt a little blush creep into his cheeks. "I think about this a lot, rehearse it in my head."

"That's good," she said. "Shows you're in the right line of business. Are you a Daffy Duck man?"

He cocked his head. "More of a Bugs man," he said, finally, wondering where this was going.

"Go download a cartoon called 'The Stupor Salesman,' and get back to me, okay?" She stood up, wriggling her toes on the mossy surface and then stepping back into her shoes. He scrambled to his feet, wiping his palms on his legs. She must have seen the expression on his face because she made all those dimples and wrinkles and crow's-feet appear again and took his hand warmly. "You did very well," she said. "We'll talk again soon." She let go of his hand and knelt down to rub her hands over the floor. "In the meantime, you've got a pretty sweet gig, don't you?"

➤ ➤

"The Stupor Salesman" turned out to feature Daffy Duck as a traveling salesman bent on selling something to a bank robber who is holed up in a suburban bungalow. Daffy produces a stream of ever more improbable wares, and is violently rebuffed with each attempt. Finally, one of his attempts manages to blow up the robber's hideout, just as Daffy is once again jiggling the doorknob. As the robber and Daffy fly through the air, Daffy brandishes the doorknob at him and shouts, "Hey, bub, I know just what you need! You need a house to go with this doorknob!"

The first time he watched it, Leon snorted at the punchline, but on subsequent viewings, he found himself less and less amused. Yes, he was indeed trying to come up with a need that this Buhle didn't know he had—he was assuming Buhle was a he, but no one was sure—and then fill it. From Buhle's perspective, Leon figured, life would be just fine if he gave up and never bothered him again.

➤ ➤

And yet Ria had been so *nice*—so understanding and gentle, he thought there must be something else to this. And she had made a point of telling him that he had a "sweet gig" and he had to admit that it was true. He was contracted for five years with Ate, and would get a hefty bonus if they canned him before then. If he managed to score a sale to Buhle or one of the others, he'd be indescribably wealthy.

In the meantime, Ate took care of his every need.

But it was so *empty* there—that's what got him. There were a hundred people on Ate's production team, bright sorts like him, and most of them only used the office to park a few knickknacks and impress out-of-town relatives. Ate hired the best, charged them with the impossible, and turned them loose. They got lost.

Carmela knew them all, of course. She was Ate's den mother.

"We should all get together," he said. "Maybe a weekly staff meeting?"

"Oh, they tried that," she said, sipping from the triple-filtered water that was always at her elbow. "No one had much to say. The collaboration spaces update themselves with all the interesting leads from everyone's research, and the suggestion engine is pretty good at making sure you get an overview of anything relevant to your work going on." She shrugged. "This place is a show room, more than anything else. I always figured you had to give creative people room to be creative."

He mulled this over. "How long do you figure they'll keep this place open if it doesn't sell anything to one of the vat-people?"

"I try not to think about that too much," she said lightly. "I figure either we don't find something, run out of time and shut—and there's nothing I can do about it; or we find something in time and stay open—and there's nothing I can do about it."

"That's depressing."

"I think of it as liberating. It's like that lady said, Leon, you've got a sweet gig. You can make anything you can imagine, and if you hit one out of the park, you'll attain orbit and never reenter the atmosphere."

"Do the other account execs come around for pep talks?"

"Everyone needs a little help now and then," she said.

•━ ━•

Ria met him for lunch at a supper club in the living room of an eleventh floor apartment in a slightly run-down ex-doorman building in Midtown. The cooks were a middle-aged couple, he was Thai, she was Hungarian, the food was eclectic, light, and spicy, blending paprika and chilis in a nose-watering cocktail.

There were only two other diners in the tiny room for the early seating. They were another couple, two young gay men, tourists from the Netherlands, wearing crease-proof sports jackets and barely there barefoot hiking shoes. They spoke excellent English, and chatted politely about the sights they'd seen so far in New York, before falling into Dutch and leaving Ria and Leon to concentrate on each other and the food, which emerged from the kitchen in a series of ever more wonderful courses.

Over fluffy, caramelized fried bananas and Thai iced coffee, Ria effusively praised the food to their hosts, then waited politely while Leon did the same. The hosts were genuinely delighted to have fed them so successfully, and were only too happy to talk about their recipes, their grown children, the other diners they'd entertained over the years.

Outside, standing on Thirty-fourth Street between Lex and Third, a cool summer evening breeze and purple summer twilight skies, Leon patted his stomach and closed his eyes and groaned.

"Ate too much, didn't you?" she said.

"It was like eating my mother's cooking—she just kept putting more on the plate. I couldn't help it."

"Did you enjoy it?"

He opened his eyes. "You're kidding, right? That was probably the most incredible meal I've eaten in my entire life. It was like a parallel dimension of good food."

She nodded vigorously and took his arm in a friendly, intimate gesture, led him toward Lexington. "You notice how time sort of stops when you're there? How the part of your brain that's going 'what next? what next?' goes quiet?"

"That's it! That's *exactly* it!" The buzz of the jetpacks on Lex grew louder as they neared the corner, like a thousand crickets in the sky.

"Hate those things," she said, glaring up at the joyriders zipping past, scarves and capes streaming out behind them. "A thousand crashes upon your souls." She spat, theatrically.

"You make them, though, don't you?"

She laughed. "You've been reading up on Buhle then?"

"Everything I can find." He'd bought small blocks of shares in all the public companies in which Buhle was a substantial owner, charging them to Ate's brokerage account, and then devoured their annual reports. There was lots more he could feel in the shadows: blind trusts holding more shares in still more companies. It was the standard corporate structure, a Flying Spaghetti Monster of interlocking directorships, offshore holdings, debt parking lots, and exotic matryoshka companies that seemed on the verge of devouring themselves.

"Oy," she said. "Poor boy. Those aren't meant to be parsed. They're like the bramble patch around the sleeping princess, there to ensnare foolhardy knights who wish to court the virgin in the tower. Yes, Buhle's the largest jetpack manufacturer in the world, through a layer or two of mis-direction." She inspected the uptown-bound horde, sculling the air with their fins and gloves, making course corrections and wibbles and wobbles that were sheer, joyful exhibitionism.

"He did it for me," she said. "Have you noticed that they've gotten bet-ter in the past couple years? Quieter? That was us. We put a lot of thought into the campaign; the chop shops have been selling 'loud pipes save lives' since the motorcycle days, and every tiny-dick flyboy wanted to have a pack that was as loud as a bulldozer. It took a lot of market smarts to turn it around; we had a low-end model we were selling way below cost that was close to those loud-pipe machines in decibel count; it was ugly and junky and fell apart. Naturally, we sold it through a different arm of the company that had totally different livery, identity, and everything. Then we started to cut into our margins on the high-end rides, and at the same time, we engi-neered them for a quieter and quieter run. We actually did some prepro-duction on a jetpack that was so quiet it actually *absorbed* noise, don't ask me to explain it, unless you've got a day or two to waste on the psycho-acoustics.

"Every swish bourgeois was competing to see whose jetpack could run quieter, while the low-end was busily switching loyalty to our loud junk mobiles. The competition went out of business in a year, and then we dummied-up a bunch of consumer protection lawsuits that 'forced' "—she drew air quotes—"us to recall the loud ones, rebuild them with pipes so en-gineered and tuned you could use them for the woodwinds section. And here we are." She gestured at the buzzing, whooshing fliers overhead.

Leon tried to figure out if she was kidding, but she looked and sounded serious. "You're telling me that Buhle dropped, what, a billion?"

"About eight billion, in the end."

"Eight billion rupiah on a project to make the skies quieter?"

"All told," she said. "We could have done it other ways, some of them cheaper. We could have bought some laws, or bought out the competition and changed their product line, but that's very, you know, *blunt*. This was sweet. Everyone got what they wanted in the end: fast rides, quiet skies, safe, cheap vehicles. Win win win."

An old school flier with a jetpack as loud as the inside of an ice blender roared past, leaving thousands scowling in his wake.

"That guy is plenty dedicated," she said. "He'll be machining his own replacement parts for that thing. No one's making them anymore."

He tried a joke: "You're not going to send the Buhle ninjas to off him before he hits Union Square?"

She didn't smile. "We don't use assassination," she said. "That's what I'm trying to convey to you, Leon."

He crumbled. He'd blown it somehow, shown himself to be the boor he'd always feared he was.

"I'm sorry," he said. "I guess—look, it's all kind of hard to take in. The sums are staggering."

"They're meaningless," she said. "That's the point. The sums are just a convenient way of directing power. Power is what matters."

"I don't mean to offend you," he said carefully, "but that's a scary sounding thing to say."

"Now you're getting it," she said, and took his arm again. "Drinks?"

—•—

The limes for the daiquiris came from the trees around them on the rooftop conservatory. The trees were healthy working beasts, and the barman expertly inspected several limes before deftly twisting off a basket's worth and retreating to his workbench to juice them over his blender.

"You have to be a member to drink here," Ria said, as they sat on the roof, watching the jetpacks scud past.

"I'm not surprised," he said. "It must be expensive."

"You can't buy your way in," she said. "You have to work it off. It's a co-op. I planted this whole row of trees." She waved her arm, sloshing a little daiquiri on the odd turf their loungers rested on. "I planted the mint garden over there." It was a beautiful little patch, decorated with rocks and favored with a small stream that wended its way through them.

"Forgive me for saying this," he said, "but you must earn a lot of money. A *lot*, I'm thinking."

She nodded, unembarrassed, even waggled her eyebrows a bit. "So you could, I don't know, you could probably build one of these on any of the buildings that Buhle owns in Manhattan. Just like this. Even keep a little staff on board. Give out memberships as perks for your senior management team."

"That's right," she said. "I could."

He drank his daiquiri. "I'm supposed to figure out why you don't, right?"

She nodded. "Indeed." She drank. Her face suffused with pleasure. He took a moment to pay attention to the signals his tongue was transmitting to him. The drink was *incredible*. Even the glass was beautiful, thick, hand-blown, irregular. "Listen, Leon, I'll let you in on a secret. *I want you to succeed*. There's not much that surprises Buhle and even less that pleasantly surprises him. If you were to manage it . . ." She took another sip and looked intensely at him. He squirmed. Had he thought her matronly and sweet? She looked like she could lead a guerrilla force. Like she could wrestle a mugger to the ground and kick the shit out of him.

"So a success for me would be a success for you?"

"You think I'm after money," she said. "You're still not getting it. Think about the jetpacks, Leon. Think about what that power means."

———

He meant to go home, but he didn't make it. His feet took him crosstown to the Ate offices, and he let himself in with his biometrics and his pass phrase and watched the marvelous dappled lights go through their warm-up cycle and then bathe him with their wonderful, calming light. Then the breeze, and now it was a nighttime forest, mossier and heavier than in the day. Either someone had really gone balls-out on the product design, or there really was an indoor forest somewhere in the building growing under diurnal lights, there solely to supply soothing woodsy air to the agency's office. He decided that the forest was the more likely explanation.

He stood at Carmela's desk for a long time, then, gingerly, settled himself in her chair. It was plain and firm and well made, with just a little spring. Her funny little sculptural keyboard had keycaps that had worn smooth under her fingertips over the years, and there were shiny spots on the desk where her wrists had worn away the granite. He cradled his face in his palms, breathing in the nighttime forest air, and tried to make sense of the night.

The Living Room was nighttime dark, but it still felt glorious on his bare feet, and then, moments later, on his bare chest and legs. He lay on his stomach in his underwear and tried to name the sensation on his nerve endings and decided that "anticipation" was the best word for it, the feeling you get just *beside* the skin that's being scratched on your back, the skin that's next in line for a good scratching. It was glorious.

How many people in the world would ever know what this felt like? Ate had licensed it out to a few select boutique hotels—he'd checked into it after talking with Ria the first time—but that was it. All told, there were less than three thousand people in the world who'd ever felt this remarkable feeling. Out of eight billion. He tried to do the division in his head but kept losing the zeroes. It was a thousandth of a percent? A ten thousandth of a percent? No one on Anguilla would ever feel it: not the workers in the vertical slums, but also not the mere millionaires in the grand houses with their timeshare jets.

Something about that . . .

He wished he could talk to Ria some more. She scared him, but she also made him feel good. Like she was the guide he'd been searching for all his life. At this point, he would have settled for Brautigan. Anyone who could help him make sense of what felt like the biggest, scariest opportunity of his entire career.

He must have dozed, because the next thing he knew, the lights were flickering on and he was mostly naked, on the floor, staring up into Brautigan's face. He had a look of forced jollity, and he snapped his fingers a few times in front of Leon's face.

"Morning, sunshine!" Leon looked for the ghostly clock that shimmered in the corner of each wall, a slightly darker patch of reactive paint that was just outside of conscious comprehension unless you really stared at it. 4:12 AM. He stifled a groan. "What are you doing here?" he said, peering at Brautigan.

The man clacked his horsey teeth, assayed a chuckle. "Early bird. Worm."

Leon sat up, found his shirt, started buttoning it up. "Seriously, Brautigan."

"Seriously?" He sat down on the floor next to Leon, his big feet straight out ahead of him. His shoes had been designed by the same architect that did Leon's. Leon recognized the style.

"Seriously."

Brautigan scratched his chin. Suddenly, he slumped. "I'm shitting bricks, Leon. I am seriously shitting bricks."

"How did it go with your monster?"

Brautigan stared at the architect's shoes. There was an odd flare they did, just behind the toe, just on the way to the laces, that was really graceful. Leon thought it might be a standard distribution bell curve. "My monster is . . ." He blew out air. "Uncooperative."

"Less cooperative than previously?" Leon said. Brautigan unlaced his shoes and peeled off his socks, scrunched his toes in the moss. His feet gave off a hot, trapped smell. "What was he like on the other times you'd seen him?"

Brautigan tilted his head. "What do you mean?"

"He was uncooperative this time, what about the other times?"

Brautigan looked back down at his toes.

"You'd never seen him before this?"

"It was a risk," he said. "I thought I could convince him, face to face."

"But?"

"I bombed. It was—it was the—it was *everything*. The compound. The people. All of it. It was like a *city*, a *theme park*. They lived there, hundreds of them, and managed every tiny piece of his empire. Like Royal urchins."

Leon puzzled over this. "Eunuchs?"

"Royal eunuchs. They had this whole culture, and as I got closer and closer to him, I realized, shit, they could just *buy* Ate. They could destroy us. They could have us made illegal, put us all in jail. Or get me elected president. Anything."

"You were overawed."

"That's the right word. It wasn't a castle or anything, either. It was just a place, a well-built collection of buildings. In Westchester, you know? It had been a little town center once. They'd preserved everything good, built more on top of it. It all just . . . worked. You're still new here. Haven't noticed."

"What? That Ate is a disaster? I figured that out a long time ago. There's several dozen highly paid creative geniuses on the payroll here who haven't seen their desks in months. We could be a creative powerhouse. We're more like someone's vanity project."

"Brutal."

Leon wondered if he'd overstepped himself. Who cared? "Brutal doesn't mean untrue. It's like, it's like the money that came into this place, it became autonomous, turned into a strategy for multiplying itself. A bad strategy. The money wants to sell something to a monster, but the money doesn't know what monsters want, so it's just, what, beating its brains out on the wall. One day, the money runs out and . . ."

"The money won't run out," Brautigan said. "Wrong. We'd have to spend at ten-ex what we're burning now to even approach the principal."

"Okay," Leon said. "So it's immortal. That's better?"

Brautigan winced. "Look, it's not so crazy. There's an entire unserved market out there. No one's serving it. They're like, you know, like communist countries. Planned economies. They need something, they just acquire the capacity. No market."

"Hey, bub, I know just what you need! You need a house to go with this doorknob!" To his own surprise, Leon discovered that he did a passable Daffy Duck. Brautigan blinked at him. Leon realized that the man was a little drunk. "Just something I heard the other day," he said. "I told the lady from my monster that we could provide the stuff that their corporate culture precluded. I was thinking of, you know, how the samurai banned firearms. We can think and do the unthink- and undoable."

"Good line." He flopped onto his back. An inch of pale belly peeked between the top of his three-quarter-length culottes and the lower hem of his smart wraparound shirt. "The monster in the vat. Some skin, some meat. Tubes. Pinches of skin clamped between clear hard plastic squares, bathed in some kind of diagnostic light. No eyes, no top of the head where the eyes should be. Just a smooth mask. Eyes everywhere else. Ceiling. Floor. Walls. I looked away, couldn't make contact with them, found I was looking at something wet. Liver. I think."

"Yeesh. That's immortality, huh?"

"I'm there, 'A pleasure to meet you, an honor,' talking to the liver. The eyes never blinked. The monster gave a speech. 'You're a low-capital, high-risk, high-payoff long shot, Mr. Brautigan. I can keep dribbling sums to you so that you can go back to your wonder factory and try to come up with ways to surprise me. So there's no need to worry on that score.' And that was it. Couldn't think of anything to say. Didn't have time. Gone in a flash. Out the door. Limo. Nice babu to tell me how good it had been for the monster, how much he'd been looking forward to it." He struggled up onto his elbows. "How about you?"

Leon didn't want to talk about Ria with Brautigan. He shrugged. Brautigan got a mean, stung look on his face. "Don't be like that. Bro. Dude. Pal."

Leon shrugged again. Thing was, he *liked* Ria. Talking about her with Brautigan would be treating her like a . . . a *sales target*. If he were talking with Carmela, he'd say, "I feel like she wants me to succeed. Like it would be a huge deal for everyone if I managed it. But I also feel like maybe she doesn't think I can." But to Brautigan, he merely shrugged, ignored the lizardy slit-eyed glare, stood, pulled his pants on, and went to his desk.

➤━◆

If you sat at your desk long enough at Ate, you'd eventually meet *everyone* who worked there. Carmela knew all, told all, and assured him that everyone touched base at least once a month. Some came in a couple times a week. They had plants on their desks and liked to personally see to their watering.

Leon took every single one of them to lunch. It wasn't easy—in one case, he had to ask Carmela to send an Ate chauffeur to pick up the man's kids from school (it was a half day) and bring them to the sitter's, just to clear the schedule. But the lunches themselves went very well. It turned out that the people at Ate were, to a one, incredibly interesting. Oh, they were all monsters, narcissistic, tantrum-prone geniuses, but once you got past that, you found yourself talking to people who were, at bottom, damned smart, with a whole lot going on. He met the woman who designed the moss in the Living Room. She was younger than he was, and had been catapulted from a mediocre academic adventure at the Cooper Union into more wealth and freedom than she knew what to do with. She had a whole Rolodex of people who wanted to sublicense the stuff, and she spent her days toying with them, seeing if they had any cool ideas she could incorporate into her next pitch to one of the lucky few who had the ear of a monster.

Like Leon. That's why they all met with him. He'd unwittingly stepped into one of the agency's top spots, thanks to Ria, one of the power-broker seats that everyone else yearned to fill. The fact that he had no idea how he'd got there or what to do with it didn't surprise anyone. To a one, his colleagues at Ate regarded everything to do with the vat-monsters as an absolute, unknowable crapshoot, as predictable as a meteor strike.

No wonder they all stayed away from the office.

Ria met him in a different pair of jeans, these ones worn and patched at the knees. She had on a loose, flowing silk shirt that was frayed around the seams, and had tied her hair back with a kerchief that had faded to a noncolor that was like the ancient New York sidewalk outside Ate's office. He felt the calluses on her hand when they shook.

"You look like you're ready to do some gardening," he said.

"My shift at the club," she said. "I'll be trimming the lime trees and tending the mint patch and the cucumber frames all afternoon." She smiled, stopped him with a gesture. She bent down and plucked a blade of greenery from the untidy trail edge. They were in Central Park, in one of the places where it felt like a primeval forest instead of an artful garden razed and built in the middle of the city. She uncapped her water bottle and poured water over the herb—it looked like a blade of grass—rubbing it between her forefinger and thumb to scrub at it. Then she tore it in two and handed him one piece, held the other to her nose, then ate it, nibbling and making her nose wrinkle like a rabbit's. He followed suit. Lemon, delicious and tangy.

"Lemongrass," she said. "Terrible weed, of course. But doesn't it taste amazing?" He nodded. The flavor lingered in his mouth.

"Especially when you consider what this is made of—smoggy rain, dog piss, choked up air, and sunshine, and DNA. What a weird flavor to emerge from such a strange soup, don't you think?"

The thought made the flavor a little less delicious. He said so.

"I love the idea," she said. "Making great things from garbage."

"About the jetpacks," he said, for he'd been thinking.

"Yes?"

"Are you utopians of some kind? Making a better world?"

"By 'you,' you mean 'people who work for Buhle'?"

He shrugged.

"I'm a bit of a utopian, I'll admit. But that's not it. You know Henry Ford set up these work camps in Brazil, 'Fordlandia,' and enforced a strict code of conduct on the rubber plantation workers? He outlawed the Caipirinha and replaced it with Tom Collinses, because they were more civilized."

"And you're saying Buhle wouldn't do that?"

She waggled her head from side to side, thinking it over. "Probably not. Maybe, if I asked." She covered her mouth as though she'd made an indiscreet admission.

"Are—*were*—you and he . . . ?"

She laughed. "Never. It's purely cerebral. Do you know where his money came from?"

He gave her a look.

"Okay, of course you do. But if all you've read is the official history, you'll think he was just a finance guy who made some good bets. It's nothing like it. He played a game against the market, tinkered with the confidence of other traders by taking crazy positions, all bluff, except when they weren't. No one could outsmart him. He could convince you that you were about to miss out on the deal of the century, or that you'd already missed it, or that you were about to walk off onto easy street. Sometimes, he convinced you of something that was real. More often, it was pure bluff, which you'd only find out after you'd done some trade with him that left him with more money than you'd see in your whole life, and you face-palming and cursing yourself for a sucker. When he started doing it to national banks, put a run on the dollar, broke the Fed, well, that's when we all knew that he was someone who was *special*, someone who could create signals that went right to your hindbrain without any critical interpretation."

"Scary."

"Oh yes. Very. In another era they'd have burned him for a witch or made him the man who cut out your heart with the obsidian knife. But here's the thing: he could never, ever kid *me*. Not once."

"And you're alive to tell the tale?"

"Oh, he likes it. His reality distortion field, it screws with his internal landscape. Makes it hard for him to figure out what he needs, what he wants, and what will make him miserable. I'm indispensable."

He had a sudden, terrible thought. He didn't say anything, but she must have seen it on his face.

"What is it? Tell me."

"How do I know that you're on the level about any of this? Maybe you're just jerking me around. Maybe it's all made-up—the jetpacks, everything." He swallowed. "I'm sorry. I don't know where that came from, but it popped into my head—"

"It's a fair question. Here's one that'll blow your mind, though: how do you know that I'm not on the level, *and* jerking you around?"

They changed the subject soon after, with uneasy laughter. They ended up on a park bench near the family of dancing bears, whom they watched avidly.

"They seem so *happy*," he said. "That's what gets me about them. Like dancing was the secret passion of every bear, and these three are the first to figure out how to make a life of it."

She didn't say anything, but watched the three giants lumber in a graceful, unmistakably joyous kind of shuffle. The music—constantly mutated based on the intensity of the bears, a piece of software that sought tirelessly to please them—was jangly and poplike, with a staccato one-two/onetwothreefourfive/one-two rhythm that let the bears do something like a drunken stagger that was as fun to watch as a box of puppies.

He felt the silence. "So happy," he said again. "That's the weird part. Not like seeing an elephant perform. You watch those old videos and they seem, you know, they seem—"

"Resigned," she said.

"Yeah. Not unhappy, but about as thrilled to be balancing on a ball as a horse might be to be hitched to a plow. But look at those bears!"

"Notice that no one else watches them for long?" she said. He had noticed that. The benches were all empty around them.

"I think it's because they're so happy," she said. "It lays the trick bare." She showed teeth at the pun, then put them away. "What I mean is, you can see how it's possible to design a bear that experiences brain reward from rhythm, keep it well-fed, supply it with as many rockin' tunes as it can eat, and you get that happy family of dancing bears who'll peacefully coexist alongside humans who're going to work, carrying their groceries, pushing their toddlers around in strollers, necking on benches—"

The bears were resting now, lolling on their backs, happy tongues sloppy in the corners of their mouths.

"We made them," she said. "It was against my advice, too. There's not much subtlety in it. As a piece of social commentary, it's a cartoon sledgehammer with an oversize head. But the artist had Buhle's ear, he'd been CEO of one of the portfolio companies and had been interested in genomic art as a sideline for his whole career. Buhle saw that funding this thing would probably spin off lots of interesting sublicenses, which it did. But just look at it."

He looked. "They're *so happy*," he said.

She looked too. "Bears shouldn't be that happy," she said.

➤◄

Carmela greeted him sunnily as ever, but there was something odd.

"What is it?" he asked in Spanish. He made a habit of talking Spanish to her, because both of them were getting rusty, and also it was like a little shared secret between them.

She shook her head.

"Is everything all right?" Meaning, *Are we being shut down?* It could happen, might happen at any time, with no notice. That was something he—all of them—understood. The money that powered them was autonomous and unknowable, an alien force that was more emergent property than will.

She shook her head again. "It's not my place to say," she said. Which made him even more sure that they were all going down, for when had Carmela ever said anything about her *place*?

"Now you've got me worried," he said.

She cocked her head back toward the back office. He noticed that there were three coats hung on the beautiful, anachronistic coat stand by the ancient temple door that divided reception from the rest of Ate.

He let himself in and walked down the glassed-in double rows of offices, the cubicles in the middle, all with their characteristic spotless hush, like a restaurant dining room set up for the meals that people would come to later.

He looked in the Living Room, but there was no one there, so he began to check out the other conference rooms, which ran the gamut from superconservative to utter madness. He found them in the Ceile, with its barnboard floors, its homey stone hearth, and the gimmicked sofas that looked like unsprung old thrift-store numbers, but which sported adaptive genetic algorithm–directed haptics that adjusted constantly to support you no matter how you flopped on them, so that you could play at being a little kid sprawled carelessly on the cushions no matter how old and cranky your bones were.

On the Ceile's sofa were Brautigan, Ria, and a woman he hadn't met before. She was somewhere between Brautigan and Ria's age, but with that made-up, pulled-tight appearance of someone who knew the world wouldn't take her as seriously if she let one crumb of weakness escape from any pore or wrinkle. He thought he knew who this must be, and she confirmed it when she spoke.

"Leon," she said. "I'm glad you're here." He knew that voice. It was the voice on the phone that had recruited him and brought him to New York and told him where to come for his first day on the job. It was the voice of Jennifer Torino, and she was technically his boss. "Carmela said that you often worked from here so I was hoping today would be one of the days you came by so we could chat."

"Jennifer," he said. She nodded. "Ria." She had a poker face on, as unreadable as a slab of granite. She was wearing her customary denim and flowing cotton, but she'd kept her shoes on and her feet on the floor. "Brautigan," and Brautigan grinned like it was Christmas morning.

Jennifer looked flatly at a place just to one side of his gaze, a trick he knew, and said, "In recognition of his excellent work, Mr. Brautigan's been promoted, effective today. He is now manager for Major Accounts." Brautigan beamed.

"Congratulations," Leon said, thinking, *What excellent work? No one at Ate has accomplished the agency's primary objective in the entire history of the firm!* "Well done."

Jennifer kept her eyes coolly fixed on that empty, safe spot. "As you know, we have struggled to close a deal with any of our major accounts." He restrained himself from rolling his eyes. "And so Mr Brautigan has undertaken a thorough study of the way we handle these accounts." She nodded at Brautigan.

"It's a mess," he said. "Totally scattergun. No lines of authority. No checks and balances. No system."

"I can't argue with that," Leon said. He saw where this was going.

"Yes," Jennifer said. "You haven't been here very long, but I understand you've been looking deeply into the organizational structure of Ate yourself, haven't you?" He nodded. "And that's why Mr. Brautigan has asked that you be tasked to him as his head of strategic research." She smiled a thin smile. "Congratulations yourself."

He said, "Thanks," flatly, and looked at Brautigan. "What's strategic research, then?"

"Oh," Brautigan said. "Just a lot of what you've been doing: figuring out what everyone's up to, putting them together, proposing organizational structures that will make us more efficient at design and deployment. Stuff you're good at."

Leon swallowed and looked at Ria. There was nothing on her face. "I can't help but notice," he said, forcing his voice to its absolutely calmest, "that you haven't mentioned anything to do with the, uh, *clients*."

Brautigan nodded and strained to pull his lips over his horsey teeth to hide his grin. It didn't work. "Yeah," he said. "That's about right. We need someone of your talents doing what he does best, and what you do best is—"

He held up a hand. Brautigan fell silent. The three of them looked at him. He realized, in a flash, that he had them all in his power, just at that second. He could shout *BOO!* and they'd all fall off their chairs. They were waiting to see if he'd blow his top or take it and ask for more. He did something else.

"Nice working with ya," he said. And he turned his back on the sweetest, softest job anyone could ask for. He said *adios* and *buena suerte* to Carmela on the way out, and he forced himself not to linger around the outside doors down at street level to see if anyone would come chasing after him.

●—●●

The Realtor looked at him like he was crazy. "You'll never get two million for that place in today's market," she said. She was young, no-nonsense, black, and she had grown up on the Lower East Side, a fact she mentioned prominently in her advertising materials: A LOCAL REALTOR FOR A LOCAL NEIGHBORHOOD.

"I paid two million for it less than a year ago," he said. The 80 percent mortgage had worried him a little but Ate had underwritten it, bringing the interest rate down to less than 2 percent.

She gestured at the large corner picture window that overlooked Broome Street and Grand Street. "Count the FOR SALE signs," she said. "I want to be on your side. That's a nice place. I'd like to see it go to someone like you, someone decent. Not some *developer*"—she spat the word like a curse—"or some corporate apartment broker who'll rent it by the week to VIPs. This neighborhood needs real people who really live here, understand."

"So you're saying I won't get what I paid for it?"

She smiled fondly at him. "No, sweetheart, you're not going to get what you paid for it. All those things they told you when you put two mil into that place, like 'They're not making any more Manhattan' and 'Location location location'? It's lies." Her face got serious, sympathetic. "It's supposed to panic you and make you lose your head and spend more than you think something is worth. That goes on for a while and then everyone ends up with too much mortgage for not enough home, or for too much home for that matter, and then blooey, the bottom blows out of the market and everything falls down like a soufflé."

"You don't sugarcoat it, huh?" He'd come straight to her office from

Ate's door, taking the subway rather than cabbing it or even renting a jet-pack. He was on austerity measures, effective immediately. His brain seemed to have a premade list of cost-savers it had prepared behind his back, as though it knew this day would come.

She shrugged. "I can, if you want me to. We can hem and haw about the money and so on and I can hold your hand through the five stages of grieving. I do that a lot when the market goes soft. But you looked like the kind of guy who wants it straight. Should I start over? Or, you know, if you want, we can list you at two mil or even two point two, and I'll use that to prove that some *other* loft is a steal at one point nine. If you want."

"No," he said, and he felt some of the angry numbness ebb. He liked this woman. She had read him perfectly. "So tell me what you think I can get for it?"

She put her fist under her chin and her eyes went far away. "I sold that apartment, um, eight years ago? Family who had it before you. Had a look when they sold it to you—they used a different broker, kind of place where they don't mind selling to a corporate placement specialist. I don't do that, which you know. But I saw it when it sold. Have you changed it much since?"

He squirmed. "I didn't, but I think the broker did. It came furnished, nice stuff."

She rolled her eyes eloquently. "It's never nice stuff. Even when it comes from the best showroom in town, it's not nice stuff. Nice is antithetical to corporate. Inoffensive is the best you can hope for." She looked up, to the right, back down. "I'm figuring out the discount for how the place will show now that they've taken all the seams and crumbs out. I'm thinking, um, one point eight. That's a number I think I can deliver."

"But I've only *got* two hundred K in the place," he said.

Her expressive brown eyes flicked at the picture window, the FOR SALE signs. "And? Sounds like you'll break even or maybe lose a little on the deal. Is that right?"

He nodded. Losing a little wasn't something he'd figured on. But by the time he'd paid all the fees and taxes—"I'll probably be down a point or two."

"Have you got it?"

He hated talking about money. That was one thing about Ria is that she never actually talked about money—what money *did*, sure, but never money. "Technically," he said.

"Okay, technical money is as good as any other kind. So look at it this way: you bought a place, a really totally amazing place on the Lower East Side, a place bigger than five average New York apartments. You lived in it for, what?"

"Eight months."

"Most of a year. And it cost you one percent of the street price on the place. Rent would have been about eleven times that. You're up"—she calculated in her head—"it's about eighty-three percent."

He couldn't keep the look of misery off his face.

"What?" she said. "Why are you pulling faces at me? You said you didn't want it sugarcoated, right?"

"It's just that—" He dropped his voice, striving to keep any kind of whine out of it. "Well, I'd hoped to make something in the bargain."

"For what?" she said, softly.

"You know, appreciation. Property goes up."

"Did you do anything to the place that made it better?"

He shook his head.

"So you did no productive labor but you wanted to get paid anyway, right? Have you thought about what would happen to society if we rewarded people for owning things instead of doing things?"

"Are you sure you're a real estate broker?"

"Board certified. Do very well, too."

He swallowed. "I don't expect to make money for doing nothing, but you know, I just quit my job. I was just hoping to get a little cash in hand to help me smooth things out until I find a new one."

The Realtor gave a small nod. "Tough times ahead. Winds are about to shift again. You need to adjust your expectations, Leon. The best you can hope for right now is to get out of that place before you have to make another mortgage payment."

His pulse throbbed in his jaw and his thigh in counterpoint. "But I *need* money to—"

"Leon," she said, with some steel in her voice. "You're *bargaining*. As in denial, anger, bargaining, depression, and acceptance. That's healthy and all, but it's not going to get your place sold. Here's two options: one, you can go find another Realtor, maybe one who'll sugarcoat things or string you along to price up something else he's trying to sell. Two, you can let me get on with making some phone calls and I'll see who I can bring in. I keep a list of people I'd like to see in this 'hood, people who've asked me to look out for the right kind of place. That place you're in is one of a kind. I might be able to take it off your hands in very quick time, if you let me do my thing." She shuffled some papers. "Oh, there's a third, which is that you could go back to your apartment and pretend that nothing is wrong until that next mortgage payment comes out of your bank account. That would be *denial* and if you're bargaining, you should be two steps past that.

"What's it going to be?"

"I need to think about it."

"Good plan," she said. "Remember, depression comes after bargaining. Go buy a quart of ice cream and download some weepy movies. Stay off booze, it only brings you down. Sleep on it, come back in the morning if you'd like."

He thanked her numbly and stepped out into the Lower East Side. The bodega turned out to have an amazing selection of ice cream, so he bought the one with the most elaborate name, full of chunks, swirls, and stir-ins, and brought it up to his apartment, which was so big that it made his knees tremble when he unlocked his door. The Realtor had been right. Depression was next.

●━━●

Buhle sent him an invitation a month later. It came laser-etched into a piece of ancient leather, delivered by a messenger whose jetpack was so quiet that he didn't even notice that she had gone until he looked up from the scroll to thank her. His new apartment was a perch he rented by the week at five times what an annual lease would have cost him, but still a fraction of what he had been paying on the LES. It was jammed with boxes of things he hadn't been able to bring himself to get rid of, and now he cursed every knickknack as he dug through them looking for a good suit.

He gave up. The invitation said, "At your earliest convenience," and a quadrillionaire in a vat wasn't going to be impressed by his year-old designer job interview suit.

It had been a month, and no one had come calling. None of his queries to product design, marketing, R&D or advertising shops had been answered. He tried walking in the park every day, to see the bears, on the grounds that it was free and it would stimulate his creative flow. Then he noticed that every time he left his door, fistfuls of money seemed to evaporate from his pockets on little "necessities" that added up to real money. The frugality center of his brain began to flood him with anxiety every time he considered leaving the place and so it had been days since he'd gone out.

Now he was going. There were some clean clothes in one of the boxes, just sloppy jeans and tees, but they'd been expensive sloppy once upon a time, and they were better than the shorts and shirts he'd been rotating in and out of the tiny washing machine every couple days, when the thought occurred to him. The two-hundred-dollar haircut he'd had on his last day of work had gone shaggy and lost all its clever style, so he just combed it as best as he could after a quick shower and put on his architect's shoes, shining them on the backs of his pants legs on his way out the door in a gesture that reminded him of his father going to work in Anguilla, a pathetic gesture of respectability from someone who had none. The realization made him *oof* out a breath like he'd been gut-punched.

His frugality gland fired like crazy as he hailed a taxi and directed it to the helipad at Grand Central Terminus. It flooded him with so much cheapamine that he had to actually pinch his arms a couple times to distract himself from the full-body panic at the thought of spending so much. But Buhle was all the way in Rhode Island, and Leon didn't fancy keeping him waiting. He knew that to talk to money you had to act like money—impedance-match the money. Money wouldn't wait while he took the train or caught the subway.

He booked the chopper-cab from the cab, using the terminal in the backseat. At Ate, he'd had Carmela to do this kind of organizing for him. He'd had Carmela to do a hundred other things, too. In that ancient, lost time, he'd had money and help beyond his wildest dreams, and most days now he couldn't imagine what had tempted him into giving it up.

The chopper clawed the air and lifted him up over Manhattan, the canyons of steel stretched out below him like a model. The racket of the chopper obliterated any possibility of speech, so he could ignore the pilot and she could ignore him with a cordiality that let him pretend, for a moment, that he was a powerful executive who nonchalantly choppered around all over the country. They hugged the coastline and the stately rows of windmills and bobbing float-homes, surfers carving the waves, bulldozed strips topped with levees that shot up from the ground like the burial mound of some giant serpent.

Leon's earmuffs made all the sound—the sea, the chopper—into a uniform hiss, and in that hiss, his thoughts and fears seemed to recede for a moment, as though they couldn't make themselves heard over the white noise. For the first time since he'd walked out of Ate, the nagging, doubtful voices fell still and Leon was alone in his head. It was as though he'd had a great pin stuck through his chest that finally had been removed. There was a feeling of lightness, and tears pricking at his eyes, and a feeling of wonderful *obliteration*, as he stopped, just for a moment, stopped trying to figure out where he fit in the world.

The chopper touched down on a helipad at Newport State Airport, to one side of the huge X slashed into the heavy woods—new forest, fast-growing carbon sinkers garlanded with extravagances of moss and vine. From the moment the doors opened, the heavy earthy smell filled his nose and he thought of the Living Room, which led him to think of Ria. He thanked the pilot and zapped her a tip and looked up and there was Ria, as though his thoughts had summoned her.

She had a little half smile on her face, uncertain and somehow child-like, a little girl waiting to find out if he'd be her friend still. He smiled at her, grateful for the clatter of the chopper so that they couldn't speak. She shook his hand, hers warm and dry, and then, on impulse, he gave her a hug. She was soft and firm too, a middle-aged woman who kept fit but didn't obsess about the pounds. It was the first time he'd touched another human since he left Ate. And, as with the chopper's din, this revelation didn't open him to fresh miseries—rather, it put the miseries away, so that he felt *better*.

"Are you ready?" she said, once the chopper had lifted off.

"One thing," he said. "Is there a town here? I thought I saw one while we were landing."

"A little one," she said. "Used to be bigger, but we like them small."

"Does it have a hardware store?"

She gave him a significant look. "What for? An ax? A nailgun? Going to do some improvements?"

"Thought I'd bring along a doorknob," he said.

She dissolved into giggles. "Oh, he'll *like* that. Yes, we can find a hardware store."

▬▶ ◀▬

Buhle's security people subjected the doorknob to millimeter radar and a gas cromatograph before letting it past. He was shown into an anteroom by Ria, who talked to him through the whole procedure, just light chatter about the weather and his real-estate problems, but she gently steered him around the room, changing their angle several times, and then he said, "Am I being scanned?"

"Millimeter radar in here too," she said. "Whole-body imaging. Don't worry, I get it every time I come in. Par for the course."

He shrugged. "This is the least offensive security scan I've ever been through," he said.

"It's the room," she said. "The dimensions, the color. Mostly the semiotics of a security scan are either *you are a germ on a slide* or *you are not worth trifling with, but if we must, we must.* We went for something a little . . . sweeter." And it was, a sweet little room, like the private study of a single mom who's stolen a corner in which to work on her secret novel.

Beyond the room—a wonderful place.

"It's like a college campus," he said.

"Oh, I think we use a better class of materials that most colleges," Ria said, airily, but he could tell he'd pleased her. "But yes, there's about fifteen thousand of us here. A little city. Nice cafés, gyms, cinemas. A couple artists in residence, a nice little Waldorf school . . ." The pathways were tidy and wended their way through buildings ranging from cottages to large, institutional buildings, but all with the feel of endowed research institutes rather than finance towers. The people were young and old, casually dressed, walking in pairs and groups, mostly, deep in conversation.

"Fifteen thousand?"

"That's the head office. Most of them doing medical stuff here. We've got lots of other holdings, all around the world, in places that are different from this. But we're bringing them all in line with HQ, fast as we can. It's a good way to work. Churn is incredibly low. We actually have to put people back out into the world for a year every decade, just so they can see what it's like."

"Is that what you're doing?"

She socked him in the arm. "You think I could be happy here? No, I've always lived off campus. I commute. I'm not a team person. It's okay, this is the kind of place where even lone guns can find their way to glory."

They were walking on the grass now, and he saw that the trees, strangely oversized red maples without any of the whippy slenderness he associated with the species, had a walkway suspended from their branches, a real *Swiss Family Robinson* job with rope railings and little platforms with baskets on pulleys for ascending and descending. The people who scurried by overhead greeted each other volubly and laughed at the awkwardness of squeezing past each other in opposite directions.

"Does that ever get old?" he said, lifting his eyebrows to the walkways.

"Not for a certain kind of person," she said. "For a certain kind of person, the delightfulness of those walkways never wears off." The way she said "certain kind of person" made him remember her saying, "Bears shouldn't be that happy."

He pointed to a bench, a long twig-chair, really, made from birch branches and rope and wire all twined together. "Can we sit for a moment? I mean, will Buhle mind?"

She flicked her fingers. "Buhle's schedule is his own. If we're five minutes late, someone will put five minutes' worth of interesting and useful injecta into his in box. Don't you worry." She sat on the bench, which looked too fragile and fey to take a grown person's weight, but then she patted the seat next to him, and when he sat, he felt almost no give. The bench had been very well built, by someone who knew what she or he was doing.

"Okay, so what's going on, Ria? First you went along with Brautigan scooping my job and exiling me to Siberia—" He held up a hand to stop her from speaking and discovered that the hand was shaking and so was his chest, shaking with a bottled-up anger he hadn't dared admit. "You could have stopped it at a word. You envoys from the vat-gods, you are the absolute monarchs at Ate. You could have told them to have Brautigan skinned, tanned, and made into a pair of boots, and he'd have measured your foot size himself. But you let them do it.

"And now, here I am, a minister without portfolio, about to do something that would make Brautigan explode with delight, about to meet one of the Great Old Ones, in his very vat, in person. A man who might live to be a thousand, if all goes according to plan, a man who is a *country*, sovereign and inviolate. And I just want to ask you, *why*? Why all the secrecy and obliqueness and funny gaps? *Why*?"

Ria waited while a pack of grad students scampered by overhead, deep in discussion of telomeres, the racket of their talk and their bare feet slapping on the walkway loud enough to serve as a pretense for silence. Leon's pulse thudded and his armpits slicked themselves as he realized that he might have just popped the bubble of unreality between them, the consensual illusion that all was normal, whatever normal was.

"Oh, Leon," she said. "I'm sorry. Habit here—there's some things that can't be readily said in utopia. Eventually, you just get in the habit of speaking out of the back of your head. It's, you know, *rude* to ruin peoples' gardens by pointing out the snakes. So, yes, okay, I'll say something right out. I like you, Leon. The average employee at a place like Ate is a bottomless well of desires, trying to figure out what others might desire. We've been hearing from them for decades now, the resourceful ones, the important ones, the ones who could get past the filters and the filters behind the filters. We know what they're like.

"Your work was different. As soon as you were hired by Ate, we generated a dossier on you. Saw your grad work."

Leon swallowed. His résumé emphasized his grades, not his final projects. He didn't speak of them at all.

"So we thought, well, here's something different, it's possible he may have a house to go with our doorknob. But we knew what would happen if you were left to your own devices at a place like Ate: they'd bend you and shape you and make you over or ruin you. We do it ourselves, all too often. Bring in a promising young thing, subject him to the dreaded Buhle

Culture, a culture he's totally unsuited to, and he either runs screaming or . . . *fits in*. It's worse when the latter happens. So we made sure that you had a good fairy perched on your right shoulder to counterbalance the devil on your left shoulder." She stopped, made a face, mock slapped herself upside the head. "Talking in euphemism again. Bad habit. You see what I mean."

"And you let me get pushed aside . . ."

She looked solemn. "We figured you wouldn't last long as a button-polisher. Figured you'd want out."

"And that you'd be able to hire me."

"Oh, we could have hired you any time. We could have bought Ate. Ate would have given you to us—remember all that business about making Brautigan into a pair of boots? It applies all around."

"So you wanted me to . . . what? Walk in the wilderness first?"

"Now you're talking in euphemisms. It's catching! Let's walk."

—•—••—

They gave him a bunny suit to wear into the heart of Buhle. First he passed through a pair of double-doors, faintly positively pressurized, sterile air that ruffled his hair on the way in. The building was low-slung, nondescript brown brick, no windows. It could have been a water sterilization plant or a dry goods warehouse. The inside was good tile, warm colors with lots of reds and browns down low, making the walls look like they were the inside of a kiln. The building's interior was hushed, and a pair of alert-looking plainclothes security men watched them very closely as they changed into the bunny suits, loose micropore coveralls with plastic visors. Each one had a small, self-contained air-circ system powered by a wrist cannister, and when a security man helpfully twisted the valve open, Leon noted that there were clever jets that managed to defog the visor without drying out his eyeballs.

"That be enough for you, Ria?" the taller of the two security men said. He was dressed like a college kid who'd been invited to his girlfriend's place for dinner: smart slacks a little frayed at the cuffs, a short-sleeved, pressed cotton shirt that showed the bulge of his substantial chest and biceps and neck.

She looked at her cannister, holding it up to the visor. "Thirty minutes is fine," she said. "I doubt he'll have any more time than that for us!" Turning to Leon, she said, "I think that the whole air supply thing is way overblown. But it does keep meetings from going long."

"Where does the exhaust go?" Leon said, twisting in his suit. "I mean, surely the point is to keep my cooties away from," he swallowed, *"Buhle."*

It was the first time he'd really used the word to describe a person, rather than a *concept*, and he was filled with the knowledge that the person it described was somewhere very close.

"Here," she said, and pointed to a small bubble growing out of the back of her neck. "You swell up, one little bladder at a time, until you look like the Michelin man. Some joke." She made a face. "You can get a permanent suit if you come here often. Much less awkward. But Buhle likes it awkward."

She led him down a corridor with still more people, these ones in bunny suits or more permanent-looking suits that were formfitting and iridescent and flattering.

"Really?" he said, keeping pace with her. "*Elegant* is a word that comes to mind, not awkward."

"Well, sure, elegant on the other side of that airlock door. But we're inside Buhle's body now." She saw the look on his face and smiled. "No, no, it's not a riddle. Everything on this side of the airlock is Buhle. It's his lungs and circulatory and limbic system. The vat may be where the meat sits, but all this is what makes the vat work. You're like a gigantic foreign organism that's burrowing into his tissues. It's intimate." They passed through another set of doors and now they were almost alone in a hall the size of his university's basketball court, the only others a long way off. She lowered her voice so that he had to lean in to hear her. "When you're outside, speaking to Buhle through his many tendrils, like me, or even on the phone, he has all the power in the world. He's a giant. But here, inside his body, he's very, very weak. The suits, they're there to level out the playing field. It's all head games and symbolism. And this is just Mark I, the system we jury-rigged after Buhle's . . . *accident*. They're building the Mark II about five miles from here, and half a mile underground. When it's ready, they'll blast a tunnel and take him all the way down into it without ever compromising the skin of Buhle's extended body."

"You never told me what the accident was, how he ended up here. I assumed it was a stroke or—"

Ria shook her head, the micropore fabric rustling softly. "Nothing like that," she said.

They were on the other side of the great room now, headed for the doors. "What is this giant room for?"

"Left over from the original floor plan, when this place was just biotech R&D. Used for all-hands meetings then, sometimes a little symposium. Too big now. Security protocol dictates no more than ten people in any one space."

"Was it assassination?" He said it without thinking, quick as ripping off a Band-Aid.

Again, the rustle of fabric. "No."

She put her hand on the door's crashbar, made ready to pass into the next chamber.

"I'm starting to freak out a little here, Ria," he said. "He doesn't hunt humans or something?"

"No," and he didn't need to see her face, he could see the smile.

"Or need an organ? I don't think I have a rare blood type, and I should tell you that mine have been indifferently cared for—"

"Leon," she said, "if Buhle needed an organ, we'd make one right here. Print it out in about forty hours, pristine and virgin."

"So you're saying I'm not going to be harvested or hunted, then?"

"It's a very low probability outcome," she said, and pushed the crashbar. It was darker in this room, a mellow, candlelit sort of light, and there was a rhythmic vibration coming up through the floor, a *whoosh whoosh*.

Ria said, "It's his breath. The filtration systems are down there." She pointed a toe at the outline of a service hatch set into the floor. "Circulatory system overhead," she said, and he craned his neck up at the grate covering the ceiling, the troughs filled with neatly bundled tubes.

One more set of doors, another cool, dark room, this one nearly silent, and one more door at the end, an airlock door, and another plainclothes security person in front of it; a side room with a glass door bustling with people staring intently at screens. The security person—a woman, Leon saw—had a frank and square pistol with a bulbous butt velcroed to the side of her suit.

"He's through there, isn't he?" Leon said, pointing at the airlock door.

"No," Ria said. "No. He's here. We are inside him. Remember that, Leon. He isn't the stuff in the vat there. In some sense you've been in Buhle's body since you got off the chopper. His sensor array network stretches out as far as the heliport, like the tips of the hairs on your neck, they feel the breezes that blow in his vicinity. Now you've tunneled inside him, and you're right here, in his heart or his liver."

"Or his brain." A voice, then, from everywhere, warm and good humored. "The brain is overrated." Leon looked at Ria and she rolled her eyes eloquently behind her faceplate.

"Tuned sound," she said. "A party trick. Buhle—"

"Wait," Buhle said. "Wait. The brain, this is important, the brain is *so* overrated. The ancient Egyptians thought it was used to cool the blood, you know that?" He chortled, a sound that felt to Leon as though it began just above his groin and rose up through his torso, a very pleasant and very invasive sensation. "The heart, they thought, the heart was the place where the *me* lived. I used to wonder about that. Wouldn't they think that the thing between the organs of hearing, the thing behind the organs of seeing, that must be the me? But that's just the brain doing one of its little stupid games, backfilling the explanation. We think the brain is the obvious seat of the me because the brain already knows that it is the seat, and can't conceive of anything else. When the brain thought it lived in your chest, it was perfectly happy to rationalize that too—*Of course it's in the chest, you feel your sorrow and your joy there, your satiety and your hunger . . . The brain, pffft, the brain!*"

"Buhle," she said. "We're coming in now."

The nurse-guard by the door had apparently heard only their part of the conversation, but also hadn't let it bother her. She stood to one side, and offered Leon a tiny, incremental nod as he passed. He returned it, and then hurried to catch up with Ria, who was waiting inside the airlock. The outer door closed and for a moment, they were pressed up against one another and he felt a wild, horny thought streak through him, all the excitement discharging itself from yet another place that the *me* might reside.

Then the outer door hissed open and he met Buhle—he tried to remember what Ria had said, that Buhle wasn't this, Buhle was everywhere, but he couldn't help himself from feeling that this was *him*.

Buhle's vat was surprisingly small, no bigger than the sarcophagus that an ancient Egyptian might have gone to in his burial chamber. He tried not to stare inside it, but he couldn't stop himself. The withered, wrinkled man floating in the vat was intertwined with a thousand fiber optics that disappeared into pinprick holes in his naked skin. There were tubes: in the big highways in the groin, in the gut through a small valve set into a pucker of scar, in the nose and ear. The hairless head was pushed in on one side, like a pumpkin that hasn't been turned as it grew in the patch, and there was no skin on the flat piece, only white bone and a fine metalling mesh and more ragged, curdled scar tissue.

The eyes were hidden behind a slim set of goggles that irised open when they neared him, and beneath the goggles they were preternaturally bright, bright as marbles, set deep in bruised-looking sockets. The mouth beneath the nostril-tubes parted in a smile, revealing teeth as neat and white as a toothpaste advertisement, and Buhle spoke.

"Welcome to the liver. Or the heart."

Leon choked on whatever words he'd prepared. The voice was the same one he'd heard in the outer room, warm and friendly, the voice of a man whom you could trust, who would take care of you. He fumbled around his suit, patting it. "I brought you a doorknob," he said, "but I can't reach it just now."

Buhle laughed, not the chuckle he'd heard before, but an actual, barked *Ha!* that made the tubes heave and the fiber optics writhe. "Fantastic," he said. "Ria, he's fantastic."

The compliment made the tips of Leon's ears grow warm.

"He's a good one," she said. "And he's come a long way at your request."

"You hear how she reminds me of my responsibilities? Sit down, both of you." Ria rolled over two chairs, and Leon settled into one, feeling it noiselessly adjust to take his weight. A small mirror unfolded itself and then two more, angled beneath it, and he found himself looking into Buhle's eyes, looking at his face, reflected in the mirrors.

"Leon," Buhle said, "tell me about your final project, the one that got you the top grade in your class."

Leon's fragile calm vanished, and he began to sweat. "I don't like to talk about it," he said.

"Makes you vulnerable, I know. But vulnerable isn't so bad. Take me. I thought I was invincible. I thought that I could make and unmake the world to my liking. I thought I understood how the human mind worked—and how it broke.

"And then one day in Madrid, as I was sitting in my suite's breakfast room, talking with an old friend while I ate my porridge oats, my old friend picked up the heavy silver coffee jug, leaped on my chest, smashed me to the floor, and methodically attempted to beat the brains out of my head with it. It weighed about a kilo and a half, not counting the coffee, which was scalding, and she only got in three licks before they pulled her off of me, took her away. Those three licks though—" He looked intently at them. "I'm an old man," he said. "Old bones, old tissues. The first blow cracked my skull. The second one broke it. The third one forced fragments into my brain. By the time the medics arrived, I'd been technically dead for about 174 seconds, give or take a second or two."

Leon wasn't sure the old thing in the vat had finished speaking, but that seemed to be the whole story. "Why?" he said, picking the word that was uppermost in his mind.

"Why did I tell you this?"

"No," Leon said. "Why did your old friend try to kill you?"

Buhle grinned. "Oh, I expect I deserved it," he said.

"Are you going to tell me why?" Leon said.

Buhle's cozy grin disappeared. "I don't think I will."

Leon found he was breathing so hard that he was fogging up his face-plate, despite the air-jets that worked to clear it. "Buhle," he said, "the point of that story was to tell me how vulnerable you are so that I'd tell you my story, but that story doesn't make you vulnerable. You were beaten to death and yet you survived, grew stronger, changed into this"—he waved his hands around—"this body, this monstrous, town-size giant. You're about as vulnerable as fucking Zeus."

Ria laughed softly but unmistakably. "Told you so," she said to Buhle. "He's a good one."

The exposed lower part of Buhle's face clenched like a fist and the pitch of the machine noises around them shifted a half tone. Then he smiled a smile that was visibly forced, obviously artificial even in that ruin of a face.

"I had an idea," he said. "That many of the world's problems could be solved with a positive outlook. We spend so much time worrying about the rare and lurid outcomes in life. Kids being snatched. Terrorists blowing up cities. Stolen secrets ruining your business. Irate customers winning huge judgments in improbable lawsuits. All this *chickenshit*, bed-wetting, hand-wringing *fear*." His voice rose and fell like a minister's and it was all Leon could do not to sway in time with him. "And at the same time, we neglect the likely: traffic accidents, jetpack crashes, bathtub drownings. It's like the mind can't stop thinking about the grotesque, and can't stop forgetting about the likely."

"Get on with it," Ria said. "The speech is lovely, but it doesn't answer the question."

He glared at her through the mirror, the marble eyes in their mesh of burst blood vessels and red spider-tracks, like the eyes of a demon. "The human mind is just *kinked wrong*. And it's correctable." The excitement in his voice was palpable. "Imagine a product that let you *feel* what you *know*—imagine if anyone who heard 'Lotto: you've got to be in it to win it' immediately understood that this is *so much bullshit*. That statistically, your chances of winning the lotto are not measurably improved by buying a lottery ticket. Imagine if explaining the war on terror to people made them double over with laughter! Imagine if the capital markets ran on realistic assessments of risk instead of envy, panic, and greed."

"You'd be a lot poorer," Ria said.

He rolled his eyes eloquently.

"It's an interesting vision," Leon said. "I'd take the cure, whatever it was."

The eyes snapped to him, drilled through him, fierce. "That's the problem, *right there*. The only people who'll take this are the people who don't need it. Politicians and traders and oddsmakers know how probability works, but they also know that the people who make them fat and happy *don't* understand it a bit, and so they can't afford to be rational. So there's only one answer to the problem."

Leon blurted out, "The bears."

Ria let out an audible sigh.

"The fucking bears," Buhle agreed, and the way he said it was so full of world-weary exhaustion that it made Leon want to hug him. "Yes. As a social reform tool, we couldn't afford to leave this to the people who were willing to take it. So we—"

"Weaponized it," Ria said.

"Whose story is this?"

Leon felt that the limbs of his suit were growing stiffer, his exhaust turning it into a balloon. And he had to pee. And he didn't want to move.

"You dosed people with it?"

"Leon," Buhle said, in a voice that implied, *Come on, we're bigger than that.* "They'd consented to being medical research subjects. And it *worked.* They stopped running around shouting *The sky is falling, the sky is falling* and became—*zen.* Happy, in a calm, even-keeled way. Headless chickens turned into flinty-eyed air-traffic controllers."

"And your best friend beat your brains in—"

"Because," Buhle said, in a little Mickey Mouse falsetto, "*it would be unethical to do a broad-scale release on the general public*"

Ria was sitting so still he had almost forgotten she was there.

Leon shifted his weight. "I don't think that you're telling me the whole story."

"We were set to market it as an antianxiety medication."

"And?"

Ria stood up abruptly. "I'll wait outside." She left without another word.

Buhle rolled his eyes again. "How do you get people to take antianxiety medication? Lots and lots of people? I mean, if I assigned you that project, gave you a budget for it—"

Leon felt torn between a desire to chase after Ria and to continue to stay in the magnetic presence of Buhle. He shrugged. "Same as you would with any pharma. Cook the diagnosis protocol, expand the number of people it catches. Get the news media whipped up about the anxiety epidemic. That's easy. Fear sells. An epidemic of fear? Christ, that'd be too easy. Far too easy.

Get the insurers on board, discounts on the meds, make it cheaper to pre-scribe a course of treatment than to take the call center time to explain to the guy why he's *not* getting the meds."

"You're my kind of guy, Leon," Buhle said.

"So yeah."

"Yeah?"

Another one of those we're-both-men-of-the-world smiles. "Yeah."

Oh.

"How many?"

"That's the thing. We were trying it in a little market first. Basque country. The local authority was very receptive. Lots of chances to fine-tune the message. They're the most media-savvy people on the planet these days—they are to media as the Japanese were to electronics in the last cen-tury. If we could get them in the door—"

"How many?"

"About a million. More than half the population."

"You created a bioweapon that infected its victims with numeracy, and infected a million Basque with it?"

"Crashed the lottery. That's how I knew we'd done it. Lottery tickets fell by more than eighty percent. Wiped out."

"And then your friend beat your head in?"

"Well."

The suit was getting more uncomfortable by the second. Leon won-dered if he'd get stuck if he waited too long, his overinflated suit incapable of moving. "I'm going to have to go, soon."

"Evolutionarily, bad risk assessment is advantageous."

Leon nodded slowly. "Okay, I'll buy that. Makes you entrepreneur-ial—"

"Drives you to colonize new lands, to ask out the beautiful monkey in the next tree, to have a baby you can't imagine how you'll afford."

"And your numerate Vulcans stopped?"

"Pretty much," he said. "But that's just normal shakedown. Like when people move to cities, their birthrate drops. And nevertheless, the human race is becoming more and more citified and still, it isn't vanishing. Social stuff takes time."

"And then your friend beat your head in?"

"Stop saying that."

Leon stood. "Maybe I should go and find Ria."

Buhle made a disgusted noise. "Fine. And ask her why she didn't finish the job? Ask her if she decided to do it right then, or if she'd planned it? Ask her why she used the coffee jug instead of the bread knife? Because, you know, I wonder this myself."

Leon backpedaled, clumsy in the overinflated suit. He struggled to get into the airlock, and as it hissed through its cycle, he tried not to think of Ria straddling the old man's chest, the coffee urn rising and falling.

She was waiting for him on the other side, also overinflated in her suit.

"Let's go," she said, and took his hand, the rubberized palms of their gloves sticking together. She half-dragged him through the many rooms of Buhle's body, tripping through the final door, then spinning him around and ripping, hard, on the release cord that split the suit down the back so that it fell into two lifeless pieces that slithered to the ground. He gasped out a breath he hadn't realized he'd been holding in as the cool air made contact with the thin layer of perspiration that filmed his body.

Ria had already ripped open her own suit and her face was flushed and sweaty, her hair matted. Small sweat rings sprouted beneath her armpits. An efficient orderly came forward and began gathering up their suits. Ria thanked her impersonally and headed for the doors.

"I didn't think he'd do that," she said, once they were outside of the building—outside the core of Buhle's body.

"You tried to kill him," Leon said. He looked at her hands, which had blunt, neat fingernails and large knuckles. He tried to picture the tendons on their backs standing out like sail ropes when the wind blew, as they did the rhythmic work of raising and lowering the heavy silver coffee pot.

She wiped her hands on her trousers and stuffed them in her pockets, awkward now, without any of her usual self-confidence. "I'm not ashamed of that. I'm proud of it. Not everyone would have had the guts. If I hadn't, you and everyone you know would be—" She brought her hands out of her pockets, bunched into fists. She shook her head. "I thought he'd tell you what we like about your grad project. Then we could have talked about where you'd fit in here—"

"You never said anything about that," he said. "I could have saved you a lot of trouble. I don't talk about it."

Ria shook her head. "This is Buhle. You won't stop us from doing anything we want to do. I'm not trying to intimidate you here. It's just a fact of life. If we want to replicate your experiment, we can, on any scale we want—"

"But I won't be a part of it," he said. "That matters."

"Not as much as you think it does. And if you think you can avoid being a part of something that Buhle wants you for, you're likely to be surprised. We can get you what you want."

"No you can't," he said. "If there's one thing I know, it's that you can't do that."

•—•—•

Take one normal human being at lunch. Ask her about her breakfast. If lunch is great, she'll tell you how great breakfast is. If lunch is terrible, she'll tell you how awful breakfast was.

Now ask her about dinner. A bad lunch will make her assume that a bad dinner is forthcoming. A great lunch will make her optimistic about dinner.

Explain this dynamic to her and ask her again about breakfast. She'll struggle to remember the actual details of breakfast, the texture of the oatmeal, whether the juice was cold and delicious or slightly warm and slimy. She will remember and remember and remember for all she's worth, and then, if lunch is good, she'll tell you breakfast was good. And if lunch is bad, she'll tell you breakfast was bad.

Because you just can't help it. Even if you know you're doing it, you can't help it.

But what if you could?

•—•—•

"It was the parents," he said, as they picked their way through the treetops, along the narrow walkway, squeezing to one side to let the eager, gabbling researchers past. "That was the heartbreaker. Parents only remember the good parts of parenthood. Parents whose kids are grown remember a succession of sweet hugs, school triumphs, sports victories, and they simply forget the vomit, the tantrums, the sleep deprivation . . . It's the thing that lets us continue the species, this excellent facility for forgetting. That's what should have tipped me off."

Ria nodded solemnly. "But there was an upside, wasn't there?"

"Oh, sure. Better breakfasts, for one thing. And the weight loss—amazing. Just being able to remember how shitty you felt the last time you ate the chocolate bar or pigged out on fries. It was amazing."

"The applications do sound impressive. Just that weight-loss one—"

"Weight-loss, addiction counseling, you name it. It was all killer apps, wall to wall."

"But?"

He stopped abruptly. "You must know this," he said. "If you know about Clarity—that's what I called it, Clarity—then you know about what happened. With Buhle's resources, you can find out anything, right?"

She made a wry smile. "Oh, I know what history records. What I don't know is what *happened*. The official version, the one that put Ate onto you and got us interested—"

"Why'd you try to kill Buhle?"

"Because I'm the only one he can't bullshit, and I saw where he was going with his little experiment. The competitive advantage to a firm that knows about such a radical shift in human cognition—it's massive. Think of all the products that would vanish if numeracy came in a virus. Think of all the shifts in governance, in policy. Just imagine an *airport* run by and for people who understand risk!"

"Sounds pretty good to me," Leon said.

"Oh sure," she said. "Sure. A world of eager consumers who know the cost of everything and the value of nothing. Why did evolution endow us with such pathological innumeracy? What's the survival advantage in being led around by the nose by whichever witch doctor can come up with the best scare story?"

"He said that entrepreneurial things—parenthood, businesses . . ."

"Any kind of risk-taking. Sports. No one swings for the stands when he knows that the odds are so much better on a bunt."

"And Buhle *wanted* this?"

She peered at him. "A world of people who understand risk are nearly as easy to lead around by the nose as a world of people who are incapable of understanding risk. The big difference is that the competition is at a massive disadvantage in the latter case, not being as highly evolved as the home team."

He looked at her, really looked at her for the first time. Saw that she was the face of a monster, the voice of a god. The hand of a massive, unknowable machine that was vying to change the world, remake it to suit its needs. A machine that was *good at it*.

"Clarity," he said. "Clarity." She looked perfectly attentive. "Do you think you'd have tried to kill Buhle if you'd been taking Clarity?"

She blinked in surprise. "I don't think I ever considered the question."

He waited. He found he was holding his breath.

"I think I would have succeeded if I'd been taking Clarity," she said.

"And if Buhle had been taking Clarity?"

"I think he would have let me." She blurted it out so quickly it sounded like a belch.

"Is anyone in charge of Buhle?"

"What do you mean?"

"I mean—that vat-thing. Is it volitional? Does it steer this, this *enter-*

prise? Or does the enterprise tick on under its own power, making its own decisions?"

She swallowed. "Technically, it's a benevolent dictatorship. He's sovereign, you know that." She swallowed again. "Will you tell me what happened with Clarity?"

"Does he actually make decisions, though?"

"I don't think so," she whispered. "Not really. It's more like, like—"

"A force of nature?"

"An emergent phenomenon."

"Can he hear us?"

She nodded.

"Buhle," he said, thinking of the thing in the vat. "Clarity made the people who took it very angry. They couldn't look at advertisements without wanting to smash something. Going into a shop made them nearly catatonic. Voting made them want to storm a government office with flaming torches. Every test subject went to prison within eight weeks."

Ria smiled. She took his hands in hers—warm, dry—and squeezed them.

His phone rang. He took one hand out and answered it.

"Hello?"

"How much do you want for it?" Buhle voice was ebullient. Mad, even.

"It's not for sale."

"I'll buy Ate, put you in charge."

"Don't want it."

"I'll kill your parents." The ebullient tone didn't change at all.

"You'll kill everyone if Clarity is widely used."

"You don't believe that. Clarity lets you choose the course that will make you happiest. Mass suicide won't make humanity happiest."

"You don't know that."

"Wanna bet?"

"Why don't you kill *yourself*?"

"Because dead, I'll never make things better."

Ria was watching intently. She squeezed the hand she held.

"Will *you* take it?" Leon asked Buhle.

There was a long pause.

Leon pressed on. "No deal unless *you* take it," he said.

"You have some?"

"I can make some. I'll need to talk to some lab techs and download some of my research first."

"Will you take it with me?"

Leon didn't hesitate. "Never."

"I'll take it," Buhle said, and hung up.

Ria took his hand again. Leaned forward. Gave him a dry, firm kiss on the mouth. Leaned back.

"Thank you," she said.

"Don't thank me," he said. "I'm not doing you any favors." She stood up, pulling him to his feet.

"Welcome to the team," she said. "Welcome to Buhle."

Afterword

My father, a Marxist all his life, had been an avid science fiction reader in his boyhood. But by the time I started reading the stuff, he had been off SF for years and years. But he had a number of half-remembered, highly politicized recollections of his old favorites: "*The Door into Summer* is propaganda for planned obsolescence," for example (he also used to tell me the Conan stories with Conan replaced by a gender- and racially-balanced trio called "Harry, Larry, and Mary" who would usurp evil kings and establish workers' paradises in their place).

He always had good things to say about *The Space Merchants*, though. A satirical anticapitalist masterpiece and so on. I totally disagreed about *The Door into Summer* (and continue to do so, though I do think that the Maker's Manifesto and its cry of "Screws not glue" and "If you can't open it, you don't own it" are good implicit critiques of Hired Girl, Inc.'s engineering decisions). But Dad, you are totally, 100 percent right about *The Space Merchants*. That thing is a damned masterwork: comic, scathing. The gender stuff is more than a little dated (as Jo Walton pointed out in a recent review on tor.com), but that's endemic to the period. The fact remains, *The Space Merchants* was country before country was cool—presaging Naomi Klein and Adbusters both.

The financialization of the twenty-first century's economy means an ever increasing polarization of wealth. The superrich are in danger of speciating from us Homo suckerus. They run the financial system. Ikea registered itself as a charity and pays 3.5 percent tax on 551 million euros in annual profits, while its founder (likely the richest man on Earth) hides out in Switzerland, dodging tax on the millions he presumably extracts from his "charity." The megarich can afford Götterdämmerung, rising seas, and climate devastation. They'll just hop from mountaintop to mountaintop in harrier jets, carefully breeding their offspring while we tread water. It's far more darkly comic than even Pohl and Kornbluth imagined.

I first met Fred at a birthday party in Judy Merril's honor in Toronto. We were both smokers at the time, and it was a golden time to be a smoker, since there were so few of us that you'd get to meet and converse with people who'd otherwise be way out of your league (case in point: I met my wife because we were the only two smokers at a Nokia think tank in Helsinki; I quit immediately afterward, thus ensuring that I wouldn't ever meet anyone as wonderful as her again). I was about nineteen at the time. I was in awe. Fred was Fred: nice, funny, gracious. The veritable template of what a gentlemanly SF writer could be. It's an honor to write this story for him.

Hope you like it, Fred.

—CORY DOCTOROW

FREDERIK POHL:
HOMAGE TO THE MASTER

I'm the invisible man in this book, the in-house editor. My job (at Tor Books) is to work with the wonderful Betty Anne Hull to make sure the publication process goes smoothly. When there's an editor whose name is on the front of the book, the in-house editor *should* be invisible.

Betty has done all the heavy lifting, from the very start of the publishing process, way back in March 2009. One day she called me up and said something like: "Fred is going to be ninety in November. I'd like to put together a book to honor him. Stories, reminiscences, by writers and others he's known, friends, family, all sorts of things, in time for his birthday."

My first thought was that this was impossible. November! Normally it takes ten months to go from having a finished manuscript to when finished books hit the stands. Nothing had been written, no contracts signed—not even a deal had been agreed upon. Even as I despaired about the timing, I told Betty I loved the idea of this book. I've worked with Frederik Pohl for more than fifteen years, and have been a great admirer of his work for much longer than that. I can't think of anyone else in science fiction who is more deserving of this kind of a book. As Betty mentioned in her introduction, he's done just about everything you can do in science fiction, and I'm merely one of the many, many people who know and revere him and his contributions to the field over the past—gasp!—seventy years.

But, as I said to Betty when she called me, there was no reasonable way we could have a book such as she described ready for November. Could we, I asked, possibly publish this sometime in 2010? She very kindly let on as how that would be nice. In the best of all possible worlds, sooner would have been better, but a terrific book in 2010 would be better than a hastily cobbled-together book in November 2009.

With this mandate from her, I told her I'd do what I could to get the okay to buy the book—and as quickly as possible. So I called our publisher

Tom Doherty who, like the rest of us at Tor, is a huge fan of Fred both on a professional and personal level. When I suggested this project to Tom, he said, without hesitation, "For Fred, yes, of course!"

I immediately conveyed this message to Betty, and we were off to the races. Now she had to contact a bunch of writers and others in the field who have either worked with or been influenced by Fred. That includes a lot of people, and it took her a while to get hold of everyone she thought might be interested in being involved with the book. Some people were hard to track down; others were easy to contact. But altogether, there was an enormously positive response to her e-mails, letters, and phone calls.

As you've seen from the stories and appreciations, not everyone she contacted had the time to write a story for this book. All the people represented in these pages are, after all, writers, and most of them are busy working on novels, most of them with deadlines, and some of them were late and trying desperately to finish other projects. But despite that, Betty—offering them a chance to express their love and appreciation of Fred and his enormous body of work as editor, agent, writer, and all-around SF legend—has gathered a collection of fictions and personal anecdotes I hope you have enjoyed as much as I have.

April came, and people started responding. A few sent their regrets that they couldn't write a story, but shortly I started getting e-mails from Betty with stories from various writers, and appreciations from a few people who, for one reason or another, simply could not write stories for the book. Along with the stories came afterwords about Fred. You've read them already, so you know what fun these many afterwords are, along with the stories and appreciations. For me, it's been a constant joy to open my e-mail, see two or three e-mails from Betty, each containing yet another delicious piece of fiction or nonfiction for the book.

Betty—well, she's just so sweet. When Cory Doctorow submitted his twenty thousand word novella, she apologized to me. "Sorry it's so long." I had to suppress my impulse to laugh, to scream with delight. What a tough thing to deal with: A wonderful, amazing novella from Cory. Somehow, I told her, we'll manage to find room for it.

It wasn't just Cory, of course. David Brin's novella is even longer, and also extremely cool. And Frank Robinson's novelette, not quite as long, is also quite wonderful. And it wasn't just these, of course. The next six months witnessed a steady influx of stories from many other favorite science fiction writers: Brian W. Aldiss, Greg Bear, Gregory Benford, Ben Bova, Phyllis Eisenstein, Neil Gaiman, James Gunn, Joe Haldeman, Harry

Harrison, Larry Niven, Jody Lynn Nye, Mike Resnick, Sheri S. Tepper, Vernor Vinge, and Gene Wolfe.

It is very rare (you can look it up!) for an in-house editor to giggle with delight, but *Gateways* caused me to do this on more than one occasion. After the first few times, I had to restrain myself, lest people think I was stranger than they already knew.

Get the picture? This was more like fun than work. Really.

But more to the point, I hope you'll understand that getting superlative original stories from as many wonderful writers as have contributed to *Gateways* was nothing short of a miracle, if for no reason other than the odds against it, given the demands they all have on their time and talent. At Tor we publish a fair number of anthologies, and we always want to get the best writers to contribute. But most of the time we receive stories from only a small number of the authors we'd most like to contribute. So *Gateways*, with its "Who's Who" of science fiction has been a uniquely wonderful, satisfying experience for us. And we hope it is equally wonderful for one particular reader: Frederik Pohl. More than once, it has occurred to me that the success of this book as an artistic venture depends on Fred liking the results. And that scares me just a little.

Frederik Pohl's accomplishments have been mentioned by various writers in their afterwords or appreciations. As an editor myself, I'm all too keenly aware of the fact that we're making this book to honor not only a writer, but also, most emphatically, an editor. A hard-nosed, grizzled veteran who is nobody's fool when it comes to judging good science fiction. So I'm hoping that you're still reading, Fred, and you haven't thrown the book against the wall in disgust, thinking—*Hell, I could do better than this!* (Hey, Fred, if you really don't like it, just please don't throw it. It might put a dent in a wall.)

I've left out what everyone else in the book has talked about: what Frederik Pohl means to me. I haven't known Fred nearly as long as some of the others who have provided reminiscences of him. (I was amazed to read Frank Robinson's afterword, in which he referred to him as "Freddy.") As happens between authors and editors, Fred has become a dear and valued friend, but I have other friends. What Fred has given to me that is unique to him, is his work, to which I relate as an editor, but even more, as a grateful reader.

There is a common thread in the afterwords and appreciations, whether they talk about his editing, his agenting, or his writing. In everything he does he gives maximum effort. So Fred gave Bob Silverberg grief, even when he was buying his short stories, when he thought they should be better; he turned the magazine *Worlds of If* into a Hugo Award–winning machine; he invented and defined the term *original-story anthology* with the *Star Science Fiction Stories* series; he bought, edited, and helped market Samuel R. Delany's remarkable, bestselling novel *Dhalgren*; he's written close to a million words of thought-provoking, entertaining short fiction. And when he'd already been writing longer than most people in the field, he began to write the string of startlingly original novels that began with the multiple award-winning, bestselling *Gateway*.

All these endeavors illustrate his drive for excellence in himself and in others, a big reason why he's a living legend, and why all the people who have contributed to this book were eager to jeopardize other deadlines so they could be included.

Others have discussed many aspects of his career; I will add only one thing that has struck me, which marks Frederik Pohl as unique in the annals of science fiction and perhaps all of modern literature.

He started writing at the end of the 1930s. The "Golden Age" of science fiction was in full flower, John W. Campbell was editing *Astounding Stories*, and World War II was on the horizon. He has written stories in every decade since. What so impresses me is not his longevity, but rather that he is what I think of as a "complete" science fiction writer. By that I mean to say that his best work functions on many levels.

More specifically: from his early work to this day, he has demonstrated an ability to tackle a range of subjects and styles that has developed and matured throughout the course of his career. He has an uncanny talent for creating viewpoint characters that fit the needs of the story, whatever they require.

Many of his stories are political, not surprising considering, as Betty pointed out, his strong interest in politics. But even in his blatantly political fiction his humanism, as expressed through his characters, is never sacrificed to an agenda. In his stories and novels, his nonfiction and in his editorial decisions as well, he is consistently mindful of the things that make us human, for better or worse.

Most particularly important to the science-fictional validity of his work over the decades, he has successfully integrated science and technology into the fabric of his stories. He has continually found new and diverse ways to cogently present possible outcomes of a mind-boggling variety of potential scenarios inspired by new scientific theories, discoveries, or technological advances.

Science fiction readers are fond of dividing the genre into hard- and soft-SF. But Frederik Pohl defies that distinction as do few other writers.

He has the skills of those who write soft-SF—i.e., stories with the social sciences as their basis. But he also uses the tools of hard-SF—works with plots that are inspired by an idea based in one of the physical sciences—to craft stories that readers find both accessible and challenging, tales that intrigue them, that make them *think* and consider the possibilities inherent in the story's premise. That may sound easy but it isn't.

When you put together all these virtues, you get what I think of as a "complete" writer. A writer for the last century, and for the current millennium.

One last thing: if you are familiar with Frederik Pohl's *oeuvre,* you may already have noted that among the stories in this book some are, essentially, Fred Pohl stories. Not stories written by him, but ones that use some trope, style, or technique that reflects his influence. This is only fitting. His stylistically diverse work, wide-ranging in subject matter, has provided the marvelous authors who fête him in these pages ample food for thought, as it does for all of us, the lucky ones who read and enjoy his work.

So I'll say the thing I have to say. It's not original, but the sentiment is real: Thank you, Fred. (And finish *Pompeii*, that new novel, soon, man!)

Madison, WI